About the author

Cedric Paul Foster was born in Leicester, studied at London and Liverpool (Chester) Universities and later took up a position at the University of Heidelberg, Germany, where he was able to extend his interests in East Asian culture. This led to the publication of several scholarly works that link the thinking of East and West, including *Beckett and Zen* (Wisdom Publications) and *The Golden Lotus* (Book Guild). He lives with his German wife near Heidelberg.

By the same author

Beckett and Zen (Wisdom Publications, 1989)

The Golden Lotus (Book Guild, 1998)

Jesus - Buddhist Fact and Christian Fable (Upfront Publishing, 2004)

Feb. 2020
For Glenda with love from Paul

A ROGUE LIKE ME

and other true short stories

Cedric Paul Foster

Book Guild Publishing
Sussex, England

First published in Great Britain in 2015 by
The Book Guild Ltd
The Werks
45 Church Road
Hove, BN3 2BE

Copyright © Paul Foster 2015

The right of Paul Foster to be identified as the author
of this work has been asserted by him in accordance with the
Copyright, Designs and Patents Act 1988.

All rights reserved. No part of this publication may be reproduced, transmitted, or stored in a retrieval system, in any form or by any means, without permission in writing from the publisher, nor be otherwise circulated in any form of binding or cover other than that in which it is published and without a similar condition being imposed on the subsequent purchaser.

All characters in this publication are fictitious and any resemblance to real people, alive or dead, is purely coincidental.

Typesetting in Sabon by
Keyboard Services, Luton, Bedfordshire

Printed in Great Britain by
CPI Group (UK) Ltd, Croydon, CR0 4YY

A catalogue record for this book is available from
The British Library.

ISBN 978 1 909984 68 4

Contents

Introduction		vii
1	Exit	1
2	Light Under a Bushel	9
3	Nina	31
4	Mrs Manship	73
5	Harlingford House (1928)	93
6	A Rogue Like Me	111
7	Gypsy Boy	151
8	The House at Starost	183
9	Over Tea One Hot August Afternoon	197
10	Grandfather	203
11	Well, Fancy That!	219
12	The Last Dance	227
13	Saturday	247
14	Ann (1947)	259
15	Still Life (1938)	273
16	Vincenzo	289
17	No. 14 Cavendish Street, Spring 1958 and Thereafter	329
18	The Vision (1871)	349

Introduction

However unlikely some of the events depicted in these narrations may appear, they are in fact true accounts of what actually happened. That is to say that all names and some places have been changed to avoid embarrassment, but that the detail and sequence remain, and that these events once affected real people in real situations. Most of them occurred in the last 100 years, and most of the people involved are now dead. Some of the stories are more dramatic than others and, with one exception, they are either based on authentic written accounts, which have later been furnished with fictional detail while leaving the essential incident unchanged, or were related to me personally. While one or two are straightforward enough, one historical and one autobiographical, all of them reflect the true experiences of normal people living in an apparently normal world that is sometimes oddly interwoven by the strange and inexplicable.

1

Exit

Suddenly I was awake, finding it so dark in those first seconds of consciousness that I thought I had died and was in that deepest of hells where there is no light, not a beam, nor a sliver, nor even a suggestion that light could ever be or ever was in that ultimate hell, but where there is intense feeling, for which there is no description in this world, only an appalling premonition, and I there, ensconced, gelled and terrified in the cool sheets, waiting for these terrible moments to pass in the pitch blackness of that place, Mollstrasse 12, waiting for my heart to beat again, in that large, well-proportioned, heavy, dark-red, stone building erected at the turn of the century, whose frozen slate roof had protected me for a day or two from the enormities outside, awake, waiting for normality to return, for the blood to flow once more, for the dead mind to give the cold, trembling hand a signal to scramble and scratch for the wristwatch and the cigarette lighter on the table at the side of the bed at ten past four in the morning, the question in my mind asking why I had woken up so unnaturally in the bitterly cold room with its high ceilings invisible above me, not knowing why I must rise, must move, an imperative without a name, without cause, a provocation without reason in the icy bedroom with its invisible, oaken, black-and-brown, 100-year-old, stalwart furniture around me which had heard so much and seen so much, listening, implacable, like ancient trees that have withstood the test of time against changing temperatures, damage and human carelessness, against gravity, the woodworm and the mouse, me in that room now, an alien fumbling among the furniture and fittings of a past age for the lighter, then the thing hot in my fingers as I search for the candle, and then snapping it to in the darkness, in the darkness beyond the bed, a dimness and an obscurity more palpable than the blankets around my shivering bodily existence, and then, like someone under orders, swinging out of the bed, placing my feet on the icy linoleum, automatically flicking the lighter on again, pawing for the candle in the dancing gloom like one blind, fumbling for where I had put it the night before, and then applying the living flame to the wick, its slow ignition immediately throwing bizarre caricatures on the walls as I dress quickly in its meagre light, not knowing why, but tossing the half-frozen water from the bowl on the commode into my face, drying my face quickly, standing there for a second or two more, not knowing what to do next and with ever the same question in my mind as the water on my shirt collar trickles to my chest, realising that the stub of a candle wouldn't last long and then as I look at it that strange feeling of urgency which had overcome me and within a few seconds I was dressing again, glad of the thick pullover my mother had knitted me, for the socks and the heavy overcoat as I hear the sound of a vehicle, first one and then another in quick succession coming to a stop outside in the frost-bitten street and the subsequent slamming of doors accompanied by voices, and a moment later, only a moment later it seems a thunderous knocking on the heavy oak door of that building in Mollstrasse 12, four storeys below and I know they are there in the wide, flagged hall under the bronze chandelier below and my body freezes with the coldness of the air around me, my mind racing as I retreat to the lounge, where, opening the window to the frost and silence of the other side of the house, I see the one great tree spreading

EXIT

seventy years of growth over the courtyard four sets of stairs below, wondering in the seconds left to me whether what Kristof had shown me in the way of a ladder of knotted blankets was still a feasible means of flight, but then asking myself what if I found myself hopelessly caught up in the winter branches of the beech tree or if they would groan and snap under my falling weight to let me stream down to the heavy flags of the courtyard below, when I hear voices above me, a short, sharp cry and the twitching of legs right in front of me only a metre away, swinging towards me, yes, barely a metre, then swinging away from me, kicking violently, senselessly trying to find footing where there is none and I looking on for precious seconds, not knowing how to help, quite unable to help, to grasp the swinging bundle of ebbing life and then me closing the window with all the force of fear and terror which had seized me, running back into the room and to the massive wardrobe for the forage cap I had worn in these last few days, an angel-given inspiration surely to God and a mighty decision in my mind, finding then the courage of a lion and feeling the truculence of desperation, the turmoil of not knowing what to do having suddenly vanished like smoke in the air to give way only to an iron will and a set determination, the twisted-up strength and fortitude of a man in the face of an enemy, ready to strike, kill or be killed, with no thought of anything else but to prevail, treading with a cat's stealth through the thin light of the modest candle out to the carpeted hallway beyond the room with its silent, watchful furniture towards the front door under the high, white ceiling and tired wallpaper, past the faded, light-brown photographs and the sombre prints in their black frames on the high walls depicting inconceivable times past with lucent, placid lakes and quiet trees, grazing sheep and cud-chewing cows under summer skies, stags and deer under the mountains, men and women reclining in unlikely positions and abundant finery unsuitable to their bucolic surroundings and on to the bolted door, listening the while to the muffled, general noises coming up as if from a funnel below, punctuated here and there by sobbing and by short screams of protest, the noise of shuffling feet, of struggle, of panic, of protest and remonstrance, the gruff replies and retorts, the dull sound of something heavy striking the human body and the harrowing shouts of pain, the staccato clattering of determined boots on the stairway, the lights on the landings now full on, blinding me for a moment as I leave to descend into the abyss beneath me with my outrageous ruse, which aims to upset the routine of tyranny for a second, to guide the suspecting eye to a symbol of alliance, a cheap ploy garnished with a smile, a brief and fragile subterfuge, the pullover warm about me, the dark-blue overcoat clean and creased and heavy on my shoulders, my forage cap set straight on my short-shorn head, descending the stairs without hurry, my mind tight but secure, my feet in their polished boots, Kristof's boots, treading the stairs in measured steps, my view now as I approach the third floor taking in the others of this building's community, half-clad in pyjamas and other night attire watching the scene below them, half in fear and apprehension, half in self-satisfaction, whispering among themselves, rasping whispers, their eyes wide and staring, their breath short, eyeing me as I pass, fluttering among themselves in their night apparel like harboured chickens, some leaning over the stair rail, peering down to get a better view of what was going on downstairs, and wondering at my sudden appearance so early in the morning, a man dressed to face the day in an overcoat and a forage cap, a man whom they'd seen coming and going up the steep stairs for a day or so, a man who had greeted them as now with half a smile and a nod of recognition and here and there among the medley of gapers and bogglers, someone returning my discreet '*Guten Morgen!*' and I passing on down the many steps, how many steps, steps leading down, down to the tumult at the bottom of the stairs, to the dead-eyed officers and their bullying assistants and offering a courteous '*Guten Morgen!*' to those who noticed my passage by and between them in the commotion and rendering a cordial '*Heil Hitler!*' to the captain and an NCO who registers my passage, who looks keenly but lets me pass and whose attention coincides in that precious, unbelievable second with the appearance of another of their kind ascending the white, granite steps to the open door of the house, another of his rank and persuasion who, by his manner and his brisk, determined step clearly has a message of importance to deliver just, just, I say again at that very intersection of circumstance, at that critical, hair's breadth constellation of events, neither a fraction of a second before nor after, a silken thread timing between life and death as our ways traverse in opposite directions, he ascending, holding a board and a clip in his black-gloved hand, the other halfway up, lifting his hand in salute, the black-clad arm rising as he still mounts the hard, stone steps, the sound of his steeled heels clacking hard on the stone, the arm rising, the impeccable uniform, the belt and the revolver rucking slightly as he does so in the direction of the arm, the captain putting one jackbooted foot forward to greet his comrade in iniquity, the curl of his breath congealing on the cold morning air, God's air, our air, his mouth open, curt, military phrases issuing on the curdling morning air, awaiting the essence of the message contained on the board he carries in his left hand, I on the third step of ten descending, one, two, three, four to the street, at whose kerb a small, grey-green army vehicle has parked and whose engine I notice in that instant is still turning over, its exhaust fumes spuming and boiling upward, folding and playing in a whitish grey harmony over the road in smarting cold air on this January morning, my heart pumping like an engine within me, the fifth step and the sixth and hear as I descend to the seventh and eighth, hear a sharp exchange above me then the bark of an order and I am on

A ROGUE LIKE ME

the ninth of ten – I am there and the name 'HORVATH!' barks upon the air followed by 'HALT!' and, seeing that neither flight to the left nor right will save me, seize the grip of the door of the general purpose vehicle and I know as I open it that a well-aimed bullet now will certainly finish me off, but the gears are easy and the wheels turn and out of the corner of my eye I see them as they both reach for their revolvers, turning furious faces towards the pavement, descending the better to take aim, and me in a toiling plume of exhaust which hinders their vision, I who am underway realise in that cathartic, that explosive, indescribable moment of freedom, which is like the moment of death itself, in that fragment of an instant that the massive, vigilant trees in the park opposite will not this time be the patient witnesses of another murder as I grind through the gears and away, with bullets shattering the rear window and my forage cap holed and flying onto the dashboard, and I see with inexpressible relief that the road in front of me is clear as I gain speed, ramming the gears one after another into their respective positions, turn right, turn left and on like fury while my mind clears to the recollection of a driveway about a mile from my present position, one that is always open and may the gods that play with us scorn our ignorant ways, permit that this place is as accessible as it was yesterday, and I see as the small back street alongside the cemetery comes into view and I close in on it that the garage doors are open as usual and that the driveway which descends under the house is free, and the engine is still now as I sit and wait in its dark interior for a minute, listening intently, sitting quite still, listening for the slightest stirring that might give me away, opening my eyes and my mind to the benediction of darkness here in the empty garage, waiting for a minute, for two perhaps, three, waiting there until I'm assured there is nothing untoward, and then out into the relative light of the street, after divesting myself of my overcoat, looking both ways as

EXIT

I go, running for all I am worth for the bus-stop I know is somewhere not far in the distance, passing a man with a dog, and another with a newspaper in his hand, and, after a few hundred yards, there it is in the distance, I think, yes, I am on the right way, slower now, slower, but as I arrive I am out of breath and the knot of human beings waiting for the bus think I've been running for the bus, having wrongly judged the time of its departure and one woman in the queue says I needn't have run so hard as it's only five-twenty and I try to smile and nod between drawing my breath and then another, eyeing me, tells me it's too cold to go out without a coat in midwinter, that I must have forgotten it in my hurry and there's mild amusement and I am deeply thankful for the remark, look silly and nod to the truth of it, panting, drawing my breath, my eyes watering, my mouth full of saliva, drawing in the breath of life in great gulps while some others in the group of those who wait look askance and we wait together in silence while an age passes under the leaden skies of Berlin's reluctant dawn.

2

Light Under a Bushel

Many years ago, in the city of Chesterfield, England, there once lived an elderly couple. At the time I speak of, he was seventy-two and she was sixty-nine. To see them stroll in the park of a Sunday it would be quite easy to assume that they were married. But they were not married. Mrs Thornton, *née* Heseltine, had been married, but was widowed in 1917 when her husband, Elias Thornton, fell at the Battle of the Somme. The man she walked with in the park and occasionally in the town was called Jack Roebottom and he hailed from a place a good deal further north of Chesterfield, like Mrs Thornton herself, and he had been a bachelor all his life. The fact was that these two were landlady and lodger for nigh on thirty years. In this relationship they had experienced two world wars together and all the changes, social, economic and technological that had taken place during that period. At times life had not been easy, God knows, but somehow they had got by and together managed to keep the little household afloat. He, Roebottom, had twice been out of work, for example, and she had once been taken to hospital where she stayed for six months. Mr Roebottom had visited her there every day, even though at the beginning Mrs Thornton had lain unconscious in her hospital bed for weeks and Sunday visitors and other folks went by on tiptoe as if out of respect for the dead. That had been a hard time for Jack and during it he had learned to cook for himself – well, a little, let's say. He could boil an egg, for example, and toast bread, make tea, and this until the day Mrs Thornton returned from Turnpike General Hospital. Since then he seems to have gone off egg and toast. Aye, that was a day, the day when she returned. He had had the whole of the little house, two up and two down, decked out with flowers and sweets. Even the kitchen looked like an arbour. He had made a frame of flowers for the picture of Corporal Thornton, VC, in uniform standing alone, rifle in hand, near the barracks where he was once stationed. It was a good picture. Two months after it was taken, he was dead. This brown photograph stood on the sideboard and had been witness to the lives of these two in the parlour from the very beginning. And now, Jack Roebottom had threaded flowers round its frame and, I must admit, with success. And then Mrs Thornton arrived. He heard the taxi door click to, and as he moved towards the front door he could hear the engine running. She crossed the pavement into his open arms and he noticed how thin she had become. This encounter was the only intimacy they had ever indulged in all these years. Mrs Thornton had often looked back to that moment and had also often wondered if Jack Roebottom had done the same. Occasionally, she yearned for such moments. But he could be so distant, this Jack, content enough with his pipe and his pint three nights a week down at the Working Men's Club. How she longed to know more about him. The years, however, had caught up with them and she had adapted herself to his long silences and his self-sufficiency.

'Another cup of tea, Mrs Thornton?'

'Aye, don't mind if I do, thank yer.'

He was always civil, one of nature's gentlemen.

Every weekend, or almost every weekend, weather permitting, he would take her out either on Saturday or Sunday, and this was always a treat because then she would meet his cronies and they'd always end up at some pub or other and almost always a different one. He seemed to know everyone and every bar, this Jack. And then they'd return to the little house in a row of sixty houses and each would retire for the night to a separate chamber. Nothing serious ever really happened to disturb the routine of their lives except for the occasional visit of one of her relatives together with the children and, these days, their children's children.

'I've become old,' said Mrs Thornton one day to the mirror and she was aware at the same time that, somehow, many of the good things in life had passed her by. 'Young folks go on holiday these days,' she said, again out loud. 'Wouldn't that be lovely, to go to some romantic place like Paris or Rome or even some sunny place in Spain? Everything's possible these days,' she added as she looked at herself carefully close to the glass. It made her sad, this thought, and she turned from her reflection with a sigh.

Jack's life had been a regular one, too. He had worked at the same printing shop for fifty years, starting work as a lad of fourteen and, except for four years' service in the army during the First World War, his life had been relatively uneventful. But he read a good deal, Mr Roebottom, read and read. His eyesight was extremely good and even now, at seventy-two years of age, he needed no assistance from a lens to read or to focus on objects near or at a distance. Often when they were out together on some Saturday or Sunday afternoon, he would point out something to his consort, something which had caught his attention, and Mrs T. would stare and stare in the direction indicated only to discover the cause of his enthusiasm much later as they approached the object.

Yes, this reading of his – very often in what for her was very bad light, she felt – and the subject was nothing which she could share. This fact disappointed her deeply. It would have been so interesting and for her so satisfying if they could have shared a mutual subject of interest, but she couldn't, simply couldn't work up any enthusiasm for – what was the last book he had borrowed on the inter-library service some time ago? Something so bizarre that she had taken the trouble to note the title: *The Interference of Ultra-violet Light on Colour in Stamp Production*. Ah yes, and then there was another, she recalled: *Refractive Indices and Colour Change in Fluids*. A mixture of astonishment and curiosity had moved her to open the book, but what she found therein was for her quite unreadable, a book full of tables, graphs and mathematical formulae. 'How very odd,' she had thought to herself on that occasion, 'not the kind of reading one would associate with an ordinary individual. I mean, this kind of thing was more for educated specialists. Was he educated?' she asked herself. She would pump him about it when he came home from his pint. Although never drunk on these occasions, his returns from the pub were marked by a certain inclination to talk and these moments of communication were often the best of the day.

Thursday evening around eleven, she heard his heavy step towards the door and then the key turning in the lock. He had become just a little corpulent of late, she noted, but then, hadn't we all? It was always reassuring to know that it was him after all coming down the short, dark corridor that led to their parlour. Even after all these years she still entertained the secret fear that it could be someone else. His policeman's step now brought him into view.

'Still up, then?' he enquired cheerfully.

'Oh yes, been doing some knitting and listening to the wireless. Good programmes tonight. Quite entertaining. Would you like some warm milk before you go to bed?'

'No, no, not on top of the beer, I'll wait a while.'

They chatted about how nice the weather had been and about his new acquisition, a bicycle.

'Problem is where to put it,' he said simply.

'Leave it in the entry. It'll be all right there. Mrs Copeland's kitchen window looks onto it and she'll keep an eye on it I'm sure.'

'Nevertheless, I'll buy a lock and chain for it. You never know these days.'

She liked his northern accent, the 'knaw' of 'know'. He'd never lost his northern burr and it always charmed her. Bolton was the place where he had been born. She had never been to Bolton. When she considered for a moment, the furthest she had ever been was to her sister's place in Torquay. Dorothy, though, had long since been dead. Poor Dorothy. Cancer.

'Did you go to the library today? You said you were waiting for a new book from Interloan. Did you get it?' she asked.

'Naw, dear. Tomorrow.'

She liked him to call her 'dear'. He was, after all, a dear man himself. But she was curious, and continued her ploy.

'What's the new book about? I can never make hog, dog 'n' mutton of the stuff you read. I like a nice romance myself. You know, for the first time since you've been in this house I've had a peek at the titles of the books you read. Odd stuff. Really odd, I say.'

Roebottom coughed and cleared his throat as though about to deliver a lecture. 'Printing stuff, Mrs Thornton, printing technology. I'm still interested in it, you know. Been in the business all my life and finally rose to be departmental manager.'

'Aye, I remember that,' she said, 'you've told me more than once, I think. But I would have thought you'd have finished with all that by now. Give yourself a rest like. A bit of light literature would do you good I reckon.'

He laughed gently at this. 'Well, it might at that,' he concurred. But now it was time for the milk and bed.

She watched him drink the milk slowly and appreciatively.

'Aye, good, this,' he said, nodding over the glass. She was pleased.

They listened to the midnight news on their old radio and

then, when it was over and they were informed of tomorrow's weather, they took leave of one another.

'Good night, Mr Roebottom.'

'Good night, Mrs Thornton, sleep well.'

'Thank you, I take my little nightcap,' by which she meant a little herbal pill which helped her get off to sleep quickly.

After twenty minutes or so, the full moon appeared at her window like a gentle visitor, soft and yellow. She peered at it from the comfort of her pillow. It seemed to be telling her something. But how absurd! And yet... She lay there fascinated by its round, peaceful quiescence, it seemed never to be in a hurry, this moon, she reflected, and despite the little green pill she lay awake for another hour at least. 'What *are* "refractive indices"?' she asked herself before falling asleep. Tomorrow, she would look for the dictionary she once owned and find out.

Another twenty minutes passed and the moon had arrived at Jack's window. First, it touched the old curtains and the half-yard of netting stretched across the lower part of the window. And then, little by little, its light moved over to the fine mahogany chest of drawers, the upper drawer of which was closed while all the others were partially open. The truth is that the key to the upper drawer was in the pocket of a pair of trousers that hung over a chair together with their owner's undergarments. And, slowly, slowly, the moonlight illuminated the bed and its sleeping inmate, the coverlet drawn up to an ear. Not a sound, not a movement, and it was difficult to say whether anyone was there at all. The rest of the room exhibited that untidiness resulting from too many things in too small a space, an apologetic untidiness. All that this man possessed was in this room and there were many books, journals and papers piled up at the side of the bed some four feet high. On the small door leading to the attic there was a picture of a human body showing the internal organs and the circulatory system. All in all, this room resembled a student's den. Moreover, it was a place to which this man, Roebottom, often retired for hours on end. Mrs Thornton never set foot in here. It was a tacit agreement between them never to enter each other's rooms. The cleaning, therefore, was left to its occupant, and for him was an activity undertaken once a year.

Mrs Thornton, wondering whether the incumbent was all right, would frequently knock on the door, cup of tea in hand, which she would then offer him at the threshold. She would often find her lodger simply reading or tinkering with a watch or clock, which was a hobby of his. Folks would often bring their small jobs to him for repair, a clock here, a hair-dryer there, a typewriter or a faulty electric razor, and once he had even lugged part of a motorcycle engine up the steep, dark stairs for treatment on his broad desktop. At the time, Mrs T. had considered this too much of a good thing. 'Eric Tranter is just putting on you. It's not right to ask a man of your age to do a big job like that,' she had protested. But Jack Roebottom, a man of infinite patience, had taken it upon himself to repair the defect, and what he had said he would do he would do and there was an end to it.

The motorcycle, as far as I know, is still roaring through the town.

Then came the Day of the Plumber. Mrs Thornton had gone downstairs to make a cup of tea for breakfast as usual when she discovered to her surprise that no water was forthcoming from the tap in the kitchen.

'Ugh! Funny,' she said, her arms akimbo before the offending faucet, and wearing that expression common to all womankind when confronted with a technical problem. 'Mr Roebottom! ... Mr Roebottom!' she called upstairs.

Roebottom's heavy foot found the first step of the descent. 'I'm coming.'

'The tap won't work. No water.'

Once in the kitchen, Mr Roebottom twiddled and fiddled under the sink, but to no avail. After a moment or two of this activity he straightened himself with a groan and announced, 'Water's been turned off.'

'Well, I'm blowed. They usually tell us before they turn the water off,' said Mrs Thornton in annoyance. She was referring to the local water authority.

Jack shrugged his shoulders. 'Hmm,' he said, 'can't shave either. Better fetch t'plumber.'

'Aye,'

So Jack lumbered out of the house to call upon Whitworth, the plumber. 'Then I'll go on t'post office,' he added after a few steps on the pavement outside.

Mrs Thornton merely nodded at this and took up the daily paper from the hall floor, stooping a second time after Mr Roebottom's departure to bring in the milk bottles from the street.

"Ere, you can wash in milk!' she called after him with a smile as Jack headed towards Whitworth's.

'Aye – like Pompeia,' Jack replied and then he was round the corner out of sight.

'Like who?' Mrs Thornton asked herself as she re-entered the house. 'Pompeii? Isn't that some place in Italy? Sometimes he is really queer,' she mused.

Whitworth arrived within the hour, a small, round man with a magnificent head of hair and a handlebar moustache.

'From my days in the Royal Air Force,' he would say when folks admired the moustache. A cheerful, balanced, practical man, this Whitworth, with a twinkle in his eye and a wry sense of humour. Indeed, if one knew nothing of his professional activity, the last thing one would have associated him with would have been pipes and cisterns, tanks and stopcocks, threads and clack valves. He seemed rather a man born into the world of entertainment, a man of repartee, a master of ceremonies at any do up and down the country, a slick comedian perhaps, but now here he was in his boiler suit with his first words of blithe inquiry.

'And what appears to be the trouble, Mrs T?' he said, that twinkle in his eye.

'Tap won't work,' Mrs Thornton said laconically.

'Umm.' Samuel Whitworth made a few perfunctory checks of the kind Jack had made half an hour before. Then, suddenly, he assumed an earnest expression.

'Is any water coming through the ceiling upstairs?' he asked.

Mrs Thornton was taken aback by this suggestion. 'Goodness me, I hope not!'

'Could be, though,' said Whitworth enjoying for a moment the superiority born of professional experience, 'I'll have to check in the roof.'

'Mr Roebottom isn't here at the moment, Mr Whitworth. I don't like to go into his room, without his knowing. The door to the roof's in that room.'

Whitworth acknowledged this, but at the same time pointed out that should the overflow cock not be functioning properly, there was the likelihood of several hundred gallons of water responding to the call of gravity and slowly but surely making their way to the drains below the house.

Whitworth's pompous rhetoric was lost on Mrs Thornton as she ushered the plumber up the stairs to Jack Roebottom's room.

'The door to the attic's there,' she said, indicating the small door with the picture of the human circulatory system on it, below which some books were stacked.

'You'll have to move the bed to one side, I think,' Mrs Thornton suggested.

This was soon done since Mr Whitworth was a strong man. But then he found the door locked and, turning to Mrs Thornton, he asked for the key.

'I haven't got one. He has the key, I suppose. Don't know when he'll be back.'

At this moment, Mrs Thornton felt slightly ill at ease. Although it was certainly interesting to once more be in this room after thirty years or so, it was, she had to admit, a little embarrassing as well. There were feelings of betrayal and conflict within her.

'Well, it could be a matter of urgency,' Whitworth continued, turning to her once again after another attack on the door. 'I'll have to force the thing.'

Mrs Thornton winced, but she realised that it had to be done. In no time at all Whitworth had the door open and shone his torch into the gloom above. The beam revealed a switch just behind the door and he flicked it on and then went up the narrow wooden steps to the attic above. What met his eyes at this instant would fill the ears of the town for the next decade. It was, if you will, like suddenly setting light to a haystack. The very strong light in the attic revealed that water had indeed overflowed from the cistern there and that it had not yet seeped through the ceiling below because heavy boards had been laid on the rafters at some time or other to cover about fifty square feet. On top of these boards was a very firm, collapsible steel table and, a little to one side, a high-voltage heavy duty printing machine. About forty or fifty one-pound notes had been placed on a large sheet of glass next to this machine to dry. Some crisp ten-shilling notes had also been placed on clean paper for subsequent use as tender. Forgers' tools were scattered about and a range of colours, dyes and solvents were lined up along one edge of the steel table. After taking all this in, Whitworth retraced his steps and appeared once again in Mr Roebottom's bedroom. The light in the workshop had been so intense that this little room now appeared almost gloomy.

'Er... Mrs Thornton, could you come a moment?' Whitworth's usual joviality had left him. 'The place must be flooded,' thought Mrs Thornton as she entered the attic. Then the two of them were standing there, speechless under the glare.

'Roebottom?' said Mr Whitworth at last.

'Who else?' returned Mrs Thornton. 'Oh dear, this will land him in jug for many a year, that's for sure. Oh dear, oh dear,' she thought to herself in the next moment.

Mr Whitworth had turned slightly pale and his eyes studied Mrs Thornton's expression. 'What shall I do?' he asked simply.

'Mend the leak or whatever it is and I'll see to the rest,' she replied succinctly.

The plumber drew himself up, a reflex he had learned in the RAF. 'Of course. Immediately.' And he set about finding the right tool to adjust the valve. It took him some time and when he had done the repair work, had switched off the light, closed the door and was ready to go downstairs again he met two policemen coming up the stairs, closely followed by the good Mrs Thornton. They greeted each other curtly in the obscurity of the stairway and Whitworth was obliged to turn and go upstairs again since there was no room to pass each other at that point of their encounter. Once in Roebottom's room, the two policemen consulted Whitworth about his discovery.

'And you have left everything just as you found it?' one of the policemen asked.

'Oh yes, I pick my money up elsewhere,' he replied before he could check himself. The quip was not lost on the police constable and he looked at Whitworth sharply. 'So you do, do you?' he said in that way policemen have when their suspicions are aroused.

'I mean, I *earn* it, Officer. I don't manufacture it,' Whitworth added hastily and with emphasis.

'We shall need you as a witness this afternoon at the police station, Mr Whitworth, if you don't mind,' said the constable, ignoring his remonstration.

'And you too, Mrs Thornton,' the senior officer added with a smile.

This policeman, a sergeant, had just returned from the forger's workshop with a satisfied look on his face.

'He'll get ten years for this, that's for sure,' he said with an air of accomplishment.

Mrs Thornton felt a traitor as they descended the stairs to the parlour below. A moment later, Mr John Ernest Roebottom stepped into the room.

If he was surprised to see the police officers there, he didn't show it.

'Is your name Roebottom?' the sergeant asked, taking out his notebook.

'Yes,' Jack said quietly.

'Is this tool kit yours?' He indicated a bag full of tools.

'Yes.'

'You know why we are here?'

'Yes.'

'Very well, I must arrest you in the name of the law on a charge of forgery.'

Jack humbly submitted himself to being handcuffed and without further ado was then led out of the house to the waiting police van in the road. A little crowd had gathered to watch the proceedings. Mrs Thornton felt more and more like Judas Iscariot as each minute passed. She was crying. The tears were tears of sadness and confusion. Should she have conspired with Whitworth not to mention the whole thing she asked herself? But such a thing was impossible, she knew, and would have only made things worse. She had known the plumber for years, knew him as a man who liked to tell a story, liked a laugh, drank his fill in convivial company and sat easy to life. It was highly unlikely that he'd hold water despite his trade, she considered bitterly. And to be found out later would have resulted in a catastrophe, a catastrophe of huge proportions. What could she have done in such a situation she asked herself? Nothing. There was a witness after all. Had she discovered Jack's clandestine activity herself, perhaps things would have been different. Perhaps.

* * *

LIGHT UNDER A BUSHEL

Two months passed before Jack Roebottom's case came up before the court. Mrs Thornton was not allowed during this time to visit her paying guest, because of a law pertaining to collusion. She missed his heavy footstep in the hall and the sweet-smelling tobacco of his pipe, his patience and his unvarying kindly courtesy, his generosity, his frankness and humour. The house was empty without him and she was beginning to feel lonely. To make up for this loss she sent him the kind of cake he liked and a pot of jam that she had made that summer. And after the press had got over its paroxysms of joy at finding a real forger among the residents of Chesterfield, she sent him the paper each day. She never received an answer to her many little gifts, but, she surmised, he was probably not allowed to send letters from prison. And perhaps, after all, she could not expect a reply. Perhaps he hated her now for betraying him to the police. Often she sat down and wept as Iscariot is said to have wept. Unlike him, however, she did not hang herself, but instead went out and spent some of her hard-earned savings on a new costume and coat in order to appear properly dressed in court.

Months passed. Finally, Mrs Thornton was informed personally that the case was to be judged on February 1st at the local assizes. Mr Justice Graymore was to preside. The day arrived and the case opened with the usual questions put with a view to establishing identity. Mr Whitworth, the plumber, and Mrs Thornton were in turn asked about the circumstances of their discovery on the morning in question. All this was taken down and later they were cross-examined by Mr Roebottom's defence. Interrupting for a moment, the magistrate asked how long Mrs Thornton had known the offender.

'Thirty-two years, sir.' she replied.

'And in all that time you never suspected that there might be something going on upstairs?' the judge queried.

'No, sir.'

'No idea at all? I mean, did the accused ever display a great deal more money than would be normally the case in his circumstances, for example? That is to say, did he show off with his money?'

'No, sir,' Mrs Thornton said simply.

'I see. So you never benefited materially from this extra income?' There was subdued laughter in the public gallery at this. 'I mean, did you receive expensive gifts from the accused, of gold or silver, let's say, or were you treated to a long holiday and such?'

'No. He always seemed to have enough, paid his rent regularly and I never had any trouble with him. All we did was to go out together from time to time.'

'Does that mean that he spent a lot on you at such times?'

'No, not at all. We would sit in the Black Swan and drink of an evening, that's all.'

The judge raised his eyebrows. 'The "Black Swan", I take it that this is a public house in the neighbourhood?'

'Yes, sir.'

Mrs Thornton looked across the courtroom towards Jack Roebottom sitting with his lawyer. He seemed unperturbed by the proceedings and sat there, resigned to his fate, his large hands folded between his knees. It crossed her mind how clever these hands were to make pound notes that could pass as legal tender.

The judge continued, 'So I understand you are telling me that to all intents and purposes you had not the slightest idea that the accused could in fact be a rich man?'

'That's right. He never gave me that impression and swanking's not his way.'

Finally, Roebottom himself was questioned. For the prosecution, Mr Algernon Pettifoot addressed himself to the accused. 'John Ernest Roebottom, how old are you?'

'Seventy-two.'

'Will you give an account of your activities in the attic of 21 Marlborough Street in this city? How long, for example, have you been a forger?'

'About twenty-five years.' Jack answered without expression. A murmur of astonishment ran through the court at hearing this.

'Making money good enough to deceive those accepting it is not an easy matter. Where did you learn to do this?'

'I was employed at a firm which made stamps, bonds and foreign money.'

'I see. But for effective printing you need expensive equipment, do you not?'

'Yes.'

'So that, initially, obliged you to invest quite a lot of money. Is that correct?'

'Yes, it is.'

'And you saved this from your salary I presume?'

'Yes, I did.'

'Mr Roebottom, what were the reasons for you to need to break the law in this way?'

'I was never paid enough for the expertise required to do a good job of this kind,' Jack replied with a hint of emphasis in his voice.

'Do you mean to say that your wages were inadequate?' Mr Pettifoot continued.

'Yes, I noticed very early on that the owner of the firm for which I worked drove a huge car, lived in a large house in the suburbs of the city and could afford everything he desired, while those who actually did the work for him lived meanly by comparison.'

'So you thought you would increment your income somewhat, is that it?'

A ruffle of amusement again in the public gallery. Roebottom remained unconcerned. 'Not all at once, no. The idea only occurred to me after I'd worked there for many years.'

'When would that have been, would you say?'

'When I was getting older and my thoughts were turning to what lay in store for me in the future.'

'Did you feel that your pension would have been too little, then?' Mr Pettifoot asked coolly.

'Yes.'

'And is it?'

'It's just enough to live on very modestly like the salary I once earned,' Jack replied with equal coolness. There was an exchange between Mr Justice Graymore and Mr Algernon Pettifoot. The latter then continued his interrogation.

'Would you describe yourself as a man with high aspirations?'

'No, I don't think so,' Jack replied, looking at his questioner sturdily. 'I live modestly, as has already been noted in this court. I don't own a car or go to Bermuda for six weeks, entertain a troop of servants or live it up generally.'

'Are you referring by this remark to the habits of your former employer?'

'Yes.'

'Could it be that you are jealous?'

'No, but the crass difference between the way he lived and the way his employees had to live is an indictment on society and on labour conditions as a whole in this class-ridden land.'

The courtroom was electrified by this. One didn't talk about class in England at that time, and it was quite obvious to every single person sitting in the room that the classes, as Roebottom envisaged them, were talking to each other at this very moment in the shape of Mr Pettifoot and the accused. Mr Justice Graymore, himself a conscientious, thoughtful individual, was also one who did not delight in the superiority of his position nor use his place to evoke the embarrassment of others as some of his colleagues might have done in a similar situation. He intervened to ask, 'Are you a communist, Mr Roebottom?'

'No, I am not a communist,' Jack replied.

'But I can tell by your manner and speech that you are a well-read man. Is that so?'

'I've done some reading, yes,' Jack replied with dignity. There was another pause. Mr Pettifoot continued his inquiries.

'I might assume, then, that what you did was a considered action and not just an experiment in view of Mr Justice Graymore's question. Nor, apparently, were your actions provoked by a desire to get rich. Is that so?'

'Yes, that is so. I could have become rich and left the country, but I didn't want to end up being somebody like my boss.'

'You don't seem to like your boss much,' Mr Pettifoot smiled with kindly amusement.

'I didn't like his arrogance if that's what you mean,' Jack countered with some warmth. 'He had no grounds for arrogance that man. He was mean and stupid.'

At this, Mr Pettifoot raised his eyebrows. Then he said, 'Now let us get down to brass tacks, Mr Roebottom. You have sworn on oath to tell the truth. How much did you make per week or per month on your machines?'

'Enough to supply me with beer and cigarettes.'

'Is that all?' Mr Pettifoot's voice showed surprise.

'Yes, about three pounds a week, reckoned by today's money.'

'Then how do you explain the piles of notes discovered by the police in Mrs Thornton's attic? That was a good deal more than the three pounds you speak of.'

'There were more favourable times than others to work. In the winter it was often too cold or too damp for the paper to dry properly and in the summer it was frequently too hot upstairs or the humidity wasn't right for a good job. So I laid up a job in advance when printing could be carried out in good conditions. I never spent more than three pounds a week, as I say, or its equivalent today.' Jack Roebottom made a slight bodily gesture as though to continue and then hesitated.

'Do go on, Mr Roebottom. You have something more to add?' Mr Pettifoot probed.

'There was a lot of research and experimentation connected with my work,' Jack Roebottom went on. 'The design or colour of notes would change at the Treasury and this needed quite a lot of attention. Many of the notes found by the police, for example, were experimental notes, quite worthless on the market.' Again there was a rustle of interest among those observing the proceedings.

'I see. And where did you change your banknotes when they had met with your specifications?'

'At the station or at Lyall Street Bank.'

'But that's a long way from Marlborough Street where you live, isn't it? You could have changed them at the local newsagent's.'

'They're friends,' Roebottom said simply.

It was some time before the laughter in court could be suppressed. Mr Graymore threatened to clear the public gallery. Jack for his part witnessed the whole thing calmly, never changing his expression or removing his hands from the bar in front of him.

At this point Mr Justice Graymore intervened again to remind Jack Roebottom of the seriousness of his crime and to tell him that, as he put it, 'I am obliged to commit you to the High Court for trial there. You are also aware, I hope,' he added, 'that the maximum penalty for forgery is not less than ten years' hard labour, although at your age I dare say such a term may well be commuted to something less.' His face became earnest as he said this, looking over his glasses at the culprit. He dismissed proceedings for that day.

Later, Jack Roebottom was tried at Sheffield High Court and given three years' imprisonment. His lawyer pleaded for a fine in view of the age of the accused, but it was found that the criminal in question was not in a position to pay any sum at all and even if the fine were to be levied over a period of time it was possible that he might die in the interim. Thus, he was handed over to the jailer to serve a term of imprisonment.

Jack Roebottom didn't die. Instead, about eighteen months later he was discharged from prison for good conduct and arrived at Chesterfield station to be met by none other than his former landlady. Mrs Thornton was too overcome by emotion to greet him as he stepped from the train onto the platform. Her eyes were filled with tears. 'Oh Jack,' said Mrs Thornton, 'I'm so sorry, so sorry.'

'Don't take on so, girl,' Jack said kindly, laying an arm round her shoulders. No one recognised him as they walked slowly to the station exit. At last she recovered enough to be able to say: 'I've missed you, Mr Roebottom.'

'Aye.'

'Did they treat you properly? Did they give you enough to eat?'

'Oh yes, simple stuff, but enough. Last Sunday we had chicken. One of the warders had a birthday,' he remarked briefly.

They moved through the station ticket office and reached the road and the taxi rank outside.

'Let's not go home yet,' Jack said, looking at her suddenly at the same time touching her arm. 'I suggest we have a cup of tea and I know a nice café not far from here.' Mrs Thornton brightened. 'What a good idea. Let's do that.' They walked on arm in arm.

Once inside the café, Jack removed his heavy grey coat that he had had for years and helped Mrs Thornton to get out of hers, hanging it up on the coat hangers that were supplied near the stairs. It was warm inside the little café. They found a table, sat down and ordered tea.

'Do you still take sugar in your tea, Mr Roebottom?' she asked, smiling.

Jack smiled too and then he said, 'Call me Jack. Nobody's called me Roebottom recently.' A large smile spread over his face. She, too, smiled. 'And I've been thinking,' he said. He lifted his spoon thoughtfully. Mrs Thornton waited with interest.

'Can I call you "Joan"? I mean... I mean we've known each other a long time?' The pitch of his voice rose slightly to a question that needed confirmation.

'Oh Jack,' was all Mrs Thornton could say.

They sipped their tea in silence for a few minutes more. Then he enquired, 'What are your plans for the future, Joan?'

'What do you mean, Jack?' She looked at him curiously. It was strange, this getting used to Christian names.

'Well, we, er ... er could go on, er like we did or, er ... do something else... I mean...' Jack paused for a moment before continuing. 'I mean...'

'Yes, Jack?'

He paused again after clearing his throat and changed tack. 'Mmm, you remember Bill Finney?'

Joan Thornton was visibly disappointed at this diversion, and it was only with difficulty that she recalled the burly figure of Bill Finney, his loud laugh and his huge hands.

'Yes,' she said crisply. 'I only saw him once, I believe.'

'Well, he's dead,' Jack said without the slightest emotion.

'Dead?'

'Yes, dead. He died a few weeks ago at Burlington Hospital, Rochdale. I learned this while eating my bread in humility,' he said, smiling faintly.

She noted the turn of phrase. Then she said: 'Oh.'

'Thrombosis.'

Jack looked at her for a long moment. 'He was the best mate I've ever had. Close as a clam. He was into this with me, you know.' He looked at her intently for a second. 'I learned it all from him.'

Joan was silent. Jack moved his heavy body to look round the little café, at folks reading papers and watching the rain that had started to grime the windows. He sighed. Then he turned again to look at his companion.

'Yes, Bill. He'd been ill for years. Kept having to go to hospital for checks and operations and the like.' Again he paused. 'You know how it is with these things?' Joan nodded. 'Well, he, ah, he gave me a stack of money to keep for him. All good stuff, you understand.' He paused and again looked around the smoke-filled room before continuing. 'None of these were forged notes, nothing like that, and now he's dead and ... well, I've still got the money,' he added quickly.

Mrs Thornton looked hard at him for a moment over the table.

'What do you mean, "got"?' Jack Roebottom looked embarrassed. She had never seen him embarrassed before.

'Must be about a hundred thousand quid, I reckon. Bill wanted to collect it and live somewhere else, but it wasn't to be, you see,' he said with resignation. Again there was a long silence between them. Thoughts chased one another in Joan's mind. She decided finally not to ask him any more questions and just to sit there waiting for him to continue. But Jack Roebottom didn't continue. He finished his tea with a loud gulp.

Finally, she said: 'Where?'

'In the sofa. You've been sitting on it for years.'

At this, Joan was dumbstruck. 'How did it get in there?' she asked at last.

'When you visited your sister a few years ago in Torquay I sewed it up in there for safety.' He said this in such a matter-of-fact way that she couldn't help laughing out loud. People turned their heads in her direction.

'Well,' she said, 'you're a dark horse, you really are! Who have I been living with all these years?'

Jack looked sheepish and apologetic at the same time. This only made her laugh all the more.

'And who does all this belong to now, if I've a mind to unstitch the sofa – his heirs I suppose?'

'He has no one,' Jack replied quickly. 'He's a bachelor, like me. Was, that is...' and here Jack hesitated again, 'so, it's ours.'

'Ours?'

'Yes, well...' Now he was thoroughly flustered, embarrassed and quite unable to say anything else but 'so' and 'well'. She loved him for it. 'I mean, er... I thought we could, er, get, er, er, get married or something?' The last was added hurriedly, almost by way of an apology.

'Or something?' Joan answered, her forehead creasing in irritation.

'Well, you know what I mean,' he added in a tone of self-defence.

'Mr Roebottom. Are you suggesting I marry a jailbird, an ancient forger, a custodian of ill-gotten gains?' She asked this so seriously that he was touched to the quick. He sat there crestfallen at this retort, and she nearly cried to see him so. At least by this she knew that he was sincere, but she nevertheless continued in the same vein.

'Are you asking me to marry you after all these years, Jack Roebottom?'

He recovered himself manfully and said, 'Yes, dear, I am.'

'Well, then, ask!' Again she was speaking quite loudly so that again heads turned to look at them.

So Jack Roebottom formally asked Mrs Joan Thornton to marry him. Then they held hands across the table while the rain spattered merrily against the window. Outside, the evening was drawing in and the town lights were already aglow.

3

Nina

Once upon a real time there lived two children who attended a school in Gloucestershire, England. Although it was only just over seventy years ago, so much has taken place in the meantime that their existence seems now to have belonged to another age. Another age indeed, when he, though not much more than ten years old at the time, helped a little girl after finding her in tears and desperation on a very cold winter's day in 1942. It was snowing hard along the country lane which led from the village school to the neighbourhood, a mile or two away, where they lived not far from each other.

She had lost her scarf, she said as he came upon her in the gloom of that early evening, and although this today would be nothing much to be concerned about, in those days it was truly a loss. War raged in Europe and relations were tense everywhere. The time had not yet come when one could simply drop in at the next supermarket and pick up a scarf for a few shillings. There were no supermarkets. Clothing was expensive.

'Have you left it at school?' he asked the little girl.

She shook her head. Tears filled her blue eyes. She had not dared to see whether she had lost it in a snowball fight down the road a few minutes before, for now it was nearly dark and she was afraid. The other children had all disappeared, laughing into the white, whirling, all-enveloping snow. It was snowing heavily, so much so that neither of them could see beyond about thirty feet from where they were. They stood there quite alone in the half light of a silent, snow-filled world.

'What's your name?' enquired Eric, the little boy.

'Nina,' she sobbed.

He considered for a moment. 'I think you've dropped it on the way,' he said shortly and sensibly in the way his mother would speak, and then, 'Wait here and don't go away. I'll see if I can find it.' So saying, he turned back the way he'd come, quickly vanishing into swirling oblivion.

Her fear of reprimand at home was added to by the apprehension that the boy might not return, that she would lose her way in the snow and perhaps not survive the oncoming night. Overhead, she heard the muffled sound of an aircraft plying through the night. Terror seized her. She stood very still like a frightened rabbit while the snowflakes tried to reduce her to another soft mound in the landscape like the hedges and trees and gates around her. Then, suddenly, the boy appeared again, her snow-laden scarf in his hand.

'That's the enemy upstairs,' he said wisely, recognising the sound of a German bomber and pointing upwards. It was his uncle's phrase. 'We'd better get home quickly. Where do you live?'

She was so relieved to see him again and have the wet scarf firmly round her neck that she could hardly answer. Then she said, 'I live at The Hayes.'

He knew the house. It stood in its own grounds just beyond the housing estate where his father had a shop, a relic from the nineteenth century, large and imposing. He had often wondered who lived there. They walked on with difficulty through the snow, which was now up to their knees, saying nothing more, she clutching her scarf and her satchel, he with his school cap pulled over his eyes into his rosy face.

After a few minutes, they gained the main road which cut

through their part of the village, and he took her elbow gently. 'Better to cross here. It's safer.'

She didn't know why, but followed his instructions. Once on the other side of the road, they heard the familiar whine of an army truck as it rolled past them on bandaged wheels, its dimmed, slotted lights like eyes in the darkness, its form metamorphosed by snow to a mobile, featureless packet of snow. A moment later, a blizzard struck them so that they were temporarily blinded by it and had to stop. Eric, acting on instinct, took his small charge protectively in his arms, and guided her into the direction of a nearby bus-stop shelter. The snowstorm did not make him abandon his resolve to get home. For ten minutes or so they watched as the swirling flakes coalesced with what had already fallen to destroy every feature of identity. On the way to where they were now resting, he had managed to recognise certain landmarks despite the stifling embrace of the blizzard, here a gate, there a tree, and after a while the two of them set forth again. Nina was by this time so truly frightened that all she could do was follow helplessly, her large eyes staring from inside her hood.

'Not far now,' Eric said to encourage her, stamping forward courageously into the whiteness.

It took them a further twenty minutes before they arrived at The Hayes and its wrought-iron gate. Without a word, Nina grappled with the latch, which had six inches of snow piled on it, and pushed. Snow crashed down on them that had been loosely attached to the spikes above. Reluctantly, the gate opened as the two of them pushed mightily against it. Once it had opened wide enough to allow access to their small bodies, Eric said, 'I gotta go back home now. You can find your way to the front door.'

'No, no, come with me to the door!' Nina pleaded. 'It's not far.'

The lad threw his weight against the gate once more to close it, and then they stepped forth into the white, formless garden. Although night had fallen, the whiteness everywhere strangely reflected what little light there was as though it were a moonlit night, and so they soon found the wide steps which led up to the large, oak front door. There were no welcoming lights in the house. Wartime blackout was in force. The steps were slippery and difficult to mount, but once at the door, Nina pulled the heavy brass-ended knob which hung on a wire to one side of the massive door. Seconds passed. Then, suddenly, light appeared from the hallway at the door's ornamented window. A woman opened the door to them, and behind her in the yellow dimness of the hall, another, older woman looked anxiously towards them. One of them was Nina's mother and the other her grandmother.

'Oh, my darling!' said the mother, scooping Nina up into her arms, 'we were so worried. We nearly informed the police. And who's this?' She looked curiously at Eric, half-hidden in the snow which had fallen from the high gate.

Nina explained that Eric had taken her home.

'Come in, come in, both of you!' the women said together, ushering the two children inside, and the front door was closed with a bang. 'Go along now into the living room where it is warm. Here, give me your coats.'

The young people were divested of their wet coats, scarves, shoes, gloves and headwear and soon found themselves in what for Eric was a very large, high-ceilinged room. At one end was a roaring wood fire.

'Er, I must go soon, Mrs...' Eric ventured, feeling a little uneasy.

'Lavelle-Dumois,' the younger woman said kindly. 'Ah, but that's difficult for you, my pet, call me Anita.'

'My mother will be worrying about me, and...'

'Yes, yes, of course, my dear, I understand. Have you got a telephone at home?'

Eric said that they had; they were among the few who possessed one as Eric's father was the local electrician and such a gadget was needed for the business. He gave Anita the number. This was duly called and from the hall Eric could hear the ensuing conversation.

''Allo, it's Lavelle-Dumois at The Hayes. I have your little boy here... Yes, he's all right. He rescued my little girl, Nina, and brought her home through the snow. She'd lost her way. He's quite safe, yes, in the lounge here. Would you like to speak to him?'

Eric was called to speak to his mother and was told that his father would pick him up in a few minutes. The telephone was handed back to Mrs Lavelle-Dumois, who was still standing at his side.

'Very good, Mrs Shipstone... Yes... we're most grateful. Thank you so much. Yes... A young hero... Yes...' She laughed. 'Goodbye, so kind. Goodbye. Thank you.' The phone was replaced and Nina's mother reappeared in the lounge.

'So, young feller, you won't say no to a cup of cocoa, will you?'

Eric acquiesced to this, relieved that his mother wouldn't punish him for being late, a thought which had occupied him throughout the slog uphill in the snow from the school. He had time now to consider the way these two women spoke. It was different. What they said was correct and comprehensible, but unfamiliar. You didn't say ''Allo' like that into the phone. You said 'Hello'. Still, he mused, they were kind folks, that was clear. He sipped at the hot chocolate when it arrived and answered the routine questions about his age, what form he was in at school, what had happened to make them so late (the buses weren't running), whether he knew Nina at school, where he lived, whether he liked school and so on. Eric was bored by such interrogation, but had to admit to himself that the cocoa was welcome. A towel was brought to dry his face and feet.

'Are you in the same class as Nina?' the older woman asked as she reappeared from fetching the towels; her name was Lena. Madame Lavelle-Dumois put more wood onto the fire.

'No, he's a year or two older I think,' she said, straightening from this labour. 'Isn't that so, my dear?' she added, answering her mother's question and turning to Eric for confirmation.

Eric nodded.

'Nina's only eight, Eric must be twelve... Is that not so?'

Eric noted this antique formulation, smiled inwardly, but said that he was eleven-and-a-half and that he'd be twelve in June. Anita seemed inordinately pleased with this answer, the boy thought.

'Nina's birthday is in June, too.'

Nina, who had been wrapped in a blanket and placed nearer the fire in the meantime, looked up from her own cup of cocoa and smiled. The flames danced merrily in the grate.

'We're very proud of you, Eric. You're a real gentleman, did you know that?'

Eric didn't know. He felt just a little embarrassed about all the fuss being made of him and was looking forward to sitting down to his tea at home, but he smiled and nodded, as he had been brought up to be polite to adults at all times, especially customers, regardless of his own feelings. Some minutes later, his father arrived to take him home. More of those adult exchanges which bored him stiff followed. When, during them, he was referred to, smiled at and praised for his heroism, he nodded and smiled himself, but was glad when, at last, he was trundling awkwardly through the night with his father in the firm's cold van. During the short journey home his father said nothing, all his attention being given to negotiating the way back over the slippery, snow-banked roads.

Winter passed, the summer came. Another winter; another summer. Eric grew in strength and in 1944 helped to bring in the harvest on the fields where he met Nina again and hardly recognised her. She was becoming a young woman. He was not yet half a man, but she was half a woman in those days. They talked as young folk do as they helped to bring in the hay. During a break in the afternoon, they sought shade under a stack and she reminded him of the day she lost her scarf. They both laughed as they reminded each other of the details of that day. It seemed from another age and time and they said what a difference a few years can make. Soon she would be finishing school, she told him, and then she'd be off to France for a year at a school there. For him, France was at the other end of the world. Only rich people travelled in those days; 'tourism' was an unknown word. The sun shone on their young faces and the sandwiches their mothers had prepared for them.

Slowly, very slowly, another year passed. Then the war was over. It was as if spring had come again to the nations after a long, dreadful winter. He had himself left school for some time when she returned from France. It was the summer vacation again for her, and for him the period between school and getting a job, during which he was giving a hand to the local farmer as in the war years, since the farmer, Abel Fletcher, and his family were distant relatives and good friends. The strange thing was that he met her quite accidentally at the station where she was waiting for a taxi to take her home. But the one and only taxi was elsewhere at the time. Eric had just delivered goods at the station warehouse and was atop a noisy, smoky tractor. He waved as he caught sight of her. She told him that she had been waiting some time, but that no taxi was in sight and the only telephone was out of order.

'Aw, don't take the taxi,' Eric said loudly over the fumes, 'that's too expensive; I'll take you. Come, hop up here and I'll put your luggage in the truck.' And so he did, and the two of them tuckered up the hill to her home. She laughed and felt it was a great idea.

Lena had seen them coming up the hill towards the house from the garden and as Eric drove up to the gate at last, she welcomed them excitedly. Eric thought that she looked much older than when he had last seen her, but was touched by her happiness at seeing him again. Anita, Nina's mother, soon joined them in the front garden on the other side of the house to welcome them. There was much merriment at the tractor idea and Eric was asked in for a cup of tea.

'Mustn't be too long,' Eric said, 'I'm on a job, but I'll have a sip and then I'll have to go.' And so it was.

'That's the second time you've helped our daughter,' Lena said.

'Eric replied, 'Ah but this time she wasn't in so much distress. I think she was just a bit irritable that no one was there to pick her up!'

'I came on an earlier train and thought I'd surprise you all,' Nina explained.

Eric noticed that her voice was no longer that of a child. He liked her voice. He liked the way she carried herself as she went to fetch the cups for her mother. He liked her face, her figure, the way she moved. All this he noticed in a few fleeting seconds as everyone laughingly agreed that this had been his second knight's mission.

Nina's father appeared for a moment or two from his study to join them as they sat on the shaded balcony in the south wing of the house.

'So you're the young feller called Eric,' the father said amicably. 'I guess you've grown somewhat in the meantime!' he added, and Eric agreed.

Tea and scones were brought by a maid as if from nowhere and everyone tucked in to enjoy the reunion. They were joined by another pair, young people who were on holiday from France and staying with the family, and who shook his hand on being introduced. Eric liked them immediately. In all the conviviality which followed, Eric noticed as she moved about serving one with tea and the other with coffee or a scone how womanly Nina had become and for a moment he looked wistfully around him, wondering why he had not kept up his association with her over the intervening years. She must now be about seventeen, he surmised.

As he looked back into the room from time to time, he familiarised himself with the objects he remembered seeing so many years before. There had been changes, but not enough to render the room wholly unfamiliar. On entering the house, for example, he had noticed the same old-fashioned telephone used on the night he had taken Nina home and, along with this, the tall, equally old-fashioned hat-and-coat stand just inside the door. He also saw the stairs leading up to the bedrooms above and had noted that the carpet had not been replaced by a new one. Today, the old house breathed early summer and it made him happy. The large trees in the garden were already in full leaf, the air warm and balmy. He was glad to be here, he said to himself, and it was good to be alive.

Conversation turned for a time to Nina's intended studies at the Sorbonne in Paris. She hoped to emerge from these as an accomplished cellist, they told him. Eric had never heard her play or even suspected that she played an instrument sufficiently well to attend a university for instruction. From time to time and very briefly for clarification purposes, or so it seemed, phrases were exchanged in French with the visitors, visitors who bravely and for the most part successfully coped with the peculiarities of English, and there was many a laugh when they failed to do so. Eric was asked about his aspirations and replied that he was enjoying his time at the city's technical college, where he was studying electrical engineering. He didn't know, he said, whether he would eventually take over his father's business, but it was likely. They were interested in his activities as a saxophonist with the local band. Nina especially was interested in this side of his life and asked him a number of questions.

'Is it a difficult instrument to learn?' Nina's father wanted to know, and Eric explained that the formation of the right lip shape and the need to coordinate the breathing were most important. This required practice, he said. Leon, the father, pursued the matter with other questions and Eric was glad that his knowledge was put to the test. Moreover, there was a feeling on Eric's part that he was for the first time talking to a man who regarded him as an equal. For the first time in his life he realised that there was no patronisation in the older man's manner, neither in his speech nor his manner, and this endeared him to Eric. They talked of other matters, too – of the political and economic situation, during which Leon warmly recommended he visit France and said that, opportunity arising, he would be glad to take him and introduce him to the country. This was a generous offer at a time when people didn't travel much. It was clear to the young Eric that Leon was sincere in his suggestion.

'Our folks live in the south for the most part. Beautifully warm at this time of the year. You'd like it, I'm sure. Stay for a month or so. You'd never forget it, and I know you'd enjoy it, Eric.' Leon was an uncomplicated personality. If he liked someone, he showed it. If he said something, he meant it.

Nina appeared through the door to the balcony, saw the two of them in conversation and sat down next to them. Once, between male exchanges, she smiled at Eric, and it was at this moment that a chord was struck between them. Perhaps her father had noticed too, for a second later he excused himself politely and joined the others in the garden. The two young people were left alone. They looked into each other's eyes for a moment, only for a second or two, only for that length of time one needs for another to answer a question or before reaction to a remark takes place – one second perhaps? Not more. The time it takes to reply to a request or understand something which for that very short length of time had not been understood. There was a silent communication in the look. Eric received the communication, not knowing fully what it meant, but knowing quite certainly that it was a positive transmission. In it there was something which he interpreted as: 'I like you; let's see more of each other.' After Leon had left to join the others, Eric's ability to say anything sensible or relevant to their being there together for that moment had totally abandoned him. Nina, however, was a true mistress of the situation and promptly asked him whether he would like to go with her and the others into the garden. He rose without a word and the two of them went through the door, down the steps and out into the open air.

On his way home, Eric reviewed his feelings. Nina had not spoken much to him, since courtesy had required her to spend time as an intermediary with the others, but what she had said – and even more important, how she had spoken to him – had left a deep impression on his mind. It was as though their schooldays, although not entirely eclipsed, were now informed by something wonderfully new, the past not quite forgotten, but marvellously metamorphosed and enfolded in a new world of having grown up. Although she was four years younger than he, she was quite as mature. The disparity between them as children had vanished completely. They had wandered together in the garden and both of them, he knew it, had experienced the same happiness, the same joy at being young, the same pleasure in each other's company. This made him determined to see her again. By hook or by crook he would find some means to see her again, he repeated to himself as he went along.

And he did see her again. Not long after the encounter in the garden he rang The Hayes. Nina's mother answered the phone.

'Ah, young Eric! How nice of you to ring. I was thinking about you this morning. Isn't that strange? How are you?'

Eric announced that he was well and asked after Madame's health, hoping against hope that she would ask him whether he would like to speak to Nina.

'Now I'm sure you'd like to speak to Nina. She's here. Just a moment. *Au revoir!*'

'Eric?'

'Yes. Er ... I was wondering whether you would like to come with me to see a film ... er ... on Tuesday evening.' He felt silly. Perhaps he had already done and said the wrong thing. He stumbled on. 'It's supposed to be good. You might like it.' He paused.

'Yes, Eric, why not? I'd love to go with you. Thank you. What film are we going to see?'

Eric had recovered himself sufficiently at this to be able to say, 'Well, let it be a surprise, and I hope you like it. I'll pick you up in Dad's car around seven o'clock.'

'Oh, I like surprises!' she said. 'That's wonderful. I'm looking forward to seeing you.'

'See you then at seven,' he repeated. 'Till then.' Eric left the telephone kiosk feeling ten feet tall. She had said, 'to go with *you*', not merely and only to see the film. She must feel something for him, then, he reasoned. Again, he noted, she had said the right thing. She was in charge of the situation again, whereas he felt as nervous as a butterfly. He smiled to himself.

As the summer months passed gently into autumn they saw each other many times. Her cello practice was the only thing that had priority in her calendar. Both had agreed to work at their studies in the morning during the holidays and meet only in the afternoon or evening. It wasn't long before they were both deeply in love with each other. The countryside was part of their love; the great cedar of Lebanon which stood alone in what was once parkland not far from where they lived; the long, shaded gloom of Sheldon's Walk, whose arbour of high trees had given fronded umbrage to countless lovers, was theirs; the evening air, full of birdsong; the smell of hay; the tall hedgerows with the fair fields behind them; the animals of the field; the friendly wave of a farmhand cycling home to tea; and the bench where they so often sat to talk of many things – all these were intimately interwoven with what they felt for one another in a time which is now past.

Winter came and spring; their respective terms began, but they kept in touch on high days and holidays, returning home to meet each other again, she from Paris and he from London, the intervening absence having sharpened their longing for each other. On their long summer walks they often stopped to kiss under the waning sun, and on the occasion related here they had come across a brick building in the countryside which served as a barn and, in front of it, a yard to contain animals as need arose. At ground level there were stalls and above the barn, floored storage room for hay and the like. They went up into the loft. The warmth of the day's heat reflected from the wooden boards on which there were several bales of straw. Laughing and larking, they threw themselves down onto these and kissed each other passionately. Consumed with desire, Eric cupped her breasts in his hands and after a while freed them slowly from her clothing.

'Someone might come,' she whispered, her eyes misty with love.

'No – we're safe here,' Eric replied. He removed his shirt and pressed her firm pear-shaped breasts against his chest. Within a few moments they were nude, caressing each other ecstatically. He knew after a few moments that she was ready for him, but instead of parting her thighs, she cried bitterly, pressing her nails into his arms and clawing at his back as though in pain, resisting him, pushing, clawing him so that he was astonished at her strength. For a moment or two they struggled like this.

'What's the matter? Let me into you ... now... What's the matter? ... Why?'

'No, no, you mustn't, you mustn't, not yet ... not now, please, dear, dear Eric. No.'

He came in a great tidal wave of sighing and gasping in which he all but lost consciousness, his heart beating like a steam hammer in his chest and eyes and ears, his mind empty, his mouth uttering 'Ohs' and 'Ahs' as the gigantic wave of feeling ebbed to indescribable warmth and gratification. She held him very tight now and then he saw that she was weeping, the tears were streaming down her face to mix with his ejaculation. He straightened to look at her.

'Nina, Nina, have I hurt you? What's the matter?'

She shook her head vigorously, her thick black hair flowing into his face as she did so.

'What then? Have I done something wrong?'

She shook her head again, but didn't stop crying, and as she did so she gave vent to small cries of desperation as though in pain. He held her in his arms and, looking up, saw that the sun had become visible as a red ball at one of the openings in the wooden wall above them.

They clutched at each other for some time in this position until she disentangled herself from him, took the handkerchief he had found for her, wiped herself, rose and dressed. He looked on, ravished by her superb figure, but remained where he was, abashed and defeated, unable to understand what made her so miserable. 'She doesn't want to get pregnant,' he thought and resigned himself to this reasonable conclusion. That was fair enough, he felt, and with this he dressed too, and then helped her down the wooden ladder to the stable door leading out into the yard. It was deliciously cool outside. Nina stood still in the yard.

NINA

'Do I look dishevelled?' she asked him, brushing away a last tear from the corner of her eyes. Without answering, he removed bits of straw from her hair and brushed her back.

'You look OK now,' he said, making a last inspection, and she thanked him, smiled and put her arm in his and they crossed the fields in silence the way they had come.

They must have gone a mile homewards like this before she stopped again suddenly, turned to him and said: 'I'm Jewish, Eric.'

He looked at her without comprehending, so she continued. 'That means that I can't have intercourse with you just like that. I must be married first. And I can't marry you because you are of a different faith. You're a Christian.' She said this simply as though she were relating something which was common knowledge.

Eric's face was a question mark. A few seconds elapsed before he said, 'What's that, Jewish?'

She told him. 'It's not usual for us to intermarry, although it's possible,' she added. Again the manner and the tone was formal. He tried to interrupt, but she continued. 'Either you would have to adopt my faith or I yours, and my father certainly wouldn't allow that,' she added firmly.

Eric could say nothing to all this. He was completely unarmed for such an encounter. He'd heard about these things, of course, but at the moment he wasn't in a position to comprehend such issues, much less debate them. He just stood there like a fool, noting as he did so, however, that she had the upper hand again. By now she was quite in control of herself – or so it seemed. He could not say the same for himself. It briefly crossed his mind that he had somehow been tricked into a situation which he could not deal with. His face darkened.

She knew his thoughts and looked at him with all the love she could summon. But he turned away, his face to the west where the sun's rim was sinking in fiery glory among the evening clouds. He was dumb. She put her arm round him as they stood there in the approaching twilight. A few minutes passed; Eric's heart was full of pain, his mind full of things he wanted to say that were unutterable. Angrily, he resisted the tears that welled into his eyes, brushing them away impatiently, releasing his arm from her grip in annoyance and frustration. They stood there sadly for some time, each with their own thoughts. After a while she said gently, 'We must go, dear; it's getting late.'

They walked on again saying nothing to each other until they came to the field's wooden gate and the road beyond it which led into the village.

'I'll leave you here,' he said. 'I want to be alone.' So saying, he turned without another word and made off in the direction of his house, leaving her standing. He felt ashamed of his emotion, of having wept like a child. Added to this, there was the feeling that even in this ineluctable situation in which they found themselves, she was somehow in charge. She had known this all the way along. Why, then, had she let herself in for disappointment on her part and inevitable frustration on his? He blamed himself for allowing himself to get attached to her, for allowing himself to become involved in such an intractable muddle. The solutions she had mentioned were of course quite impossible. For him to accept Judaism would be like turning a dog into a cat or vice versa: it was simply idiocy. Unreasonable. And if her father would not allow her to marry outside his confession, there was an end to it. The two of them were in a cleft stick. Why, he asked himself, did folks submit themselves to such ritualistic nonsense? Why erect barriers between people where there were none?

For days he mulled and wrestled with this problem. He was off his food, mooned and moped about the house and garden without purpose, went for long walks, slept badly, and all this time wondered whether he should ring her or whether she ought not to ring him first. She did not. This only made matters worse, for now there were feelings of hate mixed with his desperation. He imagined her supremely managing her life without him, thinking: 'Well, if that's the way he wants it, he can stick with it.' The very idea inflamed him to rage, only a few minutes later to reduce him to a beggar once more with only the thought of ringing her on his mind.

He did not ring her – out of pride or what you will – and the days passed in a hell of indecision and mental turbulence. Finally, ten to fourteen days later, and by a stroke of luck, they encountered each other in the town. She was with her mother. The three of them talked as though nothing had happened; Madame Lavelle-Dumois spoke with enthusiasm of the wonderful early autumn, but said that the trees were tired after a long, hot summer and when would he be taking up his studies again and so on, but Eric knew from Nina's manner that she wanted more than anything else to speak to him.

'Mama, you said you wanted to visit Harris's. I can't be much of a help to you there. Shall we meet at Café Blanca?'

Her mother took the hint, smiled knowingly at Eric, the slightest of smiles, a mere hint of complicity, and left for Harris's furniture shop.

The two young people stood on the pavement for a long moment, looking at each other. It was immediately clear to Eric that all his worries about her indifference had been for nothing. She looked pale and sad. The day had been glorious so far, but now it had come on to rain slightly. There was a very slight wind at play in the street where they stood looking at each other with so much emotion.

'Let's go,' he said, and they walked in profound silence with each towards the café, supremely happy to be in each other's company again.

'What happened to you?' Nina almost blurted as soon as they had settled themselves in the café.

Eric just looked at her. 'I was so worried about you,' she

went on, 'and sad. I didn't want to ring as I wanted to speak to you personally, and hoped you'd come round. You can't talk about these things on the phone. I mean, can you?'

'I felt so rotten about the situation, you know. So helpless,' Eric replied. 'It's hopeless, isn't it?'

'No, it isn't,' Nina said with determination. 'I want you. I love you.' Her superb eyes flashed. It occurred to him in that second that these eyes had matured recently into two veritable weapons of intimidation. They could convince you of anything, and he was their slave. His heart leapt. 'There's a solution if we are determined enough. We mustn't back down.'

Their tea and buns arrived. Eric took her hand in his over the table. 'I've missed you terribly,' he said.

'And I you, ' Nina replied. There didn't seem much more to be said. All that had to be said was in their looks. Harmony had been restored. When Anita returned she found them laughing and was glad. It was difficult to tell from her behaviour whether she knew what had been going on between the young people – her manner was always impeccable, a perfect amalgam of dignity, courtesy, empathy, and yet a certain distance. It was as though she did not want to come too near out of respect for one's person. Warmth there was, certainly, but with a certain detachment, a certain aristocratic equanimity which was not haughty, but caring. Eric liked her. He had always liked her. She had asked him about his intended career and he had answered by saying that next year he would apply for a job with General Electric, where his father had connections.

'Well, that's wonderful, Eric,' she had said and had looked at him in a way which he found fascinating, but impossible to fathom. It was highly expressive, this look, and yet it had in it a whole array of meaningful overtones as she turned her head to raise the cup to her lips. He noted, too, in this that she was a handsome woman, very different from her daughter in looks, Nina being much more like her father. Her features were fine, everything about her lean and delicate, her carefully tended, brown hair laid perfectly in place upon her head; her expressive eyes, like those of her daughter, were clear and alive.

However, he was not sure today whether the warmth of their other encounters had not been replaced by attentive civility. It was difficult to tell. Nina for her part sat opposite them, and although pale, looked her usual beautiful self. She was becoming more beautiful the longer he knew her, he assured himself. He looked at her while she chatted to her mother. He looked at her fine, aquiline nose and her thick dark hair, her smooth, dark complexion and small ears, and above all, at her remarkable blue eyes which, by all the rules of nature, should really have been dark brown. The gods had played an unusual card here in giving her eyes that were neither really blue nor grey, but a violet which could change from one to the other, and which were capable of an astonishing range of expression. It was his joy to watch them now as she talked. He noticed, again, that she much more resembled her father than her mother and that the likeness was something that could not be overlooked.

The two young people saw each other twice after this meeting before their respective studies took them to different places on their island. Their love had been consolidated, and both of them looked forward to the time when they would be financially independent. Then, they assured each other, they would marry, come what may.

A year later, Eric passed his examinations with distinction and, as arranged, secured a job with General Electric in the city. Things were changing rapidly in England. Whether the family shop would remain independent or be taken over by a larger firm was a matter for his father to decide, but Eric's own personal advancement coincided with a change of life for him. He was no longer able to help his father in the shop. The long holidays of summer were a thing of the past, and frequently he was obliged to work late in his capacity as a young probationer with his own firm in order to satisfy his superiors. Now he was a serious candidate for further responsibility. Nina had another year to go to complete her studies in Paris, and returned home later than usual that summer. The two young people had corresponded regularly, but in June and July there had been a lull in their exchanges. Eric was too busy to enquire why this was so, since he was preparing for and finally taking his examinations at the time. August passed before he had a chance to look Nina up at home. For once, he dispensed with his usual routine of ringing beforehand and visited The Hayes unannounced.

Nina's much older brother, whom he'd never got to know, answered the door and introduced himself. Pleasantries were exchanged. Eric was ushered into the lounge from which the noise of several people laughing and talking issued. There, amid jollity and the clinking of wine glasses, was Nina, her mother and father and a tall, bearded man about 35 years of age dressed in an all-black suit. Two other people were there whom Eric did not know. The large individual was introduced as Benjamin, who regarded Eric haughtily before giving him his hand. Eric disliked his supercilious air. Moreover, he noticed, he was generally introduced by Anita as a 'neighbour's son and friend of the family'. Nina was clearly embarrassed at Eric's sudden appearance among them, and remained the only one seated. She, too, took Eric's hand as though he were a mere acquaintance. Leon, Nina's father, however, was as hearty as ever and clapped Eric on the shoulder with friendly cordiality, saying that they were a musical party today and that he must stay a while to listen. Perhaps later Eric would fetch his saxophone and give them all 'a treat'? A chair was found for him and this seemed to be the signal for a short, prearranged recital. To Eric's surprise, Nina took another instrument from a corner of the room piled with music stands, cases and scores – a clarinet – and tried her lips on it.

'I didn't know you played the clarinet,' Eric said loudly across the floor.

She replied to the effect that at the conservatoire students were expected to play at least two instruments. She said this in such a matter-of-fact way that he found himself incapable of saying anything more. The only way he could describe her attitude in retrospect was 'snotty-nosed'. He wondered what the devil had got into her. And who was this equally snotty person with her? There was nothing in her manner or tone of voice which indicated the slightest familiarity with Eric, while she couldn't do enough to please the man in black who, from what he had heard from Lena, was one of her teachers in Paris. Eric noticed with growing agitation how she followed this man's every movement, hung on his words and made herself amenable to his slightest indicated wish as they together selected the scores and later while he tuned his violin. Eric was so overwhelmed by this fawning little drama that he contemplated going, but just at that moment the other two people in the group to his left took the opportunity to introduce themselves. Friendly formalities were exchanged, but within seconds he had forgotten their names. Three other people arrived to whom he was not introduced, but who settled onto chairs brought for them. After a few more minutes, the music began. However, Eric was by this time in no mood to enjoy music. He had seen enough. Later, taking advantage of a short interval in which tea was to be served, he left without a word and went home.

Two or three days after what had been, for Eric, a shameful interlude in which he felt himself to have been snubbed, he was surprised by a phone call from The Hayes. It was Nina.

'What do you want?' Eric asked shortly.

'You,' came the prompt answer. Then she asked, 'Why did you go so early?' There was a short pause between this and her next remark. 'You could have excused yourself or rung me to say what was wrong.'

'And what about your disgraceful conduct, Miss Lavelle-Dumois?' Eric asked warmly.

'What do you mean? And don't call me that!'

'This sucking up to whoever he was...'

'Benjamin you mean?'

'Yes, but I couldn't give a damn for his name.'

There was a brief pause. Then she said: 'Eric, clearly there's something to explain...'

But Eric by this time had already had enough and he put the phone down, regretting his action a second later. Nina phoned back immediately.

'Really, what do you want?' Eric enquired irritably.

'I must see you,' Nina said, 'now. Come over. There's no one here at the moment.'

'And friend Benjamin?' Eric asked sarcastically.

'No, he's *not* here,' she replied pertly. 'Please give me a chance to explain.'

'I think I've seen enough; there's not much you can explain. It's clear how the land lies,' Eric replied.

'No, no, you're wrong,' Nina urged. 'Come over and I'll explain. It's important!'

'The way you all treated me last Thursday was enough for me. I don't want to come to The Hayes again.'

'Eric, please! I can't tell you over the phone. Come over, it's only a step. I can explain everything.'

Eric was aware that his mother was listening to the conversation from the kitchen. This embarrassed him. Not knowing what to do, he merely placed the telephone back on its cradle without another word. 'Who was that?' his mother asked.

'Nina,' he said shortly.

His mother appeared in the hall, drying her hands on a kitchen towel. 'Ah, my son,' she said kindly, 'I think you've burned your fingers. I knew there'd be trouble sooner or later with her.'

Eric looked flushed and angry. 'What do you mean?' he demanded.

'I mean that they're Jews, that's what I mean. They're not our folks. They have their own ways, these people, and they're not our ways, that's what I mean.' Eric raised his eyebrows in enquiry as she went on. 'I mean that they're all right in their way. Your dad and I've got nothing against them, but they are different and your world is not their world. Besides, if you were a good churchgoer like him, you would know that it was these people who crucified Christ.'

Eric was struck dumb for the second time that week. Then he said, 'But that was nearly two thousand years ago! That's mad!'

'Mad or no,' his mother retorted, 'it's a historical fact.'

Eric had been brought up on facts. His training had been concerned with facts. He had an appreciation for facts. He considered the matter for a moment without answering, and his mother, seeing that she had scored a hit for a moment, returned to the kitchen. The turmoil that Eric had experienced a few months before now returned to upset his balance. Should he go to The Hayes and receive an explanation or should he stay here, face the fact of rejection but preserve his dignity? The noise of their van in the yard outside and his mother's announcement that lunch was ready resolved the need for an immediate decision. His father appeared at the front door, greeting them heartily as was his way, took off his working overalls in the hall, and rubbing his hands as he walked towards the kitchen, asked cheerily, as he did practically every day of the year, 'What's for dinner?'

The three of them sat down in their small dining room.

Since his mother was a woman of integrity and could hold her peace, nothing more was said about the incident of the phone call or indeed about anything else during the meal. They ate more or less in silence like monks. Afterwards, however, and after having helped his mother wash up so that she could leave earlier to go shopping, and after his father had returned to work, the house being empty, Eric approached the black telephone in the hall. He looked at it for a long time, hoping that it would ring and so relieve him of the need to decide whether he should ring, go over to The Hayes or hold the fort of his male dignity. But the telephone did not ring. After half an hour, his mind tortured by indecision, he lifted the receiver and rang The Hayes. The phone rang for a long time. Evidently, there was no one at home. He then replaced the receiver, consoling himself with the thought that he had tried, had done her bidding, and if she were not there to receive his call, then the ball was quite clearly in her court. He wouldn't try again.

This did not silence his feelings, however. Inwardly he knew that he was acting like a child. Perhaps she would interpret his actions, his patent silliness, as immature. But then, he told himself, she started the business with this man, and he was not just a teacher, of this he was certain. You didn't behave like that with teachers. Those two were closer to each other than that. Any fool could have told you so by observing them for less than a minute. He tortured himself with the thought that he had not allowed her to explain. Perhaps, just perhaps, there was a reason for his presence that would not arouse jealousy. She had not behaved like that before. She had showed no signs either of wishing to be with another man. They had been very happy with each other. Perhaps he should have gone and talked the whole thing over. At least that would have ended the matter, if it needed to be ended, on an adult level. Anyway, what did she want to tell him that was so important? Did she want to tell him – in an adult way – that she had fallen in love with this bearded prig? Well, if that was the case, he'd prefer not to know. She could keep him. Was that the solution to their problem? Did she want to say that now she was attached to a man of her faith and tradition that this was the best way to avoid the pain, the inconvenience and all the future inconveniences that would lie in their way if they were to attempt to marry? A pretty solution!

That evening, Eric went for a long walk in the countryside so dear to him and which he knew so well. The trees, the bushes and the fields were an ineradicable part of his being, his childhood and early youth, and he was familiar with them all. He listened to the birds, which, in his garden at home, had sung him to sleep so often of a summer evening when he was a child. He crossed the railway line where, as a boy, he had taken down the numbers or crossed them off in a book of such numbers, put pennies on the line to be crushed by the weight of the locomotive, and later 'walked the plank' as a test of boyhood prowess by traversing the blue-brick parapet of the bridge while a train passed under it. A foolhardy thing to do if ever there was one, he reflected now as a young man. A little further on, at the top of a sloping field, he found himself on a patch of level ground where he with other lads from the village had played football in the winter and cricket in the summer. The lads had all gone their own ways by now and the younger ones had never kept up their tradition. Things had changed. Everything changes. Eric wondered what had happened to his classmates and friends as he walked on over the fields and through the surrounding copses. After an hour or so with these and other memories, he took the long route home.

* * *

It was already late August. In a month or so Eric would have his practical examinations, the last of a series of tests that would qualify him finally as an electrical engineer and give him the chance to apply for a job wherever he liked. Time had passed quickly over the last year, he reflected. From a height on the road he looked over the Cotswold countryside and thought lovingly of Nina. If only she could be with him at this moment. Perhaps she wanted to and couldn't. As soon as he got to the village and although it was by now quite late into the evening, he would use a public telephone to call her. All the rankling of a few hours before had left him. He was now quite ready to forgive her everything. He was sure that she had not betrayed him. If he were honest he knew that this could not be so. He found a kiosk and dialled her number. After a long time the phone was answered by Lena, Nina's grandmother. It was clear from her faltering voice that she had been woken from early retirement to bed.

'Oh, Eric,' she said, at last recognising his voice. 'Nina isn't here, my dear. She left yesterday to return to Paris. Her mother has gone with her for a few days.' There was a pause as Eric digested this information with difficulty. 'Are you there, Eric?' the thin voice then enquired.

'Yes, yes, I'm here, and thank you for telling me. When will she be back?'

Lena's voice sounded old and tired. 'Well, let me see, it's nearly September, I suppose she'll be back in May next year.'

'Thank you, ma'am. I'm sorry if I've disturbed you,' Eric said hopelessly, while nevertheless remembering his manners.

'Not at all, young man. Take care ... and good luck with your finals!'

'Thank you so much. Thank you,' Eric replied, happy that she had remembered his exams. The phone clicked. Eric left the red phone box feeling so thoroughly depressed that as he stepped into the road he was nearly run over by a passing car. The driver hooted violently. Eric tried to pull himself together, but was tormented by the thought of what she had wanted to ask him yesterday. Was it that she wanted to tell him she was going back to Paris or was it to settle with him, as he had imagined earlier in the day? He made his way home not seeing the houses he passed nor the people who passed him on the way. The next three months were to be unhappiest of his life.

In March 1956, the following year, he was called up into the army as a National Serviceman and after six weeks of basic training sent to Cyprus with the Royal Electrical and Mechanical Engineers. He was there for eighteen months before taking leave to return home for two weeks in February 1958. He had enjoyed his time in the army so far and during his sojourn there had also met Susan, a young woman who worked for the civilian authority supporting the army in the political upheavals there at this time. While at home he had also met an older school friend on the bus returning from Worcester. They enjoyed the conversation with each other and after establishing friendly confidence with her he was moved to ask what had become of Nina, knowing that his fellow passenger, Debbie Lyons, was also Jewish.

'Oh, she married a year or so ago,' she replied. Seeing the disconsolate expression at this news, Debbie added, 'I'm sorry to see you so disappointed. These things happen you know.' She smiled in a comforting way. 'I guess you weren't there and I'm told you didn't write to her, so she thought you'd given her up I suppose. But I don't know, Eric. I really don't know. Anyway, she told me you hadn't written to her, I remember that. I know she was very much attached to you at one time. Were you in love with her?'

'Why?' asked Eric in some confusion at his mixed feelings. 'Did you know we were together?'

'Of course!' Debbie laughed at the idea of possible ignorance of the fact.

'Who did she marry, then?' he asked.

'She married her teacher...'

'A big guy with a beard...?' Eric ventured.

'Yes, do you know him?' The bus swerved and lurched round a tight bend, and they found themselves leaning heavily on each other. She laughed at this. He did not laugh.

'Well, yes, in a way. Not well,' he said.

Debbie was interested in all she could learn. 'They had a super-duper marriage at Devon Hall after the religious ceremony. I was there.'

'Oh, were you?' Eric said vaguely.

Debbie was a sensitive, intelligent individual and didn't want to cause pain and so felt it was the moment to change the subject. Eric in any case had heard enough. That was all he needed for confirmation of her fickleness. He had not thought her so faithless. The contemplation of it hurt him deeply even with his own memory of his relationship with Susan, so that he could no longer listen to Debbie's further relations. After all, it was over; he was attached now to Susan, he thought consolingly. Susan was great. It was just that ... that Nina should not have acted like that.

During the last three months of his soldiering in Cyprus, Eric enjoyed sunbathing and swimming whenever he could in the warm waters surrounding that island, taking the occasional trip to Egypt with two of his companions whenever duty allowed. Finally he returned to Britain, ostensibly to be demobbed in late May, but his destiny was to stay on with the army for another three years. In that time he would most likely be promoted to captain and so have a better opportunity of getting a top job when he got out. Army experience was always reckoned as being as valuable as civilian experience. That he knew. The upshot of this decision was leave for another two weeks in the summer of 1958, one week of which he spent with relatives in London and the other at home. During the latter week, after a visit to the cinema in Worcester, he returned home one afternoon to find his mother sewing outside in the garden. He greeted her light-heartedly, kissed her and sat down heavily at her side on their scrap of lawn. His mother put down her sewing for a moment and looked at him seriously.

'I'm glad you're back so soon, my lad,' she said, and paused for a moment. 'There was a call from The Hayes this afternoon asking whether you were in. I told whoever it was that you'd probably be back later on the three-thirty train and that I'd tell you they'd called.'

'Who?' Eric asked warily.

'It was an elderly person. I don't know any of them,' his mother replied.

'What did they want?' Eric enquired, standing and entering the kitchen to put the kettle on for a cup of tea.

'I don't know. They didn't say. It seemed important though.'

'Important?' Eric said in surprise. 'What could be important from that end? I've not seen Nina or any of them for over four years.'

'Well, I don't know,' said his mother, 'but you should ring back, I feel. It's only polite to do so. She was perfectly nice to me, the woman who rang. She had class. Seemed like a request or something.'

Eric deliberated for a moment, wondering who it could have been, then made the tea mechanically, fetched the milk from the cupboard and joined his mother in one of the deck chairs.

'Was it an elderly woman, the mother perhaps or the grandmother...?'

'The grandmother died last year,' his mother said. 'It was in the papers. I wrote to you about it. You must have forgotten. As for the other lady, I don't know her except by sight. I personally have never spoken to her, strange though that it seems, the many times you've rung that place in your time.'

'I'm sorry Lena's dead,' Eric said sincerely. 'She was nice.'

Then he said nothing for some time, his mother's suggestion retaining its power over his mind. He took his time over the hot tea and revised the possibilities of what the telephone call could mean. He was reluctant to do a favour for anyone at The Hayes after what he had learned from Debbie. He had tried to forget all about the place. Yet that was small-minded. The army had taken the corners off him, he knew, and he felt as he drank the hot tea that he should really be in charge of the situation. The minutes passed in silence with his mother intent on her sewing, and he knew what that meant. Finally, after half an hour had passed, he rose and went to the telephone. The phone rang for a long time, or so it seemed, and he was beginning to feel relieved at the possibility of having done his duty once more when a small voice answered. Apparently, there was a child in the house.

'I'm Eric Shipstone,' he announced. 'Someone rang me.' There were scuffling noises at the other end. He waited. Finally, it seemed that the phone was handed over to an adult and an unfamiliar voice said, 'Hello, who's there?'

'Shipstone, Eric Shipstone. Someone rang asking for me earlier...'

'Oh yes, Mr Shipstone, thank you. Would it be possible for you to come over for a few moments? I'd be obliged to you.'

'You mean now?'

'Well, yes, if that's possible. Please. Can I expect you in the next few minutes perhaps?'

'Excuse me, but do I know you?' Eric enquired, a little perplexed.

'No, not me personally, I'm here on duty, but do, please come over. Thank you.'

'Very well; I'll come over,' Eric replied, 'but can you tell me why, I mean...?'

'Well, I'm not sure myself, or let me say that I can't divulge anything to you on the phone; the best thing is for you to come over. I know that it will be much appreciated.'

'Very well; I'll come,' Eric said.

Thank you so much, Mr Shipstone.'

Eric put the phone down. He didn't recognise either of the voices. What was going on over there? he asked himself. He put his tie straight in front of the mirror in the hall. Although it was a hot afternoon, he felt he ought to look the part. Then he said goodbye to his mother and set off on the half mile walk towards the great house.

When he got there a few minutes later, knocking on the door which he once knew so well, he was received by a district nurse. In the background stood Nina's mother and a person he did not know with a child of about four or five holding her hand. He greeted Madame Lavelle-Dumois, who came forward and gave him her hand.

'Eric, *mon ami*,' she said quietly. 'How are you?' This was said with sincerity as though she had only seen him the day before. He looked into her face for a sign of information, but received none. She merely added, 'Nina is upstairs.' She looked old as her own mother had looked in 1949, he recalled quickly. She then indicated her companion. Eric shook the other woman's hand, limp as a dead bird's claw, and returned to Anita with a question in his eyes. 'She's very ill and wishes to see you. Will you go up?' She paused as if to allow him to decline. The place had the sharp smell of disinfectant, he noticed. The afternoon was uncommonly quiet. Those keen eyes Nina's mother had once possessed had sunk into her head, he noticed. There was just a second or two of hesitation among them. The district nurse waited obediently at the foot of the stairs.

'What's the matter?' Eric enquired before moving in that direction.

Nina's mother was so moved that she could only shake her head, trying hard to stem her tears, signalling him to go upstairs. Eric, perplexed and affected by her demeanour, followed the district nurse's apron up the steps, feeling most uncomfortable. Almost at the top, and at a turn in the stairs, he touched the nurse's arm.

'Is that Benjamin man here?' he asked nervously, regretting the question a second later.

'There's no one with her. She's alone. I think the person you refer to is on his way here from Paris. We're expecting him at the station at about seven this evening.'

Once on the broad landing at the top of the stairs, they stopped at the entrance to a large room shaded inside. It smelled unpleasantly of sickness. The nurse paused before entering.

'She wants to talk to you,' she said in a whisper. 'I think she wants to tell you something, but please don't be long with her. She's very ill and shouldn't really be disturbed at all.' Gesturing him to go into the room, the nurse then turned back towards the carpeted landing, half closing the door behind her. Eric went in, wondering what he would encounter.

Nina, propped by cushions, lay very still in a white silk nightgown, her arms lying limply, uselessly, on the bedding as though after great physical exertion. She didn't turn her head as he came in, but, recognising his presence, said weakly, 'Is that you, Eric?'

He did not reply, but presented himself at her side. It was then that she turned her head slightly to look at him, her eyes glazed with fever. She smiled weakly. He still loved her mouth and felt a pang of sadness at seeing her so spiritless.

After a moment or two without saying anything, Eric sat down in the chair at the side of the bed, finding no suitable words of greeting, though devoutly wishing to. Nina seemed to understand this, and they remained silent for some minutes.

After quite some time had passed, she said, 'I have a little present for you which you can look at when you get home. Not now.' The effort to say this seemed great and she lapsed again into a state of utter exhaustion, her breathing hard and laboured. Again, the minutes passed.

'Nina,' Eric then said, for that was all he could summon

in his soul to say. Just that one word. It seemed enough to restore her for a moment and her pale hand indicated the bedside cabinet where there was what seemed to be a book wrapped in gold paper. He nodded and took the book or whatever it was in his hand.

'For you,' she said in a whisper.

He put the thin book aside in that moment and took her pale hand, unable to control the tears which streamed down his cheeks and onto the bedspread, incapable of uttering a word. He didn't know why he felt so moved. Without looking at him, she knew he was weeping. Her face was very calm and her hand squeezed his gently as he remained there wordlessly, sitting on the hard chair, his mind vacant, painful. Time seemed to stop. The sun had become hazy as high, sinuous clouds strewed the sky like gossamer in the heat of the afternoon. A sparrow twittered excitedly outside somewhere in the ivy which hung at the window. A few seconds later, another joined the altercation and within moments there was a right royal row going on in the eaves. She smiled without looking at him and he, too, wiping the tears from his face, could not help but smile wanly at the tiny theatre of fury beyond the curtains. There was a rapport between them again, and for this he felt an enormous swell of gratitude, which enveloped his body like a huge ocean wave. It was accompanied by an ineffable happiness he had not felt possible, a great surge of absorbing fulfilment. He closed his eyes, sinking into a river of euphoria whose features were blessedness and peace. The bickering at the window then stopped as suddenly as it had begun, and the ensuing silence in the minutes which followed was deeper than before.

Nina sighed and closed her eyes; Eric was happy to realise that she could sleep now. His visit had done her some good and he was glad. Perhaps she would soon gain in strength. He hoped so. Her breathing was easier. Eric released her hand and sat for a moment or two longer with closed eyes until he was roused by a gentle knock at the half-open door.

The nurse appeared with a tray which she set at the bedside table on her side and almost in the same movement took up Nina's wrist to take her pulse. Only a second or two elapsed as she did this and then she looked over to Eric. He was never to forget that look in the nurse's grey eyes and her attitude in those seconds, an equal mixture of human sympathy and professional commitment. Quickly, she took a small torch from her breast pocket, opened one of Nina's eyelids and shone the light of it into the eye. She straightened slowly and looked for a long time at him, Nina's arm in hers, the small watch in the other.

'She's gone from us, my son,' she said quietly, returning the lifeless limb to the canopy. Rising and moving towards the door, she beckoned him to follow her.

Eric, horrified, confused and unable to say or do anything else, followed the rustle of her uniform out onto the landing which linked to the bedrooms. The sun had reached the high, domed window above them and shone into their faces, heightening the emotion expressed there. The nurse turned to him, seeming to know that his mind was full of questions.

'She had a stillbirth about a month ago and since then her condition has slowly but surely deteriorated, especially in the last twenty-four hours. Septicaemia. Everyone has done the best they possibly could, the local doctor especially. She was too weak to move to hospital yesterday without worsening her condition, so we have done what we could here. Dreadful blow to you and the family.' She paused for a moment and then added, 'I must ring Doctor Macmillan.' And with that she turned away and preceded him down the stairs where anxious faces awaited them.

Eric did not attend the funeral a few days later, since he was obliged to return to his unit. The army only made provision for men to extend leave 'for compassionate reasons' in the case of relatives or soldiers engaged to be married. Eric's father and mother represented him. Nina died on Thursday, 12 June 1958, two days before her birthday. Two days later, Eric sailed for Cyprus from Southampton.

Eric Shipstone married Susan Richardson a year later in Cyprus and in the course of the next five years the couple produced two sons and a daughter. Returning to General Electric in Britain as a manager for a time, he was eventually transferred and promoted later to their sub-division in Sydney, Australia, where the young family eventually settled down and the children grew up. Two years or so after that they were joined by their respective parents. Eric became the firm's general manager at forty-five and retired ten years later. His wife died in a tragic car accident somewhere in Australia's Outback in 1998, aged 64. In 2002, before he himself passed away after returning from a visit to Europe that year, he asked me to record the following episode in his life and its sequel during my visit to an old people's home where he spent the last ten months of his life. Until then, and even during his last visit to Britain alluded to above, he had enjoyed very good health. His death was sudden and quite unexpected.

As is often the case with older people, there is a tendency to relive the past, and in pursuance of this, Eric Shipstone revisited the haunts of his childhood, knowing that it would be his last return to England. In one respect he was greatly disappointed with what he found there. The fields and woods he had once known were gone. In their place was an ugly, sprawling mess of urban housing where every house was the same as the other. These estates followed the contours of the land he had once known as wooded farmland with ponds and barns, hedgerows and copses, but now only the rise and fall of the streets was indication of what was once there. Even the railway he had once so loved had vanished. Where there had once been a thriving allotment on level ground running alongside it, now there was a sterile, dirty, half cared-for football ground. Careless youth had scattered litter wantonly on the paved path towards the clubhouse and changing rooms. A broken bottle of Coca-Cola lay on one of the windowsills. At the back was a broken window which had been boarded up years before and whose chipboard had deteriorated with time. He found it all repulsive. Not far from where he had climbed one of the highest oak trees in the neighbourhood as a boy was a loveless public house where, thirsty and depressed by what he had seen, he sat down outside with another elderly individual to whom after a few minutes of conversation he confided his astonishment and disappointment at what he had discovered.

'Yeah, things change,' the other said. 'T'aint the same as it was, but then folks gotta live somewhere.' He turned to Eric for confirmation.

'Like this?' Eric countered.

The other didn't answer.

'There used to be an old house not far from here called The Hayes,' Eric said eagerly. 'Or has that been pulled down to make room for housing, too?'

The other man was unmoved. 'Not yet,' he said flatly, 'but soon! Been there for one hundred and twenty-five years, but on Saturday it'll be pulled down. They been at work on it today all day.'

Eric hated this careless lack of feeling, this non-committed recital of fact.

'Have the people that once lived there left then?' Eric urged.

The other man smiled complacently. 'Oh that was years ago. It was owned by a Jewish family, you know, refugees from occupied France during the war. Came over on a fishing boat, they did, at the beginning of the war. Quite an adventure, I 'eard. They had good connections as these folks do and got the money together to rent the house and later they bought it, I understand. Anyway, it fell to a nephew when the husband and wife died and 'e lived there for years. His name was Lion. Funny name to give to an individual. Something of a recluse he was.'

Eric listened to this with great attention. 'And what happened then?'

'Well, as far as I know, he 'ad no heirs or anything and the will was a mix-up. The one daughter – I've forgotten her name – died at twenty-two. Tragedy, that. Years and years ago. Practically the whole village went to the funeral. Me and all. I was only a kid of fourteen at the time. Then the place was up for probate for at least six years after the old uns passed away. Then it stood empty for goodness knows how long. Ten or fifteen years I reckon. Then squatter folks moved in illegally and after that the Council took it over. And I read in the paper last week that it'll be pulled down.'

'What's going to replace it?'

'Dunno. Some folks talk of an 'otel, others that there's gonna be a park or some kind of recreation ground or a youth club. Don't think anyone knows for sure.' He took another swig at his beer, wiping his mouth unappetisingly with a dirty handkerchief.

Eric thanked his companion for the information, finished his drink, paid for them both and departed. It was a quarter to eight in the evening and still quite light and warm, although the sun was beginning slowly now to decline.

The house was still there, the garden ruined, a veritable jungle of weeds and bushes so thick that had there not been a path made by the demolition contractor's bulldozer, one would not have gained access to the front door without a machete. At the gate, which had been taken off its hinges and laid to one side, there was a large notice.

DEMOLITION IN PROGRESS. DANGER
KEEP OUT.

Regardless of the prohibition, Eric made his way to the door and up the broken steps, noticing on the way that much of the roof had already been removed. The front door was ajar as if awaiting someone. Everywhere there were broken pieces of tile, mortar and slate from the roof, so that a grinding and crunching accompanied every footstep. He recognised the design of the hallway floor and paused for a moment after fifty-five years to review the situation. The feelings which assaulted him in these first few minutes are impossible to describe. He walked on, kicking the debris from his feet as he did so, pausing to look into the empty lounge where he had once sat in happiness. Only the long dust-filled curtains still hung miserably from the high ceiling. It was a scene of utter desolation.

A few more grinding steps took him towards the staircase which, to his surprise, was still carpeted but full of minor debris, and, as he ascended it, the handrail was smoothed of its dust under his palm. He arrived at the top of the stairs to find himself under the open sky. Here, most of the roof had been removed. Tentatively, he walked along the still-solid, oak-floored landing littered with torn wallpaper, broken timber from the roof and sharp glass, appreciative nevertheless of the handiwork of a generation before his which accomplished such intrinsically fine work as this, work that, despite its desolation, could still declare its worth even in death.

The bedroom he had last entered fifty-four years earlier was empty except for a steel bedstead and a skip bag full of rubble. From it there was a rope up to the jib of a crane high above him. His back ran cold in the mild evening air.

NINA

Could this have been the bed in which she died? The skip bag contained, among its rubble of plaster, wood and brick and other trash, a whole lot of books which, he assumed, had once filled the bookshelves ranged on one wall which had not yet been removed. On the floor there were piles of other books for which there had not been room enough in the fully loaded industrial sack.

'Apparently,' Eric thought to himself as he stood there amid the debris, 'there's little interest in books these days, even old books.' He fished one out of the over-filled bag: *Isle sacrée*; and another: *La chaine d'Or*. *If Winter Comes*. Some of them were bound in leather and gold lettered, he noticed. He brushed the thick white dust off one of these. Someone had kept an unopened letter between its leaves. *The Origin of Species*. Quite a size, he thought to himself, and sadly replaced it with the rest. On an impulse it occurred to him that he would take something from the place, this yellowed letter, perhaps, 'as a keepsake'. He said this aloud as though excusing himself to the ghosts of that place and as much to salve his conscience for illegal entry, trespass, and now theft. At that moment he realised that he had no business to be there. But for all that there was no one to remember him; he was here among the dead and their dead past. He paused for a moment longer. He wondered where Nina was. What happened to all that they had experienced together? Was there anything in this idea of afterlife in which so many people believed? And what had happened to his dear wife? Where were all the people who had once walked between these walls in over a century of habitation? All very well to say they were dead. Dead, yes, and gone ... where ... ? Nowhere? Was that possible? Somewhere? Where, then?

It was getting late. The sun had already reached the horizon. Tomorrow, he reminded himself, he had thousands of miles to put behind him and he needed a good sleep beforehand. Pocketing the keepsake in his light summer jacket, he went out of the room, carefully picking his way through the dust and muck down the stairs and out once more into the wild garden. One solitary bird sang in the bushes, which tomorrow would be cleared. The evening was unusually quiet and he recalled as he stood there, half listening to the bird's song, the summer evenings he had enjoyed as a boy in those parts. That, too, he mused, had gone with the trees, the ditches and ponds and hedges and the friends of his youth. He looked back again, pausing for just a moment on his way to the road to refresh his memory of the house one more time where once there had been life and love. Then he walked on resolutely towards the opening to the road beyond. Two people, out for a walk with their dog, looked at him with suspicion as he reappeared at the entrance to the road.

Leaning back into the seat in the first class cabin as the aircraft rose powerfully into the air above Heathrow on the initial leg of its flight to Australia, Eric knew that this would be his last trip to Britain. The plane veered slightly to find its course and then steadied, and the engines ceased to roar. Somehow, he was glad to be flying home. A minute or so passed and the lights went on. Seat belts clicked. There was movement again on board.

'Would you like a drink, sir?' the stewardess asked. It was hot in the plane. When the young woman had left, he removed his light jacket and attached it to a hook above him.

'It'll be spring back home,' he thought to himself, and at this moment he noticed the gentle presence of the faded gold envelope in the inner pocket of his jacket. Retrieving it, Eric settled comfortably in his seat once more and turned the letter over in his hands. The juice he had ordered was cool and good as he took a sip and considered the thing again. He was curious. Two edges, each about half an inch wide, had been bleached by exposure to light and he concluded from this that it had long been ensconced in the book he had found containing it. The envelope was still sealed and, taking a small knife from his trouser pocket, he slit open the tired, faded paper and opened out the page inside on the small table in front of him with some difficulty, its creases having been reinforced by years of pressure. On it were large, pale letters, as though scrawled by an old person's hand: 'June 10th, 1958. Eric: I love you', it said.

4

Mrs Manship (1955)

It had been a cold, raw day with thick grey skies heavy with snow, and when Clifford arrived home at ten to six that evening from the railway station where he worked, having removed his greatcoat, he complained of tightness in the chest.

'Come, dear,' she had said, taking his coat and placing it on the peg in the hall, 'sit down by the fire; the toast is ready.' Poached egg on toast was one of his favourite evening meals.

A few minutes later, Cliff lay dead in her arms, his head strangely twisted to one side. He was forty-seven and had never been ill in his life. Mr and Mrs Manship had a boy of about six who was autistic and who at that moment was next door playing with the neighbour's children. She could hear their excited laughter through the wall of the semi-detached house she lived in, and it would be hard to describe her feelings at that moment. It was as though something had snapped within her, as though not only Cliff's life had come to an end, but her own as well. After holding him for a long time, she laid his body gently on the carpet before the crackling fire and then called the doctor.

Five years after this event, Mrs Manship realised that she and her boy could no longer live off Clifford's insurance money plus the small amount she had laid up for hard times. She would have to find work. But what work could she do? All she had ever been was a housewife and then, very late in life, a mother. This, her friends told her, was the reason why she had borne a child who was defective. It had been too late for motherhood. But Margaret Manship had loved her baby and still loved her little boy dearly. Her life had been a life of devotion, and now that Clifford was dead she gave all her love and time to Robert, her son. What would happen to Robert during the day if she had to go out to work, she asked herself? She did not relish the idea of working outside her home with people she did not know. The world outside was foreign to her. Robert was next to her, playing with a plush toy rabbit, stroking it in a way a much younger child would do. He, like his mother, was a loving person. Love was something he could understand and his mother put her arm round him. 'I have to go and find work, dear,' she said to him, and the child smiled, not comprehending. But Margaret did not mind that. Somehow, she assured herself, he would understand her need to earn money. He showed her the toy and she took it gently from his hand as one does from a baby's. She looked long into the soft, blue eyes and wished that he could really understand her predicament. She hugged the small body and Robert uttered a sound.

It took Mrs Manship eight months before she found work and by this time she was on her last legs financially. It was a job in a church, cleaning. Saturday morning and each evening after services. It was a Catholic church in Bridge Street, a few yards away from the post office. On her first evening there, the priest talked to her for a few minutes. He seemed tired after a long day. 'So many at confession this evening,' he apologised. 'I'm so glad you could come, Mrs ... er...'

'Manship,' Margaret prompted.

'Yes, of course,' he said kindly. Father Benedict was a tactful man and had much to do with people of all kinds. 'It's nice of you to help us out. Not the usual hours of work, I'm afraid, dear Mrs Manship, but there you are. I hope you will not feel too lonely all on your own in an empty church of an evening.' He smiled at her.

'No, I don't think so,' Mrs Manship said simply.

'And as for your remuneration, I shall pay you cash each Friday. When you arrive in the evening, you'll find me in my room. Will that be all right? My rooms are through here and then along the corridor to the right. That will bring you to the chaplain's house. Just knock and go in. It will be all right.' He smiled a gracious, kindly smile. She liked him.

'That's all right, sir,' she said respectfully and in this way revealed to him at once that she was not of the faith. He smiled again briefly and left.

Mrs Manship had never been in a church except on her wedding day and certainly not in a Catholic church. She looked around for a moment. It was a nice church, very clean and well appointed. To the right of the altar, there were candles burning at different lengths. She wondered what they were for and a second later her gaze rose to a statue of the Virgin to the right of the candle stand. It was a very beautiful statue. Somehow, she thought, the figure had life. And it seemed to be smiling. She smiled back at the saint in blue and white, stood there for a moment wondering what the figure signified and then commenced her work.

The job at the church was very useful to her. She managed to arrange for Robert to be looked after by her neighbour while she was away at work and as time went on, she established a good relationship with Father Benedict, who was always kindly and amenable to the occasional changes in her routine brought about by Robert's needs and her neighbour's plans. She met regular visitors to the church, and one of these was the sister of the former cleaner, a woman in her early seventies, Mrs Severin.

'Yes, dear, a French name. My father was French you know. Such a dear man, my father. Alas, long dead now. We must all say farewell one day. It doesn't last for ever, no, my word, it's not long…' And then she would go on talking and it was difficult for Mrs Manship to get on with her work.

'I must get on, Mrs Severin, if you'll forgive me,' she used to say on such occasions and make a slight gesture in the direction of the bucket she always had with her.

'Oh, of course, dear,' said Mrs Severin, 'I'm keeping you, I really do talk too much.' But then she'd nevertheless go on talking until it was embarrassing to stay any longer at the door or in front of the font or on the steps of the chancel or wherever it was she had chanced to encounter her. Mrs Severin, however, seemed to have her own inbuilt 'timer', so to speak, and would suddenly stop in the middle of a discourse on her own account and say, 'Oh, really! Yes, I really must go. So nice to have met you again, dear.' And she would be off before Mrs Manship could say goodbye.

It was in this way, then, that one weekend she came to know her predecessor. She had been invited to the Severin house for a cup of tea, and had accepted partly because she was curious as to what kind of a person the former cleaner was and partly out of politeness. She did not know many people and she felt it would be a small embellishment to her weekend, and although she dreaded the first Mrs Severin's loquacity, she had already decided to cut through it as well as she could so as to get to the second Mrs Severin (the sisters lived together). She rang the door bell at No. 16 Newberry Street. The house was one of those very substantial affairs built of red brick in the latter part of the nineteenth century for the middle classes of those times, having a simple bay window to the street and an apology for a garden in front of it. The door was opened by the first Mrs Severin, who welcomed her visitor most cordially. Mrs Manship had brought with her some homemade scones and some jam from her own pantry which she was sure they would enjoy, and after a moment or two of pleasantries they climbed the brown wooden stairs to the bedroom where the second Mrs Severin had lain now for two or three months. It turned out that at home the first Mrs Severin, Jeanne, was not so garrulous as

Mrs Manship had expected her to be. It was also clear to her from the outset that the second Mrs Severin, Colette, was a lady of considerable personal magnetism, despite the disadvantage of her largely supine position.

There is no need of course to report on all that passed between them in the course of the next two hours, except perhaps to mention the very short exchange which occurred while they were enjoying their second cup of tea and which has a bearing on our narrative. No one as yet had made any reference to Colette's condition. Mrs Manship felt that it was not her place to enquire, while Jeanne considered it best for her sister to bring up the matter if and when she felt obliged to do so.

'I think it will rain soon, Colette,' said the older sister on glancing out of the window. Colette turned her head with difficulty to look out of the window. Large, black clouds had formed above the city.

'Well, I suppose so,' said Colette with a faint smile. 'After the rain the sun and after the sun the rain. This is the way our lives pass. Is it not so, Mrs Manship?'

Margaret nodded.

'Before me Mrs Tyler, the former owner of this house, lay here and finally died here in this room and now it is me. Just a little longer with a little patience.' And she sighed.

'Oh!' said Mrs Manship, alarmed and concerned at the same time.

'Oh, don't trouble yourself, my dear,' Colette replied, 'it's all in the natural way of things. What once was is no more and what will be will appear in due course. It's all very natural,' she repeated.

'My sister has accepted her fate,' Jeanne said simply.

'More than that – I've accepted everything. Just as it is.' Colette continued, stroking the coverlet of the bed with one pale hand, 'That way lies happiness. Just accept what God offers and be content.' There was a moment's silence in the room during which Margaret Manship quickly turned this thought over in her mind.

'It's true. You're right,' she said suddenly, surprising herself by the note of conviction in her voice.

Colette smiled and looked at her visitor for a long moment, nodding her head ever so slightly in appreciation of this affirmation. Again, there was a pause in their conversation, then Colette said: 'You, too, Mrs Manship, have something which troubles you like so many people who come and visit me. Such kind people. I know it. Something – how shall I say – undigested, unaccepted. I feel it intuitively, you know. It is strange, this intuition.'

Margaret replaced the cup to its saucer and was silent.

'You shouldn't probe, dear, it's not nice,' Jeanne intervened, perturbed by the direction the conversation was taking and a little anxious about the wellbeing of her guest.

'You're right, dear Jeanne,' Colette said. 'I'm sorry, Mrs Manship. Do forgive my little submission to a desire to help. It's the way I am. I'm sorry.'

She looked very sweet as she asked for Margaret's pardon, so that Mrs Manship said, 'Well, but it's not always so easy to accept things as you suggest, that's all I wanted to add,' she said in her simple way.

'Indeed, how right you are!' Colette responded warmly.

And there the matter would have ended in the normal way of things had it not been for the fact that Mrs Manship, after having gratefully taken leave of her hosts, turned this over and over in her mind on the way home by tram. There was indeed something in her life which she had not digested, but which she would never admit to a stranger, or even for that matter, to her sister and friend, Grace. Perhaps Grace knew anyway. Yes, Grace knew. Rain had begun to speckle the window, she noticed with half her mind as the tram slid on its way through the city. It was Robert. She had never accepted the fact that he wasn't normal and she had never accepted Cliff's death. Forty-seven was no age to die, and why had she been singled out among women of forty to have an autistic child? It seemed unfair, especially because she and Cliff had so wanted a child in all their younger years and nothing had happened. And then, when they weren't expecting it, came Robert. It seemed like a mean trick of fate, an unwarranted backlash from the hand of God. God? Could that have been an act of God? For the first time in Margaret's life, feelings of resentment stirred deep within her. And how could all those church people be so deferential to a God like that? How often had she seen them kneeling, even on the hard stone floor when the church was full, bowing and crossing themselves and singing so lustily in praise of the same God that had dispensed her so much sadness? Perhaps it was because she wasn't a Catholic. Perhaps it was because she never went to church after she had grown up. Perhaps that was it.

She felt the tram's rapid acceleration in her body as it snaked towards Moor Street, Trentham Row and the Fish Market. Margaret Manship could tell these people a different story about the God who they thought guided their lives. Deeper within her mind, she recalled the bitter poverty of her childhood, her father's black face at the door when he came home from the pit, his eyes strangely alight in that coal-besmirched face. She recalled her fear of his mood at that moment. Would he be fair or foul? Would he drink in the evening after his dinner? Would he hit their mother and beat the dog in the kitchen? The dog would howl and the neighbours knock on the wall. The children, Grace, Annie, and Trevor, would hug each other in terror. And our mum would come home on another occasion from the shops and tell us that there were only potatoes to be had and that he would devour those and we'd have to wait till tomorrow for something to eat, and we'd go to bed hungry like the kids next door whose dad was in prison. Our mum, our mum who laboured and scrimped and saved for a penny or two or more for Christmas so that we could enjoy God's festive season and then he would come and see that as an opportunity to drink all the more, take the money and leave us comfortless in a dark house listening to our mum crying in front of the dead fire, and we'd huddle together again under the living-room table with a rag of a blanket for warmth and the only cosiness we knew. When he was sober, he was a different man. It was difficult to imagine that at other times he could be so heartless.

And then Mum died suddenly in the night and how inconsolable he was then, this six foot of muscle! And dear Mum lying there like a straw doll, her life and her paps sucked dry and her cold, listless hands folded over her breast. Our mum, the only loving light in this rotten world. Only the rich could talk of a loving God, for they had something to thank Him for; they had time for Him, but we only had time for work, and after work, to eat and sleep. And who was He anyway, this God who lived in the dark chapel she had been brought up to attend on Sundays during the few precious hours they had to play in, this dark God in His dark chapel, this foreigner whom we children hardly knew and didn't like and who could be angry like Dad and who promised us eternal damnation if we didn't look out? All this and damnation to follow. As though this life wasn't hell enough. Who the devil did He think He was, this God?

She caught herself up in her thoughts. 'Blenheim Hill, Broughton Street, Drayton Street, Grand Hotel, Barnham's Shoeworks; change here for Central Station. The Parkway, Jermyn Street and Beaumont Villas.' It wasn't right to have such thoughts, she told herself. She would be punished for entertaining such thoughts. Punishment. Ugh! These things were true, she consoled herself. God ought to be able to see that. And if you just accepted this awful mess with no rhyme or reason in it, with all its injustice and horror, like Jeanne, then you were just a worm. The least you could do was to turn to your executioner and spit in his face.

The resentment caused by these thoughts made her heart beat faster. Anger warmed her. She looked out of the window at the fierce rain beating the pavement. Even the tram had slowed down in the face of it. They passed the Colonial Store in Burdock Street and the word colonial immediately reminded her of Annie, her other sister, who had emigrated as a GI bride to the United States and who rarely wrote to her now, even at Christmas, and then of Trevor, the youngest, who was on a farm in Australia and who now seemed from there to have vanished from the face of the earth. She couldn't blame them. They had wanted to get away from this town and its memories as soon as their mother had died. Even Grace lived two hundred miles away and a six-hour trip by train for either of them.

And as for Dad, why, he had married another poor fool and lost interest in them all. She didn't even know where he lived. Bitterness fell upon the heels of anger. Yes, there were things undigested all right, but at the centre of her pain was loneliness, loneliness now more than ever before. Grace was far away, the others as good as dead, Cliff was no more, Cliff who had meant so much to her, who had given her life meaning, and now there was Robert whom she could love and look after, but with whom she would never be able to communicate. A large tear fell at her feet to join the rainwater from many shoes on the floor of the tram. She began to sob quietly to herself.

'Pardon me, madam, can I be of assistance? Hazelwood's my name. You seem to be rather distressed.' The gentle voice came from the man who sat next to her and she was suddenly awake to her circumstances again. She looked at her enquirer without a word. 'If I can be of any help, dear lady...'

'No, no, that's all right,' Margaret said, hastily wiping the tears from her eyes and face in urgent embarrassment. 'I'm sorry,' she added and tried to smile.

'No indeed, it is I who am sorry to see you so distressed,' the man answered, looking under the brim of his large green hat.

'Bridge Street, Bigglesworth and Bailey, Crown End...'

'My goodness! I've missed my stop!' said Margaret in sudden confusion, getting up from her place. The stranger also rose to allow her into the gangway. She moved off towards the exit. The stranger followed, and the two of them together, with about half a dozen others, stepped down into the rain from the tram which then glided off into other far-flung suburbs of the city.

'Have you far to go?' the tall man in the long brown coat and green hat enquired. Mrs Manship looked up into a sun-tanned, elegant face with the hint of a smile in it.

'Not very far,' Margaret said half-heartedly.

'Come, dear lady, allow me to accompany you some of the way under this voluminous umbrella here,' and he unfolded a very large black umbrella and placed it over their heads. 'Show the way!' he said breezily.

Although, as we have said, Margaret had her umbrella, she was nevertheless pleased at that moment to avail herself of male assistance. It was not often that men showed such manners these days, and so together they bore against the slashing rain and wind, he with his mighty umbrella to the fore and she tripping along as best she could to keep up with him. At last they came to 67 Prince Street and she thanked him kindly for his chivalry.

'I thank you very much. You have been so kind,' she said as they arrived at her front door. She turned to him once more and noted the long face and the dark eyes under the huge expanse of the umbrella before finally putting the key in the door. 'Thank you... Mr...'

'Hazelwood,' he repeated and then, 'I very much hope you will soon be feeling better, ma'am. Goodbye,' he said with a smile.

MRS MANSHIP

'Goodbye, Mr Hazelwood, you're very kind.'
Then he turned on his heel and went down the street. She watched his retreating back for a moment and the water lifting at his heels, glad that he had not been oppressive or too talkative. So there were still some gentlemen left, she thought as she went into the hall and made towards her modest living room. Hilda, her neighbour, met her in the dark hall, closely followed by the boy, Robert.

'Ah there you are, dearie, 'ere he is, your son and heir. 'E's been a good boy, 'aven't you, lad.' Turning to Robert and then again to Margaret, she said, 'Done some painting this afternoon, he has. I did the drawin's and he filled 'em in with paint.'

'Oh, Hilda, you're a gem!' Margaret said, and meant it. 'Especially as this afternoon was a bit of a joyride. I really didn't mean to be so long, but I missed the tram stop and had to walk back, can you believe it? I must be getting old!'

'I'm always doin' it, girl,' Hilda said. 'It ain't got nothing to do with age either; it's the only time you get some time to yourself and I usually go to sleep. One day I ended up in Bellthorpe five miles away and when I got out I was wondering why it was so dark. Street lamps ain't come as far as that yet.' They both laughed at this. Hilda was indefatigable and she never lost her sense of humour, not even during the war when Margaret and Cliff would go over to her house during an air raid while enemy bombers were overhead and she'd say in her Londoner's way, 'Come on, gal, let's have another cup o' tea before the buggers find us thirsty.'

Shortly afterwards Hilda left to go next door and Margaret was left with the child. She was especially kind to him this evening, because she felt rested after the change afforded by an afternoon off despite the weather and despite her reflections on the tram. Indeed, precisely because of these, she gave the boy a special treat by baking a cake with him in the evening. On these occasions he loved to help her. She often took him in her arms that evening and kissed him. He was, after all, the only thing she had now.

Not many weeks after the events recounted here, Colette died in her sleep at the house Margaret had visited. It was only at this point that Margaret realised that she had not seen Jeanne since that time. The funeral took place on a Saturday morning and Margaret Manship attended it in the wings, as it were, since she was not sure of herself as a member of congregation. The church was packed and she could see Jeanne in a black veil right at the front of the church. Father Benedict conducted the service and spoke in his eulogy of Colette's deep faith and courage in the face of pain right until the end. A true representative of Christ, he said. Margaret was moved. The service ended with a stirring hymn promising everlasting joy and as the congregation moved off she noticed to her surprise that Mr Hazelwood was one of their number. Noticing her, he smiled and lifted his hand in friendly greeting like someone whom she had known many years. She was warmed by this small gesture and afterwards returned home at midday in sunshine for lunch and a short rest before returning to the church in the late afternoon to clean and tidy in preparation for Sunday.

Since the weather had improved, Robert would be allowed to play in their very small back garden for a couple of hours until she got back. After their meal, Robert occupied himself with a wooden puzzle designed for five-year-olds. He could appreciate the object of the puzzle and what was required of him, but made the same mistake over and over again. He made noises of disapproval and his frustration mounted. 'Why, why?' he kept saying. 'Not right. Silly! Why not fit?' His mother knelt down and placed the offending piece into the right hole, but this did not please the youngster and he tore the piece from its place and flung it against the wall. 'There!'

he said in anger and sat pouting at the jigsaw piece on the floor. His mother knew that the only thing to do in such a situation was to leave him to his own devices. She rested for an hour and afterwards the children came to fetch him so that they could play in the garden. She gave the still-sulking head a kiss and left the house.

It was Father Benedict's instruction that the church be locked for two hours after a funeral and so Mrs Manship had been given the keys of the church so that she could carry out her duties. 'Please move about quietly and carry out your work with the least fuss,' he had said. It was his conviction that the soul of the dead person still dwelt in the church for a time after the service and that, strictly speaking, no one should be allowed into it for an hour or two. Her entry today was an exception owing to the pressure of time. Margaret was glad, however, of the opportunity of being able to work alone without interruption. In fact there was not much to do. She scrubbed and dusted, arranged the prayer and hymn books, checked the supply of holy water, adjusted the flowers on the altar and descended to the row of candles, standing for some time in front of it, fascinated by the warm light which issued from the many candles. High above through one of the small windows above the stained glass, sunbeams from outside had found their way into the church interior.

It was at this moment that, having nothing more to do, Mrs Manship felt moved to light a candle for her friend Colette. 'Why shouldn't I?' she said to herself, and she was pleased as she placed its cheery light with the others on the stand. It was then that something rather strange happened. She had stood there for a few seconds looking at the candle without thinking of anything in particular, but merely absorbed by the joy of the little light, when she became distinctly aware of Colette's presence. She turned her head slowly in the direction of the altar as though expecting to find her standing near it, but there was only a presence, a feeling which she had twice encountered in moonlight when she had been a girl. But this time there was something which invested the warm light that poured in from the high windows. Something was communicated to her and that something was the personality of Colette. Suddenly she knew what Colette had meant by 'acceptance' on the occasion of her visit. It was not, she knew now, mere passivity; it was unconcern. Not indifference, for Colette was, as far as the welfare of others was involved, more concerned than anyone she could imagine. No, she touched the world, but was not touched by it. That was it. For a moment or two longer, Margaret stood quite still with the awareness of her new insight. She knew that Colette was somehow still alive. It was strange. Margaret then retrieved her hat and coat from the small room where the cleaning utensils were kept and left the church, locking the door quietly behind her.

A week after this event Robert took seriously ill. He was violently sick and complained of a terrible headache by wailing and holding his hands to his head. He then grew listless and passed into a fitful sleep, and slowly his eyes glazed over. The whole transition from health to delirium took just a few hours. The doctor was called at night and diagnosed meningitis. He asked a lot of questions, comforted Mrs Manship, but warned her of the seriousness of the situation. For the time being, the patient was to remain where he was, he said. Margaret stayed up with the boy all night, cooling his head with iced water and giving him things to drink as the doctor had ordered. He came again the next day quite early in the morning and prescribed tablets. The doctor stayed with Robert for ten minutes or so while his mother went off to the chemist to get them. When she returned, her son was being given an injection. By now he was wild with delirium and flung the bedclothes from him with frightening strength. Dr Macpherson fairly shouted at her to hold the lad down, but it was almost more than she could do.

An hour later, Robert slept very peacefully and Margaret thought on two occasions that he had passed away and sobbed pitifully, but then some small movement later indicated that he was still alive.

Several days went by in this induced coma. Dr Macpherson came twice a day, once in the morning and once in the evening to check up on how things were progressing, his whole demeanour serious and uncommunicative. Hilda and her husband took turns to keep vigil even at night. During the day, the district nurse took charge of the boy, changed the bed from under him, washed him and poured medicine into his parched throat. Two weeks passed. There was no change in Robert's condition and it was clear that if an improvement did not come about in the next few days, he would almost certainly die. This information was kindly and tactfully confided to her one afternoon by Father Benedict, who had learned of her predicament.

'Whatever happens, you are assured of your job here and my personal support. If you need help of any kind, please contact me straight away. We are praying for him and for you,' he had said.

It was nice of him, she thought, but such promises and such prayers, sincere though they were, could not help her at that moment and she could do nothing now but accept what had befallen her. She cleaned and scrubbed and mopped and dusted, cut the flowers and arranged them, displayed leaflets at the entrance of the church, polished the brass of the great doors and, feeling tired after all this work, sat down in one of the pews to recover for a moment. There were quite a lot of people in the church gathered there for evening service. It was shortly before her time to finish. To her surprise, on that day she recognised Mr Hazelwood, whom she had not seen for many weeks, coming towards her. He asked after her in his gentle, attentive manner, and in her pain and desperation she told him how it was with her. She apologised a second time for her tears, but he only smiled and put a comforting arm round her shoulders.

'What have I done to deserve all this?' she asked in her agony. 'Why me? I'm so ordinary. As far as I know I've never done anyone any harm and have to suffer all this... Why?' She fished in her smock for her handkerchief.

Mr Hazelwood didn't say anything for a moment. Then he said gently, 'Mrs Manship, our lives are like paths in snow, crossed by the tracks of men and dogs and roes and foxes and by many types of birds, and when the snow falls and we walk out, we're always surprised to see how many other creatures are abroad like ourselves. The paths of fate are similar; they criss-cross our lives and we cannot be responsible for them. That is not God's doing. It is because we do not live alone and also because we come from somewhere and are travelling somewhere in this life.' He paused to look at her with his dark eyes. 'But we need a guide in all this, and that's where God comes in, you see. All you have to do really is to ask Him the way. If there were no God, life would be very dark and dangerous indeed.' He looked at her again to see if she was following him. 'It's really very simple. Think of your friend Colette. She accepted God and everything that happened to her, do you remember?'

Mrs Manship nodded. The church was filling up with evening worshippers. She would have to complete her few last jobs and then go home. She thanked him for his kindness and said that he was a wonderful, true gentleman and he smiled, obviously pleased with her recovery.

'Go home now. Everything will be all right,' he said and took a seat at the back of the church.

Mrs Manship attended to her last few duties and then hung up her smock on its peg, put on her coat and left the church as she had done so many times before. She smiled at Mr Hazelwood on her way out. In acknowledgement, he nodded in that friendly way of his and raised his hand slightly.

Usually she liked to walk home, but this time she took the bus as she was short of time. In it, she mused as to how Mr Hazelwood could know about Colette's remark to her. Did he know of her visit and had he and she been friends? Jeanne in her occasional encounters with her since Colette's death had not mentioned him. Her bus stop came into view and she got down from the bus and walked the rest of the three hundred yards to her home. In the distance she was alarmed to see Hilda at the door and as she gained ground she could see that there was something wrong and she ran the last few yards to the door.

'Margaret!' Hilda said, so beside herself with excitement that she could hardly speak. 'Robert's better! He's OK,' and she broke into tears. Fred, her husband, stood in the narrow hallway behind her, smiling all over his face. He nodded, tears in his eyes. Margaret pushed her way past them into the house and ran up the stairs.

'He's in the lounge. He's here in the lounge!' Hilda cried, and Mrs Manship descended the stairs again and went into the little living room. The district nurse was still in the house sitting next to a lively young boy kneeling on the floor playing with a toy bus. He turned as his mother entered.

'Mum, oh my lovely mum,' he said in a natural voice and hugged her. Margaret broke down. Hilda sobbed. The district nurse busied herself with something to hide her feelings. Fred just stood there.

'Whatever's the matter with you all?' Robert cried. 'Fred, can you help me with this wheel? It seems to be bust. I can't get it on again.'

Fred helped with trembling fingers and while the two were occupied, the nurse turned to Margaret to say, 'A miracle. Nothing else. He came out of delirium cured in every way. He's normal. About eleven o'clock.'

Margaret broke down again and the two women sobbed without ceasing. Mrs Robbins, the district nurse, then quietly took her leave. She was about to lose her professional grip and there was nothing more for her to do. She shook her head. 'Incredible,' she said to herself as she closed the front door. 'Just incredible.'

Three weeks passed. Robert had been rehabilitated to a perfectly normal life and Mrs Manship once more found herself at work in the church. Once more she had finished her work and was about to pack away her bucket and broom when she spied Mr Hazelwood sitting with a few others at the end of the church near the door in his favourite pew. She would go and tell him the good news. So she put the bucket in its place, stood the broom against the wall, laid out the floor cloths to dry, and then turned the corner into the nave of the church, but to her surprise and disappointment he had gone. On arriving at the pew, she enquired in a whisper whether anyone had seen him go out. Her question was met with surprise.

'There was no one here of that description,' somebody said. She went into detail.

'No, really, there was nobody sitting here, I'm quite sure,' said a regular midday visitor to the church whom Margaret immediately recognised. An elderly man at her side concurred. Astonished and embarrassed, Mrs Manship retreated to her broom closet once more. She scanned the church from that vantage point again for the possibility that he might have moved from his habitual seat. But there were very few in the church and he was not among them. He must have slipped out, she said to herself.

'Hazelwood?' Father Benedict echoed. 'No, there's no Hazelwood in the congregation, I'm quite sure of that. I know them all by name, all three hundred and twenty-one. And the sick and absentees,' he added with a knowing wink and smile.

Margaret did not smile. Later, she asked Jeanne and received a lecture on all the churchgoers over the last twenty years. She could account neither for the name Hazelwood nor for the description Margaret gave her, and then she added firmly, 'Nobody of that name has ever been to our house, either.'

5

Harlingford House (1928)

Permit me, Terence Amery Bannister, to step for a moment from the folds of time onto the stage to tell my story, to issue, if you will, for the course of its telling from the trees over there at the end of the park. Can you see me? No, no, not there, a little to the right, nearer the botanical garden. That's right. Good. Thank you. I was butler here and later head of household, you know. That was fifty years ago. Fifty years! And yet, and yet I remember everything that happened as though it were yesterday. So clearly, too. I remember the morning stealing into the garden, advancing very slowly over the dewy lawn long before it was light, for we servants were always up early, lighting the fires in the kitchen and preparing for the day. But I always had time while I was still busy fetching wood as a young fellow in those days to greet the natural fragrances of the morning and to listen to the birds singing everywhere in the garden and in the copse beyond. In the half light of dawn, it was easy to imagine that nymphs and satyrs had their abode there and that we mortals could only catch a glimpse of them in the twilights of dusk and dawn. For the house and garden had a magic about them – the garden, its quiet beauty full of memories; the house, built in 1572, full of history, its mysterious corners, its many books and dark furniture. And everywhere in the house this all-pervading atmosphere of settled peace lending a dignity to it which is hard to describe in so many words, try as I may.

Among those I had to deal with in those far-off days were Amy, the cook, Mrs Darlington, then about forty-five I suppose, the housekeeper, Adams the butler, then in his late sixties, and Barnaby the head gardener, also an old man, and it is with him we have to do in our narrative.

One spring morning I was adjusting the long curtains in the library with an empty-headed young fellow from the village sent up to us to assist, since Mary Scallop, our first maid, was down with influenza – a young person, I might add, who seemed not to know the difference between a turnip and a scarecrow – when Mrs Darlington appeared at the bottom of the ladder.

'What is it?' I recall saying rather irritably, with my mind partly preoccupied with the unnecessarily violent tugs of the nitwit under my immediate surveillance, partly with keeping my balance at the top of the ladder and now, suddenly, with the obvious earnestness of Mrs Darlington's errand.

'His Lordship wishes to speak to you, Mr Bannister; he's in the study at present.'

'Very well, I'm on my way. Not so hard for heaven's sake, man; you'll have me off the blasted ladder! Gently, now, that's right. Pull it through. Slowly! That's it. Not so much brawn and a little more brain, that's what's needed.' Completing the operation and, I admit, a little discomposed, I descended the ladder carefully.

'Wait here until I return,' I said.

From the library I made my way to his Lordship's study in the south wing. It must have been about ten in the forenoon, I recall, a time when Lord Sherrington generally did not like to be disturbed while he read a selection of the daily papers.

'Ah, Bannister,' he announced as I arrived at the study to find the door ajar. 'Do come in.' He had heard my footsteps along the passageway. I went in.

HARLINGFORD HOUSE (1928)

The 7th Earl of Sherrington was fifty-six at the time, still very much in his prime, had recently married his second wife, was still a splendid horseman and keen huntsman, was widely read, spoke three languages to perfection and possessed a knowledge of other cultures enough to qualify for the title of Professor of European History. He was tall and slim, his face chiselled and sunburnt, and in it were two very fine, bright blue eyes which never missed anything, neither in the matter of circumstance nor in communication, a truly admirable man.

'Umm,' he said, seeing me waiting deferentially, 'do sit down for a moment, Bannister; there's no need to stand. What I have to say will take a moment or two. How are you getting along with those wretched curtains?'

'Thank you, sir, quite well; we shall manage.'

'I'm sure you will. You always do. Truth is the things are quite old and the fittings are not what we're used to today, eh?'

'Indeed, sir, you've hit the nail on the head,' I replied. Lord Sherrington smiled his winning smile.

'Well, what I've called you in for is to tell you that we're to have a royal visitor next week and that, er, certain preparations will have to be made to accommodate him.'

'A male visitor, then, sir.'

'Oh yes, I'm sorry, yes, Prince Vladimir. Not the first time this modest residence has housed a member of a royal household, eh?' He looked at me in the way army officers look at their subordinates to know whether they have understood the implications of what is being said.

'No, sir, that's true. Is this man a Russian, then, sir? I take it from the name that that is the case?'

'Not a man exactly, Bannister, a young fellow of about twelve or thirteen, I believe. He'll be staying for a week.' He then gave me another look which I had learned to understand in all its implications over the last thirty years. The truth is that, although we were worlds apart on the social ladder and were very different in our tastes and inclinations, we nevertheless understood each other extraordinarily well.

'I take it that there might be some irregularities, sir, if I may make so bold as to read your expression.'

He smiled again realising that I had understood. 'Well, I don't think so. I hope not. We'll see.'

'There is one thing, m'lord. Does this young man speak English?'

'Gad, yes, English mother. No problems there.' He paused for a second or two before continuing. 'Umm, but I hear he's a rather, umm, you know...' I nodded.

'It's a difficult age, sir.'

'Exactly, Bannister. Tight rein.' I nodded.

It was a bright day outside. Early April. The sun had just come into the room and it was this, I knew, which pleased his Lordship so much – being able, that is, to read the papers in the sunlight which flooded the room during the morning. He went on to discuss the usual matters attendant upon the visits of distinguished guests and then he dismissed me with the instruction that I should get the young man's name right. It was 'VlaDImir' and not 'VlAdimir', as so often wrongly pronounced by people unversed in the Russian language. I thanked him and went off in search of Mrs Darlington, repeating the name correctly as I proceeded along the hallway.

On the Saturday afternoon before the arrival of Prince Vladimir on the following Monday, His Lordship's sister, Gladys, arrived quite by chance with her older husband and two of her friends, a lady and gentleman who were also visitors to the house from time to time. Since we were enjoying extraordinarily clement weather for the time of year, it was decided that afternoon that tea would be taken in about an hour on the terrace, it then being five minutes past three. His Lordship joined the party a few minutes after tea had been served. Although it is so many years ago, I can still remember the substance of the exchanges which then ensued. Miss Janice Ponting, the other lady in the party, opened the conversation by enquiring where Lady Sherrington was spending her time at the moment and received the reply from Gladys that she was visiting her mother in Sussex.

'Oh, Brighton. I love Brighton, a really lovely place to be in the summer. It's becoming rather crowded though nowadays. All sorts of people there. Not all of them nice.' She winced over her teacup. Her incredibly green eyes looked away over the garden, taking everything in with a painter's eye before replacing the cup. She was a good painter.

'Well, it's not exactly Brighton, you know, it's Lewes, a place inland which has quite a different character. You only remember that it's in that area because you used to spend your childhood holidays in Brighton,' Gladys corrected her with a smile. Janice made two or three gentle sideways movements of her head in acknowledgement of this and raised her pretty eyebrows at the same time. She was very young, eighteen, nineteen perhaps, and she looked beautiful in her long white dress with bright red brocaded roses at the hem and seams, one simple gold locket at her smooth neck and a fetching, sophisticated hat which only the young would dare to wear and which she now began to remove from its anchoring pins to let her shining brown hair fall upon her shoulders. Ronald, Lord Sherrington's friend, a man much younger than himself and the son of a relative several times removed, remarked that he had had the privilege of being able to watch the Boat Race at close quarters the week before.

'Cambridge won, and they deserved to – great show!' he added.

'That's very noble of you, considering the fact that you're at Oxford, Mr Curtis,' Lord Sherrington said in mock formality as he helped himself to a piece of cake.

'Well, fair's fair,' said Ronald, 'it was a great race.'

'Didn't you row when you were young, Harland, and for Cambridge, too?' Gladys enquired.

'Oh yes, once,' Lord Sherrington replied modestly between mouthfuls of cake.

'But that's wonderful, sir. Is that really true?' young Ronald broke in with enthusiasm.

'Oh, it's a long time ago I'm afraid. You were only a baby in my time. I'm sure standards have soared since then!' Ronald was visibly impressed and mused for a moment, contemplating his senior's past glory.

'Where are you, James?' Gladys asked, turning to her husband, a round, comfortable man turning forty and a number of years older than his spouse. He had been engrossed in what he referred to as the magical qualities of the garden and he turned to his host for confirmation.

'Yes, it is nice, isn't it?' Lord Sherrington concurred. 'Its upkeep costs me a lot though, I must say. Three gardeners. Not changed much since the seventeenth century. It was re-landscaped around 1720 after Cromwell had had a go at it a few years before.'

'Cromwell was here?' Janice said in surprise, her sharp cat's eyes focused on her host.

'Yes, this was a Royalist hideout for a time. His cannons rained their destruction from the hill over there for a couple of days. Then the Roundheads plundered the chapel, pursued the few Royals who offered resistance to the village, took them back there and hanged them all in the nave. Imagine! That's religion for you,' Lord Sherrington concluded and returned to sipping his tea. 'Talking of royalty, Harland, didn't you say to Milly a few days ago that you are expecting the son of the Dowager Empress Marie of Russia in the next day or so?'

'That's correct,' Harland replied in that simple, military, unaffected way of his.

HARLINGFORD HOUSE (1928)

'I hear he's a bit of a bounder,' Ronald chipped in before Gladys could continue.

Lord Sherrington looked briefly at Ronald. It was merely to acknowledge his remark, and it expressed the fact quite clearly that he was not prepared as yet to go to such lengths as to condemn someone he had never seen. So, turning to his sister, and at the same time answering Ronald's question, which was also Gladys's question, he said: 'Can't say. I've heard things of course. Lots of verve I believe.'

'A veritable prig,' said James, coming out of his reverie.

'Oh, really?' Lord Sherrington remarked, looking in James's direction. It was one of his favourite phrases. It meant that at that very moment his mind would race like the wheels of a very accurate machine in assessment of what had been said. It was not the light acquiescence it appeared to be to others who did not know him as well as I did. He waited for enlargement from his brother-in-law, a man of great political acumen and a good judge of character.

'Saw him at the Gala Dinner. I was only invited at all on the aristocratic qualifications of my dear wife here,' he observed, turning to Gladys, whose face had temporarily turned to stone. She knew he enjoyed such reflections, coming as he did from the people. 'The King was there, and as it happened, we sat quite close to him, didn't we, dear?'

Gladys, who was quite aware of the placement of rank on such occasions, offered a face which said, 'You must excuse him; you know what he is,' and Janice, seeing this, let out a little uncontrolled giggle like a hiccup.

James, noting this with some pleasure, continued, 'Yes, and this conceited little brat was next to his mother, a seat or so from the King himself and opposite me.' Interest deepened while the golden afternoon sun surveyed the faces of those assembled on the terrace. More hot water for tea was brought from the kitchen. 'Talked about the last war as though he had taken part in it,' James continued, helping himself to another cup. 'Never a nod to the waiters who served His Little Highness, let alone a thank you. Oh, he knew it all. Any topic that happened to be touched upon, he saw to it that we were all to receive further details. At least a dozen times during the meal his mother had to restrain him. It was disgusting.' There was an interval of silence while the new brew of tea was sampled by the others, and James's view considered.

'I haven't much choice but to receive him here,' Lord Sherrington said, almost apologetically. 'I shall have to see how things go and deal with whatever crops up.'

'I don't envy you, Harland, really I don't,' James said with finality.

And so, to avoid Harland further embarrassment, the conversation turned to other things until it became a little too cool to sit outside any more, for by this time the sun had already dipped far towards Wales, and the tender leaves on the trees in the garden were touched with red and gold.

Prince Vladimir arrived on Monday morning early. He and his mother were received at the small village station. It was a beautiful morning. A handful of people paid their respects by raising their hats to His Lordship, while others paused in their doings to stare. The Empress was a truly magnificent figure, wearing a tall hat with a feathered cockade and a light, long, deep blue coat over a frilled white dress. She carried a decorative umbrella in one hand and with the other led a young boy of about thirteen. She herself was about twenty-eight or nine, but had the unaffected dignity and bearing of an empress. The description 'every inch a queen' fitted her perfectly. Both visitors shook hands with their host on the station platform. It was a moment to remember. She had a man with her, a personal servant who packed the bags into the waiting car, Lord Sherrington's new green sedan of which he was very proud.

HARLINGFORD HOUSE (1928)

The boy took a great liking to it as well, remarked on its high polish, enquired how much horsepower it had, clambered aboard after his mother had been helped up, and soon the little party was on its way to Harlingford House. He talked all the time, this youngster, and was keenly interested in all that he saw as we passed. There was nothing one could take amiss, however, and his mother was gentleness and sweetness itself. All this I was to learn later from the chauffeur. I myself first set eyes on the young man in his blue sailor suit and matching beret with its red pom-pom half an hour later when they arrived in the courtyard. The entire staff was there to receive them. The boy was well-mannered and obviously familiar with protocol. Later, I showed him his rooms and acquainted him personally with all that was necessary for his comfort, his mother being of the opinion that he should be self-reliant in these matters. After all, she had said, he's man enough now to see to these things himself.

'Thank you, Bannister,' he said serenely when we had finished, 'that will be all.'

I went downstairs thinking that we would get along quite well.

During dinner in the evening of the same day he again behaved perfectly well, it seemed to me. He held his tongue when adult matters were discussed, only once being admonished when he lapsed into Russian with what was obviously a query and not a surreptitious comment.

'While here, we speak only English, do you understand? It is rude to use another language in the presence of our kind hosts,' admonished his mother, who looked at him severely, and he accepted the reprimand without demur. There was not so much as a sulky look. The impression I gained was, I must say, a good one and this was also the opinion of other members of the household over the next few days. It was, on the other hand, quite clear to us that our young friend was proud and spirited, but what of that? It could hardly have been otherwise considering his background. After three or four days, the Empress left us to pay a brief visit to the south coast, saying that she would return as soon as she could. She was extraordinarily grateful to us all, she said, for looking after the boy for a few more days, as she had urgent things to attend to before her return to France, where she lived in exile. All of us were greatly taken with her grace, natural charm and sincerity. When she had gone, the great house seemed to lack something.

It was obvious to us all that the prince became bored after a while. He had explored the building, had taken great interest in the animals we had on the neighbouring farm, especially the horses, although his mother had strictly forbidden him to ride. Why we didn't know. I tried on a number of occasions to interest him in this and that and his answers were polite, but, alas, the young fellow could not disguise his boredom, and I could only smile sadly.

About four days after his mother had gone away he fell in with one of the village boys who was often in the grounds, since his mother worked four days a week in the greenhouse. From then on, the two were inseparable. And then a peculiar thing happened, for it was then that our guest became a pest. Whenever he was with Victor, his peer and playmate, he became overbearing and demanding to his seniors. While not being exactly rude, his manner would say everything so that the servants began to look forward to his departure. It seemed that Victor aided and abetted him in this behaviour, and this young man was subsequently taken to task about the matter by his father. He denied relishing the advantage he had over the servants when at his friend's side, and although he was forbidden to play with Vladimir from that time forth, the two were bound to see each other each day (Victor's mother not wishing to let her son out of her sight for obvious reasons), and once they had joined up again it seemed a hard thing to insist on their separation.

HARLINGFORD HOUSE (1928)

One afternoon I found the two of them stoning one of our many cats and reprimanded the two of them sharply.

'What's this?' I said, rattled at such irresponsible conduct.

'We're stoning the cat,' said the young prince shortly and petulantly, as though I had no right to interfere, and in a manner which suggested I was foolish to ask such a question as it was obvious what they were doing. Victor was silent.

'I don't want the animal injured,' I replied. The cat was hissing at us since it had been cornered by the boys and was now a convenient target.

'It's only a cat,' Vladimir answered defiantly.

'It has feelings, my young friend,' I said admonishingly.

'A cat's feelings!' came the contemptuous reply. 'Ugh!'

'I thought you were fond of animals,' I enquired, but Vladimir seized Victor by the arm and walked away from me.

Cheeky young prig, I thought to myself while I was left there to look a fool. I had little time to ruminate over the matter, for that same afternoon something else happened which was to have serious repercussions.

They had been playing, these two, tearing through the grounds near the estate, shouting and running all over the place like a couple of excited dogs, when first one of them and then the other trampled on Barnaby's lettuce patch. The little lettuce seedlings had been relieved of their glass protection for an hour or so to receive some of the warm, late April sunshine. Twice Barnaby shouted to them to keep off and it was not until the third desperate cry that they finally stopped, still standing on the lettuce seedlings, red in the face and breathless when Barnaby came hurrying up to them.

'What the devil do you think you're doing, you young hooligans!' Barnaby cried furiously. (Not even I would have dared to challenge his lettuces.)

Whereupon, the Prince drew himself up to his full height and declared provocatively, 'Who are you calling a hooligan, may I ask?'

'Get off my damned lettuce patch, you rascal!' roared Barnaby, advancing towards the offender.

'Rascal yourself, you peasant! Get away with you!' said Vladimir with supreme contempt.

Barnaby boiled over. He seized the lad's hair in his knotty hand and dragged him off the lettuce bed, and with the other roundly boxed his ears. The prince fell ignominiously to the ground. His ears were red and his eyes blazed.

'You'll pay for this!' he said under his breath. Victor was taken into custody by Dickenson, one of the farm hands who had witnessed the scene, and was similarly dealt with.

The affair came to my ears a few minutes later. I sent the boy with Cook to his room, where he was disrobed and placed in a hot bath to await my further instruction. Meanwhile, I sought opportunity to acquaint His Lordship with what had happened. He was in fact just recovering his wits after a nap in the Orangery, where he liked to withdraw for a few minutes after lunch. He received my news with a serious mien.

'The young man swears vengeance,' I declared, 'threatens to tell his mother of all that has happened. And his ears, especially the right one, are very red and swollen, sir.'

His Lordship considered for a moment. Then he said, 'Correction is one thing, injury is another. His mother will have every right to be indignant about that when she returns the day after tomorrow.' I nodded. 'Moreover, Bannister, it will look very bad for us all should this, this er, "encounter" make its way into the papers, let alone become a rumour in elevated circles that we, a distinguished family having the honour of safeguarding and entertaining a prince of the realm while his mother is away on other business, should stoop to administering corporal punishment or even allow it to be administered.' He gave me one of his straight looks. We both knew that a mere well-deserved box on the ears for studied rudeness would not be assessed in such a measured way in the circles he had just alluded to; on the contrary, there were

HARLINGFORD HOUSE (1928)

some who would revel in such a story and the consequences would be both far-reaching and damaging.

'We must try to encourage the boy to keep his mouth shut,' His Lordship said after a pause.

'That may well be difficult, sir, knowing his temper.'

'It must be undertaken somehow, Bannister. We shall have to think of a way. Send Barnaby to me immediately. When I've dismissed him, I want to see the boy personally and alone here in this room.'

'Yes, m'lord, I shall see to it at once.'

I felt sorry for Barnaby, not the boy. He was called to the servants' entrance and informed of what was ahead of him. The possibility was that he could be dismissed from his job. He was sixty-four years of age. Although work in the garden over the past fifty years had bent him, his wizened face showed no signs of remorse for what had happened. I have always entertained the conviction that gardeners are queer folk and frequently very stubborn. This one was no exception to the rule. He was fiercely jealous of his own territory, and even Lord Sherrington himself entertained deference for Barnaby's intense commitment to his tomatoes, his peas, his greenhouse and the many plants therein. Barnaby was like a post hammered into the ground when it came to concessions as far as the garden was concerned, no matter who proposed them. I felt sorry for him, seeing the incongruity of his dirty trousers and his holed and worn pullover at such a reception. He very rarely even came near the house. As far as I recall, he had never once entered it. Now, he stood there humbled in his stockinged feet and was being asked whether he had no slippers for the occasion and was thoroughly confused. Finally, he was ushered upstairs by Mrs Darlington, who had in the meantime found a pair of clean shoes to fit him for the interview. I accompanied him and announced his presence.

'Come in! Ah, Barnaby.'

'Your Honour.' His Lordship exchanged a few courtesies and came straight to the point.

'Barnaby, er, this interlude. Very regrettable, very regrettable,' His Lordship began.

Barnaby broke in, 'He started it, m'lord; gave me some fine cheek he did and standin' on my lettuces after he'd kicked 'em to bits with that ne'er-do-well, Victor...'

'Barnaby, I know the circumstances, thank you. Your ire was certainly justified, but I did not think you would lay hands on the child with so much violence. Do you think that this was really necessary? I may have to ask you to apologise to the boy...'

Barnaby straightened his arthritic back as well as he could. 'A child? Never, m'lord, not to that snotty-nosed little rogue!'

'Barnaby! I have to ask you to curb your language. The circumstances are such that an apology for violence is, on this occasion, quite in place. After all, you have struck a prince. That is not an everyday affair, Barnaby.' Lord Sherrington's voice had acquired the tone of reprimand.

'Never! Not to 'im!' Barnaby replied in defiance.

'Then I must make you aware of the possible consequences of this unfortunate affair which, if no apology is forthcoming, may result in your dismissal, much as I deplore the idea after so many years of faithful service.' Barnaby's face was of granite. 'One thing is clear Barnaby: this must not get beyond the walls of this estate, do you understand?' To this Barnaby nodded without another word. 'Very well, we'll see. You have a few hours to reconsider your stance.' So saying, His Lordship sat down again, signifying that the interview was at an end. Barnaby returned to the garden and I to my duties.

At dinner, the prince announced to us all that he would without hesitation inform his mother on the coming Friday that he had been struck. His Lordship tried to remonstrate with him. He appealed to his budding manhood. No man, he said, would go crying to his mother. He would have to

HARLINGFORD HOUSE (1928)

take things as they were. This, while it might have appealed to an English lad in those days, in no way pleased the continental prince, who had other standards and values than we on our island.

'Mother shall hear of it, nonetheless,' he said resolutely. So as to avoid an undignified exchange between himself and a boy of thirteen, his Lordship declined to go into the matter further and left the youngster to think about the attributes of manhood while he helped himself to another slice of ham from the plate in front of him. The dinner was concluded in silence.

Afterwards, when His Lordship had retired to the library to smoke and read, Cook had a gentle word with the boy, but it was obvious that Vladimir enjoyed the limelight of importance his present position had bestowed on him and was not to be moved. Mrs Darlington, an eminently tactful woman, also tried to dissuade the prince from his intentions, even suggesting a pact which, I felt, included the elements of bribery, but all was to no avail. He remained proudly adamant.

The next day, Lord Sherrington tried again. This time I was not present, but concluded that a second overture had been made when I discovered the prince issuing from Lord Sherrington's study at about ten in the morning, a time, as I have already indicated, when he was not inclined to carry out such interviews. The prince passed me with a mere nod. At midday, lunch having been served on the lawn in the form of a light snack, we had resigned ourselves to the worst that could happen and thought no more about it. We knew that the Empress would be arriving within two or three hours at the latest. Vladimir, now having no company of his own age to keep, was found later near the aviary, admiring the birds.

'Do you like them?' he was asked by an elderly woman who used to look after the birds from time to time when Her Ladyship was away.

Vladimir tamely said that he did.

'Then come in and have a look round,' said the woman kindly.

Vladimir entered and looked around with interest. The woman watched him as he looked at the colourful variety of birds in the cage.

'Some are quite friendly,' she said. 'Look, Rosie, come to auntie's finger! Rosie, Rosie, Rosie, Rosie.' The bird came and settled first on her gnarled finger and then on Vladimir's small pink hand.

'Oh, how beautiful he is!' Vladimir said in admiration of the tiny life perched on his hand which he held very still.

'It's a little girl really, I'm told,' said the old lady with a smile. 'I don't know where the name came from, perhaps because of the fine colours. These usually belong to the male,' she added. The prince was enthralled. He looked long at the bird.

'We've lots more; would you like to come along with me and look around?' she asked. Finally, the royal guest was shown the eagles and falcons, given a leather glove and allowed to nurse His Lordship's favourite bird, Rupert.

'I shouldn't allow you to do this,' she said to the boy with a shy smile, 'but since you like him and he likes you I can't see any reason why you shouldn't let him settle for a while.'

The prince was flattered by this privilege. He sat very still while the bird perched in magnificent unconcern on his gloved hand.

After a while, the woman said, 'He's very tame. If you like, we can let him fly for a while. The exercise is good for him. Come.' And she took the boy outside and he stood with the bird still on his arm in the paddock.

'Won't he fly away?' Vladimir asked.

'No, he's been trained to return. Now let the eagle fly!' She gave a signal and the golden bird soared above the neighbouring woods and fields, wheeling and purling while the boy watched, quite entranced. Forty minutes passed and twice the bird returned to the lad's outstretched hand.

HARLINGFORD HOUSE (1928)

'Oh thank you,' Vladimir said when the bird had been returned to its perch at last. 'Thank you.'

'Not at all, young man, I'm glad you enjoyed your time with Rupert. He's a wonderful bird and seems to understand what we say to him, doesn't he?'

'Yes,' Vladimir returned enthusiastically. The old woman smiled at him kindly. Then someone outside was calling. 'Hilda! Hilda, tea is ready!'

'Well now, you'll have to excuse me, dear lad, I must be away,' she said. 'Goodbye.' She squeezed his arm, turned and walked towards the three cottages some yards away from the aviary. Vladimir watched her go, standing there a long time listening to the flutter and twittering of the smaller birds in the aviary, and then he, too, slowly walked away in the direction of the great house.

'Your mother has arrived, Your Royal Highness,' Cook announced as she caught sight of him coming towards the house. 'Where have you been, my young friend?' she asked in a fluster as he joined her. 'Come, wash your face before you greet your mum.' And she led him off to a sink in the scullery at the side of the house which was used for tradesmen. 'We'll have to make a quick job of it.' She ran a clean damp cloth round the submitted fresh young face and the firm chin, afterwards surveying her work critically before announcing, 'There, that's a bit better. What do your shoes look like? Oh, my goodness, dirty as usual.' She applied the same cloth now to the shoes and then threw it unceremoniously into the sink.

'Cookie...' Vladimir enquired as the cook rapidly adjusted his tie and coat collar, 'is Mrs Barnaby called Hilda and has she got a rosy face and a wart on her forehead?'

Amy the cook paused for a moment from fastening a button and looked down at her small charge. 'Why yes, why do you ask?'

'Oh nothing,' said the lad, 'it's nothing.'

'Now, off you go or your mother'll be wonderin' what's

keeping you,' said Amy, and Vladimir leapt up the kitchen stairs through the house to the main hall. He arrived to find his mother standing there, her servant slightly behind her and Lord Sherrington together with Adams and one of the maids in the hall. All of them were about to walk off to the dining room for late tea when the Empress caught sight of her son breathlessly approaching her. She took him into her arms and hugged him. Oddly enough, she did not notice the red, enlarged ears all at once for she had turned to His Lordship to remark on something or other in answer to his enquiry a moment before. 'Well, of course, if you wish; we can talk privately after tea...' she said. Then she turned to Vladimir again.

'My goodness, child,' she asked in terror, 'what have you been doing? Your ears are swollen! Oh dear, oh dear!' She knelt beside the boy and very gently caressed the ear nearest to her.

'Been fighting, Mamma, but I gave as good as I got. Victor, he's my friend, Victor's ears are red too, by golly!'

Lord Sherrington, who had opened his mouth to say something, now closed it again.

The Empress frowned. 'Ach, these boys, why must they always be fighting? Is it something in their dreadful male natures? These men! Dreadful, really dreadful!' She shook her pretty head in incomprehension. Then the little party passed on slowly into the dining room.

6

A Rogue Like Me

The author in conversation with former SS-Hauptscharführer *Helmut Paslowitz*

'Paslowitz' was not his real name. The interview was never intended on my part nor arranged by anyone else. It happened. The whole thing was a coincidence. I was staying with my wife's relatives for a week during the '60s in what was then East Germany.

It was late autumn. We were on our way over a rough country road to the house of an acquaintance, a woman my wife had known at school. I forget now upon what errand, but it was probably to while away an afternoon with a friend one had not seen for years. I can only remember that the women had something interesting to say to one another and as my German was not very good I anticipated another very long, boring afternoon during which I would understand very little, be required to smile or perhaps even laugh in the right places, accept the proffered cake and coffee, and wait patiently, endlessly, for the moment to come when I could at last depart. I remember feeling as dogs must do that are obliged to wait and daydream while their masters gab. After sitting there for hours on end, listening to what, after all, was just a noise in those days, I would long for the moment when it would be time to go.

This time, however, I was in for a big surprise. The car

bounced up a pitted side road and stopped outside what had once been a fine house, but was now much in need of repair. It was about three o'clock in the afternoon and the weather had turned considerably cooler. Frau Paslowitz opened the door. She was a large woman in her early fifties who possessed very bright, alert blue eyes, and her hair was still the natural colour it must have been, I assumed, some twenty years before. She was an active, energetic woman, kindly, and anxious to give us the most cordial welcome she could.

'Come in, come in. So this is the Irishman everyone's talking about.' The presence of a visitor, any visitor, in those country districts and in those days was a nine-day wonder.

'Yes, that's him,' my wife laughed.

'Come, take off your coat. Allow me. It's cooler isn't it? I think the winter will be early this year.'

The quietly tiled little hall led us to a largish living room that revealed a man rising to receive his guests. I guessed his age to be about sixty or so. He struck me as large and powerful even at this age, and he had the broad shoulders and deep chest of a boxer or a butcher. His complexion was sallow and his hair, which was still full, was swept back from a high, strong, squarish forehead. The eyes were large, brown, deep set and watchful. He assessed me briefly and, I felt, accurately in the way policemen do, routinely checking off the points they learned during their training, missing nothing. He noticed everything, not with suspicion, but, we could say, with deadly accuracy, like a machine. The dark, hairy hand that was offered to me was strong and the grip was firm. His voice was deep and vibrant so that I could imagine him as an opera singer.

'*Guten Tag.*'

'*Guten Tag, Herr Paslowitz.*' He nodded formally and turned his attention with a smile to the ladies, introducing himself to my wife as he did so. He bade us all to be seated.

The room was cosily furnished and the set of two armchairs and an ample settee were well-made and comfortable. We sat back, glad of the opportunity to rest for a while after the arduous drive dodging potholes on the way here. The room was deliciously warm after the cold wind outside. For a few moments I bathed in its warmth before the fire that busily crackled in the grate and listened to the others exchanging pleasantries. I was beginning to recognise such phrases as 'Was the journey all right? The villages are not well signposted here. Not like in the West.' Frau Paslowitz sighed. Herr Paslowitz smiled knowingly.

'Well, you know how it is,' Mrs Paslowitz added after a moment's pause. Then, 'What about some coffee?' The coffee had already been prepared and sat under a cosy on a sideboard nearby. It was then served from an elegant pot into cups of Mrs Paslowitz's best coffee service, the simplicity of the porcelain relieved by a bright gold ring on the edges of both the cups and the saucers.

'Do you like coffee?' Herr Paslowitz asked suddenly. 'Most English people prefer tea, I think.'

'You speak English, then?' I asked in astonishment. Before he could answer, his wife interposed, 'Oh, he speaks everything, Russian, too, my goodness! A real gifted linguist, my Helmut.' A moment or two followed in which all this was translated to me.

'Well,' I said, 'this is really the last place I expected to hear a word or two of English – and such good English, too.' And it was indeed good English.

'Oh, thank you,' the large man said modestly and chuckled to himself.

'Cake?' Gold-rimmed plates were brought.

'Oh yes, please,' I said in English.

'It's difficult to get cake here, even the ingredients,' Mrs Paslowitz explained to Ingrid, my wife, 'but I was lucky. Through a friend, you know; when I knew you were coming and told her about it she managed to get some for me.' All this I managed to understand quite well and took the cake gratefully.

'Where did you learn such good English?' I asked, turning to my host. The man shrugged his bear-like shoulders. Frau Paslowitz butted in again before he could answer. 'He learned by listening to the BBC; he just listened and learned it, just like that.' She made a sign in the air with her hand. Although, you know, we're not allowed to listen to "imperialist propaganda".' She made a funny face as if to punctuate the sentence. The rest was up to us to comprehend.

'I listened to the "Learn English" lessons on the BBC and tried to read a bit,' Paslowitz said self-effacingly.

'You must have put in a lot of hard work,' I said with admiration.

'The toughest part is the first part,' he said simply.

'But your English is polished as well as fluent and also correctly pronounced,' I said. 'Have you ever been to England?'

'No, I've been here all my life – that is with the exception of a brief interval during the war.'

By this time the two women were deep in conversation, so it did not appear rude on my part to continue my conversation in English.

'Do you mean you were abroad during the war?' I ventured.

This, I knew, was always a touchy point in post-war Germany on either side of the border. In general, people were most unwilling to talk about the war and there was a general feeling of shame and guilt at the time this conversation took place. Practically everyone I had met denied any part in the war and its heinous consequences except to say, reluctantly, that they were soldiers. Duty. Coercion. The times. I assumed that the same would apply in this house.

'Your wife claims that you also know some Russian?' I added quickly.

'Yes, I speak Russian.' Again the matter-of-fact acknowledgement that was part of this man's personality. Everything he did, he did with economy of movement, and his answers to my questions were friendly, short and succinct. He raised the cup of coffee in his giant hand and looked at me over the rim.

'It's not so difficult here. The language is taught in schools. Lots of folks have to learn it to further their careers, and it's easy to get Russian papers and literature.'

'I've heard that it's a fiendishly difficult language,' I said with a smile. He smiled back.

'It has its difficulties, but then so does English. Different ones.' We laughed at this and then he continued, 'Russian is not such a problem since there are resemblances between it and Polish. I was brought up in an area where Polish as well as German was spoken and so absorbed it, so to speak, at an early age.'

'Where was that?' I inquired with interest.

'Well, it's a little village on the borders of Poland. You wouldn't know it I think.'

After this, the conversation turned to the political situation on both sides of the border and more particularly to the advantages of being able to purchase anything desired in the West and how difficult it was to get things, even the simplest things, in the East. In this regard, life was difficult in East Germany. I noticed that there was no outright criticism of the regime on his part, but the question of its legitimacy lingered in the air nevertheless. It seemed to say, 'Why did they make it so difficult for us? Where is the sense in it?' Outright criticism would have been too dangerous. We were clearly guests and to all intents and purposes not politically committed, but the spaces between the words said, 'What if these strangers were to relate our true feelings to others here? What then? It is better not to risk anything.'

On the other hand, our hosts took a lively interest in developments in West Germany, and in our observations on the political and economic developments in Britain and Ireland, all of which were received with the greatest attention. This mutual exchange of information, such as it was, seemed to lift the blanket of daily political terror. This was on the one hand. On the other, our hosts felt that, beneath the capitalist rapacity about which they were so often and so well informed, there were such things as democracy and humanity.

'It's not all that bad here,' Frau Paslowitz was saying. 'There's idealism; nobody actually starves. Medication is free and so on, but I cannot see why they're so aggressive about it all.' Herr Paslowitz posed questions on Britain which taxed my knowledge and it was clear that he had been reading and thinking about Britain pretty intensively. I answered his questions to the best of my ability, realising at the same time that I wasn't as well versed in many matters affecting my own country as he was. The conversation which ensued from these questions was lively and informative for us both. Ingrid interpreted for Frau Paslowitz and so she, too, was drawn into the dialogue.

We talked for some time, an hour perhaps, I can't remember. I only remember that the exchange resulted in a very satisfactory feeling of having achieved understanding, of having established the conviction between us that we were, first and foremost, human beings with similar hopes and desires and that not even political terror could eradicate this fact from our lives. There was a comfortable pause.

'More coffee?'

'No, thank you.'

'You, Mr Lowe?'

'No, thank you very much. I enjoyed both the cake and the coffee.' Mrs Paslowitz nodded as though she understood everything and she probably did. Nevertheless, the sentence was translated to her by my wife. Paslowitz himself was visibly pleased. The crackling fire was a pleasant accompaniment to our thoughts.

'Like England, isn't it?' Frau Paslowitz noted, forgetting for the moment that our home was in Ireland – a common error.

'Yes, it is – a rare thing in Germany. Most people have central heating.'

'Ah, yes, over there,' she said with conviction, amused at my ignorance of things on this side of the border.

'This house is an old one and in the old days the open grate was common here, too.' Then an idea struck her. She turned to my wife and me and said, 'Would you like to see the rest of the house? It's quite interesting.'

The house had been originally built in 1925 and had belonged to Frau Paslowitz's parents. She had spent her childhood and youth in this house, leaving it only for the duration of the war, when she had seen compulsory service in the army auxiliary services, returning at the end of 1945 to find that her parents had fled to the West a year before. She decided to stay on and see what happened rather than join them immediately after the war. Later, she met her husband-to-be and they both decided to settle in the house, which was then legitimately hers to look after, although later it officially belonged to the state, as did all other property. In 1953, she informed us, both her parents died within a few months of each other in West Germany. The house was quite large for two people, I felt, and said as much to Frau Paslowitz. She replied that part of it had been used as a doctor's practice, and had since been modified to accommodate her husband's hobby room. There were four large bedrooms to the house, and downstairs a library stacked from floor to ceiling with books, not only in German, but also in French and English. It was quite magnificent.

'Yes,' Frau Paslowitz said, turning to me on seeing my interest. My father was an avid reader. I have left everything here as it was. Only Helmut disturbs the dust on them from time to time!'

Leading off this well-lit, carpeted room was a smaller one

which, we were informed, once served as a room where her father had kept his microscopes and medical instruments and where, she added, he used to study. Since the ladies had paused here to go into detail, I had no alternative but to look round. The personality of its former owner pervaded every corner. The design, furnishings and other objects in the room, the clock on the wall, the chest of drawers, the fine, broad desk with its line of books, the thick leather writing pad, an inkwell and other functional knick-knacks all spoke of their owner, of his meticulous care, his thoughtfulness, his studiousness. The pictures on the wall were of old town squares and one was of a woodland scene depicting the peace of summer. All these things gave the place an air of the tranquillity and social stability of fifty or sixty years ago. Taken as a whole, they were almost powerful enough to displace the influence of the present. A modem torch, for example, which lay on a chair in one corner, a few letters with contemporary stamps, yesterday's communist newspaper and some other modernities were easily accommodated into this peaceful, friendly little room. Apart from these, nothing disturbed the voices of yesterday.

It was a few minutes later as we were in one of the bedrooms that my eye fell upon a photo in a frame. It had appeared in view as my host moved on to follow the women into another room. As I was the last in file I had the chance to look at it more carefully. It showed Paslowitz as a young man in SS uniform and, to my horror, I noticed the skull above the officer's peaked cap. So Paslowitz was one of them, I thought. The reflection chilled me. As the others moved on through the door I took opportunity to linger and peer more intently at the photograph. The cold, pitiless eyes, the brutal thrust of the chin, arrogance and egotism clear to see, the complete macho in that black, pantalooned uniform of terror. It was a full-length photo and he was equipped with the infamous jackboots and ... a whip. The man's arms were akimbo and he stood as if awaiting a reply or a further order. I bent over the photo, analysing it, taking in every detail, and a moment later was thoroughly shaken to find that Paslowitz was standing behind me, smiling. I straightened and looked at him, not knowing what to make of the smile. It was a half-serious, half-bantering smile.

'I ought to have removed it before your visit,' he said, much in the manner of someone excusing himself for not having given you a serviette with your meal. There was a pause. 'I suppose you find it offensive, and I can't blame you for that.' I nodded in acquiescence to this.

'Well, it's a long time ago. It's over,' he added.

The women had moved off into the other room and I could still hear them talking, their conversation punctuated here and there with an occasional laugh.

'Over?' I whispered, and I looked again at the photo in its steel frame and then I looked at Paslowitz. He knew what I was thinking. A young ruffian like that with an ego like that who knew Polish could only have seen service in the East. I looked at him a long time and he at me. Neither of us spoke and then, at last, I said, 'The Jews?'

'Yes.'

'Auschwitz?'

'Yes.'

'What rank did you hold?'

'*Hauptscharführer.*'

It was a strange situation, the guest as brief inquisitor.

'Did you get caught?'

'I was twice sentenced by an SS court for my excesses and for extorting money from prisoners.'

'An SS court? I didn't know there was such a thing,' I said.

'Oh, yes.' He looked at me levelly.

'Helmut! Aren't you going to keep us company?'

'Yes, dear; we're on the way.'

'No, I mean the Allies. Didn't they catch up with you?'

'Not yet. In any case, this government needed rogues like me to keep its own business going.' He smiled briefly.

'You know,' I said, 'you're the first person I've ever met either here or over there that has ever admitted to being part of the regime of those days.'

'I dare say,' he said simply, looking at me for a long moment.

His manner made me reflect. He had used the word 'rogues' in that matter-of-fact way of his. His attitude was of one who was resigned to the fact of an evil past. The tone was utterly without affectation. There was, for example, no attempt either to play down the matter or to emphasise the fact that in war, anything goes, that it is all very regrettable, but such things happen. I had heard this excuse, too, in West Germany. Together we went down the stairs and returned to the warm living room and for half an hour or more our conversation turned upon the past as it inevitably does when people have not seen each other for a long time. What had become of so-and-so? And is old so-and-so still alive? And do you remember that time when...?

My burly host had lit another cigar, as was his custom in the evening, he told me. He puffed and surveyed it for some time just below eye level. 'You know,' he said at length, 'I've always wanted to set down what I lived through in those days. I've never done so here since it would perhaps be more than my life is worth – for what it's worth...' he added apologetically and with a short laugh. 'But in a few years, perhaps months even, I shall be dead anyway. Heart trouble, you know. It seems to me that you would be the ideal person to confide in. The day after tomorrow, you say you'll be returning to Britain and then over the sea to Ireland?'

'Yes,' I said.

'You could, I suppose, denounce me from there.'

'I don't denounce people,' I said.

'I thought as much. I'm a good judge of character, you know. You'd be the right man for the job, I'm sure. That is, if you want to.'

I thought for some time about this.

'What would you want me to do?' I asked at last, not knowing yet whether I was willing to accept the offer.

'Well, I suppose you could ask questions and I would answer them. At least that would be the start. You could take notes and then you would have a record of what had been talked about.'

'Rudolf Hoess has written such a book, in fact he wrote it just before he himself was hanged in Auschwitz opposite the barracks where he spent so much of his time as commandant,' I said.

'Ach, Rudolf. Yes, I know about the book. It's been on sale here, too. But I've got something to say in addition and I think it ought to be said.'

I was silent for a long time. The whole thing was a little uncomfortable, unpleasant and unexpected.

'I'll have to think about it for a moment or two,' I said finally.

'Do; take your time,' he said.

That night, three miles away from the house where I had spent the afternoon, I lay awake wondering what I should do. Did this unutterable criminal have designs on me? Would he, after having spilled the beans, entice me into the cellar, there to murder me single-handed? The question had to be answered now in my bed as I gazed through the roof window at the moon sailing through ragged cloud. It was possible. I would have no firearm to draw at the critical moment, no knife and, even so, an accomplished murderer of his distinction would certainly know how to deal with a chicken like me. But for him there remained the problem of what to do with the body. Would his wife perhaps be a willing party to the murder, the hostess at yesterday's tea-time talk, a woman suddenly transformed into a harpy? This was hard to imagine on reflection and, I asked myself, what would be the point of murdering me? Unless our former SS man was a compulsive murderer? The desire alone to talk to me of his past seemed very strange. Even if he were to die soon, as he had intimated, he had nothing to gain from such disclosures. Officially at least, such people were still eligible for trial and imprisonment, even in communist East Germany. The whole thing was fraught with danger. He knew me merely on first acquaintance and this, too, was odd. Why should he for a moment entrust the long, close-kept secrets of a criminal past with me, virtually a perfect stranger? Was it because he felt safer with someone who lived in Eire, a state a world away from communism? Again and again, I returned to this question.

When, for the second time that week, I arrived at the unprepossessing little house in the unmade-up road, the house bordered on one side by tall, shivering poplars, I still had misgivings about entering it. Some leaves had blown in front of the door in a little pile since the day before. Looking at the dull windows, it would have been easy to conjecture that no one was at home. Somehow, I hoped so; I could say then that I had kept my promise, had arrived like the traveller in De la Mare's poem, knocked and asked, 'Is there anybody there?' I knocked. For a long moment there was silence and then the door opened suddenly and unexpectedly. It was Frau Paslowitz. She looked different; she looked tired and resigned to life. There was not the glow of welcome in her eyes as there had been yesterday. On the other hand, she was not displeased to see me. In that moment it suddenly occurred to me to wonder: 'Did she know of her husband's past?' It was hard to tell from her manner. What had Paslowitz said to her in wishing to see me again today? 'Do come, in Mr Lowe.'

I entered the house and found myself in the small hallway again.

'You want to ask him some questions,' Frau Paslowitz said, smiling.

'Yes,' I said, 'men's stuff, you know.'

'Pardon?'

I thought quickly.

'Oh, politics and such things,' I hurriedly added in order to get it over with. She would recognise the word 'politics'. She, like me, was glad not to be entangled in linguistic complications. She laughed nervously as she guided me towards Paslowitz's study.

He, Paslowitz, sat there as though unaware for a moment of our presence at the open door.

'Mr Lowe, Helmut.' She closed the door. He shook himself from his reverie, apologised and stood to receive me behind the desk. Automatically he offered me his hand.

'Today, Herr Paslowitz, I am not here as your guest,' I said. He gave me a look of understanding and the hand was withdrawn.

'Very well,' he said, 'of course, of course.' He sat down again heavily. For a long moment we sat looking at each other, the naïve schoolmaster and the powerfully built former mass murderer, he a trifle embarrassed at my coolness, I a little fearful of his reaction to my manner. However, only seconds passed before he pulled himself together. 'There's one thing we should be clear about at the outset,' he declared, 'and that is that we must be quite frank with each other. Otherwise I can see no sense in this interview.' His eyebrows rose in question.

'That's all right with me,' I replied. 'Let's start with some background first. When and where were you born?'

'Yes, well, I've collected some general information for you,' he said. 'In fact, I've even drawn up a list of general information for you which might be helpful when you write your report or your book,' he added, much as an insurance agent would put the matter, his tone helpful and practical as he shifted the papers on the desk in front of him. 'I was born in 1913. My father was a railway worker, my mother a housewife and seamstress. There were five children. One child died in infancy. Looking back, there were no skeletons in the cupboard. My father was strict, but not cruel, and although life was occasionally hard on us all, so it was for every working-class family in those days. I got up to the same pranks as other children and was walloped for it just as they were, but, as far as I can tell, I didn't get twisted in the process.' He smiled.

All this was said in a simple way. He paused to see if he should continue. I nodded. 'Childhood years were marked by poverty. I learned quite early on to steal potatoes and coal when the family did not have enough to eat and the stove was short of fuel, but it was a matter of survival sometimes in those years. In one respect, however, we were lucky in that our dad was a civil servant and so permanently assured of an income so long as he was fit enough to work on the railway. That was a God-sent blessing in those days. I only had a few years of schooling and began work at twelve years of age. At work life was hard. I rose at five in the morning and was still busy at six at night; I worked at the same place where my father worked. The job itself was routine. When I was about 17 or 18 I was thoroughly tired of the work at the railway station. I had "risen", if you can call it rising, from the menial job of a locomotive cleaner's helper to a cleaner proper.'

'Cleaner?'

'Yes, cleaning the locomotives and carriages inside and out. Later I became a porter and was on the way to being a guard after taking preliminary examinations when I came across the existence of the Nazi Party for the first time. This offered me an altogether new interest in life and so I regularly attended local meetings and finally became a member. This gave my life a new direction at the time and by dint of regular attendance and interested participation, I soon had a secure place in its ranks. I was able for the first time to travel (I had never left my home before), to see something of the world as they say. I joined the SA, and even saw service as Hitler's bodyguard with several thousand others when he moved from town to town to give his speeches. It was at this time that I became acquainted with violence as a way of life and it wasn't long before I was quite convinced of Nazi lore. I suppose you can say that this period of my life was one of systematic brutalisation. I would also like you to recognise the fact that I was in a situation which offered little in those days by comparison. Here I was a young, energetic man and had the opportunity to meet others of my age committed to a cause and soon gained a sense of identification both with it and with them. It was as though I had for the first time awakened to life. At home, there was the everyday drudgery, poor food, lots of work, an inflexible hierarchy, mean lodging and a little money over at the end of the week to get drunk on Saturday night in the local pub. In short, my horizons were low. As an SA member I was part of a vital organisation which was to affect our political and social future. It was a first-class alternative.'

'Were you based at home during this time?' I asked.

'For the most part, yes, but there were many opportunities to stay elsewhere as Hitler moved around.'

'What did your father and mother think of these activities?'

'My father was an entirely apolitical man. Although he felt that the government was weak in his day and that something ought to be done about inflation and unemployment, he entertained no convictions and was in no way allied to any political party.'

'Did you like your father?'

'Yes, he was a good father. He was just and fair, but aloof. He worked long hours and worked hard. When he returned at night he was far too tired to have much time for us.'

'But he treated you well? I mean, he didn't beat you or maltreat you?'

'No, not as a habit. We would all of us get up to something sometimes as I've said, and then he would give us a beating when we were young and deserved it, but he was reasonable enough. To tell you the truth, I never knew him very well. I know this sounds absurd, but it's true. My elder brother was the one in our family whom I hated and who treated us all badly. He was innately wicked and his one aim in life was to make others miserable. He was, if you like, the cuckoo in the nest; he ingratiated himself with both Mother and Dad, terrorised us, stole from us, cheated us, set one against the other, sought every opportunity to tell tales about us and show us up to others outside. This was the last and deadliest sin within the family – I mean to be made a fool of to others, to neighbours and such.'

'As there were more of you, couldn't you have ganged up against him?'

'We did, but he was always the stronger despite that and always managed to gain support from our parents. When this failed, he'd see to it that support came from the gang of brutes and bullies who were his friends.'

'And your mother, what about her? Didn't she support you at all?'

'Mother was cowed by Hans, my brother. She was afraid of him. We all were. But it was Mother who encouraged me to stay away from home whenever I could and who was glad when I joined the SA.'

'And with the SA you found a meaning in life, as you say?'

'Yes.'

For a good minute or so my opposite number paused to reflect on this affirmation. Then he continued.

'I think it amounted to giving us an identity. We were members of a movement with a definite goal and our manners and our uniform set us apart from the rest of the community. We were tough, uncompromising, and every day we were confirmed in the ideas of the Nazi Party. As in the army, we received regular physical training each day which strengthened our bodies and brought us to a pitch of physical condition where we were ready for anything. This, together with plenty of regular exercise, as well as drill, fresh air and good food, made us into healthy young animals. We had energy in abundance and this was channelled into aggression. It was easy.'

Here, Paslowitz paused again to test my reaction. He looked at me thoughtfully for a moment before continuing. 'From here on, young man, the story becomes nasty. I hope you're ready for it as I am not going to "pull any punches" as you folks say. I've promised to be quite frank with you and I've asked you to be the same. Later, I want to make something clear to you.' He waited for my reaction to this.

'Yes, go on. I'm ready for what you have to relate.'

'Very well. In the first place you will be surprised to learn that I was not an aggressive person at the time of joining the SA. I was ignorant and I was indolent. I had learned to read and write at school. I could add and subtract, do very simple multiplication, but there the arithmetic stopped. I never did learn how to divide. At school I was an indifferent pupil, knew next to nothing about the history of my own country and even less about that of other countries in Europe. The same applied to geography. In short, I was almost illiterate and, looking back on my schooldays, the only lesson I can remember is the visit of a local welfare officer who lectured us on the basic principles of hygiene and the dangers of smoking. I found it so interesting that I can still remember it today. As at all schools in those days, I had also found it necessary to assert myself in the interests of survival, to fight when the need arose, to ally myself with stronger schoolfellows, to lie, cheat and steal. That was all part of the game. It was, if you like, a good preparation for the life I was to lead later. Work at home was the only alternative to school. I hated work and the house and the street in which I lived and was even at that time quite aware of the meanness of it all. My spare time, what little there was of it, was spent lazing in the hilly fields above the town, but although I slept a lot at such times, I never awoke to peace of mind. I was looking for something and I didn't know what it was nor where to find it. From this sense of being ill at ease grew my increasing commitment to the SA. As I indicated to you a moment ago, we felt ourselves to be somebody in those days. We felt representative of the nation. We were a force to be reckoned with, "at last," I must have thought to myself subconsciously in those days, "At last I can fulfil this curious yearning for that something which will make me happy, and the more I exert myself on its behalf, the better I shall feel." At school I'd been a nonentity; at work, too, I was a nobody; and the same went for society as well of course. Here was an opportunity to play a role, to stand out from the masses and to begin to live a meaningful life. I only half realised this at the time. I didn't realise that the price to be paid for the privilege of "being somebody" was the coarsening of my nature. This took place only slowly.

'It wasn't difficult to adapt myself to the new role of rough indifference to others, of intolerance, brutality and violence. I didn't think twice about obeying orders. Indeed, I didn't think much about anything. I felt instinctively that thinking of any kind was dangerous to my existence, and in the early years very quickly acquired the habit of immediately cancelling out any compunction I might have had in that direction. It was a simple, self-defensive mechanism. It ran something like this: "Thinking hinders action, so delaying immediate satisfaction. Thinking will disassociate you from the organisation, bring contempt from your peers and finally fling you into desperate isolation, a kind of lonely death." Hard upon these thoughts would follow the prospect of a return to my dismal home surroundings, this time in disgrace, the contemptible butt of family jokes and the punchball of my elder brother. No, thinking was to be avoided at all costs.'

'What happened to your elder brother eventually?'

'He died on the Russian Front in 1942. His last letter complained of the cold and of having no food. Yes, my brother. One of the first things I did after some training in street brawls was to seek him out in my home town together with two of my SA cronies and draw him into a row from which he couldn't retreat without losing face. We gave him the thrashing of his life. The last I saw of him was his outstretched body on a pub floor and a pool of blood at his head. He was quite still. The police were called, but by the time they arrived we were over hill and dale. Some time after this incident I was transferred to Berlin for four to five weeks of duty to supervise speeches by big fish in the party. I had then been with the organisation for just over a year. I was no longer in my teens and at this time was singled out for the first rung of promotion. I remember being enormously proud of this, and the honour did a great deal to strengthen my feelings of identity with the movement. The stay in Berlin lengthened to six months, and during it, there was strife not only between us and the public as well as the police, but also internally, too. I was twice involved in brawls with the police and members of the public, and twice reprimanded for disorderly conduct. I feared then for my promotion, but as I was to find out later, these incidents were to contribute to a posting to Sachsenhausen Detention Centre, not yet the concentration camp it subsequently became. While I was there, the political coup took place which finally led to the dissolution of the SA and its absorption into the SS. Once again I was promoted to what you would call a sergeant in the SS. We received new uniforms and insignia. By this time I felt fully established and was determined to make my career in the SS.'

'So you identified yourself with the goals of National Socialism?'

'Yes, I did. I felt that Hitler was the man to get us out of the rut in which we found ourselves at the end of the First World War.'

'And what happened after Sachsenhausen?'

'At Sachsenhausen I learned the tricks of the trade, as you would put it.'

Paslowitz paused for a moment as if he were seeking the order of priority for what was to follow. Then he said, 'You won't like what is to follow.' He looked at me coolly for a second or two and again waited for my reaction. I nodded as a sign for him to continue. Paslowitz clasped his very strong, hairy hands under his chin and put his elbows on the table.

'The majority of prisoners coming to us at that time were political dissidents, but there were also quite a number of what in those days we regarded as socially unacceptable people, like petty criminals, homosexuals, Bible thumpers and a few Jews. In addition there were also a number of high-ranking Social Democrat Party officials, the heads and managers of a number of newspapers and a few authors. The mass deportation and liquidation of Jews had not begun at that time. These prisoners arrived in groups of fifty or more and were immediately sorted out into the groups I've mentioned. They received special badges and armbands sewn into their clothing. Our intention from the very first was to make them realise that here they either toed the line or we would break them in body and spirit. Intimidation was easy; we had all the cards in our hands and with the help of wooden truncheons and short whips we were quickly able to assert ourselves. Shortly after arrival, prisoners were ordered to stand in line rank behind rank for identification, and since they had been brought off the street as it were, this was not difficult. We paraded up and down between the ranks, stiffening up those who dared to slacken their stance. Then followed what is common practice in every prison or detention camp, the deliberate provocation of prisoners. I'd already had plenty of experience of this kind of thing in the gangs I had belonged to in my youth, and my first victim on this occasion was a portly individual in his late fifties whose greatcoat was not fully buttoned up and out of which protruded a waistcoated paunch.

'"What's this?" I asked this man and poked my truncheon hard into his belly. He bent his head forward in pain, as is natural in such a situation, and as he did so he received an uppercut blow from the truncheon which damaged his chin and bloodied his nose. In his pain he moved his position and attended to his chin and nose with one hand. I hit his hand and arm several times until he yelled with pain.

'"Stand still!" I bawled. He recovered himself and stood at his place, whimpering and trembling. But he stood there. Such was the authority we had over the parade. This kind of thing was a favourite pastime with us. All of us enjoyed it. I didn't stop in those days of course, young and ignorant as I was, to consider why the whole thing was a pleasure, but realise now that it was a matter of being free to determine the course of events for myself, to exercise prerogative. It confirmed our egos. So long as everything goes along according to our desires, we thought, all is well. The ego is confirmed in such situations, but if anything occurred to throw it into doubt, as occurred on this particular afternoon, the ego in us resorted to violence in order to re-establish the comfortable feeling of being supreme.

'On that afternoon there was a man in the ranks called Stark which, as you know, means "strong" in German. This Stark, on answering to his name, was then asked to step forward. I stood a few paces away to watch my first murder. Stark seemed to me to be some kind of trade union functionary (a lot of whom, incidentally, opposed the Nazi regime) and he was fairly easily recognised by his choice of phrase and vocabulary. Donath, the officer taking the parade, put his face very close to Stark's and said, "I hope you are strong, Stark, you'll need to be in this place." Stark said nothing, but stood stiffly to attention like the other prisoners. Unsatisfied with this reaction, Donath roared, "You answer my remark with 'Yes, Herr Oberscharfuehrer!'."

' "Yes, Herr Oberscharfuehrer!" Stark said quietly.

' "Louder!"

'Stark repeated the word loudly.

' "That's not loud enough, you dirty bandit. Louder!!" Donath emphasised each of his words with a blow to the small of Stark's back making him cry out in pain. The prisoner was confused and in so much pain after these blows that his next attempt to speak was a humiliating, comical mixture of anguish which hoped to please. Stark himself was only too aware of his humiliation.

' "Louder!!" roared Donath again.

' "Arsehole!" Stark retorted and spat in Donath's face. The prisoner was then set upon by two warders and beaten to the ground while Donath stood aside. Once on the ground, Stark attempted to grab the booted leg of one of the guards and unbalanced him temporarily. A third man came to aid the other two and together they pounded and kicked Stark into silence and immobility. It took just three minutes. A couple more minutes elapsed to strip the prisoner of his clothes and string him up on the simple, moveable gallows we always had at hand. There Stark swayed for all to see, his face a red, unrecognisable pulp from which blood still ran in trickles over his bruised body.'

'What did you think about this event, your first witness to murder?'

'What did I think?' Paslowitz echoed my question and reflected for a moment. 'I think that at the moment I realised he was dead I was shocked. Yes, even I. Or shall I say, I was a bit put off. We, the thugs of the town and countryside, were used to knocking people senseless. Once they were still, they were dealt with, so to speak. I think we assumed in those days that when our victim got up again, he'd behave himself and cause us no trouble in future, but this time I realised while he was on the ground that Stark would never get up again. There was a clear difference of which I was quite aware. It didn't require a church or a set of commandments to tell me then that this was something more than a beating and that it was wrong.'

'But you swallowed it?'

'Yes, I swallowed it; I let it go. The alternative... Well, there was no alternative for me.'

'And what happened then?'

'Well, I was required to see that prisoners were regularly ill-treated, which meant that we could arbitrarily give them work beyond their capacities, tasks whose fulfilment was hardly possible in the time allowed, for example, and also to subject them to drill or long periods of standing on the parade ground. This punishment could last eight hours at a time. Everything had to be done to our utmost satisfaction, otherwise punishment would follow. And we frequently punished prisoners to entertain ourselves. One of the punishments often used in Sachsenhausen and in later concentration camps where I saw service was the flogging of prisoners. They were taken into a room where their trousers and underpants were removed and then they were forced to bend over a kind of buck in which position the buttocks were tautly stretched to receive the blows of a stick or cane. Sometimes other instruments were used such as a belt, a piece of sharp steel rod, or a length of hard rubber tubing. A prisoner could receive up to twenty-five lashes; each one would have to be counted in German by the prisoner regardless of his origins – that is to say, regardless of whether he knew German or not. If he made a mistake, we'd start from the beginning. This was often the case and so the number of lashes would exceed twenty-five and frequently the prisoner lost consciousness after a time. When this happened we threw a bucket of cold water over him and started again. It was on such an occasion that I committed my first murder – at least indirectly. The prisoner concerned was passed to me for failure to report on time. He claimed to be ill, and had stayed in his bunk bed. Everyone, ill or not, and regardless of the weather, was expected to report twice a day on roll call in the morning at 5.30 and again in the evening. Many prisoners were so ill on these occasions that they had to be supported by one or more of their comrades. The roll call could last up to four hours and sometimes even longer. Many prisoners died at these roll calls or were maltreated during them. Frequently, those who had been victims of a flogging the day before died the next day during roll call. In this respect we were heartless, as in everything else. Pitilessness was expected of us and the one thing which prisoners hated most was this daily roll call. During the hours of waiting, often, in the winter, at temperatures many degrees below zero, the prisoners, poorly clad as they were, simply passed out or froze to the ground. Later, this was especially the case with young children. No other prisoner was allowed to help them on such occasions. If he did so, it would mean death. Many prisoners who passed out in this way either died on the spot or soon after they were taken back to the barracks. One prisoner whose fate I'm about to speak of was a newcomer who had complained of diarrhoea. He was a journalist and had been sent to Sachsenhausen for slanderous reference to the regime. When we (there were always two guards present at such floggings) took his drill trousers off to flog him, he stank to high heaven. This made us all the more angry with the culprit and we laid on by turns unmercifully. Twenty strokes had been ordered and at sixteen he forgot where he was and was obliged to begin again at "one". At the third stroke this time he broke down, howling and weeping.

' "Count, you bastard!"

' "Count!"

'He began half heartedly to count, but again at the third or fourth stroke he stopped and put up an enormous howling and wailing. It sounded strange, almost inhuman, this peculiar noise.

' "Count!"

'We hit him again quite arbitrarily now and I noticed that my colleague was irritated by the noise the offender was making. I, too, felt the same and I grabbed the stick and laid on with all my force without requiring him to count any more. The victim lost consciousness and, as usual, a bucket of cold water was tipped over his drooping head. But this only had the effect of bringing him partly back to life. After a few seconds he once more lost consciousness. When this happened, my senior colleague said, "Take this bag of shit out and throw it into the nearest cell. We can carry on tomorrow when he has brightened up a bit." We threw him unceremoniously onto the concrete floor of the cell where he lay crumpled and lifeless like a half-empty sack of potatoes. He must have been about fifty-five years of age I suppose, and when we visited him the next day he was dead.'

'Generally, the victim survived the flogging, then?'

'Generally, yes, although over twenty-five strokes as a result of miscounting was usually pretty dangerous to life.'

'And you were only allowed to beat the buttocks of the victim and not the back, so I've read.'

'That's right, otherwise harm done to the kidneys would result in death pretty soon. The idea was to inflict pain by way of punishment – a lesson, so to speak – not to kill the prisoner. My second murder was a clean, quick job as they say today. As I have told you, in those days I was a strong man, full of muscle. I had long ago learned to use my hands and fists to attack and also to defend myself. It so happened on one occasion that I was assigned to a job controlling building operations at the southern end of the camp. It was bitterly cold, I recall, and every now and again flurries of snow would blow across the site. Jobs like this were a bore for us and we sought every opportunity to assert ourselves and also keep warm. One man in a gang of eight or nine was working a pulley while the others were busy transporting heavy iron scaffolding to a pile of it not far away. Every now and then when the pulley was not operating this man clapped his arms repeatedly around his shoulders to keep himself warm. I kept my eye on him for a while and then patrolled another section of the building site for a few minutes, but returned sooner than expected and caught this fellow smoking in the machine shed. I took him to task.

' "What do you think you're doing, you snipe!" I said and struck the cigarette out of his mouth, landing him a blow on the side of his head with the butt of my rifle at the same time. He fell but picked himself up almost immediately and looked at me defiantly as though to say, "But for the rifle you'd be lost, you miserable thug." This infuriated me and I made to hit him again. He dodged the blow skilfully and took two paces back.

' "Come here!" I ordered. After a moment's hesitation he did so and stood shivering in front of me. I put down my rifle and in the next moment sprang at his throat. To my surprise, and although well-built himself, since he had not been in the camp very long, he put up little resistance. I remember his red face and the way his eyes bulged as I throttled him. He fell to the floor and for a few seconds more his body twitched several times as though an electric current had been applied to it. When he was still I took up my rifle and ordered the others of the gang who were waiting outside to lug him out of the machine room and throw him into the foundations which had been freshly dug and which at the time were partly waterlogged. The mud and water swallowed him up almost immediately. I remember at this moment feeling a sense of great satisfaction and achievement. I had done the job with my bare hands.

'Some weeks later, in the same way, I killed another prisoner with a spade for hesitating to carry out an order. Moreover, I had taken an instant dislike to this particular man. The sound of the sharp edge of the spade on this man's skull and the insane cry of pain he gave as the spade sank into his brain just above the ear, I'll remember for as long as I live. He did not die at once, nor even fall to the ground, but ran about screaming with staring eyes, touching things and people around until I gave him another smack with the spade on the other side of his head as he returned and he flopped to the floor like a rag man and lay quite still. The sudden silence after these hysterics chilled most of the onlookers and even I was affected by it. People don't die like they do in cowboy films, you know. Nor do they take an injury in the same way as is shown on television. This is just American bullshit. These scenes of fist-fighting in bars for instance are so much childish nonsense. And – have you ever noticed – the injuries received by the "goodies" are always in the shoulder or the arm, never in the eye or the scrotum. Some people go mad, you know, when they are even slightly injured or feel that permanent damage has been inflicted upon them. Others scream and curse and there is always resistance. Blood spurts on walls and furniture and there are some people who acquire great strength on such occasions, so that very many times it took a number of us to finish off one individual. Very few people die at the first stroke, even if it's deadly. That's very rare. Generally speaking, there are a few minutes in which things happen very quickly and these moments can be dangerous for those inflicting the injury. The foolish idea of hitting someone on the head and expecting him to sink to the ground immediately is a celluloid fallacy. It takes a great deal of skill to scientifically administer a blow where a man (or a woman) is immediately rendered unconscious. The scenes of bank robbers and other violent criminals on TV striking people down with one blow is pure fiction for the most part. Of course, there are times where a blow can be so crippling that temporary unconsciousness takes place at once and perhaps even death. But this requires a lot of practice. We had one comrade who was adept at directing a blow just above the heart with his bare fist. He used to administer this to women prisoners in his charge and practically all of them were killed instantly. Failing this, he would give a directed blow at the jugular artery in the neck and here, too, he was so expert at it that his victim fell unconscious at his feet. He would then draw his revolver and shoot him or her through the head just to make sure that they were dead.

'I see you're silent. But I did warn you that what I had to say wouldn't be pleasant.'

'Go on,' I said grimly.

'After the first two or three murders of this kind it became easy to murder. Shooting was too easy for words. I have shot men out of sheer boredom in Auschwitz, for example.'

'So you were later in Auschwitz?'

'Yes, I was moved there in 1941 quite early on.'

'What rank did you have there?'

'*Hauptscharführer*. This is the rank of something like a senior sergeant major in the SS. In Auschwitz I had carte blanche to revel in my desire to kill and maim. I enjoyed both inflicting pain and killing. As time went by while I was there, I became the terror of that place. Every prisoner feared me.'

'And what about the Jews?'

'The mass-murders, you mean?'

'Yes.'

'They took place in Auschwitz-Birkenau about a mile away. I was stationed at the so-called home camp. Only when there was a large assignment of killing to be done at Birkenau was I required to do service there. Many of the trains came in at night and sometimes it was necessary to do overtime. Sometimes the killing of Jews went on all night and all night long the flames of the crematoriums would illuminate the surrounding countryside and the sky directly above it. The countryside stank for miles around.'

'Surely there were some who sensed the fate that awaited them as they stood on the platform after having been discharged from the train?'

'Oh yes. We were always on the lookout for the troublemaker who'd give the game away. There was a constant fear among us all that we might one day have a revolt on our hands.'

'What did you do with the "troublemaker" as you call him?'

'He – usually a he, although we had quite a lot of women reacting to the treatment they received on getting out of the train – he or she then would be quickly sorted out and dragged away. No one, as far as I remember, ever came to their support. The culprits were then dealt with quickly with a shot in the back of the head. It was easy and all in a night's work.'

'How many people did you get rid of in that way?'

'Several hundred, I suppose.'

Paslowitz passed a hairy hand over his face in a refreshing gesture.

'All with the revolver?'

'No, some of the women I killed with my own hands, I either beat them to the ground and then gave them the rest on the head with the rifle butt.'

There was a moment's pause.

'In the days before we gassed prisoners *en masse* we stripped them and shot them as they stood there, forty or fifty at a time or as many as we could deal with on the spot. There were occasions when we used the machine gun for this purpose and others when we simply picked them off with a rifle. Usually five or six SS men were engaged for this job. Many of the SS men and some others employed in this work found it so distressing that they became ill and some even went mad. Many of them reported sick and a few even deserted. In the latter case when they were caught later, we were then commissioned to execute them.'

'And you were involved in all this?'

'Yes.'

'Did you derive satisfaction from this kind of work, too?'

'Yes. And in addition to all this, I sat in on interrogations with other SS men and assisted in the tortures which accompanied them. During these sessions we were given a free hand. One of these tortures was called Boger's Spindle after the name of its inventor, an infamous SS man like myself. It consisted of a steel rod supported at each end by a trestle and standing about 1.30 m high. The victim was trussed to this so that his hands and feet were bound to the spindle tightly and close to one another. Then he was beaten regularly like a drum on the buttocks and would rotate. Because it was amusing and at the same time a satisfactory punishment it gave a lot of pleasure to the sadists who were involved in the torture. Again, as in the case of flogging, many prisoners died while on the spindle, but many survived. Their buttocks and shoulders at the end of this interrogation were usually in shreds and the centrifugal force generated by the spindle as it revolved threw the blood onto the ceiling and the nearby window so that other prisoners were constantly busy cleaning the place during and after a beating.'

'At these interrogations were there any victims who successfully resisted your questions?'

'A few, not many. There was one Pole whom we picked up in Cracow, a man suspected of smuggling arms into the camp with the intention of causing an uprising. He was denounced by one of the prisoners in the camp and there was no doubt about his involvement. During the interrogation one afternoon we broke his bones, beat his face to a crazy, staring porridge and again and again brought him round with a bucket of cold water. We squeezed his testicles to a jelly with one of the instruments we had at hand for this purpose and apart from his cries of agony he never uttered a word about his activities. He survived the afternoon, though God knows how, and we threw his broken body aside at nine o'clock in the evening for "treatment" again the next day. We were tired and in need of refreshment. Aumeier, one of the chief interrogators on that occasion, wanted to subject him to further torture the same evening, but received news quite late at night that the man's wife had been arrested. She arrived the next day with two children, one fourteen and the other twelve. The next day we maltreated them in front of him. The fourteen-year-old died within an hour and his brother in the early hours of the next morning; his wife was blinded in one eye in one of our attacks and put up a tremendous fit of screaming. This was so great that we could hardly hear ourselves speak. We stopped her mouth with a mixture of plaster of Paris taken from the medical unit, gagged her, stripped her and tied her to the table. We then lifted the table so that it faced her husband. We laid on with everything we had. After about an hour or an hour and a half she died of either asphyxia or a heart attack, I don't know which. To make quite sure she was dead, Aumeier shot her once through the head. Shortly after this our friend, the Pole, died. Later we arrested about a hundred people who we suspected were involved in the conspiracy and over the next three days hanged them all as well as the denouncer within the camp. Those who were about to be executed sang Polish national songs until the very last man.'

'What effect did this kind of courage have on you?'

'I watched the hangings from my office window. It had rained all night and the ground was muddy and slippery. The soldiers employed for this task slipped several times and were laughed at by those about to be hanged. As a result these men set about the group with the butts of their rifles and a few people were dropped on the spot for offering resistance. There was not much they could do since they had their hands tied behind their backs. Those who fell to the ground unconscious as a result of these attacks were hanged next, unceremoniously, while those who were left kept up their singing. As I watched I realised that it was a defeat for us. I yelled from the window for two more auxiliaries to help speed up the job.'

Paslowitz paused and again passed both hands over his face and head in the same way as before as people do after having woken up in the morning. Then he continued.

'For the first time then in my two-year service in that place I felt doubts about what I was doing. In some indefinable way it all seemed to be a waste of time, from my point of view, all hard work for nothing. It merely crossed my mind at the time and I let it pass and went about my ignominious business until one miserable late afternoon when I was doing duty at a store in the Birkenau camp.

'This store was an important element in the whole killing machinery at Auschwitz. Everyday when the trains arrived, the Jews were relieved of their luggage and this was left on the platform. Since it was all carefully labelled, the victims were convinced that it would be returned to them in due course after allotment to their quarters. In fact, of course, it was plundered and subsequently sorted by a special group of prisoners. The work was carefully supervised by guards and anyone attempting to benefit personally from the work was put to death immediately. Despite this fact, "theft", if you can call it that, did occur. The value in Reichsmarks procured from this work amounted to several hundred million. At that time, there was a certain Italian who worked in this particular store and who had three or four prisoners in his charge, the man had once been a senior employee in a large chain store and after doing time in other camps he was finally sent to

Auschwitz for resisting the regime in Italy. His job was to see that things were properly sorted, categorised and labelled for shipment back to the "Reich". On this particular morning I had reason to ask for the key to a cupboard inside the store which had to be regularly inspected by us during routine checking. I asked for the key and was told by one of the prisoners that it was missing. On hearing this, I immediately lined up those working there and ordered the Italian, who was at that moment outside, to be brought in. He was roughly thrown into the room by one of the corporals on duty there.

' "Where's the key?" I demanded.

' "Mislaid, *Herr Hauptscharführer*. Since yesterday!" '

' "Lost!" I roared. This was all part of the game of intimidation, the prelude to certain death in such an instance.

' "You're responsible for the key, you miserable dwarf (he was a small man). Where is it?" I thundered. "You don't lose keys!" The Italian, who was half my size, remained unimpressed and added that the smith was making a new one as we "know more or less what it looks like".

' "You do, do you?" I said in menacing tones. "Well, I want the original."

' "The original will be found, *Herr Hauptscharführer*, I assure you. It's buried safely under all this work." The Italian gestured to the heaps of clothes and personal articles lying around. His tone was calm and even. His attitude was one of respectful objectivity. He was unafraid.

' "A lot of trains recently," he added with the beginnings of a smile. Nobody smiled here. It was unknown. I lifted my arm to wipe the trace of it from his face, but he didn't flinch. This arm of mine that had killed so many and could lay him, a fellow of about five foot two or three, into his grave within seconds. But his eyes were clear and unafraid. I can still see these eyes, grey-blue, they were, and in that second I remember thinking it strange since, in my ignorance, I assumed all Italians to have brown eyes. The trace of a twinkle in his eye was still there. For a fraction of a second the two of us were aware of each other, the killer and the victim, he quite still, almost smiling, and I about to strike. He stood looking at me, this intrepid Italian, with neither hate nor fear in his eyes, the lips about to break into a smile ... but it was a smile that didn't irritate as it could so easily have done. Suddenly I was bereft of the usual desire to fell him on the spot. I stood there a moment too long with my upraised arm. The interval between thought and action, intention and fulfilment, was pregnant with absurdity. To strike him now after several seconds would also be absurd and detract from my authority. I let my hand fall, grumbled something or other to the effect that I expected the key to be found by midday and left the shed. As I did so I heard the guard bellowing orders to the rest to get back to work. Outside, the all-pervading, sweetish stench of burning flesh that hung over that place day and night met my nostrils. And it was drizzling. The rain made a strange pattering sound on my helmet that I must have heard dozens of times before in that rain-sodden, God-forsaken place, but I had never registered the fact. I listened to it and at the same time recalled a quotation I'd heard sometime somewhere about rain falling with equal impartiality upon the just and the unjust. Or was it the sun shining. I don't know which. God's rain. I smiled. This place is testimony enough that there's no God, I said to myself.

'A squad of emaciated prisoners, accompanied by a guard, were marching towards me. As they drew level they chanted the compulsory greeting to me as one man and the guard saluted. Some of the men were sweating so profusely that water was evaporating from their light clothing. They passed at the double, spades shouldered, "One, two, one two!", all of them wearing the expression that one had become used to in Auschwitz, an expression of earnestness and circumspection. Every day could be their last. They knew it.

A ROGUE LIKE ME

Theoretically, I thought at this moment they could set about the one guard and kill him with ease. So many spades against one arrogant individual with a rifle. Why didn't they? There were forty thousand of them against some two thousand of us at the time; a planned, well-timed rebellion would have in all probability succeeded. All of us knew, however, that we had nothing to fear from a concerted action against us. Each man cared too much for his own life, and there were too many traitors and informers in their ranks. The truth was that our ignobility did not produce nobility in them. Most of them were contemptible sheep, I thought to myself as I watched them pass. It occurred to me then that it was this conviction on my part that had made ill-treatment and murder so easy for me in Auschwitz and elsewhere. I had even found pleasure in it. One meets the same phenomenon in slaughterhouses; the meekness and compliance of the animals provokes a desire to maltreat them. I walked along between the rows of barracks in the rain seeking shelter. Sheep. It struck me then like a blow on the head that we, the persecutors, were sheep. We too, like sheep, capitulated unthinkingly to our lowest instincts. We blindly carried out instructions for a vicious regime. And were we not fearful, too, of the consequences? Demotion? A posting to the Eastern Front which would also certainly mean death or captivity? Yes, we were sheep as well.

'It had begun to rain rather hard and as I went along I felt a strong urge to use the toilet, A moment later I reached a building where I knew I would find what I wanted. I sat in that toilet for a long time. Something happened to me in these few moments. It seems an odd thing to say, but I was not quite the same person I was when I left that place, I felt strangely detached from everything as though I were watching life as well as my own thoughts. Like an observer. It was very strange. Finally, I pulled the chain in that stinking cubicle and emerged from the building to find that the rain had set in for the rest of the day. I splashed and crashed along the muddy path between the rows of blockhouses, the mud of Auschwitz. I had not gone far when the rain suddenly turned into stormy, gusty sheets, making further progress impossible, so I dodged into a group of outbuildings where at that time coal was stored. At the entrance I discovered two prisoners under the shelter of its porch. They stood stiffly to attention on seeing me. I joined them, ignoring their deference. They were terrified by my presence. The rain continued to pound on the path outside as I removed my helmet and dried my neck with my handkerchief. The rain threw up the mud like short, black fireworks into the air. My two companions were silent next to me. After a time, I turned to them, smiled and offered them both a cigarette. At first they hesitated respectfully. "Here," I said to them, urging them to take one. They were Poles and couldn't speak German, but after a second or two more they each took a cigarette and one smiled in acknowledgement. I lit the cigarettes for them and then my own. On looking up from my cigarette I acknowledged their grateful nodding. They said something which I presumed meant "Thank you"; we all turned to consider the rain at our feet. For the first time in my life I felt myself to be a human being. I mean that I felt pity for these two prisoners. Both were shivering from the sudden cold that the rain had brought with it. I muttered something, a noise of fellow feeling, and astonished myself again. They nodded vigorously in compliance with my sentiments. "Shit rain," I said.

'After the rain had abated a little, I struck off in the direction of my headquarters, and the next day reported sick.'

'What did you complain of?' I asked, slightly amused.

'Bad back. The cause is difficult to diagnose.' Paslowitz smiled weakly at his own initiative. 'The SS doctor told me I should keep warm and go to bed. Lumbago. He gave me something for someone to rub into my back and to keep up appearances, and I actually availed myself of the opportunity.'

'You were then in the predicament as to what to do?'

'I was. I couldn't conduct my duties with that same bestiality to which prisoners and comrades alike were accustomed. It would have roused great suspicion to suddenly appear as a tamed animal in that place. I had to get out. I feigned sickness for another week and asked for leave. At first this was refused, after which I made it clear that I was really "ill". Finally, my illness convinced the doctors and I was given a week's leave. In the four hours before my leave pass was issued I began to think hard in the sick bay and made plans to desert. I escaped on the way back to Germany and finally, by devious ways, arrived in Czechoslovakia, where I had a contact, an old comrade in arms who, I felt, would not betray me. He didn't do so and a few months later I fled to Belgium where I felt that I'd be safe in the house of a former school friend, who I knew, would certainly help me. It was a very risky thing to do since that country was, like Czechoslovakia, still occupied by German forces, but the plan succeeded.'

'What you have told me is all very strange, like a religious conversion or something like that,' I said.

'Yes, I know. After the incident at the store I never harmed another soul.'

'What do you put this reversal down to?'

Paslowitz thought for a moment.

'I can only explain it from my own point of view and it sounds a bit absurd – I woke up to what I was doing. I was suddenly aware of the fact that I was reacting to everything; reacting, reacting, reacting. Like everyone else, I rarely considered what I was doing. I just reacted and regarded it as conscious action. In fact I was no more than the sheep I spoke of a few minutes ago, an animal, so to speak, completely at the mercy of its emotions and instincts or, if you like, fast asleep.'

'Not everyone else is prone to murder as you were,' I remarked.

'No, true, but that fact doesn't exonerate them from being sunk in the mud of their desires and emotions, blown about as they are by these things like leaves in the wind. Inasmuch as they are like this, they resemble animals. All of a sudden on that day in Auschwitz, my mind stopped working. For a second or two – perhaps for a few minutes, I can't say – I realised that I was, so to speak, completely immersed in what I today call my "mechanical" mind. The shock I received in the shed brought me out of it like a gunshot at a party. All the babble stops and folks suddenly become aware again of their circumstances and of themselves. For me the state of mind persisted. I've never looked back. It's like having pulled out the extension of a telescope. Once pulled out, things are in focus and that's that.'

'Has this experience made you a religious person at all, do you think?'

'Not in the traditional sense, no. One has only to look into the history of the church to discover the same states of mind I suffered from and worse.'

'Worse?'

'Certainly. There you'll find persecution of the Jews again, for example, public burnings by the hundred, pogroms, the torture and execution of so-called witches, the persecution of non-believers, crusades, religious wars, ecclesiastical torture and imprisonment, the suppression of thought and free speech, fanatical hero worship, rabble rousing, execution, the exploitation of human beings, lying, corruption, propaganda, pride, arrogance and hate. Everything the Nazis perpetrated was done by the church in another age and it is all the worse because this crime and folly was in the interests of a man who, by all accounts, was a person who never harmed anyone except a few trying to sell their wares in the temple.'

'Christ you mean?'

'Yes.'

'Do you believe in a life after death?'

'I am not sure about this, but I don't believe in hellfire and brimstone and all that.'

'But there might be a kind of payment to be made for all our senseless deeds after death, a kind of compensation, an atonement,' I ventured.

'Perhaps. We'll see,' he said.

Helmut Paslowitz died on the 6th of January 1967. He was cremated three days later and his ashes strewn on the fields outside his home as he had requested a few weeks before.

7

Gypsy Boy

In the early summer, say by the end of April, the gypsies would arrive and park their gaily coloured horse-drawn wagons on Hallam's Meadow, where there was space enough for thirty or so high-wheeled caravans surrounded by a number of very old chestnut trees that offered them shade. I never saw them actually arrive, but suddenly on the way to school I would see the smoke of their fires rising against the sky above Mrs Cunningham's thatched cottage and I knew they were there again.

Local folk merely tolerated the gypsies. They were suspected of being dirty and dishonest. You didn't trust them either, and all that fortune-telling stuff and dancing under the moon to violins and guitars at night keeping good folk from their sleep, well... The men were sallow skinned, black haired, slim and lively, and the women were dark eyed and canny as well as good talkers. They wore long, brightly coloured dresses and came a-knocking on our doors in the daytime to sell us tins and cheap braid, wooden clothes pegs, material in many brilliant colours and sometimes fans lacquered in black and gold. As a child, I liked their bright, dark eyes that noticed everything and the free way they used to laugh, showing their ruby tongues and gold teeth.

'Tell yer fortune, now, ma'am,' one of them might say at the door, and my mother would raise an admonishing hand at such nonsense and make a face.

'No, no,' the other would remonstrate, 'she's good, that she is,' looking at her sister, and before my mother could say another word, the first would issue her prophecy: 'You'll have another bairn, that's for sure and he'll be clever and do you great credit, missus, and your old man'll live to a great age.'

'Now be off with you, girl, I want none of your lip. Come away now,' and Mum would shut the door on the giggling faces, a little piqued by their forwardness, but not before she had bought some useless braid from them and two glass balls to 'decorate the Christmas tree'. The truth is, I think, that mother was a little afraid of them.

In August the next year, after their visit, Arthur, my younger brother, was born; he in fact later went to university and studied engineering at a time when ordinary folk like us rarely had opportunity to do such a thing. And as for Dad, he lived until he was ninety-six years of age and was as perky as a sparrow until his last hour. Strange, isn't it?

But as I say, apart from these door-to-door encounters, the people in the village had little to do with the 'travelling folk'. They had their world and we had ours.

'Was a time, lad, when them gypsies were really worth their salt, when it come to 'arvesting. They'd give an 'elping 'and like billy-ho and they were good too...' Dear Grandad, a jolly man he was, with a large red face and eyes that were always smiling. Never a cross word passed his lips, and for him life was a feast from minute to minute and hour to hour. 'Good tinkers they was 'n all, mend anything, even them new-fangled tractors they 'as on farms now and they could handle the 'osses 'n all. They knew a thing or two about 'osses that these 'ere stable blokes never knew, I can tell yer. Them weren't bad folks, them Romanies, so long as you treated 'em right, see. Ah, but youm 'ad to be careful, though, by golly, youm weren't done, cos they'd be mightily sly and then yohd lose yer 'osses and never get wind of 'em again!

Ha-ha!' His broad West Country accent echoes in my mind down the years.

Although the Romanies led their own lives they were nevertheless required by law to send their children to school, and from time to time a gypsy child sat with us in class. This term the boy was called Sean Brady, and folks marvelled that the word was pronounced 'Shawn' and not 'Seen'. The lad in question wore his dark hair long and we all wore ours very short. Long hair was girlish and you were in danger of being thought a sissy. This boy was tall for his age, already muscular, as we could see at sports lessons, and quick on his feet. He seemed to enjoy the ball games we played at school and was happiest then, but in class he was a dunce and there were times, too, when he smelled badly so that classmates kept aloof from him.

'I don't think he knows he stinks,' said Jeff Robson to me one day as we watched Brady sitting alone in one corner of the playground.

'He don't care either,' said Billy Turner, a sturdy young fellow from a higher form. We watched Brady playing 'snobs' with five or six stones he had picked up at the garden edge of the playground. 'Let's go and see what he's got to say for himself,' Billy said. 'At least the wind's blowin' the right way.'

We boys strolled over to the squatting figure on the dusty asphalt and stood above him saying nothing, like the bad men we saw in cowboy films. But Sean didn't look up. He just continued to toss the stones an inch or two above his hand and catch as many as he could of those falling onto the back of his hand. We watched for a moment or two saying nothing. Then Ted Simons, who was also with us, broke the spell by kicking Brady's arm just as the pebbles fell. They spilled onto the ground and the gypsy boy looked up steadily into Ted Simon's eyes. He didn't say anything, but we could see that he was as tensed as a cat about to spring. Neither Billy nor Ted were particularly in the mood for a fight, so instead Ted said, 'You play football, Pooh?' This was the nickname we'd given him because of the stench that accompanied him most days. 'Pooh' nodded, still in the squatting position, still eyeing us all steadily, not hurt by our reference but just looking, assessing, ready.

'OK,' said Ted, 'see how good you are tonight. Our goalie's got chicken pox, so you could stand in. We'll play on Alder's Field along Church Lane – you know it?'

'I've seen you play there,' said Brady, still in the squatting position.

'OK then, after tea. See you there.' And we moved off slowly. Brady continued to play with the stones until the bell sounded. Would he come? But before the game of football after tea there was another half day of school.

Our school represented more a penitentiary than a place of learning. The afternoon began with Mr Mountjoy trying to teach us the principles of art. This was a man with not the slightest idea of how to keep a class in order and in whose material was stolen, paint amply spilled and rude words scrawled on the paper he'd given us upon which we were to depict something relating to 'gardens', the theme for this lesson. It was a two-hour lesson during which most of us did what we liked and where some of the school mafia laid plots for further disruption of school discipline. These chose protagonists for the daily playground fight, a kind of children's gladiatorial show to which teachers on duty turned a blind eye unless, as happened on some occasions, it threatened to turn into a wholesale fracas involving the entire school. Then and only then would whistles be blown and other male members of staff enlisted to stop the uproar. Every new member of the school had to go through this playground ordeal as a matter of course, so that a hierarchy of the strongest could be established. Sometimes, if a new candidate was successful against his initial opponent, he would be pitted against others until he was either exhausted or simply beaten into the ground.

And if, as sometimes happened in the case of a tough newcomer, the power of the bosses was seriously threatened, then all the gang set upon him. And that was that. This happened in the case of Brady who, since his ignominious defeat, had kept himself to himself. Mountjoy's lessons were also used for brisk dealing in marbles, shrapnel, photos of film stars, knives, badges, belts, war loot – which fetched a very good price – curious stones, all sorts of junk and knick-knacks, as well as cigarettes and lighters on occasion, the possession of which was a serious offence. A lot of this stuff, of course, was confiscated during school hours and ended up in teachers' desks under lock and key. Mountjoy never confiscated anything. He seemed only half with it as far as the nefarious activities of the school were concerned. 'Put that stuff away!' he would order upon the discovery of loot being exchanged on the back row of the class, and the older boys would look sheepish and obey. But there the matter ended.

The next lesson was Dickson and religious education. You didn't muck about in Dickson's lessons. He had a fearsome presence and a heavy hand. We sat stiffly erect with folded arms. No one dared stir. You listened or you dreamed in this position. It was better to listen.

'And God is love,' Dickson intoned, swinging round sharply at the end of the aisle of benches to find Samuel Barker smiling to himself. The teacher turned on him abruptly. 'What are you smirking at, Barker?' I looked at Dickson and saw a man near retirement. He had very short, grey, stubbly hair and an uncommonly brown complexion. His eyes were unusually dark, too, almost black, and his habit of leering into our faces revealed broken, yellow teeth. It was then that he was at his ugliest and most dangerous.

'Dunno, sir.'

'Dunno, sir,' Dickson echoed, looking up at the ceiling like an imbecile. The class laughed at his mimicry for a second or two until Dickson slammed his ruler on the nearest desk, the sound of a rifle shot. The class was immediately silenced. Not a movement. 'Have you got wind, then, Barker?'

'No, sir.'

'Then why – I ask again – why are you smirking?' Barker refused to answer this question and was visibly unnerved.

'I asked you a question, Barker, to which I expect an answer. Do you understand, Barker?' (this said menacingly). You could hear the proverbial pin drop.

'BARKER!' The teacher almost screamed the name.

'Yessir!'

'God – is – love!' And with each word, the Bible Dickson held in his hand emphasised the point on Barker's head. The blows were well directed and were testimony to years of practice. Barker's head went back and forth, three times, like a small punch ball. Then Dickson dropped back into his natural teaching voice again as though nothing had happened. Barker's eyes ran with tears, but he didn't utter a sound. You don't cry in this place.

None of the teachers suspected for a moment that we thoroughly knew their real nature. Every boy in the school knew his man. Mountjoy's lenient humanity, Dickson's embittered disillusionment with life and his hatred for the school, Wheatman's fairness and justice and his competence, so that none took advantage of him, 'Nodge' Grayson's moodiness caused by the stomach ulcer inside him which turned the man from time to time into a dangerous, unpredictable creature whose erratic swipes around the ears and chops with an edge-on ruler really hurt. It did not do to provoke him. Then there was 'Joe' Palmer, who was sly, nice to your face, but gave you bad marks and ignored you completely in church on Sundays, and Taffy Roberts, the Welshman, who was in league with us and whom we did not respect for a moment – we knew them all and none of us liked Dickson and everyone of us was afraid of him.

The afternoon bell went and he kept us in for a few

minutes, our arms folded, sitting up straight in utter silence. A cough or the slightest fidget would cost a further five minutes. That we knew from experience. We sat and waited while Dickson padded the classroom floor, roughly pushing an elbow here or prodding a back there. 'Sit up! Shoulders back!' Then, at last, it was time to go and we rushed and pushed, scrambled and punched our way to the exit and out into the playground and thence to the street. Dickson watched us grimly from the classroom window. 'Savages,' he thought as he watched.

Sean Brady turned up on time that evening for the match and proved a good goalkeeper. We laughed ourselves silly as boys will when one of us made a mistake like sending the ball into Old Man Elsemore's cabbage patch or something of the sort. Sean was as much amused as we were and this endeared him to us. And what's more, a week later, he hadn't squeaked when he got a dose of the cane from Mr Leonard, the headmaster, for someone else's misdemeanour. From that time on he became a real friend. We all admired him for that. So, despite an olfactory disturbance from time to time, he became a member of the gang, since it was only possible to survive at school if you were part of an outfit. Going it alone was really tough.

But as far as the teachers were concerned, Sean Brady did go it alone. Every day he ran the gauntlet of teachers' spite and ill-treatment. We knew they were treating him unjustly. Because he was no good at his subjects, he was submissive to all they gave him. I can remember to this day how they let him stand still under the eye of a prefect on the school playground for hours. Nobody was to speak to him when the afternoon break came. That was Leonard's doing. Really mean. When Sean came to the last lesson that day, his nose was running and he was shivering. Roy Mitchell offered help with a handkerchief

– a kind lad, Roy, but he was clouted for what the teacher called 'aiding and abetting' a 'ne'er-do-well' and a 'filthy one at that'. 'Ugh! Let him stew in his own juice!' And that was Mrs Pickard speaking, a very quick-witted, fiery woman with red hair, a stickler for the detail which maketh perfection and who made it quite clear from the very beginning that she was not going to take any chelp or cheekiness from any of us at any time. We understood. At five past four after school a group of us sympathised with Sean.

'Tomorrow's Friday, kid,' said Buddy Donavan, the school's top cricketer and a fair-minded, friendly boy. 'Just one more day and then there's the weekend, thank God.' He used to speak like an adult. Despite his brilliant performance at school, he remained one of us.

'I'll do your homework,' I told Sean. I liked geography and the task would be easy. Sean smiled in his patient way. He nodded to Donavan, who moved off towards home.

'I'll be in Church Lane at six or just after,' I told Sean.

The latter nodded, smiled his gentle smile again and said, 'OK, see you then,' and left us to join his own folk.

'You'll eat everything up before you go out to play. Everything.' Mother knew I hated rabbit. The carcass was still on the serving plate. It made me feel sick to look at it. I'd left it at dinner time and, as threatened then, it had turned up again this evening. Eating it was an ordeal and on this occasion a true sacrifice for my friend, because I was eager to keep my promise to Sean. I ate it and tried to think hard of other, nicer things as I did so.

'Have you done your homework?'

'I'm doing it with Jim Holton. Got my stuff with me,' I said and Mum seemed satisfied with this. After I'd finished the awful meal I shoved the plate away from me, dodged out the back door and leapt off across the green towards

Church Lane and Hallam's Meadow. It was already ten past six. Sean was there waiting in front of the field gate when I arrived. He was pleased to see me.

'Why didn't you come over?' he asked. He meant into the field where the wagons were stationed. I hesitated. 'Tim, we're not going to cut your head off or boil you down for sausage. Your mum'll miss you!' he said, laughing. You see, these were some of the silly rumours that floated around the village about Romanies. I smiled. Sean's brown eyes were, well, loving, you could say. He had very white teeth, I noticed for the first time. Then we walked on together into Hallam's Meadow where the caravans were parked in a rough circle. Dark-complexioned men watched me as I passed and some of the women in their gay dresses smiled, flashed their teeth and said things in a language I didn't understand. As we walked through the encampment someone called over from the steps of a nearby caravan and Sean turned to address a tall woman with very red lips and dark, smiling eyes. She said something in a playful way and Sean smiled. I hoped it wasn't a plot. For a second or two fear accompanied uncertainty.

'That's my mother,' Sean said simply, 'she's visiting a neighbour. She says we can go and eat ourselves silly on the biscuits she's just made.'

Seeing me smile at this, the woman on the steps laughed. I felt relieved as we climbed the steps of another caravan a few yards off and went through the open door and into the tiny room where Sean soon discovered the biscuits. We devoured them at once. They were delicious, ten times better than rabbit, I reflected. And then I looked around. Everything was colourful and everywhere, despite the lack of space, there were souvenirs and coloured postcards and bric-à-brac. There were shiny pots and pans made of copper and bundles of cloth, a pot of fresh flowers, a shotgun and a knapsack, two bunk beds, a rush mat on the floor, jars of jam and honey ranged in every place. Sean caught me eyeing the gun.

'That's only for the rabbits you love,' he said, looking at me with a broad smile on his brown face, 'not for people.'

I couldn't help laughing at this. He said it with such solemnity in spite of the smile and I'd already told him of my ghastly evening meal. Then he offered me another biscuit. The tin was rapidly being emptied and so I thought it polite now to refuse another; I had already eaten six. Sean didn't insist, but instead put the tin back on the small cupboard where he had found them.

'Which is your bed?' I asked suddenly, indicating the two bunks.

'The top one,' Sean replied simply.

'But where does your dad sleep?' I asked, suddenly overcome with curiosity.

'With the men,' Sean said immediately, probably anticipating my second question.

'Oh,' I said, not knowing what to make of this idea.

'No room for three,' Sean explained.

I nodded. 'That's a great stick you've got there,' I remarked, noticing it for the first time in one corner. Sean took up the stick and gave it to me.

'I carved it yesterday; it's nice, isn't it?' He ran his finger over the green bark into which he had etched various designs. I admired it, tested its weight in my hand.

'A great stick,' I said.

'You can have it if you like,' Sean said, 'I can easily make another one.'

'Oh, no, I couldn't,' I replied, 'that's not right, it's yours.'

'No,' the gypsy answered, 'take it, it's yours to keep. I can show you how to make another one if you like.'

'Oh yes,' I said, very pleased at this, 'thanks.'

Sean stood up. 'Come,' he said. 'Have you got a knife?'

'No,' I said.

'Doesn't matter. I've got two. Both are very sharp and that's what you need for a good job. Come on, let's go.'

So the two of us went into a nearby wood, selected two stout, straight branches, broke them off and carried them back with us to the wagon. When we got there, Sean's mother was busy inside. She greeted us with a smile, and although I was only twelve years of age at the time, I remember thinking how beautiful she was. Her face was loving and kind and, I thought, noble, too. I reckoned that she was the most beautiful woman I had ever seen.

'You're enjoying yourselves, I see,' she said flashing her fine teeth, Sean's teeth.

'Oh yes, Mrs Brady, thank you, yes,' I said and she smiled at us both, at the same time communicating something to her son which he silently reciprocated and which I understood to be pleasure at my visit. Sean and I sat on the steps of the caravan and he showed me how to carve patterns into the bark of the stick. It began to get dark. Suddenly, I remembered.

'The homework! I forgot to show you the homework!' I cried. A cloud passed briefly over Sean's handsome face.

'It'll be OK,' he said without much conviction. 'No, I've got to show you, otherwise you'll be in trouble and it'll be my fault. Oh heck!'

Sean's mother had heard me. 'But your mum will be wondering where you are, Tim, it's half-past nine.'

'Aw, heck!' I grumbled. 'Gotta go home. But I'll do it for you. I'll fake the handwriting.' Sean's mother was silent at this and looked at me in a way no one had looked at me before.

Sean said, 'OK, you do it in return for the stick, all right? And I'll copy it up tomorrow in the break.'

'Great idea!' I said, leaping to my feet. 'Great!'

'We'll finish the other stick tomorrow,' he added. And so it was agreed. 'You can beat off highwaymen on your way home with the one I gave you,' Sean suggested.

'Thanks ever so much for the biscuits, Mrs Brady,' I said, remembering my manners. The two of them smiled at me.

A ROGUE LIKE ME

'Bye.'

'Goodbye, see you tomorrow,' Mrs Brady said. I skipped off home happily. When I got home, my mother cuffed my ears for being late. Luckily, Dad wasn't home yet.

'And don't forget to brush your teeth before you get into bed!' my mother called upstairs. I fell happily into bed. What a wonderful day it had been.

'Am I to understand that this is your own work?' The geography master, Armstrong, like Dickson the day before, put his face very close to Sean Brady's. Armstrong, although not a sadist like Leonard, the headmaster, was a difficult man to please and a pedant where the truth was concerned. In a way, this was quite laudable, had these principles not been case-hardened by an egotistical desire for self-confirmation. Armstrong delighted in the logical triumph of the syllogism. As was his custom, he was now in the act of using unerring, infallible logic prior to delivering the incontestable conclusion to be immediately followed by a *coup de grace*. On the way towards this death blow, the victim was only allowed the privilege of saying 'Yes' or 'No' and thus was guided to his own inevitable, carefully contrived downfall. Anything in between these coordinates was evinced as delaying the moment of ultimate truth, mere cheese-paring as an idle excuse to avoid pain, or, in the worst instance, as plain lying, a grievous matter with Armstrong, dedicated as he was to demonstrating truth.

'Yessir,' Brady lied.

'I see. So, if it is your own work, you will certainly know that Ireland is at the present time divided into two political camps and you, Brady, with your Irish name, will certainly be aware of that?' Silence followed. 'Eh, Brady?'

'No, sir.'

'No sir? But it appears on page 21 of your book, *World*

Geography, the book whose indicated pages you are assumed to have read for homework, Brady.'

'Yessir.'

'Yes, sir. On page 21, sir, where, quite clearly, it tells us – give me the book, Johnson (he received the book from a pupil) – yes, here it is ... where it tells us that Belfast is the capital of Northern Ireland and ... and what is the capital of Southern Ireland, Brady?'

'Don't know, sir.'

'But Brady, you mention it in your homework. I cannot believe that you could have forgotten it so soon. Can that be so, Brady?'

'No, sir.'

'Then what is it, the capital, I mean?' Silence followed. The class was as still as death.

Armstrong then turned to the class. 'Does anyone know?' There was a shower of hands. David Martin, son of a lawyer in the next town, clean as a new pin, black, greased hair, beloved of all teachers, smart and smiling, had his hand up first.

'You, Martin.'

'Dublin, sir.'

'Of course, Dublin.' The teacher returned to his prey, the tone changing to mock courtesy and helpfulness. 'Dublin, Brady.' At this stage, perhaps for a second or two, the inexperienced boy could have hoped for mercy, swallowed the seductive sweet of conciliation, but those who knew Armstrong also knew only too well that the sword was drawn and poised. 'So you were lying, Brady?' Armstrong said, changing his tone again to one of harsh challenge. Brady said nothing. 'Brady!' Nothing. Irritated by Sean's silence, Armstrong inquired again to justify the blow that was immediately to follow. 'Are you lying to me, Brady?'

'Yes, sir.' Armstrong delivered several blows to Sean's head and to the warding hand with the chalk eraser, a thing of felt and wood, no less injurious than Dickson's ruler. An undignified scuffle ensued. Brady was injured during it. At that very moment the headmaster entered the room, immediately assessed the situation as we shot to our feet and inquired, 'Having trouble, Mr Armstrong?'

Armstrong, a little out of breath and a trifle embarrassed, replied, 'Yes, sir. One here, Brady. Caught lying.'

'A liar, eh?' Headmaster Leonard was interested. He seized Sean by the hair and drew the boy violently towards him. 'Name?' he inquired fiercely.

'Brady, sir.'

'So, Brady, you're a liar, eh?' Leonard was in his element. He would delight in every detail and entertain the crowd at the same time. Turning to them, he said, 'Sit down, sit down.' The class sat, stiff with fear. Turning to Brady once more, he said, 'You, too, may take a seat, Mr Armstrong. I'll deal with this liar for you. Tell me, Mr Armstrong, what is his crime? Behind the lie is a crime. All boys are liars. What are the particulars? Has he been feeding in school, or has he stolen something, eh?' He regarded Brady with a razor-like smile, still holding him by the ear.

'No, Headmaster, he's cheated on his homework and maintains it is his own.'

'Oho, a liar and a cheat by Jove!' Some boys began to tremble in the class and one was incontinent as Leonard swung his fish-like eyes around the class. The pat-pat of the cane on his trouser leg was the only noise in the universe. Pat-pat. Pat-pat, the only noise to be heard in the corridors of the school. He turned his attention once more to Sean. 'And who did you cheat from, you miserable liar, eh (furiously shaking the boy's head by its ear)? Who?'

'Oh-oh!' Brady cried out in sudden pain. That was unlike him.

'I'll "oh-oh" you, you heap of muck. You stink like a stable, boy.' At this, someone in the class laughed inadvertently. Leonard swung round like a tiger. 'Who was that?' the headmaster inquired, a pistol shot in the direction of the sniggerer. 'Me, sir,' said a weak voice from within the class.

'Outside! I'll give you something to laugh about in a moment or two,' the headmaster snapped. The boy disappeared obediently into the corridor. Still holding Brady by the ear, the headmaster returned to his theme. Things were heating up. 'Who is your accomplice, you smelly rat, *who*?' Brady remained silent. For this he received several blows to his back with Leonard's fist, an attack known throughout the school as being extremely painful. Sean fell to his knees, but was brought up again to the standing position a second later by a tug of his hair. We could see Sean grit his teeth. Without warning, Leonard slapped Sean twice in the face, the hand resounding so that in a moment the brown skin reddened.

'We're waiting, liar.'

Unable to put up with it any longer, I stood up and heard myself say, 'It was me, sir. It was I who helped with the homework.' And then I added, 'He's had some difficulty, sir.' The class guffawed at this and was put to silence again by a smart thwack of the cane on the desk. Utter silence followed.

'You, Wakefield, I'm surprised you have truck with this kind of public nuisance.' He looked at Sean. And then said, 'Wait outside, Wakefield, with that other nitwit. I'll deal with you both later.'

I dared to add at this moment, 'I thought I could help, that's all, sir.'

'Don't you bandy words with me, you shrimp! Stand outside my office, this instant!' I went. I waited a long time in the corridor. Finally, the beak came and administered a sound thrashing to both of us. Birtwhistle, the boy who had stood with me in the corridor, got four whacks with the cane in the old man's office and came out weeping loudly. The prefect ushered him out onto the playground to stay there for a further hour. I received six on my backside and the task of a book to read by the following day, and on which I was to answer questions fully. I was to know everything about it or I'd receive a further thrashing. 'And keep away from gypsy trash,' Leonard warned, calling after me as I made my painful way to the corridor outside his office.

On the way home from school, where I had been kept overtime for half an hour to help move some tables for the caretaker, I was suddenly intercepted near the railway level crossing by Roy Tyler, one of our gang. He looked concerned and it was clear at once that he'd been waiting for me. 'You OK, Tim?' were his first words.

'I'm all right, thanks, Roy, and thanks for waiting, but what about Sean?'

'Gone 'ome.'

'Yes, but what happened after I'd been sent out?'

There was a gleam of resentment in Roy's face before he answered my question. 'They took his pants down and caned his naked arse in front of the class. Even Armstrong was embarrassed.'

'How many?'

'Seven or eight, it was horrible. They gave up finally, because Sean struggled so much or I don't know what. But he never uttered a squeal. The old bastard wanted to hear him squeal. Sean was then ordered outside, but he made off without reporting. He'll be in for it again on Monday.'

'Poor bugger. It's a lousy shit school. But there's no Monday, brother, we've got five days holiday. It's Whit.'

'Oh yeah. I'd forgot.'

We trudged home for the last few hundred yards in silence.

'See you, Tim,' Roy said resignedly and threw open the gate to his house which was en route to mine. He gave me another look. Roy hated injustice.

'See you, Roy.' I moved on up the road to tea and an angry mother.

'Where've you been? It's five o'clock.'

Well, in those days you didn't tell your folks that you had a dose of the stick at school for misbehaving, because if you did, your old man would give you another good hiding for upsetting the teachers. They knew that at school. Imagine! So I said, 'I had to make myself useful helping Mr Cartwright the caretaker move some tables and chairs after school.' It was the truth, after all.

'A likely story,' my mother said.

'But it's true, Mum!'

'Well, I'll tell your dad when he comes home, you can be sure of that. Eat your tea. The toast is cold and the egg is hard, but that's your business.' She left for the kitchen. I couldn't have cared less about the egg or the toast. I was so damned glad it was Friday night and that I could be left in peace for a while. I kept thinking of Sean and the whole horrible affair of the afternoon. It made me feel slightly sick. I had to get into touch with Sean soon. When my mum returned to take the plates away, she said, 'Your dad left word for you to clean the shed out. Give you something useful to do instead of playing ball with those hooligans down the road.'

'But Mum...!'

'Do as you're told. When Dad comes back at nine he'll expect the job done.'

'It'll be dark at nine, Mum,' I protested. 'Anyway, the shed's clean.' But she had gone, this specialist in the Parthian shot. As I said, you did as you were told. But I was furious nevertheless. I went outside and attacked the shed like a maniac; I didn't look up for an hour. I brushed and swilled like an able seaman, cleaned and polished, tidied and ordered the shed until it looked like a chemist's shop. Even my mother noticed my industry while I was at work and asked during my efforts whether I'd like a cup of tea. I refused, thinking to consolidate my moral position by a refusal. Around eight thirty the shed was spotless. I reported to my overseer in the kitchen, who went with me to the shed for an inspection.

'Yes, that's very nice. Your dad will be pleased. Do you want a cup of tea now?'

'No, Mum, thanks. I want time off.' I said this like a trade union spokesman.

She looked at me queerly for a second and then she said, 'All right, back here at ten sharp or there'll be one hell of a row.'

I didn't wait for another word, but was off down Church Lane as fast as my legs could carry me and on to Hallam's Meadow. The gypsy folk were beginning to sing. Men were tuning their guitars, laughing and playing the fool with one another. I went through their midst. Arriving at the caravan, I leapt up the steps and knocked on the half-open door. Mrs Brady peered behind it.

'Hello, Mrs Brady,' I said breathlessly, 'is Sean here?'

The beautiful woman could see the urgency of my errand in my manner. 'What's wrong, Tim? Is there a fire or what?'

'No, Mrs Brady, I've only got till ten, then I have to go home.' All of which was true, but my primary concern was to see how Sean was faring.

Mrs Brady looked at me for a full five seconds, and then she said, 'I think he's gone off fishing, Tim. Try down by the river.'

I fled to the river bank and there indeed was my schoolmate. But he wasn't fishing. His bin and tackle were on the bank beside him while he sat naked in the shallows.

'Hey, what's up?'

Sean smiled his charmer's smile. My eyes continued to question him.

'Sore backside,' he said and then stood, turned and showed me the mean strips of red across his bottom and the small of his back.

'That bastard!' My soul was full of revenge and hatred for Leonard. 'Rotten swine!' I said in anger.

'The cool water helps,' Sean said simply. I was beyond words. Sean turned again into the shallows and half immersed himself in the cool river water. After a moment or two he said, 'Tim, you could help me. Do you know what a dock leaf looks like?'

'Of course, you clot.'

'Then get a heap of them. They're a mighty help against wounds.' I went off at once and sought out as many dock leaves as I could in the gathering twilight and returned, placing them on the bank in front of my friend.

'Here,' I said, 'do you think they really help?' Sean dragged himself from the water and shivered a bit in the cool of the evening.

'Why don't you tell your mum about the bastard, Sean? We're all sick of him. Get the police down,' I said quietly.

Sean placed the soothing docks on his reddened buttocks and seemed as if he wasn't going to answer my question for a moment. Finally, he said, 'If I tell my mum, she'll tell Dad and there'll be a murder. I don't want Dad to get into trouble. I want to keep him, do you see what I mean?' I saw what he meant. I said nothing for some time, kept handing him the leaves as the dusk gathered. 'This helps,' Sean said at last.

'Sean, I gotta go home.'

'OK, Tim. Come tomorrow, we'll spend the day together.'

'Good. OK. But I got to go now.'

I was already on the move when Sean called out to me once more. 'Thanks for owning up. You're a good guy.'

I stood still, overcome with emotion for a second or two, and then ran like a hare across the fields, home and to bed.

Dad and Mum were so pleased with the garden shed that they left me alone on Saturday to do more or less what I liked. Holiday, whoopee! I raced up to the gypsy encampment and there found my friend in good spirits, although still suffering from his injuries.

'It wasn't easy to hide things from my mother,' he said. 'She has a sixth sense for such things. But the dock leaves helped a lot anyway.' I was glad. And by getting whacked myself, I knew that I had gained his confidence. We were in fact two sufferers. And so on that note we set off over the fields that Saturday morning with a pack of sandwiches to see what we could find.

For me, it was another great day. We fished, Sean showing me how to catch fish with and without a line and how to make a hook from a thorn. He found the tracks of animals where I could see nothing but grass or soil and he told me what to look for. He showed me a herbal antidote to nettle stings which worked immediately to my astonishment, for I was stung all over my legs, and together we discovered an owl's nest high up in a tree. We could see the mother still on the nest.

'Wait till she's gone,' Sean said, 'the old girl could attack.' We waited for quite a long time and then, put off by our presence, the owl swooped off through the wood. We climbed up into the tree where, sure enough, we found the nest with two eggs in it.

'One for you and one for me,' I cried. 'I haven't got an owl's egg in my collection yet.'

Sean looked at me from a branch opposite and smiled his easy-going smile. 'Then she ain't got no family,' he said.

I looked at him and understood something that had never been pointed out to me before. So I nodded in comprehension and we made our way down again. But what an experience! Once at the bottom, Sean gazed over the cornfield at the edge of the wood.

'What's up?' I asked.

'There's a plover over there, if I'm not mistaken,' he said, scanning the movement of birds over the field. He strained his eyes keenly and then added, 'Ah yes. She don't want us to know where the nest is, see? Look, wheeling over there.' I looked, but could see little until he took my head and turned it into the right direction. 'Now plovers lay quite a lot of eggs. You got a plover's egg yet?'

'No, I haven't,' I said.

'OK. Then let's see where the nest is.' It seemed quite a hopeless task in that monotonous terrain, but I followed obediently. After a moment or two he said, 'There! There it is!' Sean ran unerringly to the nest.

'Seven eggs. Gosh!' I said as we got there, 'that's great.' Kneeling down, I put my hand on the warm eggs.

'Take one quick, otherwise she'll desert,' Sean said. I seized one of the eggs and we made off back to where we had started at the edge of the cornfield.

'What you gonna do with it?' Sean inquired.

'Blow it and put it on a string with all the others,' I replied. He smiled.

At midday we stopped to eat our sandwiches near a village situated along the river whose course we'd pursued for an hour or so. Sean had found some rope and after we'd devoured our sandwiches he showed me how to tie knots that were useful for a number of purposes. He was a patient teacher and urged me again and again to tie the knot until I knew how to tie it even on a short length and with my eyes closed. He was pleased that I got the idea so quickly.

I said suddenly, 'School's daft.'

He said, 'Why so?'

I said, 'Because it comes down on you for being a dunce. You're no dunce. It's the school that's stupid.'

Sean lifted his eyebrows but said nothing to this. After the meal we fooled about and had a friendly wrestle in which I noticed how strong my adversary was. I didn't stand a chance against his strength as I might have done against others of my age. Then we swam in the river and talked about this and that afterwards on the bank until we were dry and the sun began to sink towards Gloucester Cathedral in the west.

'You mean you've never sat on a horse?' Sean asked incredulously.

'No,' I said, 'never.'

'Then I'll teach you to ride,' Sean said. 'Tomorrow we'll begin lessons.' So we romped homewards and the next day I did learn to ride under Sean's guidance or, to be honest, in the next few days, but by the Friday following we could gallop together through the fields. By that time I had met Sean's father and his aunties and uncles, and spent many an hour round the Romany campfire, where I got to know a number of conjuring tricks at which everybody laughed heartily, especially at my lack of guile in such things. But I learned quickly and was able to make the company laugh in a different way and clap in appreciation of my later efforts. Because I was Sean's friend they readily accepted me among them. While I was there I learned two songs of theirs in the Romany language. I placed my hands on a guitar for the first time, a serious moment with Sean's uncle guiding my fingers over the strings. I managed to make fire without the use of matches. I helped clean the horses and learned a lot about their nature while doing so. Romany food was delicious, and eating it in the open air was more fun than I had ever imagined it to be. I even learned the first principles of how to cook, Sean's mother's brown hands guiding mine in the matter like those of his uncle. One night I got permission from Mum and Dad to stay up until midnight and listen to my friends singing and watch their dancing. Mother and Dad were apprehensive about this and my father took the precaution of picking me up at the gate of Hallam's Meadow just after midnight. The guitar, the singing, the whirling dances, the cross-rhythms numbed my mind, putting my soul into a strange ecstasy. What I saw and heard and learned in that week I retained in my mind for the next forty or fifty years. And, I must add, I have rarely been so happy since.

The holiday week passed. Friday the following week, Leonard, the headmaster, had taken over the last lesson of the afternoon as Mr Hutchinson, a man we all liked, was away that day. Instead of history which Hutchinson always made so interesting, we were obliged to do mathematics at the end of the day. A prize imposition! It was half-past three in the afternoon; I remember because I had sneaked a glance at Roy's new watch which he proudly displayed on every occasion. In half an hour we'd be free. It was an unwritten law at school that no one stepped out of line in the last few minutes of school. This was because all of us wanted to get away from the place as soon as possible. I began to dream as Leonard droned on about square roots.

'Wakefield!'

'Yes, sir!'

'Apparently not so awake as your name might imply,' said Leonard slyly. 'Or could it be that the "field" part of your name is more appropriate; I refer to lazing about in fields with gypsies and other riff-raff. Eh?' The class laughed heartily at this.

'Now, "Sleepfield", tell us what the square root of 121 is.' In that moment, the coarse, thick nose, the yellowish, liverish skin and the mean, dark blue eyes were alight in anticipation of ensnaring another victim. The cane plopp-plopped against the trouser leg with a trifle more animation than usual. But I had found square roots of interest the night before and knew the answer.

'Eleven, sir,' I replied briskly.

'Ah, so our "Sleepfield" really is a "Wakefield".' The class tittered at this as before. Like a shot, Leonard thrust his second question to me, 'And 81?'

'Nine, sir.'

'And 144?'

'Twelve, sir.' I knew that the class would be relieved at this. They laughed at the play on names to humour him, not because they thought it was funny. I didn't care about his puns anyway. Like them, I wanted to get away as soon as possible. Get it over with. Then, just as Leonard, pacified, turned to put the information he had received on the board, and we all thought we were on the home straight, a ruler crashed to the floor with devastating, ear-splitting, world-splitting effect. A disaster. The class was electrified. Leonard swung round in the direction of the noise. 'Who was that?' he asked, glaring with terrifying import into the class.

'Me, sir. I'm sorry.' It was Brady. You never said you were sorry in Leonard's class. Sean didn't know this since he hadn't been long enough at the school. To say you were sorry was to make matters worse with this brute.

'So you're sorry, are you, you smelly little guttersnipe.' Leonard moved quickly towards Brady, who just sat there unmoved, looking at the headmaster squarely, as was his way. He never attempted to parry the blows he received, taking them on the face like a man, without wincing. We all admired him for this. The heavy hand descended again. Twice. Three times. Sean continued to sit there looking at Leonard and for a moment you could tell from Leonard's manner, yes, just for a fraction of a second, that he was put off by the boy's courage. I think all of us loved Sean at that moment. There was not a tear in his eye nor a change in his manner. It was as though Leonard had smacked a tailor's dummy. Leonard raised his arm for another assault.

'Just a minute, Mr Leonard,' said Sean, raising his hand in admonishment. 'Why all this fuss about a dropped ruler? I didn't drop it on purpose and I've said sorry.' Sean's voice was firm.

Leonard's resentful, hate-laden eyes bulged with amazement

at this ingenuous enquiry. He paused before striking to say, 'You impudent, dirty little snake, come here to me!' Sean rose from his place in his own time without hurry or discomposure and stood in front of the headmaster.

'I am not a snake, Mr Leonard, if you please,' he said.

'Take your trousers off!' Leonard roared.

'No!' The word rang out to join all the other brave words uttered in history in the face of tyrants and torturers by those who have defied injustice in this world. Leonard then made to seize the boy, but as he did so, Sean produced a flick knife and stood tensed like a steel spring before the teacher. We had never seen such a defensive position in our lives before. 'No more of that nonsense, Mr Leonard. Keep your hands to yourself or you may get hurt.' Leonard let out a scream of rage and lay on with his cane, but after the third or fourth stroke, Sean caught the cane in mid-descent, quickly took a pace backwards and broke the stick over his knee, knife still in hand. At this, Leonard went mad and dived at Sean like a rugby player, and as he did so, he fell over a chair which had been placed in front of the desks earlier that day. He fell. As he crashed the floor he snagged himself on the very sharp knife which Sean still held in his hand. Leonard just screamed like a mad thing. At the sight of blood the class rose to its feet in tumult. All hell was let loose. Seconds later, another member of staff, on hearing the uproar, appeared in the class. The school bell rang out through the school. It was four o'clock. Then the caretaker appeared, alarm in his eyes. Other classes and teachers crowded into the corridor and into the class to witness what was going on. Their noise was hushed at seeing their headmaster on the floor, bleeding and unable to move. First aid was rendered. Blood dripped. The headmaster had become inarticulate. Blood and saliva formed on his lips and he was quite unable to explain what had happened. Then one of the boys said, 'It was Sean Brady.' And everyone looked round for the culprit, but he had gone.

Finally, the police were called. A constable arrived. Little by little, boys dribbled home. I made my way home by a devious route. When I got near Roman Way, I changed course and made for Green's Farm, which lay west of the gypsy encampment, not far from which was an ancient tree where Sean and I would often meet and sometimes climb into its deep shade to talk among the branches. It was quite a detour to get there and meant brooking a stream and crossing two fields, but I didn't want to be molested by schoolmates or teachers, much less by policemen. My intention was to reach Sean and give him my support. I kept thinking of the amazing, detached way he had broken Leonard's cane, the hated symbol of his authority, and how quickly both the cane and his authority had been smashed.

I hurried on through a small, sombre spinney where birds trilled and twittered, past the mounds where, thousands of years ago, our ancestors had buried their dead, and on towards the broad, silver band of Calcott's stream, over the cool water, slipping too often on the smooth round stones into a foot or so of water, up the bank and over the two fields. The late afternoon had brought its peculiar stillness and lengthened shadows to the pastures. I waited a moment to gather breath. At last I came to our tree.

'Sean!' I whispered up into the thick foliage. 'Sean! Are you there?' But there was no answer. I decided to wait a while. Surely he would turn up sooner or later. I waited. I gazed out to the shadow of the tree over the fields in the direction of the encampment, hoping to detect Sean's familiar form. A donkey hee-hawed from the farm nearby. Nobody came. It must be about five now, I told myself, and I was a bit on edge since this Friday evening the whole family was to leave by train for Birmingham to see Auntie Mabel and Uncle Harry. There would be an awful shindy at home when I arrived, I knew that. Dad would have left work early in the afternoon and would certainly box my ears or worse for being late, especially today, but there would be too much fuss with packing and I don't know what for them to devote much time to me, I calculated, so that they would probably leave me alone after a short skirmish. Where was Sean? It seemed hopeless to wait here and so, finally, I decided to go up to the back of the encampment and see what was what. Perhaps I would find Sean in Hallam's Meadow.

When I got to the hedge I discovered a man in a black coat and a kind of waistcoat with a watch chain hanging from it on which were gold coins. It was this man who discovered me creeping up towards the hedge and he asked me straight away what I was doing. I told him I was Sean's friend and he said then that he remembered me. In a moment he had recalled my face and smiled broadly.

'Why don't you come in?' he said. I felt ashamed, like a surprised burglar, although I had no reason to harbour such feelings.

'I can't come in by the gate because...'

The man grinned again. 'Why not?' he asked squarely.

'Well ... well, something's happened.'

The man's alert, dark eyes clouded very slightly. 'What's happened, sonny?'

'Oh, it's difficult to say in a word. I must go. Please, please tell Sean I came.' Then the man looked at me sharply and I ran away from his dark scrutiny, home to trouble and raised voices.

At six fifteen that same day I was smart and catlicked, sitting in a railway compartment with Mum, Dad and Jessica, my sister, on the way to our relatives in Birmingham. All the way there I kept thinking of Sean and the events of the afternoon. My parents dozed, innocent of what had happened at school that day and ignorant of my concerns. Jessy knitted like one obsessed. If they only knew, I thought.

Time passed pleasantly enough at Auntie Mabel's place. Uncle and Auntie lived in one of the suburbs of Birmingham and there was a boy I liked to play with there called Andrew. I told him the whole story of what had happened the day before and he was agog.

'What'll happen to him?' he asked, meaning Sean.

'Dunno. Police inquiry. Anyway, Sean was provoked. Leonard the rotten blighter had it coming to him sooner or later,' I said.

Andrew paused in our basketball game. 'Our bloke's all right,' he said. 'Never lays a hand on any of us. Nice guy. Got a sense of humour and knows what he's doing.'

When we arrived home again on Sunday afternoon, my Mum said, 'Hey, where do you think you're going?' as I tried to slip out at the earliest opportunity after tea.

'I'm off to...'

'Oh no, you're not. I've had enough of your French leave. You're going to church this evening, and before you do you can help dry the dishes.' Hell's bells! Damn the stupid dishes! I thought to myself. The dishes were washed and dried. Church followed. Some of my schoolmates were there in church squinting and peeking at me between psalms and sermon.

I didn't wait to chat with them after the service. I literally fled down the lane of great beeches that shaded the way to Hallam's Meadow. On, on, without stopping, my heart thudding in my chest. Church Lane. The field in sight. Through the gate, the meadow... The gay, high wagons had gone. Nothing remained but a few pools of water and the patches of ash where the fires had once been. Farmer Green had let his cows into the field again. I turned, shattered, and walked back towards the wooden gate, my heartbeat still thumping now in my throat. The stillness of the evening gradually sobered my excitement. Disconsolately, I trudged home to find my friend Roy at the gate of our house. He had told my parents everything.

'Fine company you keep,' my mother said reproachfully. 'Petty criminals. You stay away from those bandits in future or there'll be trouble.' Roy looked at me. Neither of us said anything. Mother continued, 'Can't understand why you don't find yourself a decent friend with so many of them around. Look at Roy here, for example, but no, you have to choose yourself a potential murderer.'

I felt that this deserved a retort and so I said, 'Well, if he's a potential murderer, so is Roy here, eh Roy?'

Mother glared, Roy smiled. I knew and he knew what the smile meant, but Mum took it the adult way.

'You see, Roy's not a fool like you. Come in now. It's nearly nine. Good night, Roy.'

'Good night, Mrs Wakefield. Bye, Tim.'

Walter Leonard, headmaster of Wainwright Council School, didn't turn up again for the rest of the summer term. The Sean Brady incident cast a long, deep shadow over school activities. Dickson and Armstrong and others reined their tempers in a most extraordinary way. Teaching improved. I wrote to Sean to tell him this, but after a week or so my letter was returned. It was, after all, a shot in the dark, I suppose. The village postmistress, a gentle woman with very thick glasses and a bun, handed me my letter back, it was full of stamps with 'Try Trucklington', 'Not found here', and, finally, 'Return to sender'. She was apologetic. 'But they've got the word "LETTERS" on the doors of their wagons and a slit for them,' I said hopelessly.

'Yes, Tim, I know,' she said kindly. 'But I think it's more of a decoration than anything else, don't you?' I had to agree and despondently left the cool post office and went out into the hot afternoon sunlight, still holding the letter.

Time passed. The eddies of Sean Brady's defending himself that July afternoon in 1943 continued to reverberate in the minds of the boys at that school right into the winter term. The knowledge that Britain was fighting for its existence against the forces of darkness and tyranny had sunk even into our youthful minds. One morning, Ivan Skinner – of all people – set up what he called a 'Distribution Counter' in one corner of the playground and even the prefects closed an eye to what was going on. Skinner had produced a key that unlocked the teacher's desk in every classroom.

'Me dad tol' me abaht it,' he said in his Cockney accent. 'Me dad knows all abaht keys,' he added. And it was true, because a long time later the village learned that his dad was a spare-time burglar. But that's neither here nor there. The point is that with this key the dauntless Skinner had opened every desk and retrieved (with the help of a list made out for him by dozens of schoolboys) all the confiscated (in the parlance of our school, 'stolen') goods piled up in staff desks over the years. He distributed all this simply and honestly every day from a leather bag according to the description each boy gave of his 'lost property'. There was little or no protest from teachers and, after all, Skinner had conscientiously seen to it that each desk was relocked after retrieval. So the teachers were left with the problem of how these items could possibly have vanished and some, I believe, were even glad of the space that the purloined goods now made available to them.

As for us, we were overjoyed to see our playthings again, the medals and cartridges, the many combs and fountain pens, the collectors' coins, the pipes and cigarette lighters, the speedometers taken from crashed airplanes or scrapped army lorries, the knives and toy soldiers, toy planes and artillery, even gloves and caps whose loss in those days was paid for with boxed ears and frozen fingers. We saw it this way: they had their desks free of unnecessary ballast and we had our property back. Thus honour had been satisfied, it was a good English compromise, but none of the young Englishmen of those days in that school will ever forget their rebel leader, an Englishman of another kind who, by his courage, had given them all a new self-respect.

8

The House at Starost

In summer, if you were to pass this way on foot towards the hamlet lying under huge blue skies flecked with stray cloud and wander past the watchful forest and the joyful, shimmering silver birches which line the roads in these parts, you would come at last to see the village in the distance and to the house of which I speak. And you would say, as others before you have said, 'How very strange to find such a fine house in such a forlorn place' or, 'Whoever could have thought of building a house like this so far away from everything?' Well, a fine place it is indeed. Or was. It stands about half a mile to the northeast of a nest of humble wooden houses and a church constructed in a rough circle round a large pond adjacent to a farm and its yard. This is the village centre, and near this pond are two massive trees that tower above it. Past it runs the untarmacked road, which, eventually, leads to Kursk. Today, over ninety years after its construction, the house looks tired as you draw near, and parts of it are sorely in need of repair. The villagers will tell you that it is haunted, and it is probably for that reason, though empty, that it was never plundered for the first twenty-five years after it was built, for superstition hereabouts is stronger than any iron bars. And yet, the architect's inspiration in his plan to build a house that was exceptional is still to be seen. It was conceived in an enlightened moment as a building unique and charming, and this not simply to contrast with the modest dwellings nearby, but as an attractive design in its own right. That design is *art nouveau* and so it represents an earlier type of building than the date, 1900, chiselled into the stone above its portal. The heavy, buff-coloured, pitted granite concedes to the ravages of time only reluctantly, and it occurs to me as I stand before it that a fortune must have been needed to bring it here. Embossed along this long façade are six classical heads with features of a serious mien, and on each side of the main door are two torches each laced with a sculptured chain cunningly worked into the surface. The door itself is of heavy oak or some such hard wood, once light brown, but darkened over the years.

Four wide windows, now deprived of their glass, face northwest and the woodwork of these has received the worst of the weather. The first storey imitates the ground-floor design and above these in the roof there are mansard windows, one on each side that enhance its good proportions. The rear of this mansion basks in the day's sunshine and to its western side there are stables and outbuildings, which have been taken over – or, to quote the district authorities, 're-possessed' – by the villagers and used today for various purposes quite alien to the builder's intentions. However, this fact has contributed at least to a path being regularly cleared of bush and other vegetation to facilitate access from the front gate to the stable yard.

The residence once sported a largish orangery to the south from which, remarkably, every splinter of glass has completely disappeared. What is left is an intact framework open to the sky, which gives one the impression that it is waiting any day now for the glazier to come and fit it with panes and so finish the job.

The house also has a spacious veranda at the back with a waist-high wall running round it on three sides and extending into the garden from the French windows. This at one time was surmounted by twelve, iron-socketed stone balls of a pinkish brown.

THE HOUSE AT STAROST

Looking back, I suppose the house once accommodated about twenty rooms, which included a sizeable foyer, a reception room, a large dining room, a kitchen, a study and a library. In the dining area, there was a long, substantial wooden table with heavy wooden chairs and dark oak panelling along the walls.

My first memory of this place goes back to a bright day in April on which it was still quite cold, heavy snow having fallen during the night, and yet, I recall, there was a hint of spring in the air despite the snow. I suppose I must have been nine or ten in those days. I had been playing with Mikhail, my friend who was a year older, when for some reason he suddenly suggested we take a look at the house standing now in the sunlight of mid-afternoon.

'But it's haunted,' I said. To this he said nothing and both of us stood looking at the building glowing brightly in the distance, which seemed somehow to welcome a visit.

'Well, we could see for ourselves – I mean, we could walk around the place, couldn't we?' Mikhail persisted.

'But we've been up there before. What makes it so especially interesting today?' I objected. Mikhail pulled a face, which meant that I was spoiling his game.

'All right, then, let's go,' I said a moment later and ran forward, knowing that he'd soon be after me. He was good on his legs even through thick snow. The going was hard, the sun intense as we struggled up the low, steady incline leading to the house. When we finally arrived at the garden fence we were puffing like two small locomotives and hardly able to speak.

'Look!' said Mikhail, 'the snow's piled up against the front like a hill!' And so it was.

During the night, the wind had blown fiercely and had succeeded in piling a large heap of snow against the lounge windows. These had given way to the weight and fury of the storm and were now wide open. We paused, astonished at this and cautiously moved forward.

'If it's open like this, maybe we can go in,' I ventured.

'Well, maybe,' Mikhail replied and we began to climb the 'hill'. Its snow was hard and compacted, since the temperature had dropped rapidly during the morning despite the sun. Both of us climbed up and laughed at being so high up and able to overlook the garden. And then we both slid down together on the other side and into the lounge. Once there, we stood on the faded carpet in silence. The snow had shut out most of the light entering the room, giving it a gloomy air. It was strange. We began to speak in whispers, too awed by the wreck of nature's intrusion and perhaps in awe of unseen presences in the dark recesses around us. We, like the uncouth wind and the careless snow, had affronted the ghosts of another world and another time. I beheld Mikhail's pale face against the sombre woodwork and he mine in the silence of that place. He turned his head very slowly in the direction of a closed door leading off the lounge and then back at me.

'Try it,' I said.

'No, you first.'

Neither of us moved.

'Perhaps there's a dead body on the other side of that door,' he suggested.

I pondered the possibility for a moment, and then a feeling of bravado seized me. 'Let's see!' I cried and, stepping forward, wrenched the door open. It squeaked in protest to reveal a hallway lit by two windows above the main door. A strange smell met our nostrils and Mikhail, looking at me, was the first to comment on it.

'Smells like soap,' he remarked.

'More like floor polish,' I said. We sniffed. It wasn't unpleasant, but something entirely unexpected. 'I know!' I said. 'It's like roasted coffee beans!'

Mikhail nodded. 'But how odd – I mean, after all these years,' he added. 'Must be something else.' We stood for a moment wondering at this and then began to inspect the place.

THE HOUSE AT STAROST

The floor was tiled with small black-and-white stones and in the middle there was the mosaic of a woman with a lute below which were words in an alphabet unknown to us. In one corner there was a grandfather clock that intrigued us both. The hands stood at a few minutes past three and on a *chaise longue* placed along one side of this hallway Mikhail discovered a child's toy. He picked it up and examined it wordlessly for a moment or two while I looked on. Then he said, 'Must be a girl's.'

'Yes,' I replied in my wisdom. 'They like that kind of thing,' and I thought of my sister. Our words left the tiniest echo in the high ceiling.

Ranged around the walls were a few pictures, one of a battle scene, another of a man in his early thirties rowing two young women on a river against a landscape that was quite unfamiliar. The other pictures were of a family of six. It seemed that the father was looking at us rather severely as one would at an intruder from his elevated position on the wall. Behind us and to one side were carpeted stairs leading to the rooms above. Mikhail plumped down on the shiny green fabric of the sofa, sending up a cloud of whitish dust into the still air.

'Why didn't they come back?' he asked suddenly.

'Dunno. Dead maybe.'

'Dead?'

'Yes, everyone's dead, who knows?'

Again, our words vibrated ever so slightly in the air, as though someone were calling to us over a great distance, over a dark lake, the words inarticulate, but the sound distinct.

'Dead,' Mikhail mused, twisting the toy he still held in his hands. I could not answer the implicit question in his repetition and instead sat down on the second step of the stairs and took off my balaclava.

'Funny, but it's warm in here.' I said.

My companion nodded. Then, looking away, he said again,

'Why didn't they come back?' There was a long pause between us. 'Where do you go when you die?' he asked, turning to me again from his place on the sofa.

I felt the need to answer his question, to say something at least, so I said, 'Dunno. To heaven or hell I suppose; you only go to hell if you've been very bad. That's what my grandad says.'

'Do you think these folks were bad?' Mikhail then asked.

'Dunno,' I said again and felt a bit foolish.

'Do you believe in heaven and hell and all that, then?' Mikhail pursued.

'For me, it's all a bit scary. Death and such. I saw my auntie Olga die. First she was my auntie and then she was like a piece of wood or a doll or something. You know what I mean? She wasn't Auntie Olga any more. Funny. I can't explain it.'

The last word bounced off the walls, almost, it seemed, in mockery of our lack of divination.

'But she must've gone somewhere,' Mikhail pursued, and the walls mindlessly returned the stress of the last word.

'Yeah,' I replied. 'Funny. Wonder if it's true – about heaven and all that, I mean?' There followed seconds of silence.

'Tell you what, Vlodya,' Mikhail said impulsively, 'let's make a pact.'

I looked at him through the soft gloom. 'A pact?' I echoed.

'Yes,' he returned. 'Let's swear now to each other that whichever of us dies first shall tell the other there's a heaven. This is a good place to make a pact.'

'You mean that the one who's dead tells the other who's still alive that he's in heaven?' I asked, perplexed.

'Yes, but we've got to have a ritual, you see. Like this!' And he picked up one of two empty glasses that had been left on a small table near the lounge door.

'We link arms. So. That's right.' Then Mikhail began to intone. 'When one of us dies, he swears now that he will tell the other that there's a heaven! By God, so be it!'

These were the words he'd heard in the wooden church

on a Sunday, the most solemn words he could muster. Ceremoniously, he flicked the glass with his fingernail. The walls faithfully confirmed the sound. Thus saying, he threw the toy on the tiles and stamped on it three times, urging me to do the same. 'Say "I swear!"' Mikhail ordered. I swore.

That was in 1925. I was about eleven years old at the time. Ten years later, it was I who helped the men from the People's Commune to force open the heavy front door of that house. With difficulty we eventually gained entry and at last four of us stood in the dim hallway where Mikhail and I had sworn our youthful oath so many years before.

'Open the shutters!' someone in our party shouted and the light of another bright, blue morning suddenly shot through the dusty curtains onto the suite of living-room furniture adjacent to the entrance. It shone on the high mantelpiece, on fine pictures hung along the walls, on the remains of a cigar in an ashtray of coloured glass, on a draped lampshade on a small table next to the fireplace. In one corner of the room stood a grand piano, and above the keyboard, open music as though it had just been used. On its top were a number of framed photographs and a vase surrounded by a perfect ring of friable dust, which had once been flowers.

Comrade Kerov surveyed the room briefly. Then he said perfunctorily, 'Get all this stuff out of here! Anyone who wants it can have it and the rest is to be loaded on the truck.' The truck, its engine running, stood waiting outside. It was minus 30°C this morning and Kerov's breath rose in clouds towards the moulded ceiling above him as he spoke. Routinely, he opened the drawers of the rosewood secretaire and rustled his hand among some papers and knick-knacks he found there. Now and again, he drew a paper out of the them, reading what was written on it, only to let it fall back into the drawer with a gesture of contemptuous indifference.

An imperious wave of his broad hand indicated to his aide that the crowd at the door could now come in and take what they wanted. To me, he said, 'Come, young feller, there might be work for you in the other rooms,' and so saying, he led the way into the next room and from there upstairs, followed by Igor Davidoff, his second-in-command.

The two soldiers who had entered the house with us had barred the way to the pushing villagers assembled at the door. My job was to open all the shutters, and so I was first to enter each room. Kerov merely stood in the doorway watching me work. Many of the shutters had been devastated by storms and some even fell to the ground below as I tried to open them. As I turned to him after this job, my glance was met with an expression of derision for what the light had revealed in the room: an unmade bed, a chamber pot, what looked like the remains of a meal, together with a bottle of wine on a side table. Then he moved his head very slightly to indicate that we should move on to the next room. Behind, Davidoff made short notes on a pad with a stubby pencil. Some of the rooms above the first storey were quite empty, including the servants' quarters, which had neither curtains nor shutters. After this, we all trooped downstairs in our wet, heavy boots and invaded the library. This was lined with a great many books of all sorts from floor to ceiling and was clearly planned as a comfortable retreat from the rest of the house. Here, light entered the room from above. Everywhere, the dust lay thick on every object.

'Ugh!' said Major Kerov, looking at his companion meaningfully. Davidoff nodded, silently acknowledging his master's unuttered sentiments on 'capitalistic scum'. Then, last of all, we entered the kitchen, which declared the same message as all the other rooms, but louder:

'We've all gone for a walk and will be back soon.'

Within half a day the house was cleared of all its moveable contents and by nightfall the rooms were quite bare. The last footsteps of the plundering villagers crashed their way out on the solid oak floorboards towards the front door, which was then slammed to and shored up. Only the books in the library were largely left in their places, and only one or two had been thrown down in contempt and left on the floor. Hardly any of us could read, and their paper and bindings were not convenient enough for kindling, so they were abandoned. Everything else had been pillaged; even the carpets had been ripped out and taken away. Those shutters which couldn't be torn from their hinges were left hanging like abandoned crucified bodies, and for the peasantry making their way home, there were no more secrets to the house, no more hauntings. The house had become public property. Kerov had said so, had he not?

Later that night, when he and his associates were abed under a frosty, starlit sky, the moon browsed for a while through the book titles embossed in silver and gold along the shelves.

Then came the war. They fetched us in an open truck, eleven of us, and took us away to fight. They gave us vodka, the officer and his driver, and the vodka warmed the innards of these young lads with their round faces and high hopes. And they sang songs on that day as they rocked and swayed, pitched and laboured through the endless Russian countryside. And glad they were when they had to stop and heave and push and pant with all their might to lift the vehicle out of some rut or other on the way. And merry they were at the prospect of fighting for their country, clawing at each other for balance as they jolted along, smoking and laughing, glad, so glad to see a bit more of the world than the confines of their own Godforsaken village whose boundaries most of them had never left in their lives.

When they had gone, the autumn wind blew across the low hills and into the valleys, howling and roaring as it had done from time immemorial, scouring the orchards of their last leaves, loosening pane and thatch, tearing at the roofs of barns, slamming the hanging stable doors, blowing up the muck of the road into a harsh veil of grit and dust in a preliminary expeditionary attack on the humble village dwellings. It rounded up the cattle in the paddock into a huddle of fear. It snapped at the fence that kept them there and stirred up the neighbouring forest to turmoil, swooping on the leaning chimney and pouring its black smoke into the yard, sniping at chained dogs before kitchen doors, nagging, scooping, spooking, scratching, whistling, by day and by night. Many a soul would be taken by the wind to the valley of darkness at this time, and now and again in all this turbulence there would be the crack of dry distant thunder above the flat, unending land, and the farmer would look up at the troubled skies and know that this was not God's thunder, but man's. Then this windy riot would suddenly cease and the skies clear for the winter to encamp in the forest nearby. Everything then would be quite still and folks would emerge from their houses and see the buzzards wheeling and purling high in the sky, calling to each other, waiting, waiting for winter. Unlike the autumn wind, the winter would first creep silently and then strike. One day there would be battalions of clouds in the sky and shortly afterwards the first snow would begin to fall. Soon, the cowering village would be covered in snow and sometimes the snow would fall for weeks until the village quite vanished under its white mantle. Those who could climbed out onto their roofs to free their chimneys of it and later clear paths to the road and to one another, to walk through roofless tunnels of head-high snow. At that time, the only house visible was that of the 'Moscow folks', as it was called. It towered above their own lodgings that were mere rounded humps in a white landscape where, here and there, a light or perhaps a curl of wood smoke were the only signs of human habitation. Each year the old house stood thus in cold isolation, a winter palace now of frost and ice where water bulged and broke the guttering and split the piping so that in spring the accumulated water from the roof flowed through the rift like blood from a wound, and on one gusty day in that season, a tile came skittering down from the roof to land hardly a foot away from one Gennadi Pollkow, the village idiot, who happened to be on the premises at the time with intent to steal, and who saw in the unexpected descent of the tile an Act of God to prevent him from realising his desire, and who, with a furious oath, seized the tile and flung it through one of the windows, where it fell with a thud on the floor, and who then took himself off back to the road.

Following this incident, and on that same spring night, Kerov, on the front two hundred miles away, fell face down in the muddy field of battle, his broad hands still clasping the gun they had given him to defend the Motherland.

Later, on a summer evening in the same year, a mother walks with her little son along the rough road to Starost. She has been collecting mushrooms.

'What house is that, Mummy?'
'An old house, dear.'
'Who lives there?'
'No one lives there now. Empty for years.'
'Have the people gone away, Mummy?'
'Yes, long ago. Come.' And the two walk on.

Birds have nested in Jelena's bedroom where Pollkow threw his tile. Above the window, five hungry mouths were fed through the early summer days, and on the day Jelena died they were ready to fly, teetering and twittering and fluttering on the window sill in the afternoon sun. Beneath the balcony of her parents' bedroom to the sunny side of the house, a young tree, now in its fifth year, thrives and struggles, incredible, incongruous, straining away from the house wall's shade towards the south.

A ROGUE LIKE ME

The mouse and the spider are in the bedrooms and the rats in the library. Little ruffles of draft have scattered their gnawings over the floor, and these have been blown under the doors and out over the mosaic of the hall where the Grecian girl with the tasselled hair forever speaks her verse and smiles her smile.

War has come to Russia and faraway Stalingrad is one hell of death and fire, and a huge pall of smoke hangs over the city. At night, the sky is sharply lit up above the horizon, and from time to time there is the thud of detonation. Flares, like gigantic fireworks, sketch the heavens in light. Aircraft scream over the quiet Starost fields of late summer. Their sound reverberates in the empty rooms of the old house. The walls tremble, its ghosts cower and cringe until silence flows back slowly into its rooms. Water seeps up the wall from the foundations and into the lounge, powdering brick to sand and loosening the colourless wallpaper that is now curling up ludicrously towards the ceiling. Then the autumn wind bangs the door upstairs at mad, irregular intervals. Bang! Bang-bang. Bang! Interminably. Insistently. It is easy to think that some maniac is there, senselessly pushing the door to and fro. Winter again. And summer. Paint peels. The worm is in the wood. Rain intrudes into the upper rooms, making puddles on the wooden floorboards, which swell and warp. Then the autumn wind again lifts other tiles and throws them into the garden. The roof sags. The flailing shutters of that season smash the remaining glass to admit the snow and sleet of spring. On frosty nights wolves wait in groups in the garden, their eyes glinting in the moonlight. Twenty million are dead and the war is over.

I sit here in a Paris café on the Quai de Louvre in the year 2000 with a companion who has just left to speak to someone he has recognised among the many old men who have time to sit and stare over the Seine. The sun shines brightly over the river and everyone is enjoying the first warmth of spring. The leaves on the ancient trees that hem the boulevard flutter in response to a passing breeze. I dream in the sunlight. At the next table a waiter taps a glass in order to catch a colleague's attention. The smell of roasted coffee beans rises to my nostrils.

9

Over Tea One Hot August Afternoon

Our master was not inclined to sit and talk. Rather, he was wont to shun conversation altogether. Later, much later, we came to realise that human talk generally didn't get one very far along the spiritual way and yet despite this, we also realised how very much he knew about each one of us and how precise that knowledge was. He was always there at moments of crisis to say exactly the right words of comfort, support or encouragement. For the rest, he went about his business, the business of bringing a handful of human beings to enlightenment without the slightest ostentation. His movements and his communication with others were quiet and economical, his attitude simple and frank. He would glide in and out of the shadows of that ancient place as though he were merely a projection of them. He also had a keen sense of humour and was ever aware of life's incongruities. A crisp reply and sometimes we burst into laughter, a reaction on our part that seemed to slightly embarrass him. When he sat with us in meditation, his stone-like figure filled the room with its vibrant presence: still, severe, inviolable and immovable. Once, the building rocked under an earthquake, the mighty rafters above us sighed and groaned and the monks in the hall ran about and shouted in panic. It was only after a few moments of this that we noticed that the master had not moved even an inch from his cushion at the top of the room. It was as if he had been poured into a mould. The earthquake passed, the torrential thunder and rain that had accompanied it ceased and life returned to normal. Or almost normal. After that episode, none of us was ever the same again. Our respect for this individual was raised to a state of awe, but he himself remained unchanged.

Thus, it was strange to find him ready to talk that afternoon. It was August in Japan and intolerably hot. I sweated in my heavy robes. Apart from the head monk, our cook, two others, and myself, there was no one else in the temple on that day and these few had been invited to join him for tea. About twenty people were expected later to attend a special meditative session at the weekend. When we had assembled in the small room reserved for the reception of visitors just off the monastery entrance, we immediately settled ourselves on the cushions provided and were handed a bowl of hot green tea.

'I want to tell you a story,' the master began. 'The first part begins when I was on a flight to the USA two years ago.' We waited while this was translated into English. 'I was to organise a largish Zen group in Los Angeles. The plane from here was to stop over in Guam. During the flight there I sat next to a woman of about sixty or thereabouts.'

There was a pause while this was translated for me. Deliberately, the master went on: 'She told me that she was suffering from terminal cancer and that she had only one wish left in life and that was to see her son's grave. This young man had died on one of the Pacific islands during fierce fighting in the last weeks before the end of the Second World War. She had been given some general information as to the cemetery's whereabouts and her present worry was whether she would ever find it.'

Now there was a longer pause following the English rendering, and during it Roshi sat there quietly, apparently impervious to the heat. We waited. High above us, we could hear sparrows quarrelling among the beams over the entrance. At that moment, our attention was focused upon their twittering when it occurred to me that just this had been going on up there for the last eight hundred years. The thought struck me as though I'd been punched.

While I was still stunned by this insight, Roshi suddenly continued, 'Frankly, there wasn't much I could say to this. What could one say that would help?' This, for him, was a very strange figure of speech, since he was always able to rise to the occasion. I listened to what followed with even more attention. 'She left the plane at Guam and I flew on. I never heard from her again. That was two or three years ago.' Pause. 'So I was particularly surprised to learn yesterday that she will pay us a visit this afternoon.' Pause. 'Actually, she'll be here any minute.' Almost as if we were witnessing a play, the sound of the small hand bell rang from outside. The head monk rose to receive the guest, and we could hear formalities exchanged at the door a few feet away. Then, bowing and smiling, a little old lady was gently ushered into the room, and was offered tea and a comfortable seat on a cushioned ledge of wood that actually formed part of the structure of the room's wooden interior.

'I followed the address on your card,' were her first words. Roshi acknowledged this with a broad smile and great courtesy. He was obviously very pleased to be able to receive her. After all, it wasn't unreasonable to have presumed her dead by this time. I think we had all assumed the same thing. But there she was, this dear old lady, sipping her tea, smiling, bowing her head in respectful deference and chuckling at Roshi's gentle humour. There was one of those pauses again and, used to silence, we drank more tea and waited patiently for things to proceed. The old woman broke the silence at last.

'I was very ill when we last saw each other,' she said, immediately returning to her cup, but looking straight at our master over its rim.

'Yes, indeed,' he concurred, saying nothing more. The pause that followed underscored the remark.

'But I completely recovered, you know,' the visitor added almost triumphantly.

'Truly remarkable,' said Roshi, 'and all of us here are very glad to hear it. What do you put it down to, do you think?' he enquired.

'I don't know,' the woman replied. After this, there was a long silence, and again we found ourselves listening to the birds above us. Then she continued, perhaps to break the silence, perhaps to expand on the matter as best she could and so help her questioner. 'I was riddled with cancer. I had about six or seven weeks to live. So the doctors, they sent me home to die. But I wanted to see my son's grave before that. Afterwards, anything could happen. I didn't care. Actually, I don't care now. Anything can happen.'

This was digested for a moment before the master continued, 'But you are all right now?'

'Yes,' she replied, 'I'm fine; absolutely fine. There's nothing wrong with me.'

'What do the doctors say?'

'They're simply baffled. No one can understand it.' She laughed. 'Anyway, they can think what they like!' She laughed so much that Osho, the head monk, was at pains to catch the hot teacup, which threatened at any moment to be projected onto the floor. To our utter surprise, Roshi, too, began to laugh. We had never seen him laugh before. Within seconds, the two of them were convulsed with laughter while we continued to sit there smiling with embarrassment. Whatever could be so amusing? At last, our master recovered himself sufficiently to say, 'And how do you feel after this incredible cure – I mean, mentally?' This was translated for me.

'I feel free,' she answered simply. She spoke quietly and soberly; her laughter had suddenly ebbed away.

'Free,' he echoed, nodding. 'Yes, I believe you,' Roshi said. Then he added, 'Let me tell you a story. At one time in the sixteenth century, the annexe to this building served as a so-called sword school. Here, young sons of samurai and others learned the techniques of survival with the sword. The country was in upheaval at the time. Practice was rigorous and utterly uncompromising. Accidents were common, and sometimes people even died from the accidental injuries they received. One evening, a visitor came to the entrance and asked if he could stay the night and was granted admission. There was generally no charge for this hospitality, but it was sometimes customary for the sword master to ask his guest to take him on for a round, and this occasion was no exception. The stranger agreed, but told the sword master he had never been taught to fight. Around fifty aspirants assembled to see the spectacle. After a brief introduction, the fight began. The guest proved himself swift and deadly, so much so that after a few minutes, the master commanded him to cease. "I thought you told me that you had no expertise in the matter!" he exclaimed. "You told me you were quite untutored, but you fight like a seasoned warrior."

' "What I told you is true," the visitor replied. "I've received no formal training."

' "Then how is it that I have my work cut out to defend myself?" the sword master asked. The guest sheathed his sword and considered for a moment, anxious to give a truthful answer to what he recognised as an earnest enquiry.

' "Well, perhaps there is one thing, and that is that I never fear for my life when I'm in combat."

' "That's it!" the master swordsman replied emphatically. "Day after day, year after year, I try by example to inculcate just this into those who seek my training, but few ever learn this first lesson. Practically to a man they're all avidly concerned to learn technique, but in so doing overlook the most important thing of all!"

'I've told you this story because its point underlies everything we do here,' Roshi continued. 'Most of the folks who come to this place are mainly concerned about "getting something", about achievement, but our essential task is not to achieve, but to let go of everything, like our friend here,' he added, nodding in the direction of the visitor. Everything is possible once you let go.'

We had entirely forgotten the heat and our former discomfort, and as for me, I'll never forget that hot afternoon.

10

Grandfather

I think I must have been about nine or ten years of age when Grandfather came to live with us. His wife, my grandmother, had died, and I remember that I had not been taken to the funeral, but had been obliged to stay with neighbours whose name I have now forgotten. Children were not told much in those days. And then, suddenly, Grandfather was there among us. He had his meals with us, but spent most of his time in another part of our large house. I remember his white hair and his white moustache and the remarkable bright blue eyes in his red face that noticed everything. Mother said he was very clean and tidy in his ways and that she was thankful for this. He walked with a stick, but his back was as straight as a mast. He said little to us children, merely noting our presence, and his communications with the rest of the family were short and to the point. Despite this, he was unfailingly courteous and grateful for everything, but formidable if crossed.

Mr Daniels came once with the groceries pressed against the green baize of his smock and said, during a brief conversation about his niece's recent visit to Germany, that at least Hitler had done something good for the Germans in building their motorways; Grandfather, hearing the remark, froze in his place at table, his eyes quite cold like blue diamonds.

'Hitler was a bounder!' he said, and Daniels, not wishing to debate the point, had left in a hurry. That was not long after the war, I imagine. His relative was a journalist working for the BBC.

You did not argue with Grandfather. It was not that he was necessarily aggressive, but with some things he was intractably dogmatic. He did not lay down the law to anyone, since he could hardly do that as our guest. Neither was he unreasonable, but we all knew instinctively that, as a retired brigadier, he had once lived in a world quite different from ours. His views and attitudes coincided with the convictions and mores of an era which no longer existed. He belonged to another age and another time, and he knew it. We knew it. The times he had seen, although he rarely spoke of them, were like palpable ghosts in the house. They were there in the way he drank his tea, in the way he spoke, in his accent, adopted by Britain's ruling classes long ago, which one seldom heard these days, in the way he greeted visitors, in the way he said 'Thank you', in the way he seated himself, and in the way he asked you questions, point blank, like a judge on a bench. They hovered around his uniform which he had brought with him from Scotland and which was now hung up for ever in a case at the top of the landing, like a regimental flag in a church together with his military cap with its red band and the tunic with its three pips and a crown on the shoulders. His swagger stick, gloves and medals were also exhibited in this window case which he had also accompanied by special carriage on the journey south to our home in Bedfordshire. The wraiths of the past swirled about his person, too. He carried his loneliness about with him, his reminiscences of which we knew nothing, the memory of comrades, campaigns, battles, victories, his aristocratic wife's relatives and friends whom we knew only vaguely because of the geographical distance, and who, as a consequence, we saw only rarely. Although he was an immediate relative, my father's father and our grandfather, he was nevertheless an alien in the house. Father had been dead three years and my mother's much

GRANDFATHER

older sister now lived with us. My brother was away at Oxford studying physics, and I and my little sister, at that time just four years old, were the other females in the house. He was nice to us all, this elderly gentleman, and never once complained about anything, but I sensed his isolation.

As I say, he used to live in another part of the house which, in the eighteenth century, had been a vicarage and was therefore quite roomy. He had a fully furnished apartment of his own on the ground floor consisting of a bedroom, a study and a large living room which he had filled with his memories. There were photographs everywhere, some of them in sepia tone and already fifty or sixty years old, people in hard hats or bearskins, all of them in uniform and armed, some standing behind cannon. Horses there were and camels, and other men in dhotis or wearing robes and little round hats, men with brown skins and inscrutable dark eyes, looking at the camera with expressions generally unfamiliar to us children, but occasionally I thought I detected fear or sometimes truculent defiance in them. Very often in the background there were white buildings and, often enough, the dome and tower of a mosque. Grandfather had spent many years in North Africa and the Middle East. On the floor of this lounge of his was a tiger-skin rug with the head preserved and so lifelike that Amy, my younger sister, had been frightened when she first saw it and had later cried because it had been killed. Grandfather was particularly proud of this trophy, having, apparently, laid it low himself, he had told us, on one of his expeditions in Bengal in the early years of his service. The tiger lived on like all the other things which surrounded his sofa – elephant tusks, a carved ebony cudgel, a splendid pair of highly polished boots with wooden shoe trees in them, another, older uniform of blue, red and white which was perhaps his father's, a large compass set in a wooden box bound in brass, a very hard, full-sized bulldog in shiny leather with a fearsome expression which stood at the hearthside, over the fireplace a long Afghan rifle, and in front of the grate a low, exquisitely carved table of reddish wood which he told me came from China, on which I would regularly place his daily afternoon tea and then retire. He would receive me on these occasions with a friendly smile and look up from the book he was reading – he was an avid reader – and thank me. Now and again on these visits, and especially in the early days of his stay, I would ask him about his treasures, whereupon he would close the book at once and gladly tell me about the history or the function of each exhibit or tell me how he came to acquire it, all of which I always found very interesting. On these occasions, he was in his element. At such times, the cloak of loneliness surrounding him fell from his shoulders. As soon as my interest was aroused, his was, too. I was then in his world. This ability to enter his world at will greatly pleased me as a child, for I was the only one who possessed it. In this way, a special relation grew up between us.

One spring afternoon, I took him his tea and scones as usual at about four thirty in the afternoon and found him folding the blanket he used to cover himself with during his regular 'forty winks' sometime in the afternoon. The refreshment was always welcome, but company not necessarily so. At this time he would often read until dinner at seven and during this time did not like to be disturbed, but today he signalled to me by his questions that he would like to engage in conversation.

'How's the homework front?' he asked me cheerfully.

'All right, thanks. Grandpa,' I replied, 'there's no great problem today. We had maths. I like algebra.'

'Do you, by Jove?' he said, a broad smile crossing his face, his blue eyes full of light and interest. 'Never could do the darned stuff myself, but admire those who can.' He said this with that tongue-in-cheek good humour which in fact was a

GRANDFATHER

characteristic of his, but unknown in the rest of the house. 'Geometry, now, I wasn't too bad at that, and anyway had to know a bit for the lads in the artillery, you know.' I didn't, but took his word for it. 'Come and sit on the couch with me and tell me how you got on at school today. Look! The spring's coming in at the window,' he added. I looked. The sun was shining in for the first time that year. It shone onto the carpet artlessly revealing how worn it was. He caught me looking at it and smiled again. 'It's seen better times, the old carpet – like me!' he said and laughed shortly, nodding his head briefly to give emphasis to his assertion. 'We've all had our day,' he added, and I wondered what he meant for a moment, child that I was. Perhaps he meant the things around him; perhaps he meant the people he'd seen and known, I thought to myself. So many people. 'The thing came from Africa, you know?' he went on, 'Taken it wherever I've travelled.'

'Africa, Grandpa?' All I knew of Africa was that it was populated by tall people who were black all over and that we once had colonies there. And lions and tigers of course. I had pictures of them in a book Uncle Cecil had given me once for my birthday. Grandfather guessed what I was thinking.

'North Africa, young lady, not central Africa.' I didn't know the difference, and without asking whether I did or not, he added, 'Where the desert is. My batman brought it to me as a gift one day in thanks for … oh, I don't know any more for what,' he concluded shortly. It was almost as if he were embarrassed by the memory. There was a moment's silence. Then he said, 'Good man, Bennett. Wonder what happened to him.' This last almost a short soliloquy. 'Yes, my dear, the northern part is desert. You've heard of the Sahara, I'm sure?' he asked, turning now to me from a moment's contemplation of the fireplace.

'Oh yes,' I said, but I didn't know more than that it was very hot and big, and to help the conversation I said, 'Camels.'

'Precisely,' Grandfather said, 'camels. Do you know that I once owned a camel?'

'No,' I replied, truly amazed.

'Oh yes, I had a camel. Used to go everywhere with it. Fine animal. Bit moody, but a good friend. Very reliable. Knew its way through our part of the desert like a bird knows its way back to the nest. Remarkable.' I listened. After a little while, he continued recollecting his thoughts and the things associated with the animal. 'Had to shoot the poor devil finally.'

'Do you mean you killed it. Grandfather?'

'Yes, my dear, I was obliged to.' Seeing that I didn't know this word, he added, 'I had to.'

'Oh,' I said, much saddened by this news. I looked up at him with a pained expression.

'Well, it's a longish story. If you like I'll tell it to you, but you must promise me that you won't tell anyone else. It's to be our secret, all right?'

I was delighted by the idea of our sharing a secret together, and readily agreed.

'Then I'll tell you,' he said with the tone of one having come to an important decision.

'In the first place I have to tell you that everything is quite true, strange though it may seem to your ears, and after such a long time. I was a major in those days and head of a platoon of men in a desert battle not far from Khartoum. That's in the Sudan.' He looked at me suddenly to see if I was properly orientated. I nodded to show him I was, but really out of eagerness for him to continue. I had not the slightest idea where the Sudan was.

'We had been surrounded by the enemy and had come off worst in that the Arab horsemen and others had attacked us in the night, set fire to our tents and harassed us in the darkness before our men could rally and locate them. The sentries had had their throats cut before they could utter a word of alarm.' I cringed. 'Well, my dear, that's how it is in war as a soldier. Anyway, after some nightmarish minutes of chaos, murder, fire, shouts and screams and the hideous warbling of these men on their steeds striking us down with their sabres, our men got themselves assembled under Sergeant Hughes and put up fierce resistance – and me among 'em.' Grandfather sipped his tea, caught up now by the memory. 'We fought on desperately until dawn. These bounders were out to destroy us completely. Well, we were not having that and gave them as good as we got, and just when we thought we'd won the day, one of them fired into a case of ammunition and the lot went up, killing about fifteen of us in one go. That worsened our situation of course, considerably.' He looked at me to see if I could imagine the situation, and seeing that I had understood, continued. 'Great thing was that none of us was ready for capitulation; we weren't going to surrender to these lawless rascals on any account. But our men were soon reduced to a pitiful handful, holding out, but knowing that their minutes were numbered, and I was one of them. Suddenly a grenade threw us all out of action.'

'Were you injured, Grandpa?'

'Yes, I was knocked out for some time, and when I came round I discovered that I couldn't use my right arm. You've noticed that I can't lift it above my head, haven't you?' I nodded. 'But the worst part of it was that, besides me, all but one of the men had been killed. He lay bleeding profusely and I knew from experience that he would not last long. I did what I could to comfort the poor chap – a musketeer, he was – but it was soon over.' Grandfather paused here to ask me whether he should go on. I nodded again and he continued. 'Well, the dreadful thing was that the tribesmen had gone round killing off the wounded when they had won the day. This is the kind of thing they do. We English and Scots don't do that kind of thing. I was only saved by the fact that I appeared to them to be dead already. Well, enough

– it was an awful business, and I continued to lie there among the dead in the sun, which was gathering strength with every hour that passed. Soon I began to wish that I had died with my men. I passed out every now and again and then came to in the appalling heat. On one of these occasions of momentary clarity, I looked into the distance and saw someone approaching on a camel. A lone tribesman, I thought, and assumed this was the end. So I prepared myself for a violent death at his hands within the next few minutes. But as he gradually approached the carnage on this beast, I discerned him to be a private soldier from another regiment. He was acting, as he told me later, as a courier and had a message for me as commander of this small platoon. I called and it didn't take him long to discover me among the appalling mess around me. He leapt from his camel and came over, greatly daunted by what he saw around him, and helped me to my feet. Together, we then surveyed the scene and checked for anyone still alive, but there was no one.

'"Ambush, sir?" he asked.

'"Yes," I said. "We were completely taken by surprise. Didn't stand a chance."

'He then gave me the message, which was to the effect that my party should decamp as soon as possible as the enemy was being assisted by wild tribesmen who were on the rampage all over the region, folks who had up to now been on friendly terms with the occupying forces. The communiqué proved to be two hours too late. The courier looked miserable.

'"It's not your fault," I said.

'"Your arm's bleeding, sir – it should be seen to. I've got medicine and bandages aboard."

'He meant aboard the camel, of course.' Grandfather winked at me. 'Anyway, the young feller went off immediately and got this stuff from his panniers and returned to bandage my arm in a very professional manner. He had water with him, bade me drink since, he said, it was necessary after being wounded, and then cleaned and bound the wound.

' "We must get you professional help," this man said.

' "Pooh," I said, "it's just a graze. What about those poor lads strewn about here?"

' "They took you for dead, like them, because some of the blood has run onto your chest," the courier said. 'And so it was. It looked as though I'd been shot though the heart. Fancy that! Now I knew why the tribesmen had not bothered to finish me off as is their custom.

' "We have to get away from here," this young man said. "The place is full of skirmishers." It was at that moment that I thought of Sammy, my camel, and looked round instinctively to find him. We found him behind a sand dune panting his last. Poor chap. He'd been shot in the back and had already suffered much. I shot him through the head and then crossed the shimmering, burning sand towards the courier and his own animal.

' "May I ask you to mount him?" this fellow asked, easily taking things into his hands. Not having anything to say against his courtesy, I mounted without a word, you know.' Grandfather looked at me again to see if I understood. This time I smiled and he took it for granted that I did.

'Well, we went on together, I on the back of the camel and he on foot. I was feeling pretty groggy by this time. Lost a lot of blood. I knew that we had a good thirty miles in front of us fraught with ever-present danger from all directions. The sun beat down on us pitilessly. The camel grumbled. I could hardly see for the haze and the strain on my eyes. I felt despondent, too, having lost my best men, and that in such a mean, demoralising manner. The courier for his part marched on fearlessly and with a determined step. I had to admire his courage and initiative, and wondered why he was still merely a private soldier.

'We had covered about ten of those thirty miles I imagine,

when it happened. There was a sharp rifle shot that hit the medicine bag. The animal started and I was knocked clean off the camel. I fell onto the wounded arm and let out a cry of pain. In the same moment I realised that what had happened some hours before was happening again. Suddenly, there was dust and the rush and commotion of horses being turned roughly in the sand. I grabbed my revolver and waited for my chance, but aiming and controlling the wretched thing was difficult with the left hand. Then, in the uproar, I felt a hand on my cap pushing me down behind the camel, which by this time was kneeling in the sand, and we were behind it as though the animal was some kind of rampart or barricade! It was about the only thing that could be done at that moment. It was a good idea. Neither of us wasted any time and either he or I laid the first of these wretches low with a single shot. And the second. In the tumult there seemed to be about five or six of them and I calculated that we'd be lucky to get out of the mêlée alive. I think we both felt this and fired at these ruffians for all we were worth. The whole rumpus must have taken about twenty minutes, but by golly, we were the victors. Imagine! The last two horsemen, seeing their comrades fall, made off as suddenly as they had come. But we were to be surprised, for not more than two minutes later they returned, firing into the air and filling it with their hooting and whooping, blood-curdling cries. My revolver had given up the ghost and I grovelled in the dust and muck for the musket which we'd taken from the previous attackers. While I was doing this, this private soldier got up and went for the one of the marauders single-handed, leaving himself open to attack, of course, from the other. He just charged at the nearest and challenged him to attack. To my astonishment, the first man fell from his horse as dead as a doornail, while the second made a mistake in the confusion as his horse fell over that of his comrade, which was already struggling to get up from the ground. My soldier went for the other, but finding him floored, out of breath and weaponless, he hesitated.

' "Kill him!" I ordered from my position behind the camel.

'The soldier had his revolver poised above his victim's head.

' "Pull the trigger, man!" I shouted. "What are you waiting for?"

But Maynard – that was the man's name – continued to merely hold the shirt of the tribesman with his strong left hand, the revolver in the other. The Arab's eyes were full of terror, knowing that his time had come, and he knelt there without struggling.

' "Shoot, man, for God's sake, shoot, you fool!" I cried, but instead of giving him the *coup de grâce*, the soldier flung him contemptuously out of the way while still training his handgun on him. In an instant, the Bedouin, or whatever he was, streaked towards his horse, and once he was in the saddle, it received a whack on its haunches from Maynard, who had ran forward to send him on his way. The two of them, horse and man, were off in a cloud of dust before you could count three. A moment later, Maynard returned.

' "Why the devil didn't you kill him off?" I roared. "He'll be back in ten minutes with a horde of others, you idiot!" I was in a rage and had quite forgotten Maynard's bravery and how he had assisted me some time before.

' "He was unarmed," Maynard said simply.

' "Unarmed my foot! Damned tribesman. You disobeyed my orders!"

' "I'm sorry, sir, I cannot kill a man in cold blood. It's against my principles." This remark only made me more furious. Who was this fellow to tell me about his principles?

' "Damn your principles!" I said, "I'll have you court-martialed for this. Disobeying an order."

' "Yes, sir," he said mildly.

'When I think back to this incident, Elizabeth, I realise he could have killed me on the spot had he wanted. He was the only one who had a weapon. He could quite easily have drawn it on me and finished me off and no one would have been any the wiser. My injury would have proved to observers stumbling on my corpse later that I had been unable to defend myself because of it. Tradition and assumption prevented me from seeing this at the time.

'Well, it turned out that there were no more attacks and we arrived safely at a little military encampment called Jabal al Seqh without more ado.' Grandfather paused and poured himself another cup of tea from the brown, homely teapot. It seemed almost that he wouldn't continue.

'What did you do then. Grandfather?' I asked after a moment or two.

Grandfather took the tea and sipped at the cup before answering. Then he looked at me very seriously. 'I court martialed him,' he said simply.

'For not obeying your order?'

'Yes.'

He watched me carefully as I turned the matter over in my mind.

'I think that was wrong of you, Grandfather,' I said at last, in wonder at my courage.

'Do you?' he said. I nodded. He looked a long time at the sun coming in brightly at the window, the half-empty cup in his hand. 'He got three years for open disobedience, was clapped in irons and sent back to England. The proceedings took place at Colchester. Remember it well. Major General Keating presided and among others, Brigadier Haig and Colonel Bambury were also there. The man pleaded his innocence, and his advocate – a man called Johnson – urged his humanity to be taken into consideration.' For the few seconds of this sentence. Grandfather was taken back forty years and one could see his manner transform to an old, familiar arrogance and authority, his face tilted firmly in a manner of assertion as he uttered the words, the phrases curt and tense. Then he was with me once more and the past had gone in the room where the April sun dappled the floor at intervals in front of us, now intense in a quick crescendo as clouds revealed the sun, only to fade again in the same way a moment or two later.

'Where would we be if in an army everybody went their own way? Eh? Chaos. There was a real chance, you see, for this Arab feller to come back with his friends and finish us off. Mincemeat then. No doubt about it.'

I shuddered inwardly and wondered why men had to fight at all. The whole business seemed absurd to me even at that age. I said nothing to his rhetorical questions and answers.

The minutes that followed were charged with self-justification while he fixed the teapot with a stare. 'Mincemeat,' he repeated, and again I said nothing.

Then, after another longish pause, he turned to me and said, 'His sentence was reduced to two years for good conduct. I went to see him when he was out of jail.' I knew quite well, even as a girl of ten, what that visit would have cost him in terms of self-discipline – nay, of humility.

'What did he say?' I asked after an interval.

'Umph. Looked thin. Haggard. Difficult to find words to say at that moment. We sat in an anteroom reserved for duty personnel. He appeared, saluted, and waited for me to signal to him to be seated. I removed my hat. It was a hot day, I remember. We sat down amid the noise of people talking loudly to each other during the shift change. I nodded to him in acknowledgement. After a moment or two he said, "How's that arm of yours, sir?"

'"Arm? Oh, the arm, ah yes, just a graze you know," I said. "These things happen." In truth, the damned arm had been a nuisance for a year. Two or three operations and it's still stiff to this day, as I've shown you.' Grandfather stretched his stiff arm in support of what he had said, smiled ruefully and after a few seconds continued with his account.

'"How was it in there?" I asked him darkly.

' "Oh, not too bad, sir. The first three months are the worst. People get used to you then and punishment is not so sharp." I remember wincing at this.

' "Look," I said, I need a good man in my office. Duty clerk. Carries a sergeant's rank. How about that?"

' "I'm sorry, sir, that'd be nothing for me. I can neither read nor write."

' "What?"

' "Yes, I'm much obliged to you for your kindness, but so it is, sir." My mind reeled in the moments that followed, because I had no immediate solution to the problem, and then he said, "I understand that the War Office won't allow promotion for the next three years, so I'd have to wait for that, sir."

'I recovered myself enough to be able to say that I wanted him in my regiment and that I would see to it that he would be billeted anonymously. Then he told me that he was married. "She's waiting for me now outside," he added.

'It's hard for me to explain to you how I felt, but I'm sure you can imagine, my dear,' Grandfather continued. Young as I was, I understood well enough. I was proud, too, at that moment that Grandfather had let me into his confidence. I nodded to show him I knew how he felt.

'Well,' he continued, 'we stepped outside and there was this young woman with a child of about four at her heels. I judged her to be about 24 or 25 years old. She was dressed for the most part in black and wore a white shawl around her shoulders.

' "I thought you were never coming," she said to Maynard directly, merely nodding to me. Maynard introduced us.

' "This is Colonel Abercrombie" he said simply. There was no deference in her manner, but no hostility either. The child hung on her hand and looked at me with large, quiet brown eyes. To tell you the truth, and for the first time in my life, I felt quite unequal to the situation. At that instant I felt the need to sit down and drink tea, and that's just what we all did, since there was a small tea room just a few yards away from the prison. We talked about nothing in particular at the tight, round table indicated by the waiter. There were worlds between us, you understand, education, wealth, social standing, rank and experience – God knows what – but after a while as we sat there and drank our hot tea, the child asked its mother a question. At first I wondered what it had said and was surprised that the child didn't speak English, but realised a moment later when the mother replied to the question that the language was Irish. She took the little girl onto her knee like mothers do all over the world as she answered its question, and then the child smiled at me. At me in my uniform. In my decorations and insignia. At me who had caused them so much harm and suffering and hardship.'

Grandfather was silent for a long time. I looked down at the carpet and I understood. It was clear that he wasn't going to say any more. The interlude was at an end. He rose and looked out of the window. The sun had disappeared, and beyond him I could see sudden snow flurrying around the gaunt apple trees, still waiting patiently for a louder call from spring. I cleared the crockery onto the tray as my mother would have done and quietly left the room.

11

Well, Fancy That!

Dr Sawyer was about 26 years old when he was called for duty one winter evening. He had done well in his final examinations, and he was doing quite well in the first two years of his practical apprenticeship. He was a conscientious, likeable young man, anxious to learn and willing to please, and perhaps it was because of this that he was frequently called upon to do the routine work that his senior colleagues were disinclined to do.

'There was a woman just on the phone, Sawyer. Says her husband died late this afternoon. She doesn't want a corpse in the house, she said, so he's been taken to Grant Street's cemetery. There's a chapel there, you know.'

Dr Sawyer didn't know, although he'd often heard of Grant Street Cemetery.

'Anyway,' his superior continued, 'you'll have to write out the death certificate. There's a wad of 'em on my desk. Man's name is Spratt. Time for me to get a bit of shuteye, I think.' And with that, Dr McCullen, 51, head of the town's hospital emergency unit, now tired after a long day, smiled formally at Sawyer and retired to his quarters, slamming the door behind him.

It was ten minutes to eleven. Outside, a rude wind blew flurries of snow defiantly at the lamps lining the ambulance yard below Dr Sawyer's window. He himself perused the street map for a moment or two, located Grant Street and went downstairs to retrieve his bicycle. Flinging his kit into the large basket on its handlebars, he navigated it through the hospital's portals and out into the street beyond. It was cold and his fingers began to freeze through his thin gloves. Added to this, the flying snow blowing into his face made it difficult for him to maintain his balance, but after a few minutes he reached Grant Street and soon came across the cemetery's half a mile of wall. Finally, out of breath and half blinded by snow that simply tipped out of the sky, he found its main entrance. Having propped up his bike as well as he could against the wall, Dr Sawyer opened the creaking iron gate to the city's graveyard. Above, a bronze angel smiled sublimely at him in the blanketing snow. The chapel was just a few steps away. Hurriedly, the doctor leaned upon the heavy wooden door of the chapel. Blackness. He fumbled for a light switch to his right, only to find it on his left after twice stumbling on the cold flagstones and cursing his luck. It was now almost midnight.

The feeble light bulb in the concrete ceiling revealed that there was a single loose white sheet on the stone slab nearest the small altar, and Dr Sawyer, after removing his overcoat and stamping the clinging snow from his shoes, drew back the sheet covering the corpse. 'They could have seen to this business long before I got here,' was his first thought. The man was quite clearly dead. His face was ashen, the body as grey as putty, the hands folded resignedly over his chest, the eyes closed. 'Still, might just as well go through the drill while I'm here' was his second.

Now, as I've said, Dr Sawyer was a diligent young man, and his third reflection mirrored his conscientiousness: 'Well, this'll decide things all right,' he thought to himself, retrieving the small but powerful torch from his medical case and lifting the man's right eyelid to peer into his eye. Spratt's pupil contracted immediately in response to the torch's penetrating ray and Sawyer jumped back in surprise. Something had to be done.

WELL, FANCY THAT!

'My God!' he announced in dismay. 'The man's alive!' Thereupon Dr Sawyer, although unable to detect the slightest sign of a pulse or heartbeat, decided nevertheless to apply another test to be one hundred per cent sure. Using the blunt end of his scalpel, he made a firm cutting motion along the sole of one foot. There was a slight reflexive jerk. 'That settles it,' Sawyer said to himself. His folks had merely assumed that he was dead. Albert Spratt was still alive.

Somewhat shaken by his experience, our doctor placed another sheet on the silent figure, leaving the head free, and hurried out of the chapel to find a telephone kiosk. At the door he was met by a blinding sweep of snow, so deep that it was impossible to use his cycle. He had no alternative but to trudge on foot in search of the nearest telephone. After battling for quite some time, he found a kiosk and dialled an emergency number.

'Yes?' a voice enquired almost belligerently.

'Dr Sawyer here. Send an ambulance and a doctor to Grant Street Cemetery immediately! It's urgent. I'll be waiting at the gate.' So saying, he stormed out of the booth and awkwardly retraced his steps to the cemetery gate and its adjacent chapel, where he was greeted once more by the angel's exalted smile.

It took the ambulance twenty freezing minutes to arrive and skid to a stop, by which time Sawyer was chilled to the bone, so that he could hardly articulate his experience through quivering lips to his colleague. This man and two orderlies were quick to rescue Spratt from his slab and rapidly transfer him into the comparative warmth of the ambulance, there to apply resuscitation, while Dr Sawyer, seeing that there was no more for him to do, turned at the door of the chapel to discover that his cycle had been buried under another fall of snow to become a mere lump in the cemetery wall. 'Damn!' he breathed, took up his bag, and walked the mile back to the hospital.

As if the details of Spratt's resurrection were not enough for a narration, there is nevertheless more to this anecdote.

Two days after this event, Dr Sawyer was moved to enquire at the intensive unit as to what had become of his 'discovery' and was informed to his astonishment that the patient was no longer there, but had been removed to a general ward where he was 'making good progress'. Sawyer decided there and then to visit the patient, not only to make his own conclusions, but also to satisfy his curiosity. Taking an hour off during his lunch break, he made his way to Ward 304 and found Mr Albert Spratt sitting on the edge of his bed noisily sucking potato soup.

'This is the doctor who saved your life,' said the nurse who had accompanied Sawyer to the patient. Spratt for his part continued to suck his soup without looking up, with the result that the sister pinched his sleeve and repeated herself. This time, Spratt looked up briefly and murmured something incomprehensible into his napkin. The sound could be described as not very enthusiastic, and the two of them, doctor and nurse, were clearly embarrassed by such a welcome. Dr Sawyer offered his hand to shake, but the gesture was ignored, so he said cheerfully, 'I'm glad that you're alive.'

'Ugh, and why not?' Spratt mumbled uncharitably.

'Otherwise you'd have been buried alive!' the sister sternly reminded him.

'That ain't true,' Spratt replied. Doctor and nurse waited while he returned to blubber in his soup and then, as they looked at him with question marks on their faces, said, 'Ah would a bin incinerated, that's what, 'cos ah paid forrit all these years.' At this, both were quite speechless.

A second or two passed and Sawyer made to turn, closely followed by Mary, the nurse, who, as they made their way to the exit, took the opportunity to apologise on Spratt's behalf.

'Well!' she said indignantly when they were out of earshot. 'There's gratitude for you!'

'Oh, don't worry, Sister, he probably hasn't got the business out of his system yet,' Dr Sawyer replied with a smile, and with that he thanked her and returned to his work on the first floor.

The fact was that Spratt didn't want his life saved, as he made clear to the nurse after being upbraided by her later for his incivility.

'Ughh,' he mumbled in response to her reasonable censure. 'Shit life! Ughh.'

'Mr Spratt! You should jolly well be grateful. This doctor put himself out to save your life. You had the luck of the devil and but for his scrupulousness you wouldn't be here!'

'Don' wanna be 'ere,' Spratt promptly replied, articulate for once, and, looking round the ward in contempt, he sneered like a cowed dog at his fellow patients who were listening intently to this exchange.

Since Albert Spratt was considerably emaciated and also rather feeble, the departmental consultant considered it wiser to keep him in for a while longer until he had gained more weight and could walk without difficulty. After about ten days of care this was achieved and the patient could at last be delivered from the reverent gaze of dozens of fellow patients all over the hospital who hobbled and shuffled to his ward on sticks or were brought in wheelchairs to gaze and gawp at the man who had 'been born again', while Dr Sawyer's reputation as a 'miracle worker' soared and his experience was the talk of the town.

Shortly after Spratt's discharge, Dr Sawyer was surprised during his consultation hours by a visit from a woman in her early fifties who introduced herself as Spratt's daughter-in-law, the older Mrs Spratt, the patient's wife, having been deceased for some years. He was glad of this visit, since there were a number of formalities that had not yet been resolved during Mr Spratt's stay in hospital. Dr Sawyer retrieved these from his in tray and turned to his visitor.

'Mrs Spratt, you can assure me, then, that your father-in-law had no other ailments other than these rather alarming asthma attacks?'

'No, he didn't, but this'n was very bad. 'E just folded up like when I was there visitin' and we thought 'e was gone.'

'That's very understandable considering his condition. Really quite alarming.'

'No, but 'e weren't dead, worr 'e?'

'No.'

'And 'e aint dead now either,' she said added with a finality in whose tone Dr Sawyer detected a distinct undercurrent of regret – not for the dreadful error which had occurred, no, but, to his disquiet, a regret that the asthma attack had not done away with him once and for all. He revealed nothing of his personal reaction to this in the way medical men everywhere are wont to do, and quickly regained his composure, to continue a moment later:

'I trust he'll enjoy better health in future, since I hear that he has been prescribed a new medication that will help him at such times.'

'Ugh,' she said. Dr Sawyer noted that this was the same noise that Spratt had made on their second acquaintance in the ward.

He smiled benignly and added, 'You don't seem very pleased, Mrs Spratt.'

'I ain't pleased.' Sawyer raised his eyebrows in questioning surprise. ''E's still got the 'ouse, aint 'e?' she asked, as though it were a challenge that needed confirmation, as if Sawyer were privy to the details of Spratt's estate. 'Could live to be a 'undred, 'e could,' she added wretchedly.

WELL, FANCY THAT!

'I see,' Dr Sawyer said, aware that he was approaching the dangerous rocks of personal privacy, and without further comment he folded a copy of the administrative paper concerning Albert Spratt's stay in hospital, put it into a long envelope, and handed it to his visitor.

Mrs Spratt then rose, and without a further word or gesture, left his office, leaving the door open behind her.

Two months later, this woman died suddenly one Sunday morning in the same kitchen where Spratt the elder had earlier collapsed. Alois, her younger brother by two years, also died at the age of 49 six months later, but much happier, swathed as he was on that occasion in a somnolent alcoholic haze.

Dr Sawyer of course knew nothing of all this, but since the incident in the city's morgue he had been thought of as a man of exceptional medical acumen, and, as I say, while this was for the most part based on popular misconstruing of the circumstances at the time, his presence of mind and the practical conscientiousness demonstrated on that notable occasion nevertheless won him acknowledgement in his profession. And so it was that he rose through the ranks to one day become a successful specialist in his own right, enjoying unique authority and widespread acclaim.

He had married a very attractive woman in the meantime, had sired two children, lived in a distinguished residential area in the town and practised the arts of medicine with diligence and satisfaction. In addition to this, and like many before him, he had naturally acquired a small coterie of aspirants, young medical men who emulated their professor and who were bent on following a similar career.

One Monday in June, this professor was enjoying a coffee in his book-filled office when there was a gentle knock at the door. It was his senior staff nurse who, along with his indispensable secretary, saved him so much administrative work.

'It's a routine matter, Doctor, but I haven't the authority to deal with it,' she announced at the half-open door.

'Oh,' Sawyer replied, 'what then?'

'Mr Spratt in Ward 2, the old man who was brought in yesterday, seems to have passed away, sir,' she said modestly, 'but we need confirmation. Do you think you could come down and check?'

Professor Sawyer never forgot names, and he was highly unlikely to forget this one, but he paused before answering, then asked, affecting faint amnesia, 'Er ... Spratt? Well, I think Robinson ought to see to that. The young feller needs some experience.'

The door closed quietly behind her.

12

The Last Dance

So in the summer of that year, and to be precise, on Friday, 20th June 1919, Mrs Rose Amery set off for her sister's house some twenty miles away. The mile walk to the station would do her good, she said to herself as she took one more look at the little kitchen to see if everything was in order. Yes, the window was closed and Mrs James would see that the cat was fed outside today and tomorrow. Poor Polly, she would miss the cushioned box in the hall, but it would only be for a day and a night. Then she took down the postcard her sister had sent her and popped it into the large basket she held in her hand, together with the pickles, the potted meat and the blackcurrant jam she had bottled last year. The key once turned in the lock of the front door, it too joined the rest of the things in the basket under its clean, white cloth. In the small garden at the front of the house, the daffodils had given way to the tulips and they in their turn to salvias, and now the many roses in that garden lining the path which led to the gate were in full bloom. She glanced back once again at the house which had been caught for a moment by the eastern sun and paused just for a second or two to admire its thatch and beam, its small, prettily curtained leaded windows, the ivy and clematis which hugged the walls. It looked so settled and so comfortably integrated into the rest of the countryside, she thought as she closed the trellised wooden gate behind her. There was a light breeze this morning which pulled at her wide-brimmed hat and the wisps of hair which were visible beneath it. It impudently tossed one corner of her shawl into her face from time to time and threatened to send the immaculate tea cloth covering the basket over the hedge to join the ruminating cows in the field beyond. 'Silly wind,' she said to herself, brushing the hair out of her face every now and then as she went along. 'Perhaps it will rain later,' she mused. But there was no sign of rain at all. The day was all blue and gold.

'Good morning, Mrs Terry!' she announced brightly as she approached a neighbour who had appeared to take in the milk from the doorstep.

'Good morning, my dear,' Mrs Terry replied. 'You're up and off early today.' The sun sharply illumined the wrinkled face.

'Off to Dorothy's today. Back tomorrow,' Mrs Amery said with her usual good cheer.

'Well, give her my kindest, dear,' the older woman said,' and we'll see you again on Saturday or Sunday, then.'

'Yes, I expect so,' said Mrs Amery with a smile, then waved and hurried on. Passing the forge on her right, she recalled her childhood, as she always did when she saw this building. She remembered Gereth Tyler, the smith of those days, could still see in her mind's eye the sweat on his strong, bare arms and shoulders as he held the horse's hoof between his knees, could still hear the regular tap-tapping of his hammer on the anvil which made its music all day long in the village. She heard his voice again raised in anger at a horse's impatience, and at other times the quiet words of comfort he uttered during a shoeing. She could still smell the strange odour of burning horn as the shoe hissed and smoked onto the hoof. 'There, there now, my beauty, steady now ... steady...' Once, as a little girl, she had peeped round the corner of the forge and looked into the darkness of its interior. It had taken a few seconds for her eyes to get used to the obscurity. Then she saw his shape in the shadows at the back, his hand on the lever at shoulder level which pumped the bellows. Red ash and sparks blew in the gloom. The smith caught sight of her standing there at the entrance to the forge and they looked at each other wordlessly in the semi-darkness. That was fifty years ago, she reflected. The forge had been closed for many years now, but she knew that his tools were still there, almost, it would seem, as though they awaited his return.

She walked on down the road, passing the Masons' house, the Barnets', the Becks', the Mitchells', the Worsleys' and the Freemans'. Then, on past the miniature post office, the grocer's, the new flower shop at the corner, Bailey's the butcher's, Brown's, the clothes shop and then to the right and down past the Brewer's Arms, a pub of dubious reputation, and finally to the last hedged stretch of road which led directly to the station. She liked Hermitage Road. There were many fine houses in it. People who lived here had butlers and servants and the like, played tennis in their own garden courts during the summer or sat in tea houses. She had once been in one of them, but that was many years ago, too, when her mother was still alive.

The station was empty when she arrived. It was hard to imagine that a great roaring monster belching steam and soot would soon enter it and take her up to Canterbury, from there racing on up to London with all those interesting people who had disembarked from the Dover packet the night before. Now she was in the wide foyer of the station with its oak-boarded floor. The sound of her shoes clacked from the walls and the high roof.

'You're early this morning, Rose, by golly,' remarked Mr Smalling, whose face now appeared at the ticket window. He wore spectacles at the end of his nose which made it easy to see both tickets and passengers.

'Yes, Robert, I'm off to see Dorothy today,' she replied,

fumbling in her purse for the sixpence which would take her there and back in a second-class carriage. She placed the coin on the scalloped wooden dish which had changed its shape over the years and become deeper through much contact with metal. Automatically, Robert took the sixpence and issued the ticket.

'Be a lot o' folks today in Canterbury, girl; there's some sort of celebration there I think,' he said.

She liked him. They had been at the same school, had both sat through Mr Bray's lessons, had grown up together, had married at similar times and had grown older together in the same village.

'There's always something going on up there,' she said laconically, snapping her purse to and letting it drop into the basket. 'Now let me see, you'll be sixty in November won't you, Robert – the 26th if I'm not mistaken?'

'You're a genius, dear girl,' Robert replied, pleased to know that someone remembered his birthday. 'You're right indeed, we're all getting on a bit now,' he added cheerily. 'You won't be so far behind either, I imagine.'

'Year after next,' she said simply. He smiled. The large clock on the wall of his office ticked with quiet dignity and for a moment or two there was no other sound. In these few seconds, she had lowered her head to look into the ticket office, taking in Robert's good-natured features and his slim figure in its uniform, the heavy watch and chain at his waist, and, at the periphery of her vision, the accessories of his profession which surrounded him in the room where he had spent most of his life. She smiled again and walked out onto the platform into the sunlight. Mrs Amery was quite alone as she waited for the seven thirty-five to find its way through the chalk hills and tunnels, the woods and shining fields of south-eastern England on that summer morning. An alien wind frolicked with everything it could find on the platform. She sat in the sunlight and let her thoughts wander. Since

Arthur's death, she reflected, her respect for Robert had deepened. No longer preoccupied with her husband's well-being, and the children being long since gone from the house, she had found the time these days for more reflection. The feeling of kinship with those with whom she had spent her life had intensified; they were a part of her life as she was a part of theirs. Soon, she thought, as her eyes fell upon the dazzling polished silver of the railway track, all that she and they had experienced would be at an end. They and she would be gone like the train which disappeared into the tunnel a few yards away or like the throng of unknown people whose names were set upon the tombstones in the shadows of the little village churchyard. She could see some of the names in her mind's eye as she gazed down into the well of light before her: 'Thomas Hamilton, died 1788, aged 63 years, and Elisa Hamilton, his wife, died 1812, aged 87 years; John Fearon Cranshawe, died 1776, aged 32 Years and Martha Shuttleworth, nee Barton, of Shepton parish, died 1842, and Annie Marston, aged Twelve Years... Howard Grant and Emily Grant, his sister, and James Freeman and his daughters, Ruth and Elizabeth, Peter Saxton, remembered here, who died at sea, and Penelope Hobson, wife of George Hobson, for forty-five years rector of this church together with...' The intense light from the steel suddenly hurt her eyes and her brief reverie was over. She looked up, glancing towards the black mouth of the tunnel to her right a hundred yards away, and for a moment a deep sadness arose in her.

Two hours later, Dorothy Thornton, a woman in her mid-sixties, opened the door to her sister.

'Ah, there you are, my dear, so lovely to see you!' she said, and kissed Rose on the cheek affectionately, at the same time ushering her inside the small house which stood as the last one at the end of the road. 'What a beautiful morning it is; a little windy today, but I'm sure it'll be warmer later. It's been a lovely summer so far,' she added, leading the way along the hall towards the airy conservatory on the other side of the house, a part which had been added as an extension to the dining room some years before. In it a table had already been set for a meal.

'I've got the kettle on the hob for the tea, Rose dear. I'm sure you're thirsty and we can sit down and have a bite to eat. Too late for breakfast and too early for lunch, but that doesn't matter, does it? Eat when you're hungry, I say – at least I do these days.' She laughed her laugh, which was a true musical interval yet quite unaffected, a characteristic which charmed everyone with whom she came into contact, and hurried off into the kitchen to see to the kettle, which was already beginning to whistle. Rose put down her basket on a small side table, took off her hat and her light coat and laid them over the sofa. Then she turned to admire the garden and the flowers which were out in a riot of colour. Dorothy was still a conscientious gardener. Another June, another year, another summer, she caught herself thinking. How quickly it all goes by! She admired the immaculate lawn which, she knew, was mowed and weeded meticulously by Mr Dobbs, a neighbour, a specialist in lawns. Dorothy herself had never married, despite the good looks of her youth. Many men friends she had had, but no husband, which, strangely, is often the case with very pretty girls.

'There we are,' her sister announced on returning to the living room. Oh, you've brought some jam I see. How lovely! Just what I wanted – and you remembered, you darling. Come now, let's go into the refectory' (she always called it that for some reason) 'and devour the good things we've assembled for ourselves!' Her pale blue eyes twinkled with the joy of anticipation.

The two women sat down to their early lunch and, as usual, chatted about everything that had occurred in their lives over the last six weeks or so. As they did so, the great sun moved slowly across the heavens, filling the room with its brilliance At a quarter to three they were still talking, sitting there among the debris of what they had eaten in the meantime.

'I told the vicar at the time that what he intended to do was rather a risky undertaking,' Dorothy was saying. She lifted her eyebrows. 'Oh yes, I told him, but you try telling a man anything. They never listen to us even when we see things ever so clearly.' Rose nodded. She recognised this failing. 'So you see, everything fell through and now he's in debt, that is to say, the church is in debt as a result of his making a foolish decision. One has to put it like that, Rose, it was nothing short of foolish.' Rose agreed by pulling a face indicating resignation to fate.

'By the way, Rose, I forgot to mention it on my card, but did you know that young Jeff Sanderson is very ill?' Dorothy asked suddenly.

'You mean the farmer's lad, Sanderson? No, I didn't. What's happened to him, then?'

'He's been ill for weeks and weeks. Too ill to move to hospital, so they say. Doctor comes every day. High fever. Delirium. Raves night and day. Nobody knows what is wrong with him. Perhaps some acute infection. Anyway, the symptoms are like those of meningitis, but it isn't meningitis. Doctor thinks it could be something he's eaten which was infected. Nobody can do anything until the fever subsides, but if he goes on like he is doing, his heart won't stand it for much longer.'

'Oh dearie me, poor lad,' Rose said, 'I do hope he gets better. I knew his mother's sister, you know. Do send my kindest love to them all.'

'Yes, you were friends for many years, I know,' Dorothy replied. 'I think she moved down to Devon and I never heard of her again,' she added.

'I will think of the lad in my prayers. I will indeed,' Rose said.

It must have been about this time – that is to say, about three or four in the afternoon – that Rose Amery began to feel very uneasy. For some reason quite unaccountable to her she wanted to be off. While Dorothy continued to talk, this time about her neighbour's arthritis, Rose's thoughts wandered. She could not concentrate on what her sister was saying. After some moments she decided that it might help if she suggested making some more tea, to which Dorothy, a little taken aback at being abruptly interrupted while unfolding the skein of her story, finally acquiesced. The table was cleared and a few minutes later the two of them were taking their ease on the lawn, each armed with a fresh cup of hot tea. Dorothy busily continued with her relation, but Rose's strange unease persisted. After perhaps twenty minutes or so, Dorothy suddenly halted in her discourse.

'Rose! You're not listening to me at all – what's the matter? Am I boring you?'

'Oh not at all, dear. I'm so sorry. Of course I'm interested. Of course, of course, do continue, dear... It's just that...' Dorothy looked concerned. She had rarely seen Rose so preoccupied, so inwardly withdrawn. It was unusual.

'What's the matter?' she enquired with a worried look on her face.

'I don't know, Dotty, I just feel I must go. It's funny.'

'Go? Go where?'

'Back home.'

'But you've come for the night as usual, Rose, and I've made your bed. It's a long way there and back just for an afternoon isn't it? I mean, that's what we've always done to avoid a stressful situation.' She looked at Rose for confirmation. Then she asked: 'Are you sickening for something, do you think?'

'No, no, I'm all right, my dear; it's just that ... well, for once, just this once, perhaps I'd like to go home earlier. I'll leave the basket and things here for the while.'

'Oh dear, Rosy, my love, I hope I haven't said anything amiss, I do hope not...' Dorothy looked disconcerted and fumbled with her cup on its saucer.

'No, of course you haven't, you silly thing. I don't know what to say to you; it's a kind of urge. A call. Perhaps someone's broken in or it's bad news from some quarter, it's strange.'

After a moment or two during which she looked at her sister very closely, Dorothy nodded slowly and sagely. 'Well, if it's like that, my sweet, you'll have to go home I suppose. I do hope everything is all right when you get there. Now I'm all worried.'

Rose hugged her. 'I'll send word via Robert on the mail van in the morning. His colleague can give the letter to the butcher's boy and he'll cycle up here with it,' she said comfortingly. She got up from the deck chair.

'Oh dear. I hope everything is all right,' Dorothy said as she accepted her sister's hand to help her up in turn.

It was about five forty-five when Rose left her sister's house and was heading for the railway station, a walk of about fifteen or twenty minutes, and having arrived there, she was informed that there would be a slow train to Dover, the last that evening, arriving in three quarters of an hour. Thus informed, Mrs Amery seated herself resignedly on one of the wooden seats in the waiting room, relieved at least to know that she would be home before it was quite dark. Again she was alone at a railway station. It was at this moment that she noticed that the urge to move which she had experienced for some hours had now suddenly vanished. She could not understand it. Should she return to her sister's house? But she had her ticket, and anyway, she would look so foolish. Her sister would think she was temporarily out of her mind. Perhaps she was. An unfamiliar word was echoing in her mind, louder now than when she had drunk tea on the lawn an hour ago. She could not eradicate it from her attention.

It popped into her mind every few minutes, *eleutheria*. What it meant she had no idea. Why she could pronounce it properly she did not know. It was there and with its sound there was a strange kind of emotion which accompanied it. It was like ... well, like a very strong conviction such as people experience when they are half drugged or in a state of trance. '*Eleutheria, eleutheria*'. It was all part of the strangeness of this day – the odd wind which had now abated, the strange word which had arisen in her mind and yet meant nothing to her, and, finally, the urge to leave her sister's house and set off for home a day early.

She boarded the train at seven twenty-two and dozed with the strange word echoing in her mind for the first half hour of the journey. She was the compartment's only occupant. The train crept through the evening meadows as the reddening sun descended to the west. Every few minutes or so, the carriages ground dutifully to a shuddering halt at a station, although there were few to either board the train or leave it, and after a time, as well as feeling refreshed from her light sleep, she also felt herself becoming a little irritated at the train's shambling tardiness like one who had an appointment to keep. At Little Morton she waited impatiently, wondering why on earth the guard didn't blow his whistle so that the train could get under way again. Whatever was going on? she asked herself. Why didn't the thing move on? What could be so important about such a place as Little Morton, totally lost as it was in the English countryside? A moment or two later, another train passed in a rush of noise and smoke on the other line as if to answer her question. The train once more wrenched itself into motion. She would disembark at Pennington Barrow and walk the rest of the way, she said resolutely to herself. To get away from this fretful, grimy, smoke-filled carriage was her only desire. Accordingly, she got down at Pennington and left the station to make the last two miles of her homeward journey on foot. Behind her, the little train puffed strenuously out of the station, belching mighty billows of dirty grey smoke from its stack as it laboured along the line to eventually disappear round a bend.

Mrs Rose Amery struck out for the track that would take her home. This led up steeply from the station through fields in which there were cows on the one side and sheep on the other. She breathed in the evening air gratefully as she came to the edge of the wood at the top of the hill four hundred yards or so from the station and stood for a moment looking down on the hamlet below. Then she turned and took to the path leading to the wood which, after a few more yards, vanished into the soft darkness of the trees. She knew that by the time she was halfway through the wood it would be quite dark, but that did not deter her. There is less to fear in the country than in the town, she often used to say. Moreover, she knew practically every inch of the way from childhood.

Mrs Amery had covered perhaps half the distance between the station and her home when, in the middle of the wood and to her astonishment, she heard children's laughter a few yards to her right. She stopped in her tracks to listen. It was very high-pitched laughter and she thought it very strange that such small children would be allowed out at such a time and in such a place. It was odd like the rest of the day. As she peered through the gloom in the direction of the sound she thought she could see light of some kind – a haze of light, a greenish glow which came and went like a light at sea masked from time to time by waves or spray. It was curious and she left the path and walked some way towards the source of the sound, picking her way cautiously through the brushwood, halting now and again to listen and orientate herself. Perhaps the children were lost and alone. Perhaps they needed help, she thought, in which case she would promptly take them home. A moment or two later she found herself on a much narrower path of soft turf which was springy to the feet, and so made more rapid progress. For the second time within a few minutes she stopped short. What she saw then was unbelievable.

In a small glade a few yards ahead she could make out a group of beings – not children, but small adults, each a little over a foot high. The light she had seen at a distance issued from what seemed to be waxen cups. At close quarters it was very intense, almost incandescent. She could not stifle an 'Oh!' as she came upon the scene and the music-makers, hearing her, stopped abruptly. Every one of them turned to stare at the intruder. Mrs Amery stood looking foolish and abashed in the shadows. The company stared at her without movement for a full half minute like roes about to spring for safety. She felt that there was a certain malevolence in their manner mixed with resentment at being disturbed, so she said quietly, 'I'm sorry, very sorry...' and turned to go. She had already taken the first step to return to the path when she heard a commanding voice behind her say, 'Stop!'

Mrs Amery turned her head and tried to smile at the figure that was resolutely advancing towards her.

'Who are you?' the voice demanded. The small man was sturdily built and wore a belt and a green cap, she noticed. His manner was that of someone in authority. 'What do you want here?' he asked in the same forthright way as before.

At that moment it was Mrs Amery who felt small. 'I was on my way home and heard voices,' she replied, and then added as he approached even nearer, 'I thought children might have lost their way, you see...'

The little man's manner visibly relaxed. 'Do you live nearby, then?' he asked, this time with less edge to his enquiry.

'Not far away, about a mile from here,' she answered. 'In Coldred.'

The man nodded and paused a while before saying, 'Well, while you're here, you might as well come this way.' And he turned and walked back to the group of miniature human beings who stood awaiting his instructions. 'It's all right,' he said to them, 'we'll move a little deeper into the wood; she won't harm us, and she's alone.' Turning to Rose, he said, 'Come a little further to where the ground slopes out of sight of the path and sit you down.' Mrs Amery followed him down into a dell of ankle-deep leaves and sat down on an old tree stump that he indicated. The group looked at her with a mixture of curiosity and fear written on their tiny faces. She noticed that there were men and women in the company, about twenty or thirty in all, and even children. They were all perfectly formed human beings in miniature, she noted. The man she had spoken to was taller than the rest of them and quite clearly their leader. After they had all assembled once more, this man turned to Mrs Amery and said, 'What's your name, ma'am?' Now there was civility in his manner, to which she promptly responded, 'Rose', she said.

'Well, Rose, we're going to sing for you,' he said and raised his arms for the others to begin. Forgetting their timidity, the assembly then sang with great gusto and accomplishment. After that, they danced as she had once seen the gypsies dance late at night as a young woman. Rose watched and listened, spellbound. After each song the little folk laughed heartily and spoke excitedly with one another as though they had quite forgotten her existence. It was then that she noticed that they were speaking a different language among themselves, but yet one which she could occasionally understand a few familiar words. Then, to her immense surprise, she quite distinctly heard the word *eleutheria*. Gradually, the little people lost their shyness altogether and came nearer to her.

'What does the word *eleutheria* mean?' she asked the nearest one excitedly.

'It means "liberation",' one of their number answered.

' "Liberation," ' Rose said, uncomprehending. They laughed at her awkwardness. The man whom she took to be their chief kindled more light in the small wax-like vessels and all of them sat in a semi-circle around her.

'My name is Kell,' the man said as he came and sat down opposite her. He lit a clay pipe of the kind she had seen her father dig up in the garden from time to time. She remembered him saying that they were used a hundred years earlier by many people in the country. The fragrance of the tobacco or whatever it was in the bowl played exquisitely in her nostrils. Kell looked up over his pipe towards her as though requiring a response, but Rose was still.

'I suppose you think it strange to have come across us small folk,' he said, studying the smoke from the pipe bowl. 'Truth is, we're used to you, but you're not to us. There was a time, though, when we were numerous and it was not so strange.' Rose nodded. He went on while the others settled themselves all around like children waiting for a story.

'We were here long, long before the Romans came to this island, you know. Some say that we have been in these parts for thousands of years and I believe it, but now our number is dwindling rapidly. Soon we'll all be gone.'

'But that's awful,' Rose commented.

The dwarf only smiled. She looked at his face for the first time carefully now in the low, flickering light. It seemed to her to be very old. The other faces round about were young by comparison, she observed.

'I've heard about you in the stories of old times,' she said.

'Aye, you must have done,' he answered, 'for once we were famed for our skill in the arts of the occult and helped the old kings here to win their battles and their brides. Our political advice was always greatly valued then, but we ourselves were never much interested in worldly power. That's what interests folks today. But there was a time when all of us lived in peace. Ah well, either you go along with the times or you pass by the board. That's the way it is in life, isn't it?' A smile crossed the ancient face again.

'It's a pity that it is so,' said Rose with conviction. 'All this senseless slaughter of young lives, all this killing for name and fame. I hate it. I could imagine better ways of getting through life than all this hateful nonsense,' she added with heat, for she had lost a brother at Verdun. And she began to cry.

Kell gave his pipe to one of those sitting next to him, stood up and touched Rose's knee in sympathy. She was greatly affected by the gesture and tried very hard to stem her sobs for his sake and for the sake of the others who were present. Sounds of sympathy and understanding came from the little group. Kell turned to them and asked a question in the language she had heard a few moments before. There was cheerful agreement to something he suggested which was shared by them all. Then he turned to her and said, 'You see, Mrs Amery, we knew you were coming. We were expecting you. I daresay that sounds strange to you. In fact, we called you here so that you could see us for the last time. We needed to tell someone of our existence before departing for ever. This shall be our last dance and our last song and then we shall disappear and never return.'

'Oh dear,' said Mrs Avery, shocked and disappointed at the announcement. She felt the tears smart behind her eyes again.

'It's all right, Rose, don't be sad. We have things in hand. That knowledge which has protected us from dogs and wild animals as well as the hand of man for so many centuries will guide our departure too. We know what to do for we know about these things,' he assured her. 'The words of our language will live on. Our legends and our designs will live on in folklore and our traditions in the lives of the Romanies, for they know all about us. But now it is time to go. Another age is upon us all in which our talents and our ways have no place, and there is no place either to flee to or to live, you see.'

Rose Amery's sad expression in the dulcet light was understood by them all. 'Where will you go?' she asked softly.

The little man did not answer her question but instead replied, 'When you go home you will wonder whether you dreamed all this, so I want to tell you something so that you can remember us and remember my words when these things come to pass. The barrows here will be opened up one day and men will find in them a treasure trove. Remember us then. Soon, men will learn to fly like birds in huge silver craft and everyone will be able to travel at great speed on smooth black roads. Men will fight another great war on the mainland and after that there will be peace. Remember what I have told you. Remember us then when you see these things. Tell men what we have said.' He turned then to the others and led them a little way off to the foot of a large beech tree. He looked back in Rose's direction and said, 'And now, farewell.'

They all began to sing then in their delightful melodious way which so affected her spirit while she sat there unable to say another word.

'Farewell!' Kell said again and as he said this the light which surrounded them all began slowly but inexorably to become weaker and weaker. She watched entranced as, very, very slowly they and their singing and the little vessels of light disappeared completely from sight, and she was left alone in the dark. Then fear gripped her. Would she find her way back to the path? She stood up in fright, strode forward, fell, slid, stumbled again, clambered up the side of the dell thick with leaves, and gained the smaller path by which she had come and then the larger one. Twice in her terror her dress was hooked by thorns as she made for the path. The spell was broken. Here she was again on the path that would lead her home. She stood still, panting for breath.

Gradually, she recovered herself and looked around. There was no one else here but her, alone and afraid in the deep

THE LAST DANCE

wood. How silly she had been to panic when there was no reason to do so. But ... but what had become of the wee folk she had seen? Had she been the victim of some sort of hallucination? Standing there in the comfortable darkness, she remained for a moment very still and recalled her adventure. She strained to hear laughter and singing, but there was nothing. There was only the whisper of an idle wind in the tops of the trees. In the seconds which elapsed as she listened, she wondered whether she were not going mad. She had happened to read of such things recently and recalled that the onset of madness is often preceded by a feeling of unease and sometimes of compulsion such as she had experienced that day. Perhaps she had had a lapse in her sanity in the early evening. For a moment or two the possibility distressed her as she walked on towards home. And yet, she told herself, and yet she felt quite well, extraordinarily well, indeed, now she had recovered from her first fright and had regained her composure. Her step was light and vigorous and her mind clear. With this thought she stepped out briskly through the quietness of the trees and arrived to find the village extraordinarily still. She took a short cut which skirted the houses, and from the meadows came upon the rear of her own house. Polly the cat met her at the garden gate.

'Polly dear, have you missed me, you lovely creature?' she asked her in the obscurity, whispering so as not to attract the attention of the neighbours. She stooped to greet her, and stroked the animal's silky black coat and held her head in her hands. 'What have you been up to, you old rogue?' The cat returned her affection. Then, standing up once more, she moved quickly through the garden and let herself into the house by the back door, Polly the cat close at her heels.

Once in the kitchen, and having lit the kerosene lamp on the heavy wooden table, she received the second shock of the last few hours. The hands of the clock over the kitchen fireplace showed twenty to four in the morning! She peered disbelievingly at this familiar piece of furniture, then took it from its place and shook it vigorously. At this there was a slight protest from its innards. She returned the thing to the shelf, and assuming the clock had stopped, ran upstairs to her bedroom where she knew the correct time would be properly confirmed by another faithful chronometer she kept at her bedside, but this too now stood at a quarter to four. Flabbergasted, Mrs Amery returned to the kitchen and began to work out her feelings. How on earth could she have spent so long in the wood and not felt tired to death by now? How could time have passed so quickly? What had happened? What had she seen? Had she really been in conversation with the Little People? No, it wasn't possible, she said to herself. None of it. It just wasn't possible.

Mrs Amery was 58 years old when she experienced the encounter related here. A day or so later, she wrote down the facts of her excursion in a child's school exercise book. The manuscript carefully records every detail. Many years later, she confided the experience to her elder sister who was then 82 years old but still in full possession of her faculties. Dorothy remembered the day in question quite clearly despite the long intervening interval in which the world had changed almost beyond recognition. At that time, the two ladies subsequently agreed to relate the incident to the Reverend George Hanbury. They gave the manuscript to him and this has remained in his possession until the present day. Dorothy passed away in March 1936.

Long before Rose died in October 1949, men had begun to fly and the tarmac road on which the motor car came into its own has since become commonplace. Rose was 88 years old when she died, enjoying good health, both mental and physical almost to her last day. The Second World War had been over for four years. In 1955, the barrows were opened at Pennington to reveal a Viking boat in very good condition. The bodies of perhaps twenty warriors were found there; among those buried were also two women, together with a great number of bronze axes, swords, silver goblets and decorated helmets, as well as much exquisitely wrought jewellery.

13

Saturday

Compiled and translated from a verbatim report in 1987 and dedicated to Herr Ludwig and Frau Magda Scherer in affectionate memory.

The following incident occurred in Germany in the summer of 1939, and before going a word further, I have to say that neither before that date nor after did I have any interest in what might be called the 'occult', or indeed in anything vaguely associated with such matters. Neither was I particularly religious, nor did I possess certain gifts, such as being 'psychic', as some people apparently do. I was in no way so inclined either then or now.

I was born of poor Jewish parents in the town of Sinsheim, Baden, in south Germany, in the year 1917. My father worked hard on the land around our modest dwelling, sired three girls and a boy, and died at the age of 47. My brother, who was three years older, died of tuberculosis a year after him, and it was these circumstances that demanded that the only male left in the family had to be the breadwinner. As a result I was quickly apprenticed at 14 to a building firm as a bricklayer, and as a further consequence, received very little education.

I worked in this trade until the early summer of 1939, when a friend of the family suggested that, because of the political developments of the time, I could avail myself of free evacuation to Israel ostensibly arranged for young men between 18 and 25 by a Jewish organisation in Stuttgart, a large town to the south of where I lived, to spare them from Nazi harassment.

The general assumption in those days was that the Nazi regime then in power would soon be at an end. My mother, still an attractive woman at that time, had caught the eye of an uncle who had recently been widowed and who was in a much better position financially than we were. This man undertook to look after her and one of my sisters, and so it came about that I was then free to avail myself of the extraordinary opportunity to emigrate. The idea had been long debated by friends and relatives beforehand, but at last it was decided that the opportunity was too tempting to dismiss, and the general situation too alarming, together with the fact that the chance to get away was free, and this finally clinched matters. I was to join a group of about twenty-five other young males at a school not far from Stuttgart's city centre.

The general idea was to make use of the school premises during the summer holidays both to allow us to become fit for the journey and to prepare us for the forthcoming voyage. Approximately a month was scheduled for these preparations. And so it was that I left my family one day in late July of that year amid tearful farewells and much sadness, but with the hope that I would certainly one day return and greet them all in triumph.

My own feelings in all this were mixed. On the one hand, it would be a wonderful adventure for a young lad like me and also something of a privilege. On the other, it was an excursion into a land about which I knew nothing other than that which my occasional acquaintance with the Old Testament afforded during my rare visits to the synagogue. There was a mysterious, exciting undertone to this imminent adventure.

It wasn't until I was actually in the slowest of trains down

SATURDAY

to Stuttgart (we couldn't afford a faster one) that I began to feel qualms at leaving my family. However, such as youth is, these were soon displaced by a change of circumstance and by the cordial welcome I received on arrival.

A makeshift reception desk had been set up at a table in the foyer of the school and behind this was a man of about 35 or so with an athletic figure and short blond hair, and dressed in white tennis flannels. Round his neck he wore a blue and red silk neckerchief with a brown toggle. He was to be our guide and companion for the next four weeks of our stay before departure to the north of the country where we would be taken aboard the *Swallow*, the vessel that was eventually to take us to the port of Haifa in Palestine. Another man of about the same age assisted him, but he was stockier and black-haired and also a representative of what was called the 'Jewish Emigration Team'. He was friendly and unassuming and immediately made me welcome, showing me 'my room', which was a classroom with four bunk beds in it. There were pictures on the wall of my future homeland and also of the *Swallow* and its crew, about eight or ten people, all of them smiling in welcome.

I unpacked and arranged my things and then studied this picture in more detail for some time before turning to review the scene below. I was on the second storey. Below was a large playground shaded by huge plane trees now in full, shady leaf and under some of them benches where one could sit. At each end of this expanse of lightly gravelled area was a netted goalmouth for football or hockey. It was here that we were later to play football or volleyball almost every day of the week.

The food was very good and every other day there were short talks, often accompanied by slide shows. Most of the material I've since forgotten, but I still recall pictures of a beach in Palestine and happy people bathing at the seaside. I loved swimming in those days. We lads in the village used to swim in the natural lakes around our home whenever we could, so I suppose it is this particular illustration that has stuck in my mind.

In the next few days, other young men joined me, until the two other beds were occupied and all of us were then divided equally into competing teams. One bunk remained empty.

I still remember the names of my roommates. There was Hans, a tall, well-built lad who was a little older than me; a young man with a square face and very black hair and light skin who had recently taken an interest in girls and who frequently regretted the lack of them here at school; and Richard, who was a little younger than us all and who had been brought up in a musical family. He, too, had fair skin, but was lightly built and quite uninterested in sport. While we kicked and raced and swung and fought, he would play the upright piano in the foyer and no one told him not to. He was encouraged in this by Heinrich, our leader to whom I've referred above.

Days at the centre were filled with physical activity of one kind or another, as I've said, but also with lively discussions in which we were entirely free to air our views about the political atmosphere of the time – a situation that would have been unthinkable outside the school walls. During them, we felt ourselves fortified in our mutuality and identity. It was a liberating and exhilarating experience. Added to these were quizzes and games, and once we were entertained by a theatre group. On this occasion we had the opportunity beforehand of helping in setting up the stage and its background, I recall. And on another afternoon there was an organised visit to the city's museum, where we all spent a fascinating time viewing the finds and the models of life, human and animal, going back some 250,000 years. It was enthralling, but it was on this particular visit that I noticed something that I

SATURDAY

later kept to myself, but which nevertheless irked me at the time.

We were taken to the museum by bus and on this bus, there was another guide, but this young fellow happened to be dressed in Hitler Youth uniform. The incident I relate here lasted not more than a second or two. It occurred as we were getting into the bus. I had already taken a seat near the front and, like the rest of our company, was full of excited anticipation. The youth I refer to was at the top of the bus steps and was organising the seating. This was all very official and proper and yet at that instant, looking at him over the shoulder of another boy sitting in front of me, I noticed an addition to the smirk of authority his office had bestowed on him. It was quite unmistakably, for a fleeting second, a look which I interpreted as undisguised contempt. Amid the general laughter and ebullience of youth, amid the jokes, the unseemly asides, the friendly buffeting, the silly squabbles for place, the shouts, the scuffles and jeers of youthful conviviality, there was this oh-so-slight leer. It was the brief glance of a basilisk, a dash of poison. Perhaps, I reflected, it was the arrogant superiority of a day's power over others. There were such people, I concluded, and turned to my companion for confirmation of my feeling, but he had clearly noticed nothing and the next moment I was diverted by the town's business on looking out of the bus window.

The visit to the museum was an overwhelming success, all the more so as we had not been out of the school precincts since our arrival. It was not that we were only at liberty behind locked doors – the gates were locked at night, but open all day – but the timetable was generally so full, and our individual needs were fulfilled, so that there was no desire to go out. Moreover, there was the shared conviction among us all that outside we might well be molested.

* * *

During my stay I found myself having more and more to do with another lad of the same age and a similar background, one Frederick, whom everyone called Fred for short. We were together in the same 'house' or team called 'Hessen' and had promised to remain together when we arrived in the land of our fathers. He was tall, open-minded, sported flaming red hair, and had a quick temper, it must be admitted, but at the same time a strong sense of fairness and justice. For this he was often chosen as referee in the games we played. We had both learned how to play chess in our short sojourn at the school and passed many happy hours together at this game. Fred had relatives in Palestine and was keen to introduce me to them on our arrival. We talked for hours about what we would do when we landed. He was all for being a member of a kibbutz, a social work-unit employed on schemes like irrigation and planting trees. He told me all about the activities of these groups and the very idea filled me with happy anticipation. Fred was much better educated than I was and knew about history and current affairs. He was a good judge of character and not given to hatred of people in general for supporting the maniac Hitler. He would often say, 'They're not all bad, you know, these Christians.' He would say this frequently, and in doing so, he would use a derogatory word to denote Christians in general, but in this connection to indicate that, although he knew all about them and their dogmas, there could also be decent human beings among them. This was typical of him: he was outspoken, but balanced in his views, clear in his condemnation of what he considered evil, but fair-minded at all times and popular with us all.

Then, after what seemed a never-ending wait, came the penultimate day of our stay at the school. I recall this day very clearly. It was the 19th of August, a Saturday.

We had all been briefed as to when we would be picked up and taken to the train and from there travel on to Hamburg.

SATURDAY

The journey, we were told, would take all day and almost half of the next. The night would be spent on the train, and for us this meant another adventure. All of us were looking forward to it. For many of us this trip was a transition into adulthood, where in the long run we would have to find a job and become independent. It was a thrilling prospect.

At midday most of us were already prepared to leave. Except for pyjamas, our kit was packed, our shoes cleaned, our best shirt ironed, ready to be donned the next day at nine. There was only this last afternoon 'to get through', as someone put it at the breakfast table. This one last afternoon! The afternoon in question proved to be very hot and sultry, despite the declining year, and by 1 p.m. most of the company were either inside the school, where it was decidedly cooler or reclining on one of the benches in the yard. An hour later, except for myself and two inveterate ping-pong specialists playing under cover at the far end of the playground, it was virtually empty. Just why I happened to be outside at this time I still can't recall.

I had sat down in the shade of one of the large trees and was watching some small, laughing intruders who had somehow found their way into the school grounds and were now calling and yelling at each other as the very young do, when under this hot, steely sky I felt suddenly cold and immediately after this, aware of an all-pervading aroma. This seemed to envelop me, and I knew in an instant where I had once smelled it. I had retained this smell in my olfactory memory many years before as a child at the house of an auntie. At a stroke, my lethargy left me and I got up, startled and intensely alert. Inside me and yet without my actually hearing with my ears, so to speak, a voice somewhere in my head quite clearly announced: 'Go away from here! Now!' The impact of this was so powerful that it was as if Auntie Anna were next to me. The words were cogent and distinct. Added to this, there was a compelling urge to move which overwhelmed me. In those seconds I wasn't the lad Ludwig leaving the bench and rapidly making for the gate. I seemed to be someone else. My legs carried me along with a speed at which I was amazed. It was just as if my feet were not mine. While on the move, an arrow of thought flashed to my room. What about my kit? My jacket? Should I go back and recover them? As if in answer, the bulge of my purse in my back trouser pocket confirmed that I had enough money and didn't need to return to the room for anything. I always carried my money with me, and so I went straight on and on until the children's cries faded in the distance behind me.

In all this there is something else that needs mention. Auntie Anna had died roughly a year before. She had always been kind to me and I distinctly remember her house in Heidelberg since, as a little boy, the old-fashioned wind-up gramophone set on a cabinet in her 'best room' there had always fascinated me. Mother and Father, as parents will, had warned me not to stand on a chair and wind the handle for the turntable to revolve. 'You might fall off,' they would say, and besides, 'Auntie won't like it if you break something', and so on. But Auntie was never too concerned about the possibility of my breaking the Bakelite records in the cabinet below the turntable. 'Let him play,' she would say indulgently, much to the uneasy reservation of my parents, 'the child's enjoying himself.'

But there was something else about that house which I still remember quite clearly, and that was the pervasive, pungent smell of the floor polish she used in the hall adjacent to the 'gramophone room', as I later called it. That smell was in my nostrils now. Ubiquitous. Unmistakable. Looking back, I think it was this presence as much as the 'voice' inside me which at that moment urged me to march so unerringly towards the city's station, which I reached within the next five minutes

Outside the station, I remember, there was some kind of celebration, I forget for whom or for what, and seconds later

SATURDAY

I was at the ticket office asking for a one-way trip to Sinsheim. 'Four thirty,' said the mechanical voice behind the grid, 'Platform nine.'

It was then ten to three. I would have nearly two hours to wait. The lads at the school would be trickling down to the makeshift dining room singly or in twos or threes for coffee or tea, and on this occasion there would be excited talk about the next day and after a time they would certainly note my absence.

And here was I amid the smoke and noise of the station waiting to go home, a Nazi newspaper under my arm to give me a sense of security and others the illusion of plausibility. Despite these reflections, I remained where I was like a dog tied to a chair and thought again of my strange experience. For the first time in my life I felt my guts churn in fear, and yet there was apparently no reason for this anxiety. It was quite inexplicable. There was no sign of uncomfortable authority. Around me, people came and went, talking and laughing. Whistles were blown, doors slammed, steel clanged as coaches were coupled, and at intervals, locomotives loudly discharged steam into the building. Trains slid into bays and out of platforms and departed. And above all this, a benign sun shone through the massive glass in the roof overhead. I had a valid ticket, was young enough to be ignored as an unimportant passenger, and yet I felt most uneasy. I tried to browse through the newspaper as a diversion. There was something about Berlin's town hall celebrating its seven hundred years of existence and something about relations between Japan and China, I remember, but I was too disturbed to take much interest. Frederick had always encouraged me to keep abreast of the times, and I remember feeling guilty about this for a moment.

Above, the station clock crept.
I walked.
I sat.
I gazed.
I waited.

And waited. At ten past four, coaches were shunted into position and after a moment or two I was free to board my train, where I found a seat and was glad to be in a corner and alone. The seat back and the side of the coach gave me a feeling of safety, but it was not until the train was well under way that I felt more comfortable. In this state of mind I was able to look back on the last few hours more rationally. 'Thank God, no one has come in search of me,' I thought. Now I was free to let the train slowly take me home.

I had received one letter from my mother during my stay at the school, informing me of what had happened in Sinsheim in my absence. Apparently, the pressure on the Jewish community there had been stronger and many people had already left for other countries, especially for the USA and Great Britain. It wasn't certain what kind of a welcome I would receive on my return, and meditating on this to the monotonous rhythm of the wheels, I resolved to get off the train one station ahead, and walk the remaining three kilometres into Sinsheim so as to be able to size up the lie of the land, so to speak, and not immediately be forced by circumstance to come into contact with people I knew or even people who might even question my flight from Stuttgart. Accordingly, a few minutes after these reflections, I jumped down from the train at Steinsfurt. From there I wandered along the railway track for a while and then gained a parallel path towards the town, as this was the shortest route.

It was a warm, balmy evening and I noticed that the nights were drawing in. Although I kept my eyes and mind open, I was worried about meeting someone I knew. In those days, such an encounter was almost inevitable. As I went along I pondered on my situation. The fact was that, although this was my home, it had become a hostile environment in which I could lose my life very easily. I passed familiar bushes and trees, sandy places and old abandoned buildings where I had played as a child. There were the trees where I had hidden

SATURDAY

trinkets and toys and the coveted cigarette cards that were collected by the children of those days. They were all still there in their hollows and niches, and the trees were still there, inviting me to come and rediscover the charm and joy of climbing them. I felt suddenly very sad. The silent embrace of evening softly revealed the contours of the places I had loved and where I had once known the careless happiness of childhood shared with my young comrades, but now the embittered hate of one man and the contemptible, sheep-like conformity of a whole nation had prevailed to spawn a monstrous coalition of hatred and persecution.

I was shocked to discover that the house was empty when I arrived, and learned later from a neighbour's child that my mother had moved with my sister to live with my uncle. This meant another footslog to his much larger house on the village outskirts. Dusk was by this time enfolding the township and, grateful for this, I set out with renewed energy, but used every opportunity to avoid people who might recognise me. This manoeuvre turned out to be an arduous and time-consuming game, with the result that I came to my uncle's house when it was already quite dark.

My sister answered the door and, seeing me, drew breath and gasped, 'Oh God! Ludwig!' This expletive brought my mother and uncle to her side within seconds and what happened then doesn't strictly belong to this narration, so, to cut a long story very short, I remained in this house like a prisoner for about three weeks before surreptitious arrangements were made for me to travel to Britain on the very last refugee scheme for young Jews seeking asylum.

I stayed in Britain as an internee and as an 'alien' until the end of the war and there met the woman I was later to marry. I finally left England to live in Israel. That was in 1948. I never saw my mother or my sisters again. In 1950, after careful research, a former friend reported that all the young people with whom I had spent four weeks at the school were taken on a long journey by train the next day not to Hamburg, but to a new, hastily and shabbily erected transit camp in Gurs, France. Here, deprivation was so great that hunger, disease and the oncoming winter's cold killed most of them. The few who survived were transferred to Auschwitz the following spring, where all of them perished a short time later.

And soon I, too, will be gone, but before I depart this world I feel I ought to add a last word to this record of survival: I want to say to those who read this posthumously that I, too, once stood up in flesh and blood like you who read these words. I, too, felt the cold of winter and the joys of summer, knew labour and hardship, hope, happiness and love, knew human kindness as well as the wickedness of humankind, and what you have felt in your life, friend, I also knew and felt.

I want to say that what I have related here is true, even though I don't know to this day how such a thing could have come about. 'Can it be,' I ask myself, 'that the dead are somehow with us? Can it be that there are such beings as guardian angels who guide our ways or unseen messengers who communicate with us in times of affliction?' I don't know.

Although nearly sixty years have passed since my comrades were so evilly betrayed, I still think of them, and this shall be their testimony.

By special arrangement, both Ludwig and Magda Scherer, his wife, today lie in the principal Christian cemetery in Sinsheim.

14

Ann (1947)

'You'll have to be very careful about what you say and how you say it,' my mother said, 'but I think you should go and see her. After all, she's your first cousin.'

'What shall I say?' I asked stupidly.

'Well, you can tell her we're all thinking of her and wish her all the best and that I'll come over and see her as soon as I can; that for a start.' We knew, however, that a recovery was impossible. All the doctors had said so.

'I don't want to go.'

'You must go. It's your duty to go and you can't funk it.'

I felt very uncomfortable. I didn't know Ann much at all these days. Life was too full of growing up and I hadn't seen her since my seventh birthday when, I remember, she played with me in the garden, an older child, half responsible for us and it was great fun. There were a lot of us, all children gathered together on that occasion, and she had been invited as well. I only had a vague idea of her these days and had not seen her since that time. Now I was seventeen and I really wanted to pick Colin up later, see what he was doing with his new cycle and then go on to the cinema. Drat! No, I had no great desire to see Ann. Everybody knew she was dying and no doubt would be gone in a few weeks anyway. What could I do to save the situation? I mean, what on earth do you say to people who are about to die? Cancer, they had said. What is cancer? How come that she had that disease at thirty-three? Wasn't it an old people's problem? Somehow, it was going to be difficult. I mean, if she had been older, you could perhaps get by with a few kind words, knowing somehow that this was the way life was: folks get old and die. It was natural. But at thirty-three years of age? What could I possibly say? What *does* one say? The very idea of death was alien to me. At my age it was a scary possibility in the background.

Mother had her arms in the sink, busy washing up. 'My God, lad, you've turned seventeen; you ought to know what to say. Take some flowers for a start. Nice ones. And don't forget to sympathise with her on our behalf. On behalf of the whole family. It's likely that Uncle and Auntie Farley have been to see her already. Heavens! What a hell that girl must have gone through! First she loses her job, then she's operated on a dozen times at least. Then the long stay at the infirmary. Then folks just giving her up sooner or later. It's all so hopeless. The inevitability. Makes you wonder if there's a God. What she must have suffered *mentally*, let alone physically, poor girl!'

I listened to all this and tried vaguely to imagine Ann's plight, but it wasn't easy. I was stuck on the thorn of obligation. It was going to be a bore and what could I possibly do to relieve Ann's condition? Nothing.

'You'll have to be tactful, my lad. It's a pity she has no husband to console her at a time like this. Why she didn't marry Ron Partridge I can't think. Such a nice lad, Ron. Mind you, she was always a bit on the independent side. Said what she thought, and all that. But she's good looking enough – or was – to have got a man.' At that moment I felt that we men were somehow the objects of women. They were out to 'get' us and we were their prey. So Ann was in the same category, I thought to myself. This made the impending encounter all the more distasteful.

After lunch I was to put on my best suit and go to Sadler's

ANN (1947)

for the flowers and from there catch the bus to Albion Street, two or three miles away on the other side of town and almost in the country. 'Drat!' I thought again. What the devil would I say to this female relative?

The flowers bought, I boarded the bus that groaned and dragged me through its schedule of stops and eventually reached the Shearson area of town, and it was then that I recalled that Albion Street stretched some way from there on to the very last outposts of the city. I hadn't been there for years, and had always previously been accompanied. Just where the house was I had forgotten in the meantime, but I had the number with me – 118. As I approached the house I passed a number of frontages, all of them different from one another and wondered if I could make myself useful in mowing Ann's lawn. Perhaps that was the answer. Yes, I concluded to myself, I would mow Ann's lawn. Ann's house came into sight. I could now recognise it as a nineteenth-century dwelling, since I'd recently developed an interest in buildings in general. At the top of the steps to the front door I rang the bell, but it was some time before the door was opened. In that moment, I had all kinds of images in mind as to what she might look like. Perhaps a half corpse or some ghostly shadow of a human being would welcome me. I recalled the pictures I had seen in books. When, finally, the door was opened, a slim young woman of about thirty greeted me with a smile.

'Norman!' she exclaimed cheerfully. I noticed the deep, dark blue eyes at that moment. It was not the unusual colour of these eyes that moved me, but their expression. This was an expression which, well, looked straight into me, not at me. I was assessed within seconds as I stood there. Briefly. Completely. In that moment she had made a decision, had come to a conclusion. I was analysed, evaluated, filed. 'Come in, do,' she said cheerfully.

The tiled hall led out into a room where I saw that she

had laid a table for us. Annexed to this, I noticed, was a veranda. 'How nice of you to come,' she said. 'Your mum told me this morning that you might look me up this afternoon as she can't come herself, so I appreciate your visit. My goodness,' she added, 'how you've grown! A man indeed!' Smiling broadly and so saying, she ushered me into her living room where we settled ourselves in armchairs set around a small, low table. After a few more pleasantries of the kind I had come to know and use in family exchanges, she poured the tea she had made a few minutes before and offered me a scone. It was delicious. I looked at the soft hands and arms and recalled that this woman was a chemist. She gave absolutely no impression that she was ill. Very seriously ill. In my ignorance in those days, I imagined chemists as people that always work in shops behind counters, ready to offer advice or medicine.

Wanting to make conversation, I made the first move. 'Mum tells me you're a chemist, is that right?'

'Yes,' she replied, 'that's right.' There was a small hitch.

Desperately, I continued, 'At Boot's the Chemist?'

A slight smile hushed across her features. 'No,' she answered simply, 'I'm an industrial chemist,' and seeing that this was foreign to me, she continued. 'I work at Glaxo in Newton in the garden fertiliser department – or *did* at one time. I suppose it's a bit like doctors; there's one down the road, a man you know, and others who work in a hospital.' This was said so simply and in a manner I was completely unfamiliar with, and the gentle smile that accompanied this information I found very charming. I smiled, too, and the slight tension between us that I always felt on encountering strangers abated somewhat. The scone was good. Noticing somehow that I'd already enjoyed one, she urged, 'Do have another one. They're fresh and I'm glad you like them.' This again was uttered with a natural simplicity that I found refreshing. I took advantage of her invitation. Looking back over the years, I surmise that at that moment I had anticipated a totally different situation, and the fact that the 'situation' was perfectly normal came as a large surprise.

Whereas I was ignorant of specialised qualifications and in dealing with people who were either very old or ill or mentally disturbed, I had acquired, even at seventeen, a certain discernment into people's character. It was difficult to explain, but it was already an acquisition quite securely anchored in my short experience of life. By 'anchored' I mean that the judgements I made about those around me were generally vindicated by fact sooner or later.

I began to like my cousin. I had never come across anyone quite like my companion and watched her drink her tea out of the corner of my eye. There was a detachment about her, but one that was not exclusive. On the contrary, it was engaging. It was clear that she was quite clearly in control of the situation. But then, I thought to myself, she's older. No, it wasn't that either. It was an invitation into the club of adults. It was an assumption that I was an equal. I was not so experienced, of course, that was clear, but I was appreciated in my own right for what I was. It was a pleasant feeling.

'I expect you'll be thinking about a career shortly, and they tell me you're good at maths. Very promising,' she said optimistically and with a certain verve that suggested it was a pleasure to get on with the future.

'Well, I hope to get a job with Rolls-Royce at Blackwell in the draughtsman's section, but there's nothing certain about it yet. I have to wait for my exam results. If I get As, I should manage it.'

'I've no doubt about that; a scientific bent is in the family, you know.' The playful violet-coloured eyes sustained the question.

'Well, I know Uncle Cyril was in research at Rolls and Jessie just laps up physics at school!'

'Oh, does she? I'm pleased to hear that.'

After we had mutually devoured the scones and the jam and drunk our tea together, Ann suggested that we then go out onto the veranda. She took up the pots from the table to the kitchen in the interim and left me for a moment to look round the room. It was literally lined on three walls with books like a library. I scanned some of the titles and came across the memoirs of Sir Winston Churchill. I was sufficiently relaxed now to take the book down from the shelf and thumbed through a few pages. I was interested in history. A few minutes later, Ann re-entered the room and found me engrossed.

'Ah, the Churchill volume,' she announced airily. 'Do you like his stuff?'

'Yes,' I answered. 'I like history, and of course we've lived through some of this,' I said, returning the book to its place.

'No, no, do take it home with you, Norman, if you find it interesting. I shan't be doing much reading in the future,' she said with a smirk. 'So please, take it with you.'

I must have winced or pulled a face at this remark, for she continued: 'All this stuff' – and here she waved her small hand at the walls lined with books – 'has to go soon anyway.'

I looked at her as she said this. Her figure was what we call 'petite' and her actions were light and free; her straight legs beneath the flowered skirt ended in high heels. Then there was a kind of rhythm in the way she did things. As she took the pots away to the kitchen a moment before, for example, I had noticed the ease and delicacy with which she did so, and the way she almost danced back to the bookshelves to find me another two volumes of Winston Churchill.

She handed them to me and there was that winsome smile of hers.

'I hope you enjoy them,' she said brightly.

'But I can't possibly take all these!' I said in protest. 'They're yours.'

ANN (1947)

'They were,' she replied quickly. 'Rather you have them than someone I don't know or that they're shredded or burned or something. I wouldn't like that.' The massive incongruity of this attractive young woman and the fate that awaited her moved me at this instant to tears. I couldn't help it. They welled up out of me as I stood there with the books in my hand.

'Come, put the books on the table and let's go out onto the terrace. The sun's shining and we should enjoy it.' So saying, she took my hand and led me out onto the veranda.

On it were two wicker chairs and another glass-topped table with a vase of flowers on it. She guided me to one of these and I sat down heavily, bashfully using a handkerchief I had with me to dry my eyes.

After a short interval, she said quietly, 'You shouldn't, you know, though I much appreciate your feelings. Not everyone has the capacity to care so much.' Nevertheless, I was not consoled by this and found it very difficult to control my feelings, so I sat there and said nothing. The sun shone on her knees and on her bright blonde hair. This glinted in its rays, and I could not help but sigh. How was it possible for the Good Lord to allocate this individual a fate such as this? I asked myself. To die in the prime of life!

'So you're going to become a scientist?' she asked quietly.

'Yes, I hope so,' I replied, collecting myself with difficulty. In saying this, I was suddenly aware of myself projected into the room as someone else answering a question. Was I going to be a scientist? I hadn't really thought about the matter.

'Do you know what being a scientist is?' she pressed gently. The question was one I'd never considered with any care. I knew that I was destined to follow in my father's footsteps, be part of the family, do what was naturally expected of me at school, do what I liked doing, do what I could do well. Was that being a scientist? I mused.

'To be a scientist is first of all to acknowledge things as they are. Face the truth as it is,' Ann said, looking at me seriously, the smile in her eyes having vanished for a moment. 'I'm looking at a fact as it is, and in this, I hope, I'm being true to myself. Things are as they are, untrammelled by what we might think they are or hope them to be. It needs courage as well as intellect.'

I nodded, but she knew that I had trouble digesting what she had said. There was another silence between us.

'Where's the problem?' she went on, her voice soft and persuasive like that of a lover. I was still so overwhelmed at her serenity, her composure and her simplicity that I found no words to describe what I wanted to say. What did I want to say? What did she want me to say? And then there was another pause while the sunshine suddenly streamed down onto us, having moved from behind the house roof in the meantime. It occurred to me at that moment with more clarity than ever before that everything was in movement and that we human beings were just as much a part of all this perennial motion as the sun itself.

'The problem is that I don't want you to go, that's all,' I said, for this was all I could find to say.

'Well, I must go and you yourself will be faced with the same thing one day, won't you?' There was a slight pause.

'I can't imagine that somehow,' I replied.

'Yes, of course.' She said this so naturally as though one had said that one was a little tired after a long journey. 'I think the space between life and death is the most important bit, not the coming in and the going out. These are only the two ends to a piece of life, so to speak. Don't you think so?' I nodded. 'What's important is the middle,' she added.

'Do you think life goes on – I mean ... afterwards?' This latter was blurted and gauche, but she ignored its clumsiness and continued in her cool but friendly interest in our conversation.

ANN (1947)

'If you mean this church stuff about an everlasting life and so on, no.' This was said with a quiet certainty which set me back a little. As a youngster brought up in the Catholic tradition, remarks like this were hard to accept.

'No?' I uttered this rather stupidly and looked at her intently, needing confirmation of what she had said.

'No,' she said again, with a trifle more emphasis. 'I think that kind of thing is a poor substitute for this life.' The sentences came simply, but with an impact behind them, and seeing my interest, she went on, 'People who dwell on that kind of thing are wishful thinkers; folks who, not having been able to manage this one, hope that it'll be better on the second time round.'

'That's a bit hard,' I managed to say, having for the moment almost overcome my shyness.

'Well, what do you think?' Ann asked in return, suddenly and so much to my surprise that I was tongue-tied again.

'Well,' I stumbled, 'because it's not always so easy to deal with this life is it? I mean, there's a lot of problems and you never know what's round the corner, tragedy and all that, and so people hope that they'll be delivered from suffering when they die... I mean, well, you know?'

'Yes, all right, but how do they *know* there'll be a better life afterwards? Is there any proof for this assumption?' Her manner was still firm and objective, her questions delivered as though she were a doctor asking about a patient's symptoms. It was a trifle, yes, just a trifle unnerving, this clear, unequivocal pursuance of what I believed and what I thought, for the truth was that I had never really considered these things. But she had asked for proof of everlasting life and I knew the answer to this one. Or thought I did, and my conditioning promptly came to my aid:

'Because Jesus rose from the dead, didn't he?' I was nervous again. I didn't like the use of the words 'dead' and 'dying' just at that moment.

'Did he?' she asked ingenuously. 'Did he give us any detailed account of what things were like on the "other side"?' she asked.

'Well, if you believe in the Gospels, you don't need a report like that. It's faith or belief if you like,' I replied, feeling then that I had represented things well.

'Belief?' Ann echoed. This one word was uttered as though I had been stabbed. In that one sound there was annihilation, interrogation, a call to arms. She saw my hesitation in the wink of an eye. 'So you're not a scientist after all!' she laughed gaily and the blue eyes were suffused with genuine amusement, the hardness of her reaction gone. Suddenly, I loved her for this. The discipline of her straight-backed posture on the chair and her uncomplicated sincerity were more persuasive than anything she could have added. She sat there for an eternal moment, looking at me, and I was never to forget this look, this frank, kindly surveillance, this gentle appraisal. In it there was unassailable self-assurance and yet, withal, compassion, both of which were woven into a knowledgeable, loving smile.

'What I *do* believe in, if we have to use this word, is a certain progression – that is to say, it seems that there is some scientific evidence for a movement through death to another life where there may be further development of the individual. The idea is tenable, even plausible, whereas "eternal life" is unthinkable, inconceivable. We just can't envisage such a thing as "infinity". It's merely a concept and of no practical use at all.' Here, my cousin was at her most formal, using words and expressions that I was proud to be able to understand. On the other hand, it was subversive and yet exciting.

'It's pretty clear that Jesus was thinking of something quite different. The idea we have of a linear, unceasing life after death subsequent to a few years on earth is an interpretation used by the Church to put the wind up us mortals and so

ANN (1947)

maintain its power. Get your ticket to heaven now or miss out and be damned for ever! There's nothing like fear as an instrument to keep folks under control, you know.' She laughed again. I didn't know. Such ideas were quite unfamiliar, Seeing my uncertainty, she added indulgently, 'Norman, I'm sorry to tread on your toes. You've never talked about these things with anyone else, have you?'

I replied that I had not.

'Then I'll shut up,' she said, 'Let's talk about the weather!'

At this we both burst out laughing and a minute passed before I could contain myself sufficiently to say, 'No, really, what you say is very interesting.'

Then her face darkened and her attitude changed so completely and so suddenly that for a second or so I felt uncomfortable. 'It's a bit more than that,' she said seriously. 'Unless you discard this armour, you'll never be free.'

'Armour?'

'Yes, this iron suit to your thinking. It hinders you. Throw it away! In that moment you'll be a man, a thinking creature, and no longer a slave to someone else's ideas.'

In the instants that followed this remark I tried to gather my thoughts and my convictions together. I was confused and troubled. I was incapable of answering her. It wasn't so much the argument that she put forward that was so coercive. Not that entirely. It was her manner. I felt a force emanating from her that was very powerful. She was indeed the free person she'd hinted at, and it was this that took me by surprise once more.

'But I can't just throw away what I believe...' I stammered.

'You mean it isn't easy to throw off your conditioning. That's what you mean, isn't it, and I agree with you. It's comfortable. You don't have to think. Thinking hurts.' She laughed and then went on. That's why most people leave it alone or leave it to others to cripple our minds until we can't think for ourselves any more. Or don't want to. It's been going on for thousands of years.' I was silent at this, and so she continued. 'If you're going to be a scientist, the first thing to do is to divest yourself of preconceived ideas, especially ideas that have no grounding in fact. That comes before anything else, the attitude, then the rational part and the logical inference. That's secondary to the prior state of mind, which, if you like, is an emotional attitude. That comes before the search for truth.' There was a tiny pause while this sank in. Then her expressive features relaxed again into that seductive smile of hers and the violet eyes glowed with good humour. 'So, the best of British!' she said, and again we laughed.

I've forgotten what we said next, our goodbyes, our friendly exchanges, but they must have taken place. What time it was when I left and how I eventually got back home is at the bottom of an ocean of memory. After all, it's now sixty years ago.

Three weeks after this interlude, Ann died suddenly and without warning while in the garden and at a time when the doctors had just come up with a drug that might have lengthened her life. But so it was. The funeral ceremony, the burial, the mass of flowers, the sadness of relatives, the black and the weeping, the preacher and the eulogies given later by local dignitaries and representatives of the firm she worked for, the articles in the paper, all this I recall only as a vague memory. Her grave is still there in the churchyard of St Mary's not far from where she lived, but what I shall never forget to my own dying day is that smile and more, the gentle, questioning light in her eye, the feeling she emitted of equality between us, a feeling of common humanity engaged in the exploration of ideas and feelings, the light, lissom way she

ANN (1947)

moved, her playful good humour and her naturalness. I had left that day with a gift that I would never lose, and with an enrichment to my life that I would always cherish.

15

Still Life, 1938

In the beginning was the garden. In truth it was not really a garden, but a glade borrowed from the green woods which covered the hills surrounding the town. In this garden glade stood our house, a strong, square house on rough-hewn granite foundations with solid, honest-to-goodness rectangular windows which, from one side, looked out over the city towards the Old Town and its famous bridge, the river and the valley beyond. My father always used to speak of that side of the house as the 'sun's eye', which was always the lighter side of the house and where, on summer mornings, he would stretch in his pyjamas and welcome the day from the small balcony which led off from the bedroom. My room was on the 'moon's eye', the other, wooded side of the house where the moon would rise in the east to look through the branches of the trees. One of my most precious memories is of watching the moon pass very slowly through the tops of the trees outside my window on summer nights. In the autumn I used to listen for hours to the rhythm of the rain falling outside, pattering on the thick carpet of leaves in the wood below. These great trees bordering the house and its garden are interwoven with the events of my early life, with the light of the moon and the sound of the rain.

Saturday, 16th July 1938 was a very warm day. That day, one of the events of my long life occurred that I shall never forget until my eyes close for ever. It is stamped indelibly upon my mind. Looking back to that sunny afternoon long ago, I see about fifteen or sixteen people in the garden, some of them chatting at the long table supplied with birthday fare, the cake, the jelly and blancmange, the salmon on a special long plate and the many meat sandwiches, the side of ham which Mother had received as a gift from friends who lived in the country and who were to arrive later. I can still see the exquisite tarts which Jocelyn had made with such loving care, each with one small red cherry in the middle. I can still recall the sea fish now so far from any coast with their open mouths and the way they had been placed upon rapidly melting ice. There were the pies and the sausages, the different kinds of fruit and the ice cream which was still packed in airtight containers, the fresh, crusty bread of various types, the melting butter and the potted jams, all of it being then covered by Elfie, our maid, with very clean, creased and laundered cloths to keep off the flies and other insects which were already interested in what was offered so abundantly. Two wasps were among these and showed considerable initiative and alacrity as well as a splendid demonstration of the aerodynamically impossible by neatly avoiding Aunt Selina's wild attempts to beat them off her glass of lemonade with a small white handkerchief. 'Damn things!' she said in exasperation after a minute or two of indecisive attack and determined retreat.

It was my birthday. I was twenty today. Two hours ago, I had walked up the cobbled hill from the town with Peter, he in a black suit and carrying a violin case and I in a summer dress, fooling around, laughing as we climbed, the two of us, stopping every now and again for breath, for the road was very steep, and eventually arriving at the iron gate to the steps which led up to a path through the garden and then to the house. 'Phew!' he had said as we arrived. 'And then steps?'

'Afraid so,' I answered practically, 'I'm used to it. Have to go up these every day.'

STILL LIFE, 1938

Peter groaned theatrically and dragged himself up the first three steps, pausing to add as I closed the iron gate behind me, 'Every day?'

'Every day.' The red walls of the stairwell threw back our light-hearted laughter as we went up the steps together. Father had met us halfway along the garden path towards the house, I remember. He was pleased to see us.

'Dad, this is Peter; Peter, my father.' The two men shook hands.

'I'm very pleased to see you, Peter. I've heard all about your wonderful playing, and as I see you with your case, I take it we're in for a treat.' He said this as he turned to me. Peter had smiled at that moment. He was particularly handsome when he smiled and he was always smiling. I loved him. I loved his tall, easy figure and his film-star face, square and manly with its straight nose and the thin furrow which developed above the root of his nose when he was in thought. I loved the unusual dark blue eyes, and yet it was not the eye colour which was so attractive so much as their peculiar lustre, their playful vitality which took you into his heart, so that you no longer felt alone in this world, but with someone who understood you. Everyone had remarked at some time or other on this fact. The only time he did not share our thoughts and our lives with his engaging smile was when he played his violin. Then you could say that he had his eye on a distant star, and the warmth of his personality was in the music for you to share. I looked at the thick blond hair cut close to his head as he exchanged a word or two about this and that with Father, and at the ears which were shaped like the scroll on his violin.

'What a hostess you are,' Father chided in mock annoyance, looking at me, 'to drag the lad all the way up from the university on a hot day like this!' And so saying, he turned on his heel, at the same time grasping Peter's elbow and guiding him towards the house. 'Come, my young friend, freshen up in the house and rest your feet for a moment; I'll take your case. Naughty girl,' he added, looking over his shoulder at me. Peter winked and I giggled like a little girl.

'This heat!' It was Mrs Goldmann, and hours later, 'It's over thirty degrees did you know, my dear? How we managed those steps the two of us I shall never know. I don't suppose we'll be doing this jaunt for much longer.' Panting, she turned to me, 'Happy birthday, dear, happy birthday! Twenty, my goodness, I remember you as a babe in arms, Marta. Ah! Doesn't seem more than a couple of years ago. Stairs weren't such a problem then, and we came to see your mother in the house.' She paused for a moment to regain her breath. Now well over seventy, she had gained weight rapidly over the last few years so that everything, even the small actions of walking and sitting down, had become a task and an encumbrance. Mr Goldmann, who was equally large, and quite bald, smiled and nodded in friendly acquiescence to all his wife said.

'She held you up for me to take in my arms,' his wife went on. 'What an experience that always is!'

Goldmann took a step forward and stretched out his plump hand towards me. 'Happy birthday, Marta!' he said, his face beaming. I hugged them both.

'Come and sit down in the shade over here,' I said. 'Rupert put this up this morning.' I indicated a large parasol which a friend of my brother had brought along for the occasion.

'So kind, Marta, dear, yes, the sit-down will enable us to recover our wits and our breath again,' Mrs Goldmann said, sitting very heavily and awkwardly down onto a light garden stool which vanished immediately under her form. Mr Goldmann did the same. He was sweating profusely, mopping his smooth, brown, hairless head every few minutes with a large dotted handkerchief. The two of them sat there panting and wheezing, somewhat apart from everything which was going on in the garden for a moment, I must say, like two giant frogs, until Elfie brought them something to drink, which both of them greatly appreciated.

Geraldine Schwartz was to be seen in the middle of the garden, and indeed in the middle of everything, as was her way. She was holding a glass of champagne in one delicately poised hand.

'And what did you do?' someone was asking at that moment. Geraldine moved her head in a way which suggested, 'Well, what does one do in such a situation?' and raised her jet black eyebrows as she looked at her questioner.

'I told him to go away of course.' This brought forth an explosion of laughter from the two young men she had angled to her side as well as the middle-aged couple who had been party to the story of Geraldine's recent discovery of a burglar in her house.

'But that could have been very dangerous. Weren't you afraid? I mean he could have become violent or something?' another in the group around her asked.

Geraldine was an attractive young woman. She worked for a textile company in a nearby industrial town and frequently modelled for the firm. She knew all about her physical plus points, but, oddly enough, was apparently quite unaware of what made her attractive to both men and women. This, to be precise, was her entire lack of affectation and the knack she had of hitting the nail on the head during conversation, a mannerism which always resulted in peals of laughter from her hearers and at the same time made her a much sought-after person to talk to.

'Well, yes,' she replied with ingenuous simplicity, 'I think we were both too surprised to resort to violence.' More laughter. 'As I said, I found him in the downstairs lavatory. He had left his kit or whatever it is outside the door and, well, I suppose...' She hesitated for a second or two and then tried to continue, but the rest of her sentence was lost in the fits of laughter from her listeners. She waited a moment with a kindly, indulgent smile on her lips, a most engaging smile that said so much about her character, until the amusement subsided. Then she continued, 'I naturally wondered what this box thing was doing in my hall and opened the door...' More laughter.

'And did he go – just like that?' John Haller, a friend of my sister's, cut in. He had just arrived and had informed himself a moment before of the substance of the encounter. He was much intrigued by the story.

'I didn't hang about myself, as you can imagine...' Geraldine continued amid more hilariousness. 'I went to the front door and left it open for him to leave – and he left.'

'Was he a big feller?' John asked.

'Oh yes, very big and ugly,' Geraldine replied quickly, and the incongruence planted in everyone's mind of a possible fifty-eight kilos of high-heeled, unarmed young womanhood suddenly placed in a situation of possible conflict with a prowling nocturnal male bear armed with his 'kit' on the lookout in the night for jewels and being thus incommoded was irresistibly funny.

Meanwhile, Aunt Salina had given up her unequal struggle with the wasps and had sought more congenial company in the person of Joachim Eckhart, my father's lawyer, who was invited to every 'do' in the family, the births, the marriages, the deaths and much more. They had known each other for years, these two, Salina and Joachim, she the actress and 'spinster of this parish', unwillingly living alone, and he a confirmed bachelor, a man for all seasons, willingly living alone, supremely capable, worldly wise, urbane and knowledgeable, and yet for all that the veriest baby in the company of any woman, no matter what her age. Aunt Salina, herself much schooled in the ways of the world, knew he needed someone to look after him and had used her womanly wiles to catch him these past twenty years past, but to no avail. He was now 58 years old, and the idea of a union with Aunt Salina had indeed occurred to him on a number of occasions, but instinctively he had always fought shy of further development in that direction. Every approach she had made to interest him in her company and her permanent support had been foiled by his excursive urbanity, by the flow of time, by the exigencies of his job and by circumstance so that now, at 51, interest had flagged and friendly resignation had taken its place. And as for their youth, of course, such had long flown from their hearts and their faces. Salina was fair, fat and fifty, but still with much of the successful actress's personal appeal. Joachim, on the other hand, had become thin and wizened. Much of the normal joy of life had been denied him by the activity of a particularly virulent stomach ulcer. This had sharpened his features and saddened his countenance. The flamboyant charm of previous years had been replaced by acid observation and pithy, ironic commentary.

'Cyril,' said Aunt Salina – for reasons only known to them both, she had called him 'Cyril' since their first acquaintance – 'you don't look the happiest of birthday heroes, I must say. What's the matter?'

'Headache,' said 'Cyril' with simple sincerity. He looked at her and he knew he was understood.

'Oh, but I have just the thing for that,' Salina replied. Cyril watched as Salina scratched in her tiny handbag for the thing she knew was there somewhere within its folds and crevices. After a moment she retrieved a very small pillbox and flicked it open with a dramatic flourish which, quite unconsciously, had become part of her way of doing things these days. The gesture exhibited two white minute round tablets. 'That's the end of the headache,' she pronounced firmly.

'And the end of me, too?' Cyril enquired playfully. 'Is this a woman's last resort – poison?'

'It could well be,' Salina replied with equal propriety. 'Are you going to take it like a man?'

Cyril looked suspiciously at the small thing she had emptied into his palm. He had known cases where such a diminutive object had indeed been the cause of instant death – sometimes, he had heard, to the accompaniment of the most appalling spasmic death throes. Cyril looked Salina in the eye.

'Somehow,' he said, 'I don't think you would want to accomplish the task here and now... I mean, not quite so publicly and on Marta's birthday. It would be acutely embarrassing, don't you think? Unless, of course ... the other one is for you.' He had not lost his old sense of humour, despite his pain.

'Aha,' said Aunt Salina, rising to the occasion, 'so now you have one of your professional quandaries; the lawyer's mind is hard at work on the legal ramifications of an issue. To take or not to take, that is the question; whether it is nobler in the mind to suffer the throbs and arrows of an outrageous headache or...' Cyril smiled weakly and swallowed the pill.

Through the net of time I see my younger sister, Corinne, her small, heart-shaped, sensitive face peeping from a cluster of neighbour's children, young people she has brought into the garden like young dogs, all screaming and giggling, flushed with excitement in all this heat. But what did it matter? They were welcome. All of them are about her age, twelve-year-olds full of fun and pranks, laughing and chattering and fluttering just like sparrows in a bush. I think of her. My sister. She was small for her age. Her little arms and legs have quickly become brown in this summer weather. I see her white ankle socks and the black shoes she wears for school, the school where she takes everything in her stride and where nothing is too difficult for her. There, she always receives great praise, but it does not change her character. Quiet and thoughtful, my little brown sister is a bookworm, an adult's head on her slight shoulders, quiet and calm, unhurried, unflustered, simple and wise. I have never known her angry or ill-tempered. She is never the slave of a mood

STILL LIFE, 1938

as we are, Sabina and I; she is never irritable, but not a saint either. While we, her other sisters, use occasional hurtful language in our daily deliberations with each other, she is always strangely controlled, but that very control coolly searches for the right word of scorn or contempt for our outbursts and her short words of criticism are deadly. Only now is she a child with other children. For a few moments, the wisdom and perception are abandoned for this gambolling frivolity. Is it not strange, these three sisters from the same womb, this small, gentle, sober, brown-eyed sage, Corinne, then Sabina, my elder sister, fair and blonde as a Scandinavian goddess with a northern warrior's temperament, strong, broad-hipped and broad busted, with azure blue eyes and her father's straight nose, characteristics which perfectly match the long, plaited, flaxen hair, Sabina with her downright, plain-spoken, robust manner. Nothing without passion with her. And then me, the girl in the middle, the dreamer, the poetry lover, the moon-gazer, my father's favourite, my mother's concern, and now the custodian of long memory.

The tinkling of a glass. My father.

'Ladies and Gentlemen!' Only gradually does the noise subside. Quite a lot of alcohol has flowed in glasses since early afternoon. 'First of all I want to thank you all for coming this afternoon to my daughter's party...' Someone is still talking and laughing. He recommences. 'Ladies and Gentlemen, Friends and Neighbours! I merely want to say that it is lovely to see you all here. Thank you for coming. Today, we have a musician in our midst, Mr Peter Horvac, who is going to play the violin for us.' My father hesitates. He is not used to public address and looks in Peter's direction in the hope that the musician will come forward now to relieve him of his dutiful introduction. He waits a moment as Peter tunes his instrument and adds, 'Mr Horvac will play us one of Beethoven's Romances, the one in G......' He forgets to say whether it is major or minor. At last, Peter comes forward and is cheered and applauded. Father seats himself and relief is written on his face.

When this enthusiastic response has died down, Peter plays. We watch and listen, enthralled. At the end of this performance we cheer and clap mightily and Peter is visibly less tense than he was a few minutes before. He plays again, but this time he walks among us as he plays. The piece is something lively, something, we suspect, that is Hungarian, and we are caught up by the rhythm. Somebody claps to the rhythm and others follow. Our virtuoso is delighted and begins to improvise in a manner which leaves us spellbound. Then, the clapping ebbs away. For a moment all thought of anything else in the world is lost in the infatuation of sound. All of us are captivated by the sound and by the dexterity of Peter's fingers. All of us in that one moment are of one mind. Even Mr and Mrs Goldman, have assumed for a moment the joyful aspect of youth, and when the refrain returns, they clap again happily with the rest of us; Peter and his music have captured us and enraptured us. The piece ends with vigour and humour. There is a resounding ovation. In the crowd which has gathered round him, people ask Peter whether he knows this or can play that and nodding his assent, he says, moving towards me: 'But what would our young hostess like to hear? Marta, you have first choice; it's your birthday, after all.'

I tell him and he plays again. I watch the slim fingers as they unerringly find the notes on the strings, the bow coaxing sound from what he calls his 'wooden box', the thing of wood and gum and varnish which is 125 years old and with which he can transport our souls. He smiles at his audience as he plays. Even Mrs Donat, who normally never stops talking, is enthralled by what she sees and hears and for a moment she is quite still. Ten minutes have already passed and no one has noticed the passage of time. When Peter has played the last note, for a second or two there is silence, so moved is his audience. Then a burst of enthusiastic clapping and shouts of 'Bravo!' and 'Encore!' from Sabina's friends. Peter plays again and again and again until the towers of the town glint like shooting points of red and yellow light as the sun begins to descend.

Evening. A few of us in the garden silently watch the red disk of the sun sink slowly and inexorably beyond the edge of the plain twenty miles away to the west. From time to time we can hear laughter issue from the open doors and windows of the house to which some of the guests have already retired. I think about my mother and my brother in Berlin, so far away from us all on my birthday. She will be thinking of us and smiling her warm smile. Mother said she would ring us, but as yet the old black telephone in the hall has not startled us with its shrill signal. It is a quarter to ten. Father, too, will be wondering why she has not contacted us. Mother is always the first to congratulate us on our birthdays. She will ring tomorrow. Yes, tomorrow she will call us, that's for sure. But why not today? Amid these thoughts of ours, the sun has sunk so far behind the horizon that only a short incandescent rim is visible above the hills of the Palatinate. After a few seconds, this, too, disappears.

A child's voice cries, 'Daddy, look, it's gone! It's gone to America!' The air is still very warm. About a dozen or so people sit at the two trestled tables among the debris of empty plates and glasses. Elfie has provided candlelight and as the darkness descends, faces are suddenly strongly illuminated by the light breeze which from time to time whispers among the trees. It is as though a spirit has moved them to say something, something earnest and urgent, a short ripple of consternation. Gregor's thin face, half in shadow, relates the story of his sister's death in January. They had been close all their lives and it was strange to see him alone today without her. His hearers are sympathetic. I cannot remember their names any more, only their umbered features, their tired, saddened faces in the flickering candlelight. 'It must have come as a great shock,' someone said.

'In the end it's always a shock, even if you're prepared for it. She knew she was going to die a few days before she actually passed away. It was strange. In fact, two days before – that would have been on the Monday – she had no pain at all and I thought she was cured. I really thought she was cured. It sometimes happens, you know. I was so pleased and told her so, but she only smiled at me patiently and said it wasn't long now and that at the end of the week I would have to do without her.' He paused in his narration. People nodded, and after a few seconds Gregory continued. 'On Thursday after lunch, I said I'd go out for a minute or two and buy cake for the afternoon so that we could enjoy it together on the veranda. She was pleased at the prospect and smiled in that resigned way of hers she had acquired in recent weeks. That smile made me feel like a small child. That was the way my mother smiled at me. I was only gone fifteen minutes. When I got back she had passed away.'

'How old was Lena when she died?' someone else asked.

'Forty-seven,' Gregor replied.

'That's no age today,' came a response in the darkness. A long silence clung to the group among the candles. Gregor retreated into the memory of that Thursday afternoon while the others were touched by the contemplation of death.

'Do you think there'll be a war?' Sylvia, my best friend, asked.

Father, who was sitting next to me, said, 'I don't think so, my dear,' and lit a cigar in complacent commemoration of a happy day and a successful party. 'This government can't last for many more months. A violent dictatorship in central Europe? Nobody's going to put up with that for long.'

Politics never interested me and my mind followed my idle

gaze across the garden. It fell upon the figure of Peter, who had ensconced himself comfortably on the balustrade of the three or four steps which turned from the terrace into the garden on its wooded side, steps which were hardly ever used. Everybody always used the steps on the other side. With the years moss and weed had competed for position there and dislodged the stones. The rising slab of the balustrade made a support for his back, while his knees were drawn up to his chest. He held a mug of beer with both hands and was very still. In the ordinary way of things I would have gone over to speak to him, the most natural thing to do in the world, but something held me back and I continued to stare. The dusk had blurred his outline, but the twilight figure spoke quite clearly of that ultimate aloneness which all of us will one day know and which occasionally accosts us even in the midst of life. Only half a dozen people were still in the garden by then. As I watched my friend, someone was talking loudly and uninhibitedly; the wine of the evening had suffused his brain. But Peter remained still in his corner, unaware that there was anyone nearby, unresponsive even to the gnat which bit his cheek, his gaze fixed on a spot before him. As I watched, a slight chill ran through my veins.

Gradually, around midnight, the last guests began to take their leave and I accompanied them down the steps to the road. There were hugs and farewells.

'It was a lovely party, Marta, thank you. Take care. See you again soon.'

'Yes, get home safely. Lovely to see you. I'm so glad you enjoyed yourselves.' The night and the knowledge that it was already Sunday morning had hushed our voices. 'Bye, dear, ... G'bye. G'bye.' Peter was among the very last to take his leave. I had forgotten him for a moment in attending to our guests. He looked tired but happy.

'I'll see you on Monday,' I said.

'Good, Monday in the university refectory, say about

midday?' I was pleased by his enthusiasm. We hastily kissed each other in the road before the last of our guests appeared at the iron gate.

'Until Monday,' I said. We hugged each other. Then, he walked off into the darkness, turning once to wave.

Returning to the garden, I found Elfie clearing the last of the plates from the tables, helped by Father, who folded the tablecloths and took them inside the house. The wind was in the trees again.

'Do you know, dear, I think it's going to rain,' Father announced, coming along the path from the house where the lights were still burning, including the two lights at each side of the front door which I loved so much and felt were so romantic. He did not wait for any comment on his remark, but turned to Elfie: 'What a help you've been to us all today, girl, I'm so grateful. I can only hope that you've enjoyed yourself as well.'

'Oh, yes, sir, it's been wonderful, thank you,' Elfie replied.

'It's we who have to thank you, I feel,' said Father with sincerity. 'I couldn't have managed all this on my own.' He gestured to what was left of the arrangements still on the grass. 'We'll leave everything now. I'm sure you're tired as well, despite your youth,' he said with a smile.

It was twelve forty-five when Elfie left to walk the short distance down the road to her grandmother's house. The first drops of rain began to fall ten minutes later. At one fifteen, Sabina kissed me and retired to her bedroom next to mine. Corinne was staying at the house of one of her friends. At one thirty the house was locked and in darkness. I opened my bedroom window to listen to the rain falling steadily outside and wondered where the birds and insects of the warm afternoon had found refuge. Seconds later, lightning cut the sky. The rain increased its speed and then thunder exploded above the house. Again and again the lightning. For some unreasonable reason I felt urged to leave the warmth of my bed and go out onto the landing to peep into the garden below. Thunder and lightning followed one another very closely and I knew that the centre of the storm was directly above the house. The flashes of lightning were so frequent that they lit up the garden with its bare tables in a sustained, savage brilliance. It was difficult to imagine that people had ever sat at them, enjoying the balmy peace of the afternoon, the friends, the food and wine, the conversation. Here was another world, another time a billion years before our world, a time before us and a time to be long after we are gone, a crashing, roaring time of elemental change and disaster where nothing is stable for long, where chaos is the slave of change. The trees were in turmoil, the garden awash in rain. So hard did the rain hammer the ground that water drops bounced six inches into the air after impact with the soil. The wind in its fury had turned over several chairs and cast them into the toiling bushes at the side of the garden. The air was full of sound, and was so loud that I could hardly have heard myself speak. Where were the others? Were they asleep or were they aware of this Armageddon all around them? Then, suddenly, I was overcome by an indescribable, inexplicable cloud of sadness which was almost palpable as I stood there alone on the landing. The feeling was so intense that for a moment – I don't know for how long – it totally eclipsed the noise and rage outside. All that was left was a small keyhole of consciousness like a very small source of light at the end of a long tunnel. It was as though for a moment or two I had died. Only gradually, like early-morning sun lifting mist, did it begin to subside, and as it did so I knew with absolute certainty that this was my last night in this beloved house. With the same certainty I knew, too, I would never see it again nor any one of those who had come to wish me well on my twentieth birthday. And so it was.

16

Vincenzo

I had arrived in the late afternoon at this bar which, like many French bars, you could walk right into from the street. Not much of a place, grubby, litter on the floor, blokes propping up the counter; smoke, an air of mild curiosity on the few faces turned my way. Two fifty-year-olds were noisily playing cards at one end. Evening sunshine had struck the glasses at the back of the bar. The man behind the counter raised his chin slightly in inquiry as I approached.

'I was told to come here,' I said and added, 'someone said that you had an apartment.'

'Gone,' he said simply, his brown eyes assessing me quickly.

'I'm a student,' I continued, 'need a place to stay. Thought you might know of somewhere.' He nodded. I hovered for a second or two. 'Thanks,' I said, and turned to go.

'Wait! I do know one place,' he said, leaving me for a moment to serve a customer. Then, returning, 'Rue de Marriot, No. 4 ... or 6, I'm not sure, it's not difficult to find. Not far from here,' and he indicated the direction briefly through the greasy glass panes of the bistro. 'About two hundred yards. Upstairs. Landlord's name is Cretille. Fat bloke.' I returned to the hot street outside, shouldered my backpack more comfortably, and took the route the barman had shown me. I found the place easily after a few minutes. No. 6.

ALPHONSE CRETILLE
AVOCAT

I climbed the dim stairway to the third floor and rang the bell. No answer. I rang again. Then, heavy footsteps behind the door. After a moment's interval it opened to reveal a very large man who still had a serviette tied round his neck. I had obviously interrupted him during a meal. Not a very good sign. He looked at me without speaking, sized me up as an intruder. I felt it was my turn to play.

'I'm sorry to have interrupted you,' I began.

'What do you want?' he enquired, cutting me off.

'An apartment,' I shot back. 'One room'll do.' He did not answer immediately, but continued to look me up and down without speaking. I asked myself in a flush of embarrassment how long I was going to put up with this, but at the same moment realised that it was already late in the evening and chose to be patient.

'You're a foreigner?' he asked in the same blunt manner. He seemed short of breath, too.

'Yes, English.'

'Ugh,' he said, not in an unfriendly way, this time, but comprehending. 'What are you doing here?' he then asked.

'Studying geology,' I replied breezily.

'Stones?' he said.

'Yes,' I said. There was a pause.

'Ain't there enough in the United Kingdom, then?' he asked, and seeing me pause for a moment to think about that one, he burst into chesty laughter before I could answer. 'Come in, come in!' he then said airily, changing his manner like an actor, and opened the door for me to enter. I went in and he followed me into a very large, high-ceilinged room, closing the door with a bang behind us. After a few steps I stopped and turned, but he said, 'Do go in and sit down, please!' He waved a fat hand towards a voluminous chair next to his at the table and came straight to the point.

'I can't offer you much, young man. If you want you can cut your expenses and stay with another young feller here. Would that be all right? Reduce the cost of things a bit; Marseille is not a cheap place to live, you know.' I nodded. 'Two hundred francs a month. Pay your own heating and light. Water's free. Furnished. All you want.' He stopped to catch his breath. An asthmatic. Then he coughed briefly two or three times, his several chins wobbling as he did so. 'Good, good. Like people who can make up their minds. The other young fellow is upstairs now. I won't come up with you,' he said, rising, 'too many stairs. Introduce yourself and if you like it, come down again in the next fifteen minutes or so and let me know. If you don't come back, I'll know you don't want it. Payment on the first of the month.' He coughed again and moved towards the door, looking at me suddenly in the frank way he had when he asked questions and made statements.

'Sounds good,' I said, 'and thank you.' He coughed again and nodded between attempts to breathe properly, but was obviously pleased about my decision.

The stairs to the next two floors were steeper than the lower ones and I was quite glad to reach the bell of App. 10. 'V. Graccini', the bell strip announcing its present occupant. 'Italian,' I noted and pressed the bell. It was some moments before the door was opened, and then, rather gingerly. A chain held the door ajar. The face that appeared over this was lean and close shaven, topped by smooth, very black hair, sleek as fur, greased and firmly brushed back from the forehead. The face smiled. It was not the custom to smile at strangers here and it revealed a row of small, even white teeth.

'Eh?' the young man enquired.

'The old boy downstairs sent me up here. Says there's a room.' The chain was lifted and the door opened wider. The smooth head gestured me to enter. I found myself in the company of a young man of about my own age, about twenty-three or twenty-four. Without another word, he closed the door and motioned me to follow him along the corridor and silently indicated a room off this narrow gangway. I looked at him as though to say 'Can I go in?' and he nodded again. It was a large room, airy and light with two largish windows in it, one of which gave onto the sea beyond, and, I noticed with pleasure, it was partially furnished. The bed was sturdy and made up. In one corner there was an ample washbasin. I looked around and saw a cupboard for my things. Compared with the doss-downs I had experienced over the last two years, it was four-star. I turned to my companion at the door.

'Anyone else live here?'

He shook his head very slightly and said, 'Nope, just me.'

'It's OK,' I said.

'It's OK,' he replied quietly.

'My name's Sid,' I said, offering my hand. 'I'd like to join you.'

'Vincenzo,' he said and nodded two or three times like a Chinese sage. His black eyes fell on me for a second. They were sharp and quick. In a fraction of a second, snick, snack, the mind behind them cut through whatever veneer I might have had in those days. Cold steel cut to the quick, missing nothing, in seconds calculating everything, weighing, assessing, cool, efficient, deadly. He took just long enough for me to feel a little uncomfortable. Then, as quick as a light is switched on, he smiled again and the brief hostility of the eyes had vanished. His manner changed suddenly to that of a comrade.

'Come into the kitchen,' he said, laying a hand on my shoulder. 'You can chuck your stuff in here. You gotta room, friend. Coffee?' He went over to the small sink and busied himself with the coffee percolator. The kitchen, too, looked out towards the sea about a mile away. A door stood open to a narrow balcony on which I could see a table and two chairs.

'Splendid view from here,' I said.
'Oh yeah, it's good,' he said, but as though he had only half heard me. The coffee was placed on the table. It was good. 'So you wanna stay for a while?' my partner asked, seating himself at the table.
'Got to finish my studies,' I said. 'Two years still.'
'But you ain't French...' he said tentatively.
'No, I'm English,' I replied. 'Hope you don't mind.'
He smiled broadly at this. 'God, no, why should I? I got nothing against English folks. You're the first English bloke I've ever met in my life,' he said. 'Yessir, the very first one, goddamn me.' And he giggled like a schoolgirl at this, spilling some of his coffee. I wondered what amused him, and sat there just looking. This seemed only to amuse him all the more. 'God save the King!' he said in English with – it was astonishing – a slightly upper-class flourish, so that I had to smile too.
'It's the Queen now,' I corrected him. 'It's 1955.'
'Ah yes, you're right. Goddamn right,' he declared and laughed out loud. 'God save the Queen!' he said, with the same brilliance as before. 'But you speak French pretty well,' he observed, and the quiet, cool, keen eye was suddenly there again.
'Yes, thank you. I've been here for five years already and learned a bit at school, too.'
'That's great,' he said, clearly impressed. 'Not many Englishmen speak other languages, and their French is usually pretty rotten I've heard,' he noted. He poured himself some more coffee. 'And you're studying what?'
I told him and enlarged on the subject a bit out of politeness.
'Not my thing,' he concluded before I could finish. There was a slight pause.
'What do you do yourself?' I enquired.
'I work down at the docks,' he replied simply and fell to biting his nails. We sat for a while longer, saying nothing to

each other. Somehow I did not want to probe further; I had the feeling he did not want to open up. He then said he would show me the whole apartment. It was large.

'How come the bed's made up?' I asked. 'Did you have an idea I was coming?' He smiled at this, a flashing, engaging, brief smile, the head slightly down, as some children smile when they feel unsure of themselves. Charming, the smile.

'No, that's for my girlfriend, Anna. You'll meet her sometime,' he said with satisfaction. 'She's OK. Then she'll either sleep with me or use the other room. The sheets are freshly laundered,' he added. 'It's OK for you to sleep in them.' Everything was clean and orderly. It was not like all the chaos I had experienced everywhere else, including youth hostels and university accommodation. Everything neat and tidy. Even dusted. I turned.

'Thanks.' I said warmly, patting the bed appreciatively. 'This is great.'

'Good,' he said absently. He had turned me off again. We passed a little bathroom on our way back to the kitchen. Again, I noticed that everything was spick and span. Without turning to address me, he said, 'When your door's open, I know you're in. When it's closed, I know you don't want to be disturbed or you're out. Understand?'

'Okay,' I said.

'I guess you'd better go tell Fatso you're interested. He goes to bed early.'

'Good idea,' I said.

'Good idea!' he echoed. 'That's real British, man,' and he was amused again. '*Bonne idée!*' he said again, and went on into the kitchen while I turned to go downstairs. I was sure that we'd get on well. At least he seemed to have a sense of humour, I thought to myself as I went downstairs a few moments later to inform my host that I'd take the place. Monsieur Cretille was pleased and formalities of my residence were completed.

VINCENZO

'Don't forget to register with the police. We don't want any trouble,' he said with a blubbery smile. These were his last words before I reclimbed the stairs to rejoin Vincenzo.

When I returned to my room I found a radio placed at the side of the bed and a few things taken out of the room that were his own property. I appreciated the radio. Returning to the kitchen, I found Vincenzo preparing something to eat. He asked whether I was hungry. Then he said, 'What's your second name, Sid?'

'Mathers,' I told him. 'What?' I repeated my name. The 'th' defeated him and he wasn't going to risk anything, so he looked at me in mock disgust that anyone should rejoice in such a foolish name and placed the cutlery on the table. When the meal came it was tasty. He was a good cook. He set to without another word. As we ate our meal I noticed that his hands were rough and scarred, especially at the knuckles, and that he had another ugly scar on his right forearm. We finished the meal in silence. Somehow his bearing forbade me to make small talk and I wondered what he was thinking. After the meal, he rose and washed the dishes conscientiously, cleaning up the sink later like an experienced housewife, even hanging the dishcloth outside on the balcony rail to dry in the late-evening sun.

'You're a good cook, Vincenzo, thanks for the meal – and the radio. Nice of you.' He merely nodded to this and I waited for a few more moments for him to say something by way of conversation, but instead he settled to read a magazine, leaving me entirely to my own devices. Turning to go back to my room, I said, 'I'll go and unpack.' He nodded again without a word.

The next morning I rose early, but Vincenzo had already gone. I helped myself to some cornflakes and milk and took them to the balcony to munch in the open air. It would be another very hot day. Soon the term would be over. What a change this was to the other place I had! I congratulated myself again. I was so pleased with my good luck. After I had raided the fridge for a second time, I began to wonder about my companion once more. What did he do down there at the harbour? His manner was not that of someone my own age. Mentally, he was decades older than I was. He had somehow skipped his twenties, I thought, and was already well into his thirties in everything he did. It was strange. Maybe it was a good thing. I had wasted a lot of my time with kids, this girl and that pal, drank into the night, neglected my studies and thought more about billiards than buffing for exams. It was high time I got down to a bit of work. An 'older' companion would be good for me. Only ... he wasn't a day older than I was. Then the phone rang. At first I decided not to answer it. But it continued to ring as though the person at the other end knew the place was occupied. At last, thinking it to be Vincenzo, I picked up the receiver. 'Allo?' The line clicked to the engaged tone and I hung up.

That morning I did quite a lot of work and was pleased with myself around lunchtime. Around 1.30 p.m. I went downstairs in search of food. I was hungry again. A pizza at the local Italian restaurant around the corner was very convenient and after that I set off to the post office bank to settle my modest finances. Mid-afternoon and very hot, even for August. I sauntered towards the city centre with no particular objective in mind, consoling myself with the thought that I had done enough for one day. I needed a drink, a long, cool drink. After a little foot-slogging I found a place, went in, settled at a table and picked up a newspaper someone had left behind, and so read for a while without a care in the world. I had sat there for about an hour, I think, when I heard a row going on outside. I looked up over the edge of the newspaper to see three young men arguing noisily on the other side of the street. One was sitting in a large red sports car. It was Vincenzo. The row grew so heated that the waiter paused in his rounds for a moment to look over the road. Others in the bistro, too, looked across at what was going on with some concern. Newspapers were laid aside for a second or two and coffee cups replaced on saucers. Bad language assaulted the air. Amid a sudden burst of fury, the red car then screamed off, leaving the two others in a swirl of tyre muck and fumes. The two well-dressed men stood where they were for a little longer, gesticulating, their gaze following the retreating car before they turned to go. After leaving the café, I browsed in a book shop before going back to the apartment, and when I returned at about six in the evening, I discovered Vincenzo busy again in the kitchen. I didn't mention the fact that I had seen him that afternoon. But a few days later, the two men I had seen that day turned up at the door of the apartment. They meant business.

'He's not in,' I said, but they roughly pushed me aside and began to comb the apartment, my room included. I kept out of their way.

When they had finished their search, one of them turned to me angrily and said, 'What are you doin' here?' The other stood menacingly at my side.

'I'm a student; I share the place.'

'Where is he?'

I told them that I had only been here for a day or so and had seen Vincenzo about twice in that time.

They stood looking at me for a moment, weighing me up, and then the older one said, 'Here, telephone number. You tell him to ring as soon as he gets back. Straight away. Understand?' He grasped my shirt in a tight fist above my breast pocket. The knuckles dug into my ribs. 'Understand?'

I understood. They left, leaving the door open, and I heard their footsteps as they negotiated the curve of the stairs. They were in a hurry. I waited until they were on the street and then went inside and tidied up the mess. I left Vincenzo's room as it was. My friend didn't return for a week, and when he did appear again he was barely able to stand. He staggered into the apartment as I clicked the door to. I didn't ask him any questions, told him about the visit and gave him the telephone number. He waved his hand to one side as though to say it was no longer important.

'What are they after?' I asked.

'Me,' he said, lowering himself very, very carefully into a chair.

'But they were looking for something, too.'

'Yeah, yeah,' he said quietly, passing a hand gently over his knee. 'I fixed them – they won't be coming back, so don't you worry. I'm sorry, boy, you got involved with that riff-raff.'

'It's OK,' I said, 'they didn't do anything to me, but you don't seem to be in very good shape. If there is anything I can do, just say the word.' I stood there in the kitchen as the huge red sun went down into the sea and I felt silly and isolated. He looked at me sharply from his low position in the chair, as sharply as he had done a week or so before, and then he winced in pain. I noticed that he hadn't shaved for some time, which was unlike him. If I had learned anything of my partner it was that he was scrupulous in such things. I wondered where he'd been. Seconds passed.

'Want anything to eat?' I asked a bit foolishly. He waited some time before answering and it was obvious that it was all he could do to speak. A minute or two later, when I tried to make coffee for us I realised that he could not get out of his chair. He tried twice and then passed out. How the hell had he managed all those stairs? I went to the sink, got some water and splashed it into his face. 'Vincenzo! Come to! Hey! You need help, Vincenzo!' I tried to manoeuvre him into a more comfortable position and felt my hand slither in blood.

'Vin...!!' He half opened his eyes. 'Hell, man, what the shit have you been doing? You're bleeding like a stuck pig.

Try and get out of this damned chair and we'll see what's up. Come on, I'll help. Heave...'

He mustered all that was left in him and half got to his feet. More he couldn't do and he collapsed immediately onto the kitchen floor with a moan.

Luckily, I had been a medical orderly during my time in the army on a two-year stint of military service and so had some idea of what to do in this situation. I removed his light jacket with difficulty and then his shirt and saw a deep wound in his side. It was so deep that I could see his liver, and boy, was I scared. Blood everywhere. There were clean tea cloths in a drawer and I seized these to staunch the blood flowing easily from the wound. To my surprise he had recovered consciousness once more in the meantime and must have been observing me.

'It's not so bad, Sid. Strap it up, that's all. Nothing new.' Then he passed out again.

I laid his head comfortably to one side on one of the cushions we had in the lounge and ran for another tea towel. I prayed that it was reasonably clean and pressed the edges of the wound together. An hour passed while Vincenzo alternately came to and then once more lost consciousness. It began to get dark. After a time he came round again and I gave him water to drink. He was very thirsty.

'Vincenzo,' I whispered, 'this needs professional treatment. I'm taking a risk.'

He looked at the towel and then at me. His eyes were glazing. 'No treatment,' he stammered. 'You treat.' And he passed out again for the fifth time since he had arrived home.

After another hour the bleeding had almost stopped, but he had not returned to consciousness and I began to wonder in panic whether he had died. Too scared to take his pulse, I flew down the stairs and out into the street in search of a chemist on night duty. The first one I came across had an announcement in the window: 'Pharmacie "La Plantaine", rue

Général Jarreau'. It was half a mile from the apartment. Forty francs for bandages, antiseptic and medical tape. It was 9.45 in the evening by the time I got back and I wondered as I leapt up the stairs like a madman what I'd find at the top. I burst through the door and into the kitchen and found that he had moved himself slightly and was conscious, but the bleeding had started again. He had recovered slightly and looked at me in his sharp way, as sharp as he could in his condition.

'Where've you been?' he asked weakly.

'Chemist's. Bandages.' He smiled his playboy smile weakly.

'You gotta keep still,' I said. 'Very still, otherwise it'll start all over again. The bleeding.' I pointed at his torso.

He nodded. Then he said, 'Ring Anna. Number over the sink.' It took me some time to find it and then I rang his girlfriend.

'Come over,' I said, 'it's urgent.'

The girl at the other end was silent for a moment or two. Then she asked what was wrong and whether there were other people there and I thought this was rather strange. So I said, 'There is just the two of us here. It's important. Please, come quickly. Bring a first-aid kit.' And before I could say anything else she had hung up on me. I turned to Vincenzo on the floor.

'You got tact. Bully boy,' he said almost in a whisper. And he nodded as best as he could on the floor in that sage way of his.

About twenty minutes later, the door bell went.

'Don't go yet!' Vincenzo ordered as I sprang to my feet. I looked at him, astonished. 'Listen!' I listened. There was a regular three-beat tap on the door. 'That's her,' he said, 'open it now.' I looked at him. 'We got to be careful, you know,' he said, trying hard to smile.

* * *

VINCENZO

In the weeks that followed, Anna and I got our friend through until he could walk again. We took turns to nurse him night and day. While he slowly slept himself well again, I had to stay put and the opportunity to study was handed to me on a plate. Not only had the patient been stabbed, he had also fractured his foot. Somehow we managed to treat this too, not very expertly, with the result that he had a slight limp from that time on. Anna was a good nurse and it was lucky for Vincenzo that she worked as a doctor's assistant in the town and so could smuggle stuff out of the surgery that we needed to attend to the patient.

One evening a few days after her arrival, when Vincenzo was asleep, I asked, 'What do you think could have happened?'

'The same old thing,' she said irritably. I looked blank. 'He's in it up to his eyes. That's why he gets injured. He shoots and stabs and kills.' She said this with an air of angry resignation.

'Kills?' I said incredulously.

'Yes, he murders and causes grievous bodily harm, that's what he does, and I'm getting sick of the whole damn thing.' It was early evening and we were sitting in the small kitchen. The evening sun illuminated the woman's fine features and the wealth of golden hair that she had recently cut shorter without first consulting her beau, much to his displeasure. She had blue eyes, too, which were the exception in these parts, and as well as having everything else in the right place and plenty of it, she was intelligent and practical. Vincenzo was very jealous and kept her on a short lead. But while she enjoyed being desired, Anna was nevertheless an independent spirit. She looked at me frankly for a long moment, hoping that the full import of what she had said would sink in. But I was too stupefied to say anything else or think about it either, so instead I continued to wonder what the hell was going on. At last, she said with a rueful smile, 'But what would you know anyway as a student? Keep to your geology or whatever it is and don't get involved with him.' And she nodded in the direction of Vincenzo's bedroom. I felt distinctly uncomfortable.

Not long after this, and having almost quite recovered, Vincenzo went to stay at Anna's place. He could get about quite well now and I was glad of the break. It was October and the term had started. For me it was going to be a hard one and already work was piling up prior to the exams. During my labours at the little desk which I had provided for myself, I often looked out to sea and wondered again about what Anna had said. Time had not eroded the sharpness of her remarks. Did he really kill, and if so, how did he get away with it and why did he kill? This thought popped up again and again in my mind like the bell that rang the quarters of every hour of the day and night at a church nearby. Why? Of course, I could find a new place; that wouldn't be too difficult, but the apartment was a boon. Anywhere else would certainly be worse than here. I pondered. Anxiety and insecurity alternated with one another. Who did he kill? Would I be the next perhaps?

A month passed and no sign of Vincenzo. The telephone was as still as if disconnected. One night I decided to lift the receiver for fun just to see if it was in fact still working and got a shock. A thick voice said in some surprise, 'Signore Graccini? Ecco Salvatore Basta. Allo... Allo...' I hung up. It gave me a turn to realise that I had at that very moment intercepted a call after weeks of silence. There had been urgency in the voice, too. I looked at the telephone a long time as if it were alive, anticipating a ring any moment. But it didn't ring. I made myself some coffee.

Three days later, I came back in the evening around midnight after a party to find the place had been burgled. Literally everything had been turned over, thrown about, taken to pieces, emptied – even the washing powder had been tipped from its carton into the sink. The place looked like the town dump. Even my books had been taken from their place, scrutinised, and I noticed that things had been spread out on the floor before having been abandoned. There was evidence of method, and whoever it was had taken time over the job and had had no fear of being disturbed. Either this person knew about my timetable or was armed. A chill ran down my spine and cold sweat pearled on my forehead. I had never known fear before I came to this house and the experience made me feel that I wanted to vomit. Every room had been ransacked but nothing removed as far as I could tell. I stood there in the dead of night and wondered whether to wake Monsieur Cretille. Where the hell was Vincenzo? After all, he was the principal tenant in this place! The rest of the hours before dawn I spent at the railway station and tramping the streets of the town. And the next few nights I spent at the house of a student who lived with his parents in the city and returned three days later with him to clear up the place. It took the two of us four hours. He and his folks said it was my responsibility to inform the police, but again I hesitated and another week passed.

Then, one evening, around seven thirty, I heard steps on the stairs. Seconds later, a key in the door. It was Vincenzo, very smartly dressed, even sporting a tie. He wore new shoes and was in the best of moods. Slamming the door behind him, he breezed down the small corridor towards the kitchen. Coming up to me, he smiled broadly.

'*Salut, mon ami!*' We shook hands. I smiled back, pleased to find him looking so well after his ordeal.

'Long time, no see, my friend. Where have you been so long then?' I asked.

'Anna's place,' he said throwing himself into an old chair.

'Great!' Then I told him of the burglary, at which his black eyes narrowed. 'I've left everything as it was in your room again. I didn't want to interfere. Sorry.' He looked at me for a moment longer. That look. And then his face broke into a smile like the sun coming out and spreading over a summer field.

'That's OK. Good. OK...' He paused for another moment as he had done once before. 'I like you,' he said at last. 'You're really intelligent. And you don't shoot your mouth off either. Anna thinks you're OK, too. You've got good nerves. Did you inform the boys in blue about the break-in?'

'No, I didn't. I thought it best to...'

'You see,' he said with conviction, 'I said you're really smart. Got tact. Keeps mum. Anna was right about you.'

'Thank you, sir,' I said. 'We geologists are all pretty intelligent.'

He leapt to his feet. 'Come, you old rogue,' he laughed, and at that happy moment he looked really handsome, like Rudolph Valentino. 'I've come to take you out to dinner.' I hesitated.

'Don't you want to look at the mess in your room first?' I asked.

'That can wait,' he said. 'First attend to the needs of the inner man. That's what my mama used to say. When your belly's full you can tackle life better. Come on, I know a good place.'

'Wait!' I said. 'I've got no money at the moment. Gotta wait till the end of the month before the bank coughs up with the grant. That's in a week's time.'

'Aw, come on, stop it, you nitwit,' he said and grabbed my arm.

'No, geologist,' I countered. We laughed.

'Come on, I'm paying for it. You're invited. *Invited.*' He spelled the word out. And then we were out down the stairs within a minute, he flying before me down the steps past the lawyer's apartment where he paused a moment to cock a snook at the door and then on down, laughing, into the street. Automatically, I turned to the right to go into town when he said, 'Here, this way,' and he signalled a bright red car parked at the kerb. 'Go in style,' he said and hopped over the side into the driver's seat. I followed. We then drove to one of the town's best restaurants, where we were received like honoured guests by an unctuous head waiter and shown to a table with extravagant courtesy. I felt slightly out of place in my student's get-up. The place oozed with affluence.

'This'll cost you an arm and a leg,' I said under my breath.

'Forget it,' he said and accepted the menu offered him by another waiter who seemed to understand my embarrassment.

'And the wine list,' this waiter announced with a flourish and placed the list on the table before us. We could, he said, choose something appropriate to the occasion.

Vincenzo played the part of a nonchalant millionaire's son as he informed the waiter of his tastes in food and wine while I played a very humble second fiddle. Seeing this, when the waiter had gone, Vincenzo whispered, 'Sid, it's all right. You don't have to pay for anything. Now just sit back and enjoy yourself. Everything's on me. Everything. Understand?' He was very fond of this word 'understand' in the interrogative mood. I nodded. The wine arrived and was sampled. 'Good,' Vincenzo said enthusiastically. '*Excellente.*' And he raised his glass slightly to the waiter in acknowledgement.

'You seem to have come into money,' I said. 'Has a relative died recently?'

'No, sir, work. Earned it. All my own work.' He put his elbow on the table to reveal an expensive wristwatch and beamed at me across the table. 'And thanks to you, I'm alive and kicking. So that's why you don't have to worry about the meal, old Sid, because I owe it to you.'

'You don't owe me anything,' I said quickly. 'Anna got you through during these weeks and swerved you through a lot of impending trouble – the burglary and old man Cretille grousing about not being paid, coming up and complaining about the rent being six weeks overdue.'

'Oh yeah, Cretille, gotta pay him sometime, I suppose,' Vincenzo said sullenly.

'Don't worry,' I said, 'I've paid him. My dad sent me some money and I paid him from that, but old Cretille thought he'd been cheated and that you'd left him without paying.'

'You paid him? God, you're a friend! Thanks – and you're cluck-clucking about this lot.' He indicated the restaurant. 'How much did you pay him?'

'About three hundred francs in all. The water for last month was included. I don't know how much that was. It was correct anyway.'

'Good lad,' Vincenzo said with warm appreciation. He leaned back in his chair and surveyed me for a long moment, then he pulled out a new wallet, plucked from it five hundred francs from a wad of five hundreds and handed it to me.

'I've got no change on me,' I said.

'Don't want any,' he said simply. 'You've earned it.'

'But two hundred francs...!' I protested.

'Forget it!' He made a gesture as if to indicate that I should behave myself and that we were in a posh restaurant where it wasn't usual to raise one's voice. The meal arrived.

The meal and the wine did much to bridge the estrangement of several weeks and smoothed over the discomforting events of our acquaintanceship.

'I must say you made an incredible recovery,' I said at last. 'I thought you were a goner. It was a pretty nasty wound you had, you know.'

'Yeah, bad do. She got a doctor in the end, you know. Had to. Delirium. Either that or I push up the daisies, she said when I came round from time to time.' I nodded. 'Tell you the truth, I didn't care one way or the other in the end,'

Vincenzo continued, 'but the doc said that someone had done a good job in the first place. Otherwise I would have pegged it. That was you, boy.' I felt embarrassed.

'Well, I did what had to be done at that moment, that's all, and I'm glad you survived to tell me what happened.' He smiled his angelic smile. 'And who's Salvatore Basta?' I enquired. The smile vanished.

'What the hell does he want. He telephoned?'

I told Vincenzo the story and he appeared relieved. Then, 'He's not important. Lawyer. You didn't tell him anything?'

'What could I have told him? It's just as I told you now. I don't know anything about your extra-mural activities anyway, what could I have told him?'

'My *what* activities?'

'Doesn't matter. University term, means what you do outside the university walls.'

'Ugh,' he said and continued, 'so you put the phone down just like that?'

'Yep, just like that; I didn't want to get involved.'

'Involved in what?' Vincenzo asked sharply.

'Well, I dunno, do I? I don't know where you go or what you do. You told me you work down at the docks. That's enough for me. The rest is not my business.'

Vincenzo fell silent.

'Like my new watch?' he enquired after a moment or so.

'Yes, it's very nice. Must have cost you a packet – or is it on loan?' I said playfully.

'On loan? Ah ... you like your little joke, don't you? I've been told that English folks have a curious sense of humour.' He smiled. 'No, friend, this is genuine.' He said this expansively and basked for a moment in my admiration. Then, 'Do you want one too?'

'What, a Rolex? Damn me, I'd look really daft wearing one of those things in the lecture hall. Folks'd think I was showing off.' He looked hurt for a second. So I added, 'Yes,

I know they're expensive; everybody's taste is different. Wouldn't suit me as a student, you see.'

'What about for best wear?' he urged. 'You could wear it for special occasions, not for school.'

'University,' I corrected him.

'Well, yeah, university then. Anyway, what do you actually *do* there? I mean looking at stones all day must be a hell of a bore,' he probed.

'On the contrary, Signore Graccini, it's very interesting; stones tell us about the history of the world and that's a revelation, I can tell you.' He was listening, alert, attentive. I continued, 'Stones tell you when and how everything came into being. How everything happened, like looking at the rings of a felled tree. You know what summers were hot and what the winters were like and what the tree experienced during them. And there are cross-references, too. You know what happened to plant and animal life, discover fossils and the like, and later up a rock scale you can find evidence of human activity as well.'

'You talk like a professor,' he said. 'Still, it's interesting. *Continuez-vous, s'il vous plaît, monsieur le professeur.*' So I told him a bit about geological time and compared this with the more or less four thousand years of our civilisation. 'So it's not true what they tell you in church about the world being created in seven days by God and all that shit?' he said.

'That's not science, but the Bible,' I replied.

'So it's not true,' he concluded.

'It's a bit odd,' I hedged, not wanting to get involved.

'I knew they were lying,' Vincenzo said with emphasis. 'People are always lying. You can't trust them for a moment. But your stones don't lie; they can't lie, can they? My mother never lied to me, but she's the only person I know who doesn't.' He said this with such quiet conviction that I felt blocked for a moment.

Then I said, 'I'm sure Anna doesn't lie either, or what do you think? She's very fond of you,' I added.

'All women lie,' he replied as the dessert appeared on the table. 'And what do you know about Anna anyway?'

'She seems a good girl to me,' I said.

'She's got good tits,' Vincenzo said and attacked his ice cream without further comment.

About a month after this dinner it was the end of semester and the beginning of the Easter holidays and as always a critical time for me since I had to get a job in order to sustain myself. I mentioned this to Vin (he had agreed to this American-style abbreviation in the meantime).

'*Non è un problema,* young man,' he said. 'I can get you a job.'

'Where?' I asked.

'Down near the waves of course,' he said with a gesture which signified that I was little versed in the ways of the world.

'Can you get me one there?'

'Of course!' he said as though it was the simplest thing in the world. But I knew it was very difficult to get work as a foreigner and jobs were rare anyway. 'You've got a job. What would you like to do, pen-push or a real man's work?'

'I guess a bit of exercise wouldn't do me much harm as I've been sitting around a lot these past weeks,' I said.

'Good. It shall be done,' he said. And it was done. As soon as the semester officially ended I had a job. Down at the docks. Following Vincenzo's advice, I went to the dockyard office and presented myself. A Monsieur Demartre gave me instructions to start the next day as if I had made a formal application weeks before. He seemed to know everything about me that was necessary and I did not even receive a formal contract, but merely signed my name to a strip of paper which stated how much I would earn. I was to start at six in the morning the next day and report in Warehouse 23 to a certain Monsieur Cillon. It was odd. The work was hard and the hours were long, but the pay was good and Cillon proved to be a fair-minded guy. There were plenty of breaks for coffee (alcohol being forbidden because of the danger of accidents, though it was drunk nevertheless), and as the weeks passed, my body adapted itself to continued hard physical work.

Vincenzo had been absent for some time from the apartment, but one day as I was crossing the compound while at work down at the docks I heard his voice say behind me, 'Hi there, how is Mr Professor today?' The voice came from the cab of a forty-ton truck. I walked over to it. The engine was idling and he looked down at me cheekily. 'Like the job?' he asked.

'Sure I do. Did you have a hand in getting me the work?' I asked over the noise of the engine.

'Yeah, got a few friends here.'

'But it was so easy,' I said. 'Nobody asked any questions. I just walked into the job, just like that. Impossible!' He smiled.

'You were lucky; my mates don't take easily to geologists.' He smiled his Valentino smile, saluted and shoved his monster into first gear.

From about that time onwards I had the apartment largely to myself. Vin turned up every ten days or so. Sometimes he would drop me a card from Paris or Milan or wherever he happened to be at the time, informing me in his small, very precise handwriting of the weather and the view and other trivia. These cards were quaint, so that at first I thought it was a joke, but I later learned that the card carried no insinuation. This, for him, was what a postcard should contain. Then he would be at our place once more with stuff which had 'dropped off the truck', food, wine in abundance, a brand-new radio or a camera, fruit and vegetables galore, and once a powerful pair of binoculars which he handed to me in his gallant way. I pulled a face.

'I can't take them, Vin, thanks.' He looked hurt and surprised.

'What d'ye mean? I'm *giving* it to you.' Anger was visible in his neck.

'Yes, it's nice of you. Nice to think of me. But I can't accept it.'

'Why not?' This flatly and loud. I sighed.

'Because it's stolen property, Vin.'

'Stolen? Who's stolen anything?' He was suddenly very angry. That was the way with him and I knew I had to be careful.

'Well, it doesn't belong to you nor to me,' I said hastily, trying to rectify the situation with a shrug.

'Are you calling me a thief, then?' he demanded, coming nearer, looking me in the eye, very close to my face.

'Look, Vin, it's not my place to judge you, or anyone for that matter…'

'No, it bloody well isn't, you student punk. Who the fuck do you think you are?' I rose to go to my room, but as I was about to walk out of the place he grabbed my shirt violently and shoved me up against the wall. Our faces were very close together, his eyes were cold, reptilian. 'Look, mister, I don't argue with people. I hurt people. Understand?' Although I was taller and heavier than he was and now fitter than I had ever been in my life before, I felt at the moment that the issue wasn't worth an escalation into bloodshed. And what's more, I knew that he always carried a very sharp flick knife with him.

'OK,' I said, 'keep your hair on. There was no offence intended anyway. I can't take anything like that, that's all.' He looked at me for a long, long time, his fist still on my chest, and then gave me a final shove against the wall and turned away to bite his nails in a corner of the kitchen. He utterly ignored me. I went to my room and for once locked the door.

The next morning to my surprise he was in the kitchen around breakfast time. It was Sunday. Usually he left early to join Anna on a Sunday or even disappeared on a Saturday night. I nodded to him.

'Hi,' I said briefly, and helped myself to cereal and milk and was on my way out to eat this in my room when he said, 'Hey, Sid, what's up with you this morning? You look as miserable as a fish on a slab.'

'Small wonder,' I replied, 'you did plenty last night to cheer us both up.'

'Oh, that,' he said with exaggerated dismissal. 'That was nothing. I'm like that.' He smiled his smile. 'Thou shalt not bear malice,' he added.

'I'll be more careful with you next time,' I said. At this he looked utterly crestfallen. I fiddled in the cutlery tray for a spoon and noticed that the kitchen had been cleaned. Turning again, I looked at him and almost laughed. He sat there like a small child wondering what it had done to deserve chastisement. 'Come, Vin, don't pretend. You were pretty unpleasant last night. Everyone has got a right to his own opinion about things, or don't you think so?'

'Sure.'

'Well then.'

'It wasn't like that.'

'Oh *no*?'

'No.'

We looked at each other in silence. Then he said, 'It was you trying to make out that I was a thief.' Immediately I foresaw the possibility of another row flashing up, so I said with emphasis, 'Well, that *wasn't* what I meant.'

'You couldn't have meant anything else.'

'Well, I don't judge you. That's all I want to say. Do what you want to do, but don't rope me into it.'

'But you've been enjoying all the food which fell off a truck, so you can't talk,' he said heatedly. 'And you needn't put on airs about bein' good 'n holy and not judging people.' He resorted now to mimicry, adopting the attitude of a righteous aunt. 'I don't stoop to that kind of thing, taking what doesn't belong to me. I'm good I am and I know I'm good...' He shook his head at this like an odd doll and I had to smile in spite of myself. But he didn't smile. 'What you don't get, my friend, is that the folks who supply the stuff to you in the shops make a nice three-hundred-per-cent profit on everything. But that's legal. That's OK. That's capitalism.' He rose and turned away in disgust at my ignorance of things commercial in order to make himself another cup of coffee. I couldn't say anything to this, so I sat down at the kitchen table and began to eat my capitalistic cornflakes. Vincenzo returned from the sink and seated himself heavily on one of the chairs opposite me. 'So when a friend of yours brings you something good that you paid for a hundred times over in terms of high prices and taxes and customs and God alone knows what – especially for essentials like food – you should be grateful and not go telling him he's a thief.' I nodded. 'Now, are you going to accept the binoculars or shall I throw them out of the window?' With this he reached for them on the table where they had been all night.

'Good, good, Vin, but I don't really know what to do with them. I don't need them, you see.' I was apologetic and I meant what I said.

'Ah, I see, now we're coming to the point. Why didn't you say that before? You could give them away, couldn't you, to a friend or someone?'

'Well, yes, I suppose so, but they'd think it mighty strange, a gift like that coming from a penniless student.' Now he smiled.

'OK, that's a good answer, I'll accept that. No binoculars in future.'

The next weekend Anna came on Saturday afternoon with another girl. This girl was supposed to be for me. Vincenzo intimated this to me after the women had made themselves comfortable in the tiny lounge which we used only very occasionally and added that the 'girl would make a good bed-fellow'. 'And don't tell me you never slept with a woman or are you going to give me all that Sunday school stuff again?' And once more he adopted this odd, snooty, middle-class pose and the voice to accompany it so that I had to laugh out loud. He seemed completely to have changed character. 'Well?' he said, reverting to his normal manner. 'Are you going to say "thank you"?'

'She's too beautiful for a bloke like me,' I said.

'Oooh,' he hooted, 'in all humility, my son. Goodness gracious me! Do be careful, you might transgress.' He was sarcastic and he knew that he had touched a tender spot. I was still callow in such matters. He pulled out two bottles of wine from the fridge and together we went into the lounge. For a moment I thought he was going to let on, but he introduced me formally and kindly to Simone, a young woman of the same proportions as Anna and, truth told, I felt mighty flattered.

'My friend here is a student of geology, a very good student, I assure you,' he said broadly and with sincerity which impressed the newcomers. Then he adopted a pose: 'He also has some acquaintance with surgery and should, in my opinion, have studied medicine, but let these things be,' he added, affecting professional tones. We all laughed. The evening passed slowly and pleasantly. I kept wondering how I would manage the situation with Simone, who, it seemed, was a good deal more experienced in the ways of the world than I was. Two or three times during the evening she placed her arm round my shoulders, which could have been a gesture of chumminess, but I suspected more in it than that. I played the game in two minds. Around nine thirty p.m. I went into the kitchen to fetch another two bottles of wine and when I got back there were three or four little cellophane packets on the table and the party had taken on a business tone.

'What's that?' I asked. 'Looks like washing powder.'

At this there was a burst of laughter from the two women. 'Washing powder! Oh my God!' There followed another hilarious shriek.

Vincenzo couldn't contain himself either and I noticed that the alcohol had done much to weaken his usual catlike alertness.

Then Anna, who was also a bit worse for wear, said, 'That's snow,' and collapsed into helpless, pulsating laughter, so much so that they held each other helplessly, swaying to and fro on the sofa.

'What's so funny about snow?' I said, but then none of them was able to speak for laughter.

That night I slept with Simone who, by two in the morning, was so drunk that she fell into bed, my bed, with all her clothes on and slept until mid-morning. Sometime around dawn I had to rise to attend to a natural call and afterwards stole into the lounge to look at the 'snow'. The packets, I noticed, were soft and the powder in them was finely divided and not granulated like washing powder. It was not a good time of day to think much about these things and so I returned to bed and slept again with the question on my mind as to what it could be.

'That's heroin, my friend,' said Vincenzo in the afternoon of the next day. He looked very pleased with himself.

'Heroin? You mean the drug?' I asked.

'Yessir, the drug,' he replied simply. 'There's a big demand for it and some has fortunately come my way. Now, ain't that a good thing, boy?'

'Why?' I asked stupidly. We were in the kitchen and the girls were busy making something to eat. They giggled to themselves.

'OK,' Vin said, 'he's never been in the business. So how could he know anything about its value?' He said this turning to the girls, and then he leaned over to me earnestly and said, 'What you saw last night, friend, is worth about half a million francs. Half a million. Understand?'

I blinked. Then, 'What are you going to do with it?' I asked.

'Well, sell it, of course! What do they teach you at that university, Sid?' The girls shrieked with laughter.

'Well, I don't want to have anything to do with drug trafficking. Count me out,' I said firmly. Suddenly, the hardness came back into Vin's eyes and the girls stopped giggling.

'OK,' he said intensely on a long breath and nodded several times, 'I'll count you out. And no dividends either. No perks. We'll see how you manage.'

'I can manage,' I said. I could see him coming to the boil and my mind raced again for something to say which would ease the tension. 'I'm scared,' I said. This did the trick. Vincenzo relaxed visibly and nodded again slowly several times like a pious Jew while surveying me quietly.

'But just one thing, my friend. One word about this stuff' – and he pointed to the packets on the table – 'and your life won't be worth a paper bag.'

'OK. I don't want to know anything about it,' I said.

From that time on, Vincenzo became more and more affluent. He bought the large red car he had previously hired to impress his Mafia friends, swaggered around in an expensive light suit, bought new furniture for the apartment, put in new lighting fixtures, had the place redecorated (all this with the exception of my room), gave up his job down at the docks, went on holiday with Anna and spent most of his time in a posh suite of rooms with her somewhere downtown. He kept his promise and I had no advantages from his business connections except for the fact that the rent was radically reduced by some arrangement he had made with Cretille. What he did with the rest was his business and not mine, he told me when I asked him about the reduction.

'You saved my life; I'm not going to forget that in a hurry,' he said finally.

'We've been through all that,' I said. 'Thanks anyway.' He seemed pleased.

About two months after this exchange, he turned up suddenly, as was his wont. He still had the key to the place. It was a beautiful day, shortly before the finals, and we sat on the balcony together, chatting like old times. I opened two cans of beer for him and myself.

'You seem to be busy,' he said, smiling wonderfully, and I knew that he had taken a look into my room in passing through to the kitchen.

'Yes, some folks have to work for their living,' I replied. He was still smiling.

'Well, if you like that kind of thing. Still, I must say I admire you for it,' he replied.

'Admire me? Now why should *you* admire *me*? that's really new!' I laughed. He nodded like a judge, as was his habit.

'Maybe it's hard to explain,' he mused, 'but I guess it's the regularity bit – the way you have an object in view and go for it, piece by piece, bit by bit.'

'Well, that isn't very difficult to explain,' I said, amused by his serious attitude, 'I have a course to follow and hope at the end of it to get a job where I can do what I like doing, that's all. Nothing to it really.'

'OK, OK, but you got persistence. You don't let go. That's good. That brings success. In the end.' He held his can of beer below knee level and gazed down at the town below us. A bell was ringing. Always a bell somewhere.

'How do you get to a university anyway?' he asked. I told him. 'And how do you come to study abroad?' I told him. He was interested and I was surprised, for it wasn't easy to interest him in anything for long. He quickly tired of listening to people. 'I left school at thirteen. Did a bunk. I hated school. Nothing for me. Outside was a million times more interesting than school.'

'I suppose so,' I said.

'What do you mean, you "suppose so"?' and he gave me one of his sharp looks.

'What I mean is that it's a temptation to leave early and earn money,' I said.

'Oh,' he said. Then he added, 'I made my first contacts when I was about fourteen.' He took a swig of beer. 'Most of it smuggling something or other, usually cigarettes and alcohol. Cigs are easier. Big jobs and little jobs. And then nothing at all for a time.'

'So the lorry-driving job was just a blind, then?'

'Well, yes, although it's a proper job as well. Very useful. How else would I transport the stuff?' It was my turn to smile. 'You can't handle that kind of thing privately. Too risky,' he continued. 'Stuffing thousands of ciggies between the double walls of a caravan, for example – I've heard about that kind of thing – that's no good.' He shook his head and pulled a face of contempt for those possessed of small intelligence. 'Get you behind bars pretty quick.'

'Sounds interesting,' I said, and I was interested, but my voice must have contained just an ounce of detachment, just a smidgen of 'but that's all very far removed from my world', when he added, 'And you've been in the business, too.'

I was startled. 'How come?' He smiled mischievously and

turned industriously to polishing his nails on his lapel and afterwards inspecting them earnestly. 'How come I've ever been in the business?' I asked again.

'Do you remember the problem you had a few months ago to get to Aubagne and your examination – the fieldwork you had to do?'

'Of course. You lent me an old car to get there. What about it?'

'Well, when you drove off to Aubagne we followed you, watched you park the car and go off to your exams somewhere. We knew that you'd be at least three hours being examined – or whatever you had to do wherever you had to do it – and in that time we took the car away to a garage where we took the tyres off and emptied them of snow. Later, we took the car back and parked it in exactly the same place where you had parked it. You were glad of the car and we were glad to use you as a decoy. Nobody – and certainly not the police – would have dreamed of shadowing you.' He shrugged his shoulders in a matter-of-fact way. 'That's business.'

'Well, damn me, and I never had the slightest inkling! A sitting duck!' I was annoyed, but Vincenzo sat there as cool as a lollipop.

'No, not really, we were quite sure you'd be safe and we got the baggings and everything was hunky-dory. It brought me a lot of money and you benefited from the deal, as well,' he said with a tone of finality. I could say nothing to this.

'Don't you feel scared in all this?' I asked him after a pause.

'Sure. There's a lot of sharp competition. A few who'd stop at nothing to lay their dirty little paws on the stuff I have for sale. Snow's pretty hot – if you see what I mean.' He smiled his smile. 'But that's life. I like it that way. Life's got an edge to it. I'd be bored looking at stones, you know.' He raised his eyebrows and gave me a cheeky, taunting look. I couldn't help but laugh.

'But man,' I said, 'you risk your neck.'

'I've got my friends. They're a bit like an insurance should things go badly wrong.'

'The Mafia, you mean?'

'Well, yes, you can call it that.' He paused to reflect. 'OK, OK, it's the Mafia – it's organised. I only get a fraction of what I peel off. The organisation gets the lion's share, but it's enough, as you can see.'

'Whew! I'd be shit scared,' I said. 'You must have good nerves, Mr Graccini. First acquisitioning the stuff and then transporting it elsewhere and then stowing it, and finally distributing it...'

'I don't distribute it. That's someone else's pigeon. I just hijack it and transport it. Yeah, but you're right about the nerves bit. When I've made enough, Anna and I'll get out and go and live in Italy. I know a nice place and next month I'll be in a position to buy a house there. Then we'll see. I guess I'm a typical Mafioso.' He said this with a peculiar kind of wistfulness and again looked down at the town dreaming in the midday heat. I waited. 'You know, all of them are unmerciful bastards, but as middle class as they come, all they want is what everyone else wants, a woman, a house and nice kids in a respectable residential area on the edge of town. Then these bastards look down on the rest of us making our way. Real snobs, believe me. No class.' He pulled a face. Then, looking away at the horizon, he added, 'Just a bunch of low-minded, small-minded materialists who want the best for their kids of course, education and university, everything, everything they didn't get back home. Most of 'em come here from some of the poorest areas in Europe.' He paused. 'Animals.' He waved his hand in deprecation.

'And what are you going to do with all the money you make, Vincenzo?' I asked.

'I've told you. Get away,' he replied simply. 'Back to Italy. God's own country. Anna is coming with me,' he repeated.

'And then?' I probed. 'I can't see you retiring just yet.' He smiled.

'I gotta do something to improve myself,' he said. 'I've got other interests than smuggling and juggling.' He sighed and looked across the town.

'Like what?'

'Like religion,' he said.

'What?' I cried, astonished at this and, for the first time since our acquaintance, I was at a loss for words. 'You're not going to become a priest or something...?'

'No fear of that,' he said, 'I don't want to join that pack of wolves, but, well, I'm interested.' I rose and got us some more beer, returned to the balcony and listened. 'There's something in it, you understand. Not all this sin and hellfire and righteousness and all that shit. I'm not talking about that. When I was young my dad fell very ill. Pneumonia. We had no more money after the doctor's first visit and we all knew that he would die very soon if he did not get some treatment or other. There was a risk in moving him to hospital about sixty miles away, so he just lay there until my brother's wife had an idea. She called on an old woman in the town who was supposed to have healing powers. She was a crazy old girl and the Church had forbidden her to practise these powers, you see. Anyway, my aunt persuaded her to come and see my dad as it was so serious. He was already quite out of his mind. Raving about. Really scary. She came late one evening and told us kids to pray in the kitchen while she went into the other room to look at my dad. After about an hour she came out again, drank a glass of wine with some of the other members of the family and then went home. She was friendly enough in her old way, I remember. She asked after each one of us, talked to us for a bit. Anyway, things got worse with my dad, despite the visit, but Mother remained calm and told us that soon Dad would get better. And he did. A week or ten days after the old woman's visit he suddenly got better and was at work again the week after. Can you imagine that?' There was something child-like in the way he asked the question. 'Since then I've been interested in religion,' Vincenzo concluded.

'I've heard of such things,' I said. 'It happens in England, too. Nobody can explain it properly.'

Vincenzo's eyes signalled interest. Then he went on, 'I've always been interested in what happens when you die.' He said this quietly, almost confidentially. 'What do you think?'

'Well,' I said, 'I take the scientific view that we change into something else when we die. That's proved by the kind of work I do. We become something good for plants or turn into stone with time perhaps, and so on.'

'No,' he said, 'you and your stones. I mean the mind: what happens to us, to our personalities?'

'The Church teaches that we...'

'Go to hell, preferably hell – they like teaching us that and if we are quite exceptionally good, well, maybe we'll go to heaven, but I can't take that stuff any more. Not the way they dish it out. They're not so perfect themselves, anyway. Eternal damnation for a few years on this earth? It's mad. Anyway, what God is so interested in us to fork out that kind of punishment? What does He gain from it? And why should He be such a bastard in this respect when He's supposed to be a God of love? Don't make sense.' I nodded. 'I mean I could understand it if you were just paid out for what you've done wrong. Like clearing a bill or something – but for ever...!'

'Yeah,' I said, 'I find that a bit hard to digest. Anyway, I gave all that up years ago.'

'You gave it up?' he asked incredulously. 'Just like that?' He looked at me in astonishment. Then he said, 'And you're not scared?'

'No, why should I be? Of what?'

'In case it's true what the Church says.'

'Well, it isn't. I've not been brainwashed as you have in this respect. In England it's different. We can take it or leave it.'

He was silent for some time, pondering on what I had said. Then he motioned that it was time to go and got up. 'By the way,' I reminded him, 'there's still some of your "snow" here left over from the party. Do you want to take it with you? I feel a bit uncomfortable about this stuff just lying around.'

He hesitated a moment before saying, 'Leave it for a day or so. I'll be back for it. It'll be all right here for a bit longer and anyway, I don't want to be arrested on a Sunday.'

Then he was gone. Hopping two at a time down the stairs. Apparently none the worse for his stabbing.

Two days later, there were other sounds on the stairs. Cretille was coming with what sounded like a delegation. Official voices. I fled to the kitchen, retrieved the 'snow' from the kitchen cupboard, tore open the balcony door and flung the four packets on the roof above me where they slithered to a stop in the guttering. A moment later, the doorbell rang, long and insistent. When I opened it, Cretille and a policeman stood there and behind them were two gendarmes with automatic machine guns.

Cretille stepped forward and said, 'Monsieur Mathers, I have a search warrant here' (he waved a piece of paper), 'I'm sorry to trouble you, young man, but we have to conduct a brief search of the premises.' Although his manner was cool, it was also apologetic as if to indicate that what had to be done in the name of the law must be done. I opened the door wider and three of them entered. One gendarme remained outside at the top of the stairs. Cretille muttered something about the possibility of drugs being in the place and hovered after the policeman into the lounge while I was asked to remain where I was in the hall. The second gendarme made his way into the kitchen and used his one free hand perfunctorily to explore the contents of drawers and cupboards, and a few minutes later I heard his boots on the tiles of the balcony. I held my breath and wondered what they would find in Vin's room. If there was more 'snow' in there I was certainly in for it. They were a long time. After about forty minutes or so I was called to the kitchen, where two of them had seated themselves and one of the gendarmes remained standing behind them as at a tribunal. Did I know anything about Graccini's activities? How long had I known him? Did he take drugs as far as I knew? Did I realise the consequences of giving false or misleading information to the police? I realised, of course. They said that this would have a disastrous effect on my career if I were trying to divert the course of the law and was I aware of the fines or possible imprisonment attendant on such behaviour? I told them that I had nothing to do with the whole affair and that Vincenzo Graccini was hardly here, which was true. They asked other questions. They were frank and matter of fact, formal. I had been warned. They went.

Another two days passed and I returned from my last examination to find Vincenzo sitting in the kitchen smoking. His face was sharp, his dark eyes quick and scrutinising. Before I could open my mouth, he said, 'Did they find anything?'

'No.'

'Where is it?'

'On the roof.' And I explained to him what had happened. He immediately went outside and said that he could see nothing. I told him that the packages must be in the guttering and that to retrieve them we would have to use a ladder. At this he turned to me and smiled, his whole body expressing relief. 'You're a good lad, Sid. That was a brilliant solution to the problem. And you didn't tell them anything about me?'

'Of course not. What do I know about you anyway?' I asked, tongue in cheek. This produced a heavy clap of appreciation on my shoulder and he guided me back into the kitchen. 'It'll be difficult to get the stuff down from there. You could break your neck,' I said. He looked pained at the triviality of this compared with what could have been.

'*Mon cher Sid*...' (he always pronounced this as 'seed') '*pas de problème, c'est trop simple*...' and he emphasised the 'too' of this so that I had to laugh. It was that wheedling aspect to his nature I had noticed before, and I was sure that this was one of the ways he managed to keep Anna. And this incredible talent for falling into a role.

That night, and at considerable risk to life and limb, we managed after a long time to fish the packets of heroin from the gutter over the eaves onto the balcony and take them triumphantly back into the kitchen.

'Do you think anyone saw us?' I asked. 'This house is interesting to the neighbours these days.'

'Can't say, *mon ami*, but I won't forget what you've done. That was the act of a true friend.'

'Ach, get away with you; I don't want to spend my youth behind bars any more than you do.'

He looked serious for a moment. 'Pity you're going into this geology stuff. We need bully boys like you in the organisation,' he said. I laughed out loud, but he didn't seem to think it funny. He simply nodded his sage head in that way of his and then he was off to his woman.

We celebrated my finals at a very fine restaurant, but not the one we had visited a few weeks before. He looked very fine. Anna too. He would pay for everything, he said, and it was a swell affair. Simone was there and there was just a tinge of sadness between us. She knew I would be off back to England in two days time and there was the feeling that we had lost the opportunity to get to know each other. This feeling was intensified as Vin gradually became more and more drunk and more and more talkative. Anna, too, for all her conservatism, was a bit tipsy at the end of the evening, with the strange effect that Simone and I felt alone with each other, alone with feelings which were the same, but unuttered. We talked and said nothing and yet conveyed everything. I had lost my chance. To sleep with her tonight would be unkind and I passed it up. I would come back one day and make up for the loss, I said to myself.

The next day was Saturday, 24 August 1957, a day I shall never forget as long as I live. I had slept until about eleven or so I suppose and was just making some coffee to really bring me to the surface, as it were, when the phone rang. I picked up the receiver: 'Allo...' An anxious voice at the other end asked for Vincenzo, but in Italian, so that I could not grasp the full message. It was Basta. Then the line clicked dead. It was then that I suddenly felt very uneasy, like a hunted tiger, and ready for action. For some reason I looked over the balcony. Below, a few children were playing, and washing flying as usual. A warm day with a breeze. Nothing untoward, but without knowing why I went into my room and collected my passport and wallet as though I were going somewhere, which was absurd since Vin had promised to pick me up at two and take me to the station. I slipped into my shoes. In that second I heard a commotion on the stairs outside and Vincenzo calling my name. I hurried to the door. He had just reached the top of the stairs when there was gunfire. I saw the flame from the barrel. Bullets splintered the door jamb next to me. One second. Vincenzo dodged in front of me, masking the fire. Next second. He slumped into the doorway. The gunman was now at the top of the stairs. Still firing. Two seconds. Three seconds. I was tearing along the short corridor to the kitchen and out through the door to the balcony. Below, children playing. A sandpit. Thirty feet. I jumped. Then I ran. And ran. I ran, for all the pain in my left foot and my bursting heart, through the winding streets of that place and on and on, the noise of splintering wood in my ears, Vincenzo's blood on my shirt, I ran. People stopped. People looked. Young and old. Buildings. Shadows. Downhill. Lungs bursting. Sound of my light summer shoes on the pavement. Vincenzo! Why? Vincenzo! Vin! My God, my God!

High above the city's tangled back streets, fleecy white clouds trailed very slowly eastwards out over the Mediterranean Sea.

17

No 14 Cavendish Street, Spring 1958 and Thereafter

Before relating what happened in the spring of that year, I would like to say to those who read this report that neither I nor my family suffer in any way from any kind of mental disease or psychological disturbance, and that both at the time the events took place and thereafter we have led where possible what everyone would recognise as normal lives.

At that time we – my wife who was then 36 years old, my oldest son, Jack, 16, my second son, Dennis 14, and my daughter, Julie, 12 – lived at the address above in the city of Worcester, England. I was employed at a large firm as a general electrician and had three people for whom I was generally responsible: another electrician, a journeyman who was just about to take his final examinations; a young apprentice aged 17; and a lad of 14 who was a trainee. The firm itself employed about six to seven hundred people. We lived in a typical council house, which consisted of two half houses. My mother-in-law lived in the other half of the house with her ailing husband, my father-in-law, and we shared the back garden and its work between us.

One day in late March or early April, I can't quite recall, I was working in the shed which occupied that garden. It had been raining, and then I remember the sun had suddenly come out very strongly, as it often does shortly after showers at this time of the year. Its powerful rays brilliantly illuminated the bench at which I was working. I was busy painting a metal tub used to catch rainwater from the shed roof. I remember using a 3-inch brush for the purpose since it was a large surface. I was getting on well when my wife called to me from the kitchen window. She said something I didn't understand and so I went out of the shed and took the few steps across our patch of lawn to catch what she said. She told me there was someone at the front door whom she didn't know and would I see to him. I went into the house through the kitchen.

The visitor turned out to be an acquaintance of mine at the Club, a man who told me that our meeting on Saturday would take place an hour later. It was clear, too, that he wanted a chat. I must have spent about ten minutes with this individual. Perhaps fifteen or even twenty, but certainly no longer. After that, we said our farewells and I returned to the shed via the kitchen. When I arrived I found to my horror that the tin of blue paint I had been using had tipped over and the brush was missing. I was furious about this, and stormed out of the shed calling, 'Dennis! Dennis! Jack! What the hell...?'

Rita, my wife, met me at the kitchen door.

'Who's been in the shed and tipped the bloody paint all over the floor?' I asked her angrily. Throwing the tea towel she had in her hand to one side, she came over to the shed to look at the accident.

'Well, blow me!' she said, ignoring my question. 'Quick, I'll get a few rags and we'll mop it up!'

'All right!' I said. 'But who did it?' But she was already on her way to the kitchen, and a moment or two later returned with an armful of old clothes to mop up the paint.

'Dunno, dear,' she said now, 'I didn't see anybody go into the shed while you were with this man. Jack's been at work two hours.'

NO. 14 CAVENDISH STREET, SPRING 1958 AND THEREAFTER

I left Rita with the paint and marched into the house. There, at the top of the stairs, I found Dennis, still in his pyjamas, bleary-eyed and half asleep. He had heard me calling, evidently, and had got out of bed. It was clear that he hadn't been anywhere near the shed. I was nonplussed and turned through the kitchen again to join Rita.

'Can't be Dennis, either,' I blurted, still very annoyed at what had happened. 'Must have been one of the neighbours' kids, just came in, jerked the tin over and vanished with the brush.'

Rita considered this for a moment. 'There'd be a trail then,' she suggested practically.

'A trail? Yes, of course.' I went out and looked for a trail of paint outside the shed, but there was nothing. Not a spot of bright blue paint anywhere. I rejoined Rita in the shed and took over the job of wiping up the mess while she cleaned the streaks of paint from her hands with thinners from a tin on the bench. I continued to curse, to which she wryly remarked that it was no use 'crying over spilled paint'. I couldn't say anything to this. I was so annoyed, and when she had returned to the house and I had taken up practically all the paint from the wooden floor of the shed I straightened my back to look once more for the brush. This was a matter of routine. It had to be somewhere. Brushes don't just vanish into thin air, especially one dripping with bright blue paint, I told myself. But to add to my annoyance, I discovered after thirty minutes of exploration that the brush had gone. Whoever it was that had spilled the paint had gone off with the brush, too. I swore.

Later that day and with a new brush I tackled the tub again and finished the job around four o'clock in the afternoon, placing the tub on a wooden block to dry. It looked good, I congratulated myself. A good job done in spite of the intervening catastrophe. The brush never turned up again.

Within the next few weeks at irregular intervals I began

to notice things which were inexplicable, but which I did not mention to anyone in the family, since they would think me 'round the bend' – one of Julie's favourite phrases at the moment. The first of these oddities as far as I can remember affected the shed again. I used to do a lot of work in the shed for a number of reasons. First, it gave me a break from the insistences of my family. A man needs to be alone from time to time. Second, and equally important to me, was the fact that I could do little jobs there which, I suppose, fulfilled my 'creative instincts', as a woman neighbour once described these retreats and, let's be frank about it, it was my little kingdom. I liked the shed and the things in the shed. I had a key and no one, not even Jack, who was a responsible lad, was allowed to potter about in there. As a consequence of this, I regularly locked the place when I'd finished work in it. I was careful about this and there were no exceptions.

Imagine my consternation, then, when, coming home from work one evening at around five o'clock about a week or ten days after the incident described above, I discovered the shed door wide open. Rita usually arrived home about an hour after me from a job she had found three years ago in Rushwick. She had to get a bus, and often these were full. She would leave the house at eight in the morning and get home at about six, so there was no likelihood of her leaving the shed door open in error. Anyway, it wouldn't be at all like her, even if she had been at home for some reason. None of the young people showed much interest in the shed and its contents. Jack occasionally wanted a spanner or some such tool for his motorcycle, it was true, but these days he had his own tools and kept them upstairs in a cupboard.

On this occasion I entered the shed and looked around. As far as I could tell everything was in its place and nothing had been stolen. With a mixture of relief, puzzlement and slight annoyance, I emphatically closed the door of the shed and locked it. 'How the hell could it have been opened?' I

NO. 14 CAVENDISH STREET, SPRING 1958 AND THEREAFTER

asked myself. It was impossible, unless, of course, someone else had a key and had deliberately opened it to annoy me. But who could that be?' I took my own key, a thing kept at the end of a chain dangling from my pocket, and locked the door carefully. I tried the door twice, knowing full well, however, that it was securely shut. Later, after tea, an evening of TV and relaxation followed and then bed.

The next morning, I rose early and looked out of the window into the half-light of the garden. I suppose it must have been something just after seven. The night had brought a sprinkling of snow. 'The last remnants of winter,' I thought to myself when, in total astonishment, I noticed that the door of the shed again stood wide open. I waited at the window, fully expecting a figure to emerge from the obscurity inside. I waited quite a time expecting this to happen. After a moment or two more, Rita joined me at the window. For a long time neither of us said anything. Then her brow creased.

'But you told me you locked the shed last night?' she enquired.

'Of course I closed the door and locked it,' I insisted.

'Then how can it be open now?' she asked.

'How the hell do I know?' We looked at each other, at a loss for words. Then I said again, louder, piqued by her logic, 'How the devil do I know!?'

'Don't raise your voice like that – it's still early!' she countered. Without answering, I went straight down to the back door, unbolted it and marched outside to the shed. The cold of the morning struck my face. There was a chill wind outside. I looked into the interior of the shed and again realised that nothing had been tampered with, nothing stolen or even moved from its accustomed place. Despite the cold, I took time to inspect the place with an eagle eye. Finally, as I say, finding nothing amiss, I closed the door, returned to the house through the kitchen, rushed upstairs for my key, retrieved it from my trouser pocket and rushed down again to the garden outside. By that time, the house was awake. Only Julie remained in bed. School started at nine for her. The rest of us had to be off around eight. Again, I locked the perfectly stable, well-built shed door, wondering as I did so who had a second key. I made up my mind at that moment to replace the lock that very day. At breakfast I mentioned the matter of the door and asked whether anyone had tinkered with the shed. As an answer I received early-morning incredulity.

'Some little bugger's having me on, spilling paint and opening the door and what not, and if I...'

'Don't use that kind of language at table, Alfred, I don't like it,' Rita objected. I felt cut off at the knees. The others showed pained faces which suggested that there could be other things of more interest at that time of day than shed doors. A day of routine for us all followed, and in the evening I replaced the lock of the shed door, threw the old keys away and secured my private key to the chain I spoke of a moment ago. I tried the lock several times with this new key, turning it this way and that. It worked perfectly, and with an air of considerable satisfaction I closed and locked the door.

Two or three days later I had taken the day off, since I was expected to work during the weekend this week. An exception. As a consequence, I was at home during the afternoon of 9 April 1958. I had taken the opportunity to clean out some drawers and was generally busy when, at around four thirty, Julie appeared in the house having just come from school. Like most people of her age, she had nothing to say for herself, and I knew that any questions on my part would be dealt with by evasive noises or, if of immediate, practical importance, the very shortest of answers. So I declined to say anything other than to greet her perfunctorily. Jack arrived from his place of work a little earlier than usual and threw himself into an armchair as though he hadn't experienced anything like relaxation for a century, and Dennis came in for tea a little later. Outside, I

NO. 14 CAVENDISH STREET, SPRING 1958 AND THEREAFTER

recall, the weather had turned fine and clear. The rain of the last day or so had cleared, and there was some evening sunshine. Rita came home about 5.45 p.m. and straightaway began to get the tea. I helped. When things were ready, she called upstairs to tell Julie that tea was ready. At around six ten or sometime shortly thereafter we were all sitting at the table. Conversation among us was lively and generally turned on the topic of the antics of a peculiar neighbour four doors away. Suddenly, talk came to a standstill. Around us, the air had become very cold in the room.

'That's odd,' said Jack, 'the sun's still shining outside, and look, Mrs Bumes is going by in an open coat.' I looked. It was a fact. Rita rubbed her arms as one does on a winter day. Jack laughed. Julie went out to put on a cardigan. I was puzzled and after a minute or so pulled out an old thermometer from a drawer which I'd discovered during the afternoon's cleaning operations and consulted it. The mercury showed plus nine degrees centigrade. Instinctively, we all went into the kitchen and then outside into the early-evening sunshine.

'What the hell's going on?' Jack asked, half in amusement and half in concern.

'Dunno, lad – summat's queer,' I replied. Rita looked as if she were about to cry and hugged Julie, whose eyes were already moist. Jack looked at the thermometer I had handed to him.

'It's warmer out here than inside,' he said, announcing what had become obvious.

At that moment, we spotted Mr Mitchell in his garden next door.

'Jim!' I called. 'Have you got a moment?' I signalled to him to come over to join us. In a moment he was with us. Jack explained the situation and the three of us went back into the house, where now it was even colder. The thermometer registered minus three degrees centigrade. Jim Mitchell wrinkled his brow.

335

'But that's incredible,' he said, 'that can't be!'
'See – or rather feel – for yourself,' I replied.
'Is it the same upstairs?' he asked.
'Let's see,' I said, and with that all of us traipsed upstairs where I can only say that it was, well, simply freezing cold. Jack, who still held the thermometer, now placed it on the dressing table and consulted it carefully. 'Here, it's apparently minus five degrees centigrade,' he said.

Mitchell was a man who worked for the Inland Revenue, a man not easily led into self-deception.

'Well, I'm damned if I can understand it,' he said, and since we were all pretty cold by now we went down the stairs and out into the garden.

'What shall we do?' Rita asked.

'Lock up and retire to the Golden Hind,' I said. 'Wait until the temperature rises – if it rises.'

And that's what we did. We went and sat in the pub until nine and then returned home to a table full of crockery and half-eaten food, but to a temperature that had risen to normal.

All of us went to bed with questions in our minds that night. How could such a thing have happened? Just what was going on in our house? However, in the next week or two nothing untoward occurred. We relaxed. The event was almost forgotten, until the house was again plunged into a refrigerated atmosphere while we were watching TV one evening about a month later. Not only did the temperature go down suddenly on this occasion, but the TV went off and all the lights in the house went out. We stumbled against each other in astonishment and confusion. I finally found a torch in the hall which I used on winter evenings when I took the dog for a walk.

And speaking of the dog, on this occasion Ernie howled in a way which made our blood curdle. I turned the torch on him to find an animal I didn't know, a creature cowed and shivering, its fur on end like a brush and his tail stiff and straight as a handle. But it was the eyes which riveted our attention. They were large and full of what I can only describe as fire. It was as though they were on fire. His mouth was full of yellowish foam. Julie screamed uncontrollably and the dog backed away from her as though she were the cause of his distress. It was a frightful moment for us all. We all made instinctively for the back door and outside. It was raining. Julie, who stood next to me at that moment, had gone up early to bed and was being comforted by her mother, who had also suffered shock on seeing the dog so distressed. Jack wrapped Julie up in one of his large winter coats and Rita had taken one of mine which hung behind the kitchen door. We looked silly standing there in the rain. It was about nine thirty in the evening.

'We can't just wait around like this,' Rita announced after a few minutes. 'Let's put the stove on full in the kitchen and bring the electric blower in and sit there until it passes.'

'What the hell is this "it"? I asked. 'Just what the hell's going on here?' It was a silly question thrown into the night air.

I went back into the house with Jack and the two of us fiddled with the fuse box situated in a cupboard under the stairs. It was pitch black in there and difficult to do much using only a torch. In a very short time we discovered that not one but *all* the fuses had blown. Again, a question arose in our minds. We struggled out of the cupboard with the blown fuses and I turned to the job of mending all six of them on the kitchen table with the help of the beam from Jack's torch. While I was doing this I could hear my mother-in-law's voice outside. The fuses had gone there, too. It wasn't cold there, though, she added. We all then decided to go next door and Jack and I carried on working in the relative warmth.

When the fuses were all mended. Jack returned alone to the house, where he was met by the dog who wouldn't let him pass into the kitchen. When he attempted to brush Ernie aside and go in he was bitten on the leg so badly that blood just poured. He returned to us within less than a minute. My mother-in-law, Betty, who had been a nurse during the war, washed and bandaged the wound. The Mitchells next door were asked whether we could use their telephone as Betty insisted the wound could be infected. The doctor arrived about an hour later. We told him what had happened and he went into the house to see for himself. It was still very cold inside and he, too, only narrowly managed not being bitten. He said that we should inform the authorities of the situation and officially register the dog bite. He looked serious. Mr Mitchell also tried to enter the house and met with a similar experience. At ten in the evening, the Morgans and the Kenneys, other neighbours of ours, came to Betty's house to offer their sympathy and to share our incredulity.

After the doctor had gone, we made a cup of tea and waited for things to change next door. I went round at half-hourly intervals to check, regardless of the dog, but it wasn't until 2.30 a.m. that I could register a rise in temperature. The dog at this time was nowhere to be found and so didn't hinder my access to the kitchen. The house was remarkably still. Inside, it was warmer. I then crept into the cubby hole under the stairs and replaced the fuses that I had repaired in the meantime. Then, creeping from there to the hall, I switched on a light. No problem. The lights in the parlour were also on and it was then that I noticed the dog shivering in a corner. I called to him gently, but he remained where he was. His expression was normal again and he allowed me to stroke him gently. He seemed to have undergone a considerable shock.

Except for Dennis, who later left for work, none of us slept well in the following hours until the grey of daybreak. There was another thing which all of us felt, but which none of

NO. 14 CAVENDISH STREET, SPRING 1958 AND THEREAFTER

us could describe – a strange, tense atmosphere in the house. If I were to attempt to describe it I would say that it was like a powerful magnetic field which held us in its tension. We were made unhappy by it, and it was difficult, if not impossible, to resist its power over us. You can't *see* a magnetic field; you can only see what it does to iron filings, and that's what this feeling – or whatever it was – did to us. It regimented us. But there was more to it than that. There was something unpleasant about it, something frightening, something immanent and, well, 'evil', you could say. We all agreed on this and each of us felt it. It was uncanny.

Jack at this time was on shift work and while all this was going on he would sleep during the day until about four in the afternoon. After that he would set off at about five for the night shift to get to his place of work at six. One late afternoon, we found him shivering on the front doorstep obviously in a state of distress. I was the first to discover him as Julie had gone off to see a friend straight from school and had not been home first.

'Dad,' he said, his face wan and his voice shaky, 'there's something in there, in the house, I mean, something ugly and frightful. It thumps around. It's there now. You can't see it, but it's there. Don't go inside!'

Without asking any more questions I went to the shed and took up a heavy hook and then entered the house. Upstairs, I could hear a strange 'thud-thud' like the footfall of a bear or some other large animal, or so it seemed, and for a moment I hesitated, hook in hand. Would I be equal to the job of slaying the beast? Like a cat on the prowl, I crept up the stairs, step by step, listening to the thud-thud coming from somewhere in our bedroom. Jack hung back at the bottom of the stairs, now also armed with a heavy hammer seized from his toolkit. I had reached the second step from the top when the thudding suddenly stopped, to be replaced by panting, the panting of a largish animal, a bear, a tiger or a lion perhaps. However, at this moment curiosity was stronger than fear and I charged into our bedroom to find ... nothing. The realisation left me feeling defenceless, even foolish. I stood there full of passionate resolve to kill or be killed, and now there was nothing but our bedroom, the unmade bed, a few of our clothes strewn about, my trousers, pressed and hanging up in their accustomed place for Sunday on the half-open wardrobe door and nothing more of the slightest interest. Jack joined me.

'You heard it, for God's sake, didn't you. Jack?' I asked almost in appeal.

He nodded and caught his breath. His nerves were as taut as piano strings and he himself near collapse. When he had pulled himself together after a few seconds, he said, 'Dad, what the hell is it?'

'I don't know, lad; I just don't know.'

We went downstairs together and there met Dennis who had just arrived home. He had a friend with him. Jack related what had happened while I made a pot of tea for us all. The friend looked sympathetic but was clearly incredulous. After all, what could we tell him that could justify our fear and anger? He said that if it was all right with us, he would stay the night with Dennis in the house, sleeping on the floor. It was clear that he was ready for a scrap with whatever it was in the house. I liked him for that. But the night passed without incident. And the next day. And the next. Later – I don't know how many days later – Rita reported that utensils had gone missing in the kitchen. All of us, every member of the family, looked for these things in our small house, but nobody ever found them. Like the paintbrush, they had vanished 'from the face of the earth' as my mother used to say. They were replaced. We waited.

One evening about seven or eight weeks later, all of us

NO. 14 CAVENDISH STREET, SPRING 1958 AND THEREAFTER

were at the table around six in the evening, as was our custom, when there was a loud bang at the *front* door. I put my serviette down beside my plate and wondered, like the rest of us, at the vehemence of the banging. I opened the door at once to this rude summons, but there was nobody at the door or next door or in the back garden or the front after forty minutes' energetic search or down the next hundred yards of road, not in the Mitchells' garden, nor in the bushes on the other side of the fence. No one. Jack and Dennis joined me in the search and even Julie helped, but nothing was discovered. A few neighbours across the way pulled back the curtains to watch us as we sprinted from one place to another. Hot and sweating from the effort, we met up again in the dining room. No one said a word for quite a time.

'It's clear this place is haunted,' Julie said simply at last.

'Haunted?' Jack said quizzically. 'What's that mean in these modern times? Anyway, there's no such thing. The Catholic folks over the way – what's their name? – believe in that kind of thing, but I mean, seriously...' No one was in much of a mood to argue with him. The facts seemed to indicate something to the contrary.

For six weeks nothing more happened and, like the last lull in these psychic activities, we were on the point of gratefully forgetting the whole affair when the banging began again. This was not banging such as is occasionally heard from a neighbour busy doing something late at night, or even the banging some folks get up to when they're annoyed, but a consistent, regular beat that seemed to issue from several sources. It finally grew so loud that we could not hear ourselves speak. Our relatives next door were so scared that they came round and joined us in our fear. It was a Sunday afternoon. All of us huddled in the kitchen. Mr and Mrs Mitchell, our next-door neighbours, joined us for a while. The police had been called, and arrived just a few minutes later in a patrol car. They entered the house and heard for themselves what was going on. They searched the house thoroughly, but both they and we knew that there was no earthly cause for the din. It was dreadful. The fearful, terrifying racket increased in such a crescendo that finally both of the police officers and the family as a whole had to go out into the street to communicate with each other. Neighbours gathered from all the houses in the vicinity to listen to the din. They gaped, frowned in incomprehension, went round the back of the house into the garden, poked their heads in at the kitchen door, sympathised, offered to help, stood around. The two police officers took notes, called headquarters, and said they would be back within an hour. They returned within only forty minutes when the banging, seemingly now came from hard steel pipes, had reached such a point that half of the street was filled with the noise.

At least, I assured myself, we were now no longer considered a group of superstitious idiots who had some bee in their bonnets about the presence of psychic phenomena. The whole street was witness to an inexplicable event.

It was ten minutes past ten, I remember, since I'd just looked at my watch and was wondering where we would have to spend the night, when, without warning, the banging ceased. The police officers were still present, together with two senior officials in civilian clothes who had come along to witness something which was probably quite alien to them. Like us, they were flummoxed. They had no explanation, but promised to give us some assistance the next day. Slowly, under a full moon, we and our neighbours drifted back into our respective houses. The night passed peacefully enough.

The next day, two representatives of the Worcester City Protestant Church came along and asked if they could perform what they called an exorcism. The ritual took about an hour, during which they entered every room and sprinkled incense or some such thing into every corner. They intoned prayers, and it was clear from their manner that they were trying to

NO. 14 CAVENDISH STREET, SPRING 1958 AND THEREAFTER

get rid of the nuisance. And, in fact, for a time it did stop. However, we were not to be duped by silence. All of us had experienced this before, and sure enough, about four or five weeks later, something else took place which was more frightening than anything that had preceded it.

At about two in the morning, Julie awoke screaming. We – her mother and I – rushed to her room and found her sitting at the edge of the bed issuing screams that were so intense and so terrifying that we thought she was out of her mind. It occurred to me in those seconds that I could not have imagined so much noise could come from such a slender body. The screams reverberated against the walls of the room. Her eyes, glazed and large, stared from her face like those of a madwoman. It was clear that she didn't recognise any of us in the room, since, by now, everyone had come to see what was wrong. Lights went on in the street. After a few minutes, there was a call from below – a neighbour asking what was wrong.

Rita tried to allay Julie's screams and fell back after touching her. She was ice cold and as strong as a bear. Moreover, when anyone approached her, her eyes were suddenly filled with hate and ugliness. Jack ushered his younger brother and his mother out of the door. I remained where I was, unable to do anything, dazed and scared by Julie's changed being. I stopped my ears to block out the intensity of her screams. Her hands then gripped mine in a clasp of steel, so strong that it hurt. Bruises formed immediately. I was at my wit's end when an ambulance arrived outside the house, its bell ringing furiously. Two St John Ambulance men jumped up the stairs and stormed into the bedroom, grasped Julie's arms, were rebutted with an enormous, animal strength, but went at her again and again until they had secured her flailing arms and legs and gagged her mouth with tape to escape her vicious bites. Again and again she kicked them, sending them flying against the furniture. After twenty minutes they finally had her violent kicking and flailing under control. Then I helped. Jack helped. Eventually, the screams subsided and Julie fell into death-like unconsciousness, her body a mere heap in our arms. Rita was crying loudly downstairs as we carried Julie's inert body out into the waiting ambulance. Dennis followed it on his motor scooter to the hospital. I went back into the house to comfort Rita. The police were there again, but different police officers this time. We explained. They made comforting noises, asked questions, nodded seriously, went away. This took place on another Sunday in the early hours of the morning between 18th and 19th June.

Julie was diagnosed as suffering from shock and given tranquillisers. After her return two days later, apparently none the worse for her experience, provision was made for Julie and Rita to sleep next door with the in-laws while we three men held fort in our own house. The doctors could make no other diagnosis than shock, since, apparently, nothing else seemed amiss as far as Julie's health was concerned. But she could remember nothing of what had happened, she said, and was shocked to hear it related to her.

We settled into a routine of sorts again, but night after night the banging continued into the last week of the month of June, sometimes so loud that none of us could sleep on any night of the week. Added to the vicious banging were voices, ugly, deep, unnatural voices which seemed to say something we could not understand. Although we could not make out a word, the tone was sufficient to put us off, like someone swearing at us in another language. This was the worst of our experiences so far and everyone was thoroughly frightened. During these onslaughts I describe, all of us sat in the kitchen huddled together. After it, we tried to sleep, but rarely with success. Finally, we sought refuge with friends and then Rita and I found assistance from friends at the Club who knew someone on the city council who found us accommodation on a camping site at the edge of the town.

NO. 14 CAVENDISH STREET, SPRING 1958 AND THEREAFTER

The house next door was also finally vacated. My mother-in-law, Elsie, and her husband, Ray, were accommodated by relatives in Derby. Julie took up residence with a friend not far away from Cavendish Street. The banging and uproar continued at irregular intervals, much to the fear and consternation of our immediate neighbours, but in early July it stopped altogether.

Two men and a woman arrived some time later from London's Society for Psychical Research, armed with recording apparatus and microphones and other instruments. Two priests also appeared from the Catholic Church at the request of the local council to exorcise in their own way whatever it was that caused so much havoc. They seemed gratified to know that their Protestant colleagues had not been particularly successful.

Thus the place was purged for a second time in a year. For those visiting our abode there was a strange sense of what one could call 'tension' in the house as I've said, which was as unnerving as anything else we had experienced. One felt ill at ease. There was the desire to shout, to call out loud at I know not what, and both Jack and Dennis noted what they described as a high-pitched, consistent humming, not like that emitted by electrical apparatus, but more resembling some unearthly 'music'. Whatever it was it was hard to put up with and none of us liked any longer to be in the house on a visit, nor indeed to be anywhere near it.

In the first week of July, I risked a visit to our old home in order to retrieve clothes and other household articles which we needed on the campsite. I returned alone one afternoon, turned the key of the door and went in. Everything seemed normal. It was a warm summer's day. Outside, the sun shone and inside and there seemed nothing out of the ordinary. I found what I wanted and turned the idea over in my mind as to whether it would now be 'safe' for the family to return. Our family had been broken up as a result of these upheavals, and all of us had been badly shaken by the events of the last few months. Now that better weather was here, life appeared to be somehow much more manageable. I looked in on our lounge as a routine gesture before departing. Within the first fractions of a second before complete awareness was established, I knew there was someone in the room. The door had been left half open. In the first instant on entering, my eyes recorded stockinged feet and then my mother sitting in an armchair beside the fireplace. My mother had been dead for seventeen years.

She turned her face to me; it wore an unpleasant expression, a mixture of accusation and pain. I remember giving out a huge cry like a man stabbed by an assassin and fell back into the hall. I caught my breath, and in the seconds that followed wondered whether I'd ever get my breath back. I yelled and choked and coughed on the floor, my eyes full of water, gasping for breath, my back as cold as a fish. Then, suddenly, there was a light knock at the front door but it was several seconds before I was able to pull myself together to answer it. It was someone off the street who had heard me yell and wondered whether there was anything he could do, since he had seen that the front door was open. He was a gentle person who appeared quite concerned about my mental state at that moment. I explained in broken sentences what had been happening to the house over the last few months. He was perplexed and kindly, and after I reassured him that I was all right, he wished me well and took his leave. He probably thought he had encountered someone who was mentally ill. I recovered from the shock in the warm sunlight of that late afternoon, sitting on the house doorstep, and then went back to the camp site.

Later that month the local council requisitioned the house for further investigation, since there was no doubt in the minds of official sources that there was something wrong with the place. Police officials, city councillors, doctors and

NO. 14 CAVENDISH STREET, SPRING 1958 AND THEREAFTER

other sane and sober representatives of society had witnessed for themselves what had been going on. Now members of the Society for Psychical Research were active for much of the time in and around the house. There were other groups, too, interested in focusing on our house. The press had taken their photographs and made their reports, and hardly a day passed without some article or other appearing in the local paper. National interest in No. 14 had also been aroused. Then something happened which caused an uproar.

One of the researchers who had been working and sleeping at the house with another scientist threw himself out of the bedroom window in the early hours one August morning, sustaining serious injuries which placed him in hospital for the next month. The other man stayed on alone in the house to continue his research and went out of his mind. All I know from hearsay is that an ambulance came one morning and took him away. The papers raved. People came from all over the country to view the house, take their own photographs and talk to people who lived in our street. For weeks after, other research was conducted and it was clear from what I read in a number of these reports that things were getting worse, not better. There was no explanation for the happenings taking place. All kinds of people were now witness to them, not only public authorities, but also ordinary people, and all of them were of the opinion that what was going on was evil and inexplicable.

On 23rd August that year the house caught fire. Since it was more or less constantly being watched, the fire was discovered early and the fire brigade was there on time to put the blaze out. How fire could have started was difficult to ascertain, since both halves of the house had been vacated. All our furniture was rendered useless either by the fire or by the water and chemicals used to put it out. I now realised that we had lost our home altogether. The next day I acquired a van, and with the permission of the council I salvaged what

I could from the house, garage and shed. While I was there, I met John Gordon and his wife, who lived in the house to the right of ours. I hadn't seen him for months. He and his pretty wife had no words to describe what had been happening. What on earth could be the cause? And why had we, ordinary people that we were, been, so to speak, 'selected' by God knows what to suffer such an appalling thing? Our conversation came to an end with this silent question and the three of us stared at the forlorn house, a house with a half-open roof and blacked-out windows, a cripple in the August sunshine.

Within a few days of the fire, the city council requested that we remove everything from the house we owned, and later cordoned it off. Neither my wife nor Julie wanted to return for any reason. On one visit, Jack, accompanied by me, found one or two articles which were dear to him. Dennis likewise. After that, the house was, as I say, cordoned off. In September, a new property was found for us in another street in the same district. Finally, on Wednesday, 12th November 1958, our former dwelling was pulled down. The plot on which it once stood is still empty today. No trees ever grew there. The few that the city council had planted in order to relieve the site of its incongruence – since in the row of houses it appeared like a gap in a row of teeth – died within three months of their planting. Only a few low, nondescript bushes and the usual weeds which cover waste land spread over the patch where our house had once stood. No official reason was ever given for the death of the trees. Jack, Dennis and Julie are all married, have children of their own and live in various parts of the country. In the winter of 1978, I retired from the firm where I had worked for thirty years and went with my wife to live on the Isle of Wight. We never returned to the West Midlands.

18

The Vision (1871)

Imagine, if you will, a snow-filled, treeless waste devoid of all those features from which we take our bearings, and indeed of all those attributes of our living world, which we take so much for granted. My companion, Graham, in his blue, woollen beret and scarf to match, in his greyish-white ski-suit and heavy, spiked black boots was the sole object in this white world.

'I reckon it's about a couple of miles from here,' he said, consulting his compass with a huge, gloved hand.

I didn't reply. Navigation was his responsibility, and we tramped on as we had done now for several hours. I was tired. I was hungry. I was depressed and remember thinking, 'All we need now is a pack of wolves to seal our miserable fate.' But we trudged on, he a little ahead of me and to this day I can still see his resolute gait in my mind's eye, and those tireless boots determinedly, rhythmically compacting the snow. After a time, tiredness gave way to resignation, and how we covered the two miles I know not. But I do remember coming upon a village issuing from this cotton wool world as if by a wonder. My companion had been right in his calculations. Not far away was an inn of sorts with a large, ice-clad sign hanging above the doorway.

'Here we are!' Graham announced blithely, as though we had put in for a pint of beer in a Gloucestershire pub at the height of summer. He carefully stamped and scraped at his boots before entering, his lightheartedness and studied patience irritating me slightly as he did so. It had come on to snow with gusto. At last, at last we were inside and were met on ringing the bell by a small individual in homespun garb displaying galloping elk on the pullover he wore. Graham knew enough Swedish to make himself understood and soon it was clear that we were welcome. They talked about the weather. I thought only of food and subsequently falling into a dreamless sleep.

The last few days had been arduous, and after we had eaten our fill, it occurred to me how well Graham had behaved on this excursion, an excursion that was certainly not without its dangers. He had never once shown signs of annoyance or impatience on the journey and had risen to challenges with magnificent clear-headedness. He had waited his turn to drink the hot tea we had with us in a flask; he never complained of either hunger of cold or fatigue and helped me on more than one occasion to rally and tramp on through the wilderness. Aye, it was as if he were travelling in England's spring countryside, and I was forced to admire his equanimity and his initiative.

When the going was even, we had fallen into long conversations about the meaning of existence, even occasionally pausing on the way to make our respective points. Yesterday, for example, had been particularly interesting and I often found myself in complete accord with his theological conclusions. At the time he was in his third year at Oxford studying divinity, although to my knowledge he never became a vicar and, as far as I know, left university later to become a diplomat with the Indian Civil Service. On the way today, we had talked about the afterlife with great earnestness. I recall that, while we respected each other's opinions, we could not agree on a 'life after death'. I remember that, as an agnostic, I had argued for a cyclic existence such as that in the material world. We died and became something else, like all other material.

THE VISION (1871)

'Yes, perhaps,' he had averred, 'that's true of the body, I'm sure; we can see the changes before our very eyes, but what of the subtle, spiritual world? We aren't just material, are we? We have a soul. Where does that go to?'

I replied that I didn't know, but suspected that this, too, would be modified in some way.

'Perhaps,' I suggested, 'we depart to ascend to a higher or descend to a lower level.'

'You mean a heaven or hell,' he answered quickly.

'No, I don't mean that,' I said. 'I don't go for that ecclesiastical stuff. My line is physics. I'm only interested in calculable facts.'

'Well, what *do* you mean?' Graham asked.

'I mean that it is likely that we land up on the spiritual level we attained in this life. If we have made advances in this life at the spiritual level, then we reap there what we've sown here. If we have failed to advance or even slipped back spiritually, then we find ourselves at a lower level, and another life will give us a chance to get back to advancement again.'

'So we can only go ahead, you think?'

'Well, I suppose that's what I mean,' I replied. 'It's probably a kind of evolution towards something more perfect.'

'So we're going somewhere?' Graham pursued.

'Well, yes...'

'Where?'

'I don't know, to tell you the truth.'

'Couldn't be that we join God?' he went on.

'Whatever that is,' I agreed and added, 'I suppose so.'

'Umm,' Graham said at this, and I can see to this day the serious expression on his face as he considered this possibility, his brown eyes caught for that moment in a fleeting glance of sunshine.

'I'd damn well like to know,' he finally announced with that young man's assurance he would display from time to time – a manner he'd acquired from his elder brother, who

351

was an army officer – and in a way almost that suggested it was God's duty to inform his creation of his ultimate intentions, and I smiled inwardly. Then, suddenly, 'Do you believe in any kind of survival after death, William?'

'Yes,' I replied, 'but I don't believe in a continuum of everlasting joy or something of that sort. For that would be illogical and impossible – and terribly boring in the long run.'

'Illogical?'

'In this relative world of ours we can't even begin to imagine pure bliss. Joy exists only in interaction with suffering. And as for the concept of infinity, the magnitude and number of the universe ... well, that's quite beyond our puny brains. And why, for heaven's sake should this miserable animal, man, be exclusively selected for such an honour? The whole idea is man-orientated and egoistic in the extreme. Quite ridiculous.'

'Well, I don't know either,' said Graham, 'but the contemplation haunts me. What happens when you die?' My companion asked slowly to give emphasis to his words.

'I think we'd better press on, lad,' I urged gently, and with this blandishment citing my three years of seniority, fearing soon to be caught in another snowstorm.

That was in the afternoon. Now, at last, at this hostelry we could wash in the cold, mountain water, eat and relax. Our host piled the fire with logs until the flames raged in the hearth to one side of us. It was good not to need to walk any more.

After dinner I felt much better in body and mind, and we stretched our legs in front of the fire. The meal had done much to overcome my fatigue and a glass of red wine did the rest to ripen my mood for Graham's next suggestion. It was clear that the exchanges we had shared on the next life during the afternoon were still very much on his mind.

'William,' he began tentatively.

'Yes?' I said, smiling.

'I know this sounds a bit odd, old boy, but for the life of me I can't think of a better idea.'

THE VISION (1871)

'What kind of an idea?' I asked sleepily.
'You'll think me a right fool.' Pausing, he then said, 'No, let's forget it.'
'Forget what?' There was another pause.
'I'll begin on another tack. Let me say this. You and I said this afternoon that there's no real proof of an afterlife. It's only a matter, you said, of believing or not believing.'
'Oh, we're back on that line,' I said wearily.
'Well, if you're not interested,' Graham said flatly, 'we'll leave the subject,' and again there was a moment's silence between us. Feeling a little uncharitable, it was I that finally took up the subject anew.
'I'm sorry, Graham, I didn't mean to choke you off. Please tell me what you wanted to say.'
'You'll only laugh me to scorn,' he rejoined, and I waited for him to say more. A longer pause followed.
'As I see it, there's only one way to solve the problem.' He recognised my interest at this and added quickly. 'And that's to swear an oath.'
'An oath?'
'Yes, let's link our arms and drink wine and at the same time swear to each other that whoever dies first shall appear to the other, this to prove that there is an afterlife.'
'And if not?' I enquired.
'Then that will be the end of the matter. There isn't one. It's as simple as that. Come on, let's swear.' This remark indicated that the matter could soon be concluded, and I felt that this rather adolescent ritual would be a convenient, if odd means of ending the matter before going to bed.
'Oh, very well, Graham, if you insist.'
'But you must be serious about it, William. This is not a matter to be taken lightly,' he warned, looking at me levelly.
Thus we took our respective glasses and linked arms, our faces near to each other.
'*We do swear by Almighty God that whoever shall die first*

shall, after death, unmistakably show himself to the other, so proving that there be an afterlife.'

There was another pause after this covenant, and during it the thought crossed my mind that Graham had earlier rehearsed what he had just said, so professionally had he intoned his spell.

Then we leaned back in our armchairs and finished our wine.

'It's late,' I said, replacing my empty glass on the long table beside us. Our host had already retired.

'I know,' Graham replied, 'but I'm not quite tired enough for bed. You go, William, if you wish. I look forward to seeing you in the morning. Let's hope that the weather will be clement enough for us to get over the border to Norway and from there catch the train to the ferry.'

'We'll see. Good night, my friend. Sleep well.'

And so I retired to my cold bedroom. Just before falling asleep I thought again of my younger companion. 'Nice young chap,' I concluded, catching sight of the one star that shone brightly through a small opening in the curtains.

The next day dawned brightly with frost and intense sunshine as we paid up, said goodbye to our host, thanking him and his wife for their friendly hospitality and the substantial breakfast they had kindly afforded us.

The details of this departure are still very clear in my mind, oddly enough, despite the fact that it is nearly sixty years ago today since it took place.

I presume we reached the border and so left Norway for England as planned, and yet all this has coalesced into the obscurity of the past like so much else. I know for sure that, except for meeting Graham and his parents at a garden party in the summer of 1862, I never saw either him or his family again. The odd thing is that I never heard anything either

THE VISION (1871)

from him or about him from anyone else after that pleasant afternoon.

It is strange, too, that we never wrote to each other, and that it was only by coincidence that I happened to read in *The Times* that he had been promoted to a high rank in the Indian Civil Service many years later.

Moreover, I kept our troth a strict secret. I never mentioned the matter to anyone, not even to my wife. And so the years passed.

In July 1870, I had been playing tennis with the younger members of my family. It was perhaps a foolhardy thing to do at my age and was more a gesture to say that I enjoyed being with them and also to vainly demonstrate that an old one was still up to a round. I must admit that it was fun, but it was hard work and so awfully hot that I was soon obliged to give up and retire to join the observers along the lines. Marie, seeing my happy, but hot-and-bothered condition, suggested that the maid prepare a bath, and to this I gladly concurred, returning to the house after a few minutes of chat with them all. When I arrived I found the hot bath ready for me upstairs, towels and a bathrobe having been put there for my convenience. The soapy water in these moments was a boon for both body and soul. Humming happily to myself, I turned to grasp the large towel on a chair next to the steel bath.

What happened then was akin to what I imagine occurs to those hapless individuals who come into contact with something carrying high voltage current. In turning, I saw Graham quite clearly sitting there on my towel, smiling calmly and looking down at me in the bathtub. At that moment I must have passed out, for the next thing I was aware of was that I was sprawled out on the tiled floor and hearing a woman's voice outside the bathroom asking me if I was all

A ROGUE LIKE ME

right. Just how I got out of that bath prior to this I know not. I remember clawing and clambering my way from the floor to the standing position, calling out at the same time that all was well and that I'd be ready in a minute.

The sun shone brightly into the room; the late afternoon was warm and still. The chair upon which Graham had sat was now vacant and I plumped down on it heavily, reviewing what I had seen, my mind in turbulence. The vision took place on 14 July. Afterwards, I recall, there was a thunderstorm in the early evening and I remember everyone saying how welcome the rain was now after so many weeks of drought.

A few days later, I returned to Edinburgh where, on arriving home, a letter awaited me in the hall. It was from India, a formal message from a relative there, informing me that Graham had passed away on the afternoon of July 14th.

Source: *The Life and Times of Lord Brougham*, 1871.